DISPATCH
from a
COLD
COUNTRY

ROBERT CULLEN

FAWCETT · COLUMBINE
New York

A Fawcett Columbine Book
Published by Ballantine Books

Copyright © 1996 by Robert Cullen

http://www.randomhouse.com

Library of Congress Cataloging-in-Publication Data
Cullen, Robert, 1949–
    Dispatch from a cold country / Robert Cullen. — 1st ed.
        p. cm.
    ISBN 0-449-91258-2
    I. Title.
PS3553.U297D57 1996
813'.54—dc20   96-4908

Text design by Ruth Kolbert

Manufactured in the United States of America

First Edition: June 1996

10   9   8   7   6   5   4   3   2   1

For Doc, with love

Chapter One

J ENNIFER MORELLI STEPPED GRATEFULLY TO the front of the checkout line at the Hotel Northern Worker, a hostelry she hoped fervently never to visit again.

It was a tired, cold hotel in a tired, cold district of St. Petersburg, a hotel that hadn't bothered to change the name it had been given in 1954, when the city was Leningrad, the country was the Soviet Union, and foreigners were carefully segregated from such places.

In the new Russia, the Northern Worker had discovered that there were certain Westerners of limited means—teachers, impecunious art lovers, and the occasional freelance writer like Morelli—willing to pay dollars, though less than a hundred of them, for a small, musty room, bath down the hall. In the era of transition from communism to capitalism, this was like learning that the frail little babushka who shared your communal apartment had real jewelry hidden under her mattress.

Behind Morelli, an old woman, wearing a parka and a black astrakhan hat, moved a dirty mop slowly back and forth over the granite floor of the lobby. In the far corner, an attendant dozed behind a portable bar marked KAFE. He had no customers; he was out of coffee.

Morelli leaned over the counter of the cashier's booth, waiting for the woman behind it to tally the surcharge for her phone calls. Dexterously, the woman slipped wooden beads back and forth on an abacus.

"Three hundred thirty-four thousand, three hundred rubles," she finally announced. It was the equivalent of about fifty dollars.

"Any discount for the days when there was no hot water?" Morelli asked.

The woman behind the counter looked at first stupefied. Then she giggled softly at this eccentric foreign attempt at humor. She shook her head.

Carefully taking two slips of carbon paper, she wrote out a receipt in triplicate, and Morelli handed over a wad of rubles about two inches thick. Laboriously, the cashier counted them. When she was satisfied, she handed Morelli the top copy of the receipt—and her blue passport. She was free to go.

Then she heard someone mention her name.

She turned to her right, startled. Twenty feet away, in front of the registration desk, stood a man in an open and openly expensive leather overcoat. He had, she thought, an odd body, a body that was all torso and arms. His legs were short and bowed, he had no neck, and his ears were like wrinkled pancakes, pressed close to his bullet-shaped head.

"Morelli," he was saying, in the kind of Russian accent she was used to hearing in peasant's markets. "Jennifer Morelli. What room is she in?" His voice was low and gravelly.

She was about to walk up to the man and identify herself, but something about him made her stop. She could not have said what it was—something in his tone of voice or the way he carried himself. So instead of identifying herself, she shrank. She was a tall woman, six feet even, always had been tall, taller than all the boys all the way through grade school. Now her body reflexively went into the stoop-shouldered posture she'd employed then to make her gangling self inconspicuous. She took a step backward, until she was screened by one of the hotel pillars.

The clerk at the registration desk said he was not allowed to give out guests' room numbers.

It was the sort of routine bureaucratic obstacle that Russians of the post-perestroika era had learned to surmount with a small packet of rubles. But the man in the leather coat did not reach for his wallet.

Instead, he laid an enormous, thick-fingered hand on the counter, palm down, knuckles lightly flexed. He put the other hand in the pocket of the coat and pushed it open a bit farther.

He was wearing a gun in a black leather holster.

"Don't give me trouble," he said to the clerk. "Give me the room number."

The clerk looked furtively behind him, perhaps checking to see if the hotel director was within earshot. There was no one there. He took a scrap of paper and picked up a pen. He scrawled something on the paper and handed it to the man in the leather coat.

The man looked at it, nodded, and walked over to the stairwell, rather than the hotel's single, creaking elevator. He pushed open the fire door and disappeared.

Jennifer Morelli did not recognize him. She did not know whether he was aware of what she had in her camera and her computer. But she could calculate her own interests, and saw no way those interests would be served by finding out who the man was and what he wanted.

She picked up her black canvas traveling bag and carefully put her passport in a zippered pocket. Looping the bag's strap around her left shoulder, nestling the bag under her right arm, she walked out the front door of the Northern Worker. She decided against claiming the suitcase she had checked with the doorman ten minutes earlier. Those clothes, she thought, were old and out of style. They were the clothes of the woman she had been, not the woman she wanted to become. She was better off without them. Everything she truly valued was in her shoulder bag.

Outside, it was snowing lightly. The winter sun barely managed to illuminate the top side of the solid cloud bank that hovered heavily over the city, so the light in the streets was gray, diffuse and dim, like dusk in Pennsylvania.

She looked for a taxi and saw none. But a yellow and red tram, its steel wheels clanking on uneven, buckling rails, rolled through the Square of Peace and stopped twenty yards from the hotel. Hopping aboard, she pushed her way into a crowd of Russians smelling of damp wool and diesel fumes. She bent down and peered through the tram's grimy window as it clanked away from the hotel. She did not see the man in the leather coat, and she relaxed as the hotel disappeared from sight.

She imagined that it would be another two minutes before he returned to the lobby from her empty room. She hoped he would then find out that she had checked out but left her suitcase, intending to return for it before noon, after a last morning's sightseeing. She hoped he would then learn that she was booked to leave on the two o'clock Lufthansa flight to Frankfurt.

When the tram reached Nevsky Prospekt, with its better class of hotels, she got out. A short line of four cabs stood outside the Nevsky Palace Hotel, and she got into the first one.

"The airport. Right away," she said to the driver.

"Fifty dollars," he replied.

Jennifer Morelli sighed. It was ten times the legal fare, and her supply of cash was all but exhausted. "All right," she said. "But fast."

———————

The airport smelled of cheap tobacco, vodka, boredom, and despair.

Morelli sniffed as she stepped through glass doors shrouded by grime and a filigree of frost, still holding the black canvas bag carefully under her right arm.

She glanced at her watch: nine-thirty. She had half an hour. The cab had taken forever.

Ahead of her, in a dim light that bespoke dozens of burned-out bulbs, was a throbbing mass of Russians in dull blue, brown, and gray overcoats. Some stood stolidly on lines. Some sat, haunch-to-haunch, on brown wooden benches resembling church pews, eating bread wrapped carefully in newspaper. Others lay sprawled on the floor, mouths open, snoring, trickles of spittle dribbling down their chins. She could only guess how long they'd been waiting for flights.

She scanned the vast room for a moment, orienting herself, until she spotted the sign INTERNATIONAL SECTOR, fifty meters away.

Before she could move toward it, however, a short man with a lined, stubbled face, the butt of a cardboard cigarette dangling from his liver-colored lips, scuttled in front of her. He flashed a smile that showed off two steel crowns and a gap where one of the front incisors had been. His breath reeked of alcohol.

"*Mozhno?*" he asked, and without waiting for her reply, reached for her black bag.

Morelli jerked away as if he'd shoved her. She was as slender as she was tall, but her arms had a wiry strength, and her grip on the bag was firm.

"*Nyet,*" she said loudly.

She flushed, then, for her voice had carried over the muted din of the terminal and caused people to turn and stare. The man, she realized, had probably meant only to earn a tip by carrying the bag of a woman who, dressed like a foreigner, would have hard currency. Her lips set in a thin line, Morelli turned and walked purposefully toward the door at the end of the cavernous room, her right arm clamped tightly over the bag.

But the man did not give up. He followed her toward the international sector, breathing heavily. "German?" he asked her, in Russian.

"No," she replied, unwilling to engage him in any more conversation than necessary.

"American?"

She nodded.

"Like to change dollars?"

She was tempted to ask why he thought she'd be selling dollars as she prepared to leave Russia, but instead merely shook her head.

"Buy souvenirs?"

"No," she said, letting the anger into her voice, hoping the man would shut up. She still had a few thousand-ruble notes in the pocket of her jeans. Angrily, she fished them out and shoved them toward him. The man accepted them, but his face showed that he thought a foreigner was capable of giving more, much more.

"Dollars?" he said, looking at her from under the bill of his sodden cap.

"Go away," she said, angry now.

They brushed past the crowd at the last ticket line, a group waiting dolefully for flights south, to the Black Sea. They ascended a grimy granite staircase.

Gratefully, she reached the door marked "International Sector," opened it, and shut it very deliberately in the man's face.

Once, when the city was still Leningrad, this part of the station had been a privileged oasis for foreign visitors to the Soviet Union. Now it was just a shabby adjunct of the main terminal, with the same grimy floors and peeling paint. A faded, backlit Players cigarette sign provided most of the illumination. But the room at least had its own ticket windows.

Morelli looked at the display board on the far wall. Aeroflot 1036 to Frankfurt was listed as on schedule, departing at 1000. The Lufthansa flight was 1400.

International flights were among the last Russian enterprises to keep to a schedule. She knew time was short, and she strode quickly to the Aeroflot window. A group of five people were clustered in front of her. They looked to be emigrants, Jews or Volga Germans most likely, leaving Russia for good. A husband, a wife, two silent, wide-eyed children, and a bent, withered old woman. The man wore a porkpie hat and shoes of a peculiarly Russian, mouse-gray leather. The women wore dirty fur *shapkas* and black galoshes. They were surrounded by half a dozen cheap, plastic valises, pink and blue, and a couple of large bundles tied up with cord and covered with brown paper.

They were arguing with the clerk on the other side of the window. Voices rose and fell as exasperation and boredom gave way to anger. The clerk was demanding an additional hard currency payment for each ticket. First the little family's patriarch, and then his wife, tried talking the clerk into accepting the tickets as they were.

Jennifer Morelli knew the history of the Jews in Russia, and the equally tragic story of the Volga Germans, invited to settle by Catherine the Great and persecuted by nearly all of her successors. She was sympathetic to anyone from either group who wanted to emigrate.

But not this morning. She had no patience. She half listened to the debate for a couple of minutes, impatiently tapping her foot, her eyes flitting from her watch to the door she'd just come through and back to the ticket window. The window next to it, she noticed with irritation, was closed. That was always the way in Russia.

Morelli usually managed not to think about unpleasant things, to force herself to stay focused on what she could manage. Maybe that was why her marriage had lasted as long as it had. But now her thoughts ran back to the man in the hotel lobby.

Maybe he was just a local thug who heard there was an American staying at the Northern Worker and decided to rob her or shake her down.

Maybe he came from the Hermitage. Maybe they had changed their minds.

But with a gun?

She swallowed. She had only one certainty. She could not risk losing the story she had. Everything she had worked for since the divorce depended on it.

A woman's voice, scratchy and loud, erupted from a hidden speaker: "Aeroflot 1036 to Frankfurt is ready for boarding. All passengers complete customs formalities and board now."

Twenty or more people in the waiting area on the far side of the customs barrier stood up and started shuffling toward a gate that she could not see. She looked at her watch. Twenty-three minutes till ten.

The argument in front of her had switched from whether an additional payment would be required to how much.

"Can't you please hurry?" she asked the cashier, raising her voice and thrusting her head over the shoulder of the old woman. "I have to make that flight."

The cashier shrugged indifferently.

The head of the little family looked at his own watch then and decided further haggling would be counterproductive. Grudgingly, he reached into his pocket and extracted a roll of bills. Morelli could see it was a mixed lot: dollars, marks, a few yen.

The man began peeling bills off the pile, and the cashier stacked them in separate piles.

Morelli looked at the clock above the customs barrier. Nineteen minutes till ten.

Slowly and deliberately, the cashier went through the calculations required to convert the various currencies.

At least she wasn't using an abacus, Morelli thought. She might not have been able to tolerate watching that. Feeling the last remnants of her patience evaporate in the heat of nerves and frustration, she bit her lip to keep from yelling.

Finally, the family was done and Morelli stepped to the cashier. "I want to switch to the ten o'clock flight on Aeroflot," she said.

The cashier nodded and picked up a large, green plastic phone. She began to talk.

Morelli stifled an urge to ask her why she bothered. Clearly, no more than thirty people were going on the flight. And she'd paid for her ticket with hard currency. Aeroflot ought to be happy to snap it away from Lufthansa.

For once, she was right.

"Da, pravilno," the woman said, and hung up the phone. She smiled briefly. "It's okay," she said in English. Morelli sighed and smiled back weakly. She looked again at the clock. Quarter till ten. She was going to make it.

The woman wrote the new ticket, using a ballpoint pen, and thrust it across the little counter. Morelli snatched it up and strode rapidly toward the customs barrier.

Two inspectors were working, and the little family was occupying the attention of one. She headed for the second, straightening her shoulders and telling herself she had no reason to be nervous. She'd broken no laws that she knew of.

She pulled her passport and papers from the shoulder bag and handed them to the inspector. He was sallow and stoop-shouldered, with greasy black hair that fell in half curls from the band of his cap. He had a little potbelly that flowed over the buckle of his web belt and pushed his green uniform shirt upward, leaving a sliver of gray undershirt showing beneath it. He was three inches shorter than she.

He picked up the passport, looked at her picture and smiled crookedly. "Jennifer Morelli," he said, sounding out the syllables slowly.

"That's right."

He riffled through the passport idly, looking at her old visas. "Tourist?"

Her visa said she was a tourist. She nodded.

"You look better without glasses."

Her passport picture, three years old, had been taken when she still wore glasses, when she was still married. Her husband, for some reason, had preferred glasses.

The inspector leered. "Hair looks lighter, too."

She sighed. Try to look interesting, and inevitably some goon would hit on you.

"Prettier now," he said.

Once, she would have been glad to hear a compliment from any man, even this one. But that was once, when her doubts about herself had all but overwhelmed her. She glared at him. "Thank you, but is this necessary?"

The inspector's leer disappeared and his face hardened. Morelli silently berated herself. If he wanted to be a pig, the smart thing in this situation was to let him. "No other bag?" he asked.

"My husband," she said. "My husband is coming later with it. On the Lufthansa flight. I'm leaving early so that I can do some shopping."

Damn, she thought, why had she lied? She'd never been good at it. And why lie about a husband? Was it because she wished she were still married?

The inspector was looking coldly at her, and she followed his eyes downward, until she realized he was looking at the fourth finger of her left hand. It was bare.

She felt her forehead get hot and prickly, and knew that her freckles stood out when that happened. His eyes moved up over her sweater and back to her face, and she knew he had noticed her blush, too.

He picked up the customs declaration she'd filled out when she arrived in Russia two weeks ago and read it. Then he gestured toward the canvas bag. She picked it up and placed it on the aluminum bench.

Casually, the man drew the zipper open and riffled slowly through the contents. Morelli watched from the corner of one eye, trying to maintain a posture of bored indifference.

The inspector's eyes narrowed.

He pulled out her laptop, a five-year-old Toshiba. She watched silently. Next out of the bag was her camera.

The corners of the guard's mouth turned up slightly.

He looked again at the declaration, laid it on the bench so she could see it, and pointed to the blank spaces under the heading "Valuables to Declare."

"Where is computer?" the inspector said in English. "Camera?"

"I didn't write them down," she said in Russian. Her throat was dry and her voice raspy. "I didn't think you had to. I thought you just had to declare currency and jewelry."

The inspector glowered at her, satisfaction showing clearly in his face. "It's obligatory."

"How can you—" she began, but he was already putting her shoulder bag under his beefy arm.

"Come with me," he said over his shoulder. And he walked off, waddling slightly, toward an unmarked door.

She looked at her watch. She had less than thirteen minutes now. She looked around hurriedly. The other inspector was studiously looking at the cigarette ad on the opposite wall. There was no one to turn to.

"Damn it," she muttered, and followed the man.

The inspector pushed open the door and entered a dimly lit corridor. He walked past one closed door and stopped next to a second, which had a wire mesh window and a brass lock. He pulled a key from his pocket; it was on a ring, linked to a metal chain attached to his belt. He turned the key in the lock, pulled the door open and gestured for her to enter. Trembling, feeling her empty stomach twist like a dry towel, she did.

It was a storage room of some kind. Deep shelves lined the walls, filled with luggage. A scuffed brown desk and two chairs of cracked brown vinyl with stuffing leaking out occupied one corner. A dim fluorescent bar provided a greenish illumination.

She turned and saw the inspector pull a dirty brown shade down over the mesh window. Fighting panic, Morelli resisted the urge to flee. He sat down behind the desk and lit a cigarette, a Marlboro. He looked arrogant and relaxed. She hated him.

Morelli made another effort to be assertive. She strode to the front of the desk. "Look, I've been traveling in and out of Russia for six years," she said. "I know the rules. You only have to declare currency and jewelry and weapons."

The inspector pulled open a lap drawer and extracted a black, loose-leaf ring binder. He opened it and wet a thumb with his tongue. Then he started leafing slowly through the pages.

"Sit down," he said.

She sat, uncertain, and glanced at her watch. Eleven minutes. "Look, I've got a flight to catch," she said, trying to keep her anxiety from cracking her voice.

The man ignored her for another thirty seconds. Finally, he came to the page he was looking for, turned the binder around and pushed it toward her. "You read Russian?" he asked.

She nodded.

He pointed a thick finger with a split nail halfway down the page to the left. She leaned forward to read it.

Under "Items to Declare," it listed various kinds of heavy machinery, oil rigs, airplanes, photo equipment, and computers.

"But the form didn't say that," she said.

He shrugged and took a long drag off his cigarette. "Hasn't been printed yet."

"But that's not fair," she protested, her face reddening with anger. "I want to talk to your supervisor."

The man blew a stream of smoke her way. "All right," he said. "He is in St. Petersburg. I will call and ask him to come out here."

By then, of course, her plane would be gone. Aeroflot would not refund her money. Worse, she would have to remain at the airport, where the man from the hotel lobby might soon be looking for her.

She sucked in her breath, took in some of the smoke from his cigarette and coughed. She needed a moment to regain her composure. The man blew smoke across the desk again.

"All right," she said. "Is there a fine or something I can pay here?"

The guard looked her in the eye, his face devoid of emotion. "One hundred dollars," he said.

She grimaced. That would leave her with barely enough for a phone call from Frankfurt to Burke in Washington and then a bus home from Dulles. But she could see no alternative.

She fished the wallet from her shoulder bag and counted out one hundred dollars in twenties and fives. She had fifteen left.

She handed the money to the inspector. He stashed it carelessly in the desk drawer and put the computer back in her black bag.

"Now may I go?" she said, letting some of her anger back into her voice.

"Now the camera," he answered her. He flicked some ash on the floor.

She felt the blood rush to her face, felt both anger and fear, and made a conscious effort to stop twisting her fingers together.

"I thought," she said, "that the hundred dollars took care of it. It's only one customs declaration."

The inspector shook his head gravely, not bothering to hide how much he was enjoying his power. The cigarette ember glowed as he inhaled again.

"Separate items," he said. "Separate problems."

This would never have happened to her, she thought, if she were not a woman, traveling alone. But she was; she had chosen to be. And now she would have to get herself out of this. She resisted the urge to look at her watch again.

She decided she could afford to sacrifice the camera, an old Nikon.

"All right," she said. "You can keep the camera. Just let me remove the film."

The man's eyes widened. "What's on the film?" he asked.

She realized she'd erred in letting him know how important the film was to her. But she couldn't take the words back.

"Nothing important," she said quickly. "Just some pictures I took in the Hermitage."

The inspector's eyebrows fluttered, and she sensed she'd said the wrong thing again.

"It is forbidden to take pictures inside the Hermitage," he said.

She remembered that he was right. "But I had permission from the director, Mr. Vasiliev."

"He gave a tourist permission to take pictures?"

"But I—" she said, and caught herself. She couldn't tell him she'd been working as a journalist. She had a tourist's visa. "I did have permission," she said weakly.

"In writing?" he asked.

She felt her stomach knot again, and when she tried to swallow, her throat felt dry and raw. "No," she said.

The inspector removed the three yellow rolls of film and the camera from the bag and laid them on the desk.

"Bring a letter from the Hermitage and you get the film," he said. "Bring a hundred dollars for the camera."

She fought to stifle a feeling of nausea. Though the room, like the whole airport, was chilly, she felt suddenly hot and dizzy. She had less than eight minutes left.

"There must be some way we can settle this here," she said.

The inspector said nothing, waiting for her offer.

Her mind, she found, had slowed down. It seemed to take forever for her to think of the things she had to offer.

"A book?" she said. "I have a good English translation of *Anna Karenina* in my bag."

The inspector slowly shook his head.

She thought some more, conscious of time slipping away. "My watch," she said. "I would leave you my watch for the film."

His eyebrows flickered upward, suggesting some interest. She unfastened the buckle to the leather strap on her watch, wishing it was one of those fake gold bands, assuming this man would not know the difference.

The inspector turned the watch over slowly in his thick fingers. The smoke drifted up from the cigarette. Then he shook his head no.

"Cheap watch," he said, and handed it back to her. She had five minutes.

"Well, you saw I don't have much money left," she said, trying desperately not to whine. "I'm not some rich tourist. I've given you what I could."

The guard shook his head again. He stood up, dropped the cigarette, and slowly crushed the butt under his boot, twisting.

She felt the beginning of a tear welling in her eye, and she blinked, fighting to keep it from rolling down her cheek. She was damned if she would let this man, or anyone else, see her cry. The blood in her head made her temples throb and her ears feel hot.

He walked toward her and stopped when his belt buckle was directly in front of her face.

He pulled his zipper down. She could see some ragged underwear behind it.

She nearly gagged. Desperately, she tried to put him off. "You don't want it like this," she said. "Wouldn't you rather meet me in a hotel somewhere?"

"You're leaving the country," he said.

"But I'll come back," she offered. And at that instant she was certain she would come back, if only to find this bastard and file charges against him.

He shook his head. He wasn't believing it.

She felt a shudder starting deep within her abdomen, shaking her to the tips of her fingers.

"All right," she whispered. "But first the film goes into my pocket and you stamp the declaration."

Grinning, the inspector complied.

Then he leaned back so that his buttocks were propped against the edge of the desk. She could smell him now, a moist, grimy smell that made her feel faint.

"Not through the pants," she said. "Let me pull them down."

She forced herself to unbuckle the man's belt and pull the trousers and grimy underpants down his legs.

His penis was small and uncircumcised. It protruded from underneath the crease where his belly hung over his groin. As she pulled the pants down toward his ankles, it started to rise, until it was half erect.

She got to her knees and shuffled forward until his penis was only inches from her face. She closed her eyes.

"I can't get close enough," she said, gesturing at his bunched-up trousers. "I need to get these off." She looked up at him and tried to make her face a neutral mask.

He grinned down at her, showing a single steel incisor. The head of his penis started to erupt from his foreskin.

She worked the right cuff and then the left cuff over his shoes. He moved his feet until she had the pants completely off. Light brown socks drooped over his ankles.

"All right," she said.

She raised her hands as high as they would go on the inspector's chest and slowly rubbed them over the fat little mounds of his breasts. He grunted his approval. She took a deep breath.

And then she shoved, as hard as she could.

The inspector fell backward, yelling in surprise, his back on the desk and his legs standing ludicrously in the air, upside down. Rising and grasping in a single motion, Morelli grabbed the man's heels and pushed again. He tumbled backward and she heard him land head first on the floor behind the desk.

Frantically, she scooped up the bag and the trousers, then bolted for the door.

She could hear him thrashing, and her hand grasped desperately for the key attached to the trousers. She found it.

She stepped outside as he crawled from behind the desk, looking both stunned and ludicrous, his fat white buttocks naked.

She locked the door. She wasn't sure whether it could be opened from the inside or not. Even if it could, she figured it would take him some time to find trousers to cover himself with.

She stuffed the pants inside the black bag, next to the camera and the film and the computer. Then she ran for the door at the end of the corridor, and the flight home.

Her seat was toward the front of the plane, next to a gray-haired man reading a copy of *Handelsblatt*. He nodded politely to her. She did not return the gesture, sitting rigidly in her seat, her hands clutching the armrests, her eyes flickering constantly to the windows.

A nervous flier, he thought. Almost a pretty one, with blue eyes and short red hair that fell nicely about her long, graceful neck. In fact, she could be very pretty if not for something about the way she carried herself.

The young woman's eyes welled and tears began to drip down her freckled cheeks as soon as the wheels cleared the ground. The plane labored upward and banked toward the west.

"Are you all right?" the man asked, in English.

She nodded, and smiled a ragged, half smile before returning her gaze to the seat in front of her. The tears continued to fall silently from her eyes. But she said nothing.

As the plane passed over Pskov, headed out of Russian airspace, the man returned to his *Handelsblatt*.

Chapter Two

Hᴇ ᴡᴀs ɪɴ ᴀ ғᴏʀᴇsᴛ sᴏᴍᴇᴡʜᴇʀᴇ, ᴀ ғᴏʀᴇsᴛ whose floor was covered with clean, white snow, and he was skiing. He didn't know how long he'd been skiing, nor how he'd come to be in the forest. But the trees were all spindly white birches and towering green larches, so he knew the forest was somewhere in Russia. It was very old, and a wind made the birch trees bob back and forth, their bare black branches waving against a sky blotted out by clouds the color of steel wool.

The snow underneath his skis was very heavy, and he had to break the trail since no one had skied this way before. The long muscles in his thighs were starting to ache, his breath was raspy, and he could feel a cold dampness where the sweat was soaking his hair.

Then he saw someone skiing in the woods, skiing much faster than he, approaching on a diagonal path. The skier crossed his path a hundred yards ahead of him. He could see long, black hair streaming out behind her, and he thought that her name must be Marina. She had on a white parka and black tights that matched the colors of the birch trees. When he reached the point where she'd crossed his path, he turned into her tracks and tried to follow her.

If she knew he was behind her, she gave no sign of it. She kept skiing straight ahead, gliding easily through the snow the way some Russians do, the way he never could. Each stride took her farther from him, but he kept going, fixed on the idea of catching up. The sun was a smudge of silver behind the dark gray of the clouds in the west, and he knew it would soon be dark.

He skied through a herd of reindeer, which parted in front of him the way small fish make way for a large one, then regrouped behind him. Just beyond the herd, up ahead, was a log cabin, with a light on in the amber window and elaborately carved wooden filigree about the yellow lintels, eaves, and shutters. Smoke curled from a stovepipe.

He stopped in front of the cabin and took off his skis. The door was unlocked, and he went in. As soon as he stepped inside, he knew he was home, home in a way that gave his soul rest.

Marina was standing between the door and the stove, dressed in black tights and a white, cotton shift embroidered with blue trim. Her hair hung, shining, down her back, and her purple eyes reflected the bright orange glow of the coal burning in the stove grate and the white and indigo tiles behind it. Near her was a bed piled high with reindeer fur.

When she saw him, she smiled and stepped into his arms. Her kiss tasted like honey mixed with wild raspberries.

Then she reached behind her and found a glass, which she offered to him. He put it to his nose, but even before he could smell it, he knew it was vodka. She was holding an identical glass.

"To love," Marina said, lifting hers.

He hung his head. "I'm sorry," he mumbled. "I can't."

Her face froze into an expression of horror and fear. "But Colin," she protested, pronouncing his name with a long O. "If you don't drink, the reindeer will die."

Trembling, he took the glass and raised it to his lips. But as soon as the fumes filled his nostrils and the liquid touched his tongue, just as it started to burn its way into his system, an alarm of some kind went off.

Startled, he spun around. The alarm kept ringing. He looked for the lights of police cars outside, but saw only the shadows of the reindeer, pawing at the snow. The alarm rang louder and he spit the vodka out.

Shuddering, Colin Burke woke up.

He looked at the ceiling and recognized the crack that ran from the window to the closet door, and the flaking paint in the corner where the roof had leaked during one of the winters he'd spent abroad.

He looked through the gap between the shade and the bedroom window. Judging by the brightness of the sky, either it was already nine o'clock or the dull gray skies of February had blown away. He raised his arm and looked at his watch. It was already nine o'clock.

And the phone was ringing. He picked it up.

"Burke," he said.

"Colin, it's Jennifer. I hope I didn't wake you."

She sounded like she was talking from the bottom of a swimming pool.

"Hey, kid, no, you didn't wake me," he said. He coughed, conscious of the fact that his voice was hoarse. He sat up in bed. "Where are you? Still in Russia? This is a terrible connection."

"Oh, I'm sorry," she said. "I did wake you."

"It's all ri—"

"I'm in Frankfurt, at the airport," she said. "I waited as long as I could to call you, and now I've just got a minute before I have to catch my flight."

"On the way back?"

"Yes."

"How was it?"

She was silent, and he thought for a second that the connection had been broken.

"Hello."

"It was fine," she said, but her voice sounded tiny and distant.

"You okay? You sound a little tired, maybe."

"I'm fine," she repeated. "I got a great story. You'd call it a 'holy shit story.' In St. Petersburg. I want you to publish it."

"Congratulations," he said. "What is it? They took a secret vote to rejoin Sweden?"

"Colin," she said.

"What, then? If it's about Nazi paintings or Catherine the Great and her horse, it's been done already."

"Please don't tease me." Her voice quavered.

She had a tendency to take him literally, he remembered. And a tendency to take him seriously.

"Sorry," he said. "What is it?"

"I want to show you," she answered. "Not tell you. Okay? I have some film I want you to see."

"Sure," he said. "But are you sure you're all right? You sound a little—"

"I'm fine," she said, and he knew she wasn't. "I get into Dulles at four. I'll take the film to a lab I know. Can I show it to you tonight?"

"Sure," he said. "You want to bring it to the office?"

"All right," she replied. "When's the best time?"

"Right after deadline. About nine o'clock."

"All right," she said. "I've got to catch the plane. See you to-night. You're going to love this. It's a great story."

Burke hung up the phone and stood. He shook his head lightly, noting with satisfaction the way his brain clung firmly to the inside of his skull. He stretched, listening to the joints pop. His lower back had a dull ache and his left knee still creaked. Whatever else he could expect from going on the wagon, physical rejuvenation was apparently not one of them.

The house was, as always, not quite quiet. Somewhere, a beam creaked. Something skittered across the tin roof. He turned on the radio, and smiled when he heard Diana Ross and the Supremes. Baby love. In the ten years he'd been abroad, radio had regressed twenty.

He pulled a robe from a hook on the inside of the closet door and walked downstairs, past a series of framed snapshots of himself and his son, all taken during the boy's annual summer visits to Moscow, visits that started when Sam was twelve and barely five feet tall, and ended when he was a college senior, two inches taller than his father, and a pleasant stranger.

Burke opened the front door and stepped out into the tiny yard, looking for the paper. He glanced up and down the street, seeing only a couple of loose pages, blowing against a spindly maple tree in front of the house next door. That was the way of Capitol Hill. Anything not bolted down was community property. At least his lost paper might be building readership.

He went back inside the house, up the staircase and into the bathroom, where he hung his robe on a hook flanked by framed letters that said he'd been nominated for the Pulitzer Prize and expressed regret that he hadn't won, but the field was exceptionally strong and it was a great honor just to be nominated. He stepped inside the shower and let the water run hot over his body for a long time. One of the pleasures of living alone, he thought. No one else needed the hot water.

As the water cascaded over his shoulders, he wondered what Jennifer Morelli could have discovered in St. Petersburg that would make such a hot story. With pictures. Most likely, he thought, it was an old story that she wasn't aware had been done by somebody else. That was what new correspondents in Russia typically came up with.

He stepped out, naked, dried himself, and did twenty-five push-ups and twenty-five sit-ups on the floor of his bedroom, grunting with the final few of each.

He dressed, pulling a blue blazer and khaki pants from a plastic dry-cleaning bag and adding a new tie with cream-colored skyscrapers of some kind painted on a midnight-blue field, telling himself that he'd planned to wear fresh clothes even before he knew Jennifer Morelli would be coming by the office, but not believing it.

Downstairs again, he bypassed the living room. It was bare of furnishings since he'd thrown out the wicker chairs and shag rug he'd gotten a dozen years ago, when his marriage ended. They'd been stored during the years he spent abroad, growing musty and slightly ludicrous.

In the kitchen, he poured out yesterday's coffee and started a fresh pot, whistling along to Stevie Wonder on the radio, then went into the study.

It was the only room in his little row house that felt entirely comfortable to him. It had an old brown leather couch he'd bought from a government sale of surplus furniture from the State

Department. A deep red rug, woven where he'd bought it in Kazakhstan, covered the floor. Pictures he'd taken hung on one wall: Chernenko's funeral, with Gorbachev walking beside the casket, looking pensive; kids facing tanks on the streets of Moscow in 1991; tanks firing at the Russian White House in the summer of 1993. Books, half of them in Russian, lined the other walls. He favored history.

With no paper to read, he sat down in front of his computer and logged into the *Tribune*'s system. Quickly, he scanned the list of foreign stories published that morning. Nothing on the story list had changed since he'd left the previous evening, just after the first edition deadline.

Burke pursed his lips. In his six weeks as an editor, he'd learned that late remakes of the story list rarely led to happy mornings. They usually meant that the *Tribune* had been playing catch-up on a story in the *Times* or the *Post*. But the routine of editing was beginning to bore him. A little crisis might be nice, he thought. Maybe somewhere in the Pacific, with late news and no deadline pressure. Or maybe Jennifer Morelli would actually have something unusual.

He put on his overcoat, walked outside, and fired up his vehicle, a 1984 Ford Crown Victoria. It was a practical car for Washington: less valuable on the street than a newspaper. The car belched once, then turned over, and he went to work.

————

An electrician, toolbox in hand, wearing a reproduction of an old Washington Senators cap turned backward, plodded up to Burke.

"Gonna have to use your desk for a minute," he announced. "Gotta check some wiring overhead."

Burke wheeled his chair to one side and allowed the man to climb up. The *Tribune* newsroom was a constant construction site. A new computer system required tearing up the floors to install new wiring. Then the new computer needed new air-conditioning, which required dismantling the ceiling. That work loosened asbestos in the old ceiling tiles, which required a new ceiling. Then someone invented a new computer system, and the cycle started over again. The 442 editors and reporters who worked on the vast, open third floor of the Tribune Building learned to ignore exposed ducts and pipes and to push papers around sheets of black plastic and electricians' feet.

He tried to focus on a dispatch from Paris that had arrived in the computer, but the electrician kept shifting his feet on the desk, leaving gritty footprints.

"How much longer?" he asked the pair of legs and torso that were all he could see of the electrician before his shoulders and head disappeared into the ceiling.

The electrician waited a moment before answering. "Don't know," he said. His voice echoed slightly above the ceiling tiles.

Burke grunted.

He had a message from Cairo on his desk, marked URGENT. Someone had stolen the bureau car, and the correspondent wanted authorization to buy a new one for $26,500. It had fallen to Burke, as deputy foreign editor, to persuade a fifth-floor accountant named Duane Walls that the off-budget expense was justified. Walls, whose mission in life was to hold down the cost of foreign news, had demanded to know why a Toyota that cost $19,969 on the Motor Mile in Falls Church, Virginia, cost $26,500 in Cairo. Burke had failed to find out. Now he had a message informing him that tourists were being shot in the Upper Nile Valley, and if the *Tribune* wanted a story, it had better buy a car, since rental agencies wouldn't let their cars go into areas controlled by the Muslim Brotherhood, and what kind of a penny-ante operation was the paper trying to run, anyway?

Burke ground his teeth together, but the mastication failed to make him feel any more enthused about dealing with the Cairo bureau's transportation problems.

Harry Press, an old baseball writer who had somehow landed on the foreign desk rim editing copy, walked up to the flanking desks of the editors and coughed.

"Something on CNN we need your help with," he said to Burke.

Burke walked the twenty feet to the small television that the desk used to keep track of breaking events. He looked at the screen and recognized the Russian deputy defense minister, Marshal Vladimir Rogov, speaking from what looked like a conference room in a hotel. A crawler on the screen said the broadcast was live from Riga, Latvia. Burke looked at the image on the little screen. Rogov had not changed in the months since Burke had last seen him. He was still short—his shoulders barely cleared the lectern, and the microphone covered his lips and nose. He still tilted perceptibly to the left, the result, Burke knew, of the steel rod that held his right leg together. Burke still did not like him.

Burke looked at his watch. It was just after eleven at night in Riga, an extraordinary time to be holding a press conference. Even more remarkably, CNN was transmitting a live, untranslated audio narration from Russian television. Normally, it provided a voice-over translation.

"CNN's carrying this live, like it was hot shit," Press said. "But they've lost the feed from the English translator."

". . . Russian troops cannot complete their withdrawal from radar stations in Latvia under the present circumstances," Burke said, beginning to translate what Rogov was saying. "Until the government of Latvia takes steps to protect the human rights of Russians, the troops will remain in their bases. They may be reinforced."

A local Latvian reporter jumped up and started shouting a question in Latvian, which Burke did not understand. Rogov ignored him and kept reading his statement, but the cacophony kept Burke from translating.

Abruptly, two thick-shouldered men in suits appeared next to the Latvian journalist and began to drag him from his seat. Another journalist jumped up, apparently to protest, but one of the pair, with a neck the size of a trash can, shoved him aside with one hand.

"Huh," Press snorted. "This isn't a press conference. It's dictation."

Rogov made a few terse closing remarks about Russian honor and immediately folded his paper and strode off the stage, his back as stiff as his right leg. The single gold star on his epaulets gleamed dully in the television lights.

CNN's screen went blank for a moment, then cut to a picture of

correspondent Stu Jorgenson, sitting in a studio at the CNN bureau in Moscow, trying to think of something intelligent to say by
way of instant analysis.

Ken Graves, the foreign editor, walked up behind Burke and
Press, pointed a remote control at the set and turned the sound off.
He had his own instant analyst.

"So," Graves said. "Tell me what it means."

Burke hated instant analysis. The more experienced he got, the
more he realized that most quick commentary was the journalistic
equivalent of a soufflé—more hot air than substance. The only
right way to answer Graves's question would be to start digging in
Moscow until the right sources explained it.

"Well, it's hard to say," Burke temporized. "If I were reporting
it, I'd want to know first why Rogov made this announcement."

"Who's Rogov?"

"The deputy defense minister. Vladimir Rogov. Nickname is
Zhezl, the rod, for the iron in his leg, but also for his personality.
He's a little guy, and he fit in their airplane cockpits, so he became
a pilot. One of the few heroes they had in Afghanistan. Shot down
and got his leg broken. Survived, even though the leg was ruined
by the Afghan doctors. Got back to Russia in a prisoner exchange
and went back to Afghanistan. Ran air combat operations until
Gorbachev pulled the troops out. He was on the fence in the '91
coup, but he's risen in the ranks since then, apparently because he's
got a big constituency among the junior and middle-grade officers
who really got the shaft when the army shrank in the last few
years. Became deputy defense minister last year. I talked to him
once. Cold son of a bitch, but very shrewd, I thought."

"But why is it interesting that he's making this announcement?"

"Well, it's not his job to announce that sort of thing. It's the
president's job, or the minister of defense."

"So why's he doing it?"

Burke shrugged. "Could be that it's not serious. A false alarm.
Maybe he's just gone off the reservation, and in a few days someone will quietly tell everyone to disregard what he said."

"Worst case?"

Burke sighed. "Worst case is that it means the army's taking a
much tougher line than it has in the past, and forcing the president

to accept it. That Rogov's somehow pushing the minister aside. That they're doing all this despite knowing that the United States and the West very much want them to complete their withdrawal from the Baltics. That they don't care very much anymore what the West thinks."

"That sounds right to me," Graves said. He smiled. "Now we have something to push for the front page."

"Return of the Red Menace," Burke said, trying not to let too much sarcasm into his voice.

"Answer me one question, pal," Graves said.

"What?"

"Does sex help Madonna sell records?"

"I know, I know."

"Good. You can come to the four o'clock meeting and help me and the Red Menace sell a little foreign news."

It was the first time in his six-week career as an editor that Burke had been invited to the session where the paper's section editors met to review the news of the day and decide what to put on the front page. He tried to look pleased.

The four o'clock meeting took place in the office of Lyle Nelson, the executive editor. His office had a glass wall that gave him a view of the newsroom, and it was known to the lesser denizens of the building as the shark tank. The four o'clock meeting was generally called, by them, the feeding. Reporters and sub-editors, gazing through the windows like children at an aquarium and reading the expressions on the senior editors' faces, liked to bet on whose pieces were making the front page and whose were being consigned to the back sections of the paper.

Nelson liked being the top shark, but he sensed that a somewhat more benevolent image was appropriate for a *Tribune* editor in the mid-nineties. So, in contrast to the suspenders and tailored shirts and Wall Street ties favored by his predecessor, he wore khaki pants, plaid shirts, knit ties, and tweed sport coats to the office, affecting the look of an associate professor in one of the environmental science departments at a small but very elite eastern college.

Now he leaned back in his swivel chair and propped his feet on the edge of his long, oval meeting table; they were shod in L.L. Bean hunting boots. One by one the section editors presented their offerings, vassals paying tribute to their liege.

"Sarah?" he said.

Sarah Nussbaum, the national news editor, leaned forward over the table. She took a quick glance at a legal pad in front of her. "We've got Senator Dickson's resignation. And the AARP is also firing the lobbyist Dickson went to bed with. We've got the new CBO projections on the cost of the health plan; the White House is very upset with them. We've got rumors that the President is going to ease Strobridge out at State and put McAllister in. . . ."

"How solid?" Nelson asked.

"Very. We got it from the White House. Very deliberate leak." Nelson nodded.

"And we've got the deaths of four drug runners and two agents in that DEA shoot-out in Miami this morning."

"The agents Americans?" Nelson did not explain why the nationality of the shooters interested him. He didn't have to.

Nussbaum smiled. "One."

She sat back, satisfied. All her candidates were shoo-ins for front-page play, and one of them would probably lead the paper.

Nelson shifted his gaze one spot lower down the table. "Charles?"

Charles Cobb, the metro editor, glanced at his own legal pad. Unlike the rest of the male editors, he'd ignored Lyle Nelson's taste in clothes and remained true to Armani suits, He had the kind of wispy body that showed them off well.

Cobb had two candidates. A woman in Prince Georges County had gone down to the jail where her husband was being held on charges of beating her. She had paid his bail, taken him home, and blown his head off with a shotgun. The local chapter of NOW had rushed to her defense, and the police were still trying to decide whether to charge her with murder. And he had a feature on a District public school where children had improved their reading scores twenty percent after six months with an Afrocentric curriculum.

Lifestyles had one offering. Princess Diana was back in town, visiting the Brazilian ambassador and shopping in Georgetown. This time, the ambassador's wife was out of town.

"Ken?" Nelson turned to Graves.

Graves had a weak list. There were more atrocities in the guerrilla fighting between Ukrainians and Russians in Crimea, but that was old already. The Chinese had threatened to send troops into Hong Kong, but no one thought Britain would do anything about it if they did. His only realistic hope for cracking the front page was bumping one of metro's stories with Rogov's announcement.

"And we have a late-breaking story from Riga and Moscow. A Russian general, Vladimir Rogov, says that the Russians aren't getting out of those radar bases they still have in Latvia, and they might reinforce them."

Nelson said nothing. His silence carried a clear message to Graves.

"Colin knows Rogov, so I asked him to sit in and flesh it out for us," Graves said.

Burke, sitting in a chair along the wall, stood up. "This could be a sea change in Russian policy," he began.

" 'Could be'?" Nelson interrupted.

"Has all the signs of being a sea change," Burke amended. "Rogov is the hero of the hard-line faction within the army. His nickname is the 'Rod.' "

He could see Nelson perk up. The executive editor liked colorful details in his news stories. He liked slightly salacious colorful details even better.

"It's significant that he took center stage for this announcement," Burke went on. "It's going to cause an immediate pissing contest with the United States. Congress has already said no more aid to Russia unless the pullout from the Baltics is completed. It suggests that the hard line is so ascendant in Moscow that they don't care about that anymore."

Nelson nodded.

Charles Cobb broke in. "Well, I can tell you that very few people in the District even know who this Rogov or whoever is, let alone care about Latvia. But the whole city is interested in Afrocentric education. And this is a good, positive story."

Cobb did not have to remind anyone that Wilhelmina Norton, the *Tribune*'s owner, had recently emerged from a meeting with the District's political leaders and pledged to look harder for positive stories from the inner city.

Graves made a careful effort to question Cobb's story without looking like a racist. "Well, is the improvement in this school's test scores because of the Afrocentric curriculum or all the extra money and attention it's been getting?"

Cobb shrugged. "Does it matter?"

"Well, yes—" Graves said. But Nelson cut him off.

"I think Charles is right," he said. "We'll lead with Dickson, and we'll make the DEA shoot-out the off lead. Then I like Diana, the State Department, the health care numbers—but keep that one column and jump it—the vengeful little woman in P.G., and Afrocentric schools. We can let this Rogov guy lead the world news page inside. And let's maybe do a feature on the teachers or something in this Afrocentric thing. Charles, coordinate with Lifestyles," he said.

In the newsroom, copy editors on the foreign desk looked at Cobb's face and Graves's scowl through the window of the shark tank. Then they paid off their bets to the copy editors on the metro desk.

Burke walked back to his desk and slid into his chair. He hoped Jennifer Morelli actually did have a holy shit story.

Chapter Three

IVAN DMITRIEVICH BYKOV PRESENTED HIS PASS-
port to the rotund black man behind the counter marked NON-U.S.
CITIZENS. The clerk opened it and scanned it quickly. Then he
picked up his heavy steel stamp and put a visa in the passport with
a solid and official thunk. The sound reminded Bykov of a cell
door shutting.

"Have a nice stay, Herr Mueller," the clerk said.

Bykov nodded and smiled pleasantly.

He walked forward to the baggage claim area and located the
carousel with *Lufthansa 61* glowing above it in red letters against a
black field. He was mildly surprised that his bag had not yet arrived on the carousel. He expected more efficiency in the West.
Its absence, however, pleased him. He felt more at ease with
inefficiency.

The bag came and he took it through the green line. As he expected, the inspector did not bother to open it.

Bykov was out in the terminal building, the first hurdles behind
him. His next thought was of clothing. He needed something very
American. He walked upstairs to a concourse where departing passengers awaited their flights under a soaring concrete canopy supported by glass walls that let outside light cascade in. He looked at

it briefly, then spent a few minutes studying the clothes of waiting passengers until he felt confident he could pick the Americans out from the foreigners. Then he found a row of shops. One sold books and magazines. The next one sold candy. The third dispensed souvenirs and clothing. He selected a hat and a jacket. Both were colored an odd shade of red and both had an insignia, a profile of an Indian with a feather. He didn't know what the Indian meant, but within three minutes on the concourse, he'd seen no fewer than a dozen men wearing clothing of the same color and insignia.

Bykov took the hat and the jacket to the cashier and handed her a hundred-dollar bill. The cashier rang up the purchase, then held the bill up to the light and examined it.

Bykov felt a tightening in his bowels and thought about escaping from the store. As far as he knew, the bill was genuine. But he did not know for sure. He took a step backward.

But the woman completed her inspection and wordlessly slipped the bill into the register, under the smaller currency drawer. Though Americans carried hundreds while they were abroad, Bykov decided, they dealt in tens and twenties at home. He would have to do the same.

He walked into the men's room and found an empty stall. He took his knife out of the bag and slipped it into the pocket of his pants. Then he took his overcoat off and stuffed it into the bag, and ripped the tags off the maroon jacket and hat and put them both on.

Bykov left the terminal through the door with a taxi sign overhead. There was only a short line, and the temperature felt very mild, at least three or four degrees above freezing.

In the cab, he gave the driver a piece of paper on which he had carefully copied the address he had bought from the clerk in the Hotel Northern Worker, St. Petersburg.

It read: 1475 R Street NW.

Bykov reacted calmly to the first problem he encountered. Her building had four apartments, one on each of the three main levels and a smaller basement unit. None of the mailboxes bore her name, and he decided she must be living there illegally. That was all right. He would wait until he saw her coming in. He preferred a wait anyway. It let the expectation build slowly. He retreated across the street. R was a short street of Victorian town houses with rounded turrets, wrought-iron front steps, and large bay windows. Down the block, an alley interrupted the facade of windows and front steps and doorways. In it he saw a group of men, homeless from the looks of them, standing around a small fire in a garbage can. He drifted toward them. If he stayed in their vicinity, he decided, he would not be noticed as he waited, particularly since it was getting dark. He checked his watch. Six o'clock.

It was remarkable, he thought, how patient he was. Normally, waiting more than a few moments for anything caused his temper to fray and then break. But now he felt a kind of serenity. Nothing else he did made him feel serene. That was why, despite everything he had to do in St. Petersburg, he had come to Washington to handle this himself, rather than sending someone.

The door to 1475 R Street opened again, and he peered across the street. A woman came out, very tall, dressed in a sleeveless, light blue down vest, jeans, and brown leather boots that reached up to her knees. She was hatless and her hair was red. As she passed through the light over the door, he checked the photocopy of the passport picture he had bought from the hotel clerk in St. Petersburg along with the address. There was no question. It was Jennifer Morelli.

It would have been more efficient, he thought, if she had been entering the building rather than leaving it. Now he would have to follow her. But that had its own pleasures.

He waited until she crossed the intersecting avenue and headed toward Dupont Circle before he fell in behind her. After a block or two the row houses began to give way to storefronts, and the number of pedestrians on the sidewalks increased, leaving Bykov confident she would not notice him. He maintained a pace that kept him a block behind her, making certain there were always other pedestrians between them. She was walking purposefully, but not too quickly, and showing no signs that she suspected anyone was following her.

She turned right under a street sign that, with his limited knowledge of the Roman alphabet, Bykov appreciated, since it did not require him to read anything. It said 19th Street NW. That was easy to decipher. The back ends of a row of stores fronted on this street, which was full of parked cars.

A shop window caught his eye, and, despite himself, he stopped to look. It had mannequin torsos, all male, all wearing black leather garments with steel or silver studs. By stopping, Bykov almost lost her. But from the corner of his eye he saw her disappear into a store a block farther up the street. He could not read the sign, but as he drew closer, he could see that it sold groceries.

Bykov had seen American grocery stores on television and in movies, and this one disappointed him as he passed by it and gazed through the window. In contrast to the stores on television, all large and bright and stocked with fruits and vegetables that threatened to spill out into the aisles, this one was small and cramped. Some of the produce had turned brown around the edges. There must be Negroes living nearby, he thought. In the old days, the television news in Russia had rarely failed to mention that Negroes got the worst of everything in America, and that must have been one of the few true things the television news reported.

He took up a position across the street, camouflaged by people waiting for a bus, and watched as she paid for her purchases with a plastic card.

She retraced her steps down Nineteenth Street. But just as he expected her to turn left toward R Street, she headed west, toward Dupont Circle. On Connecticut Avenue she turned south, into a store whose window was filled with photographs and picture frames. He recognized the Kodak sticker in the window. It was the same sticker the tourist shops in St. Petersburg displayed if they sold film.

Bykov leaned against a streetlight, keeping her in sight. She received an envelope over the counter, offered some money, and left the store.

But again she frustrated him by not heading for R Street. Instead she walked down the block to a bookstore and entered. Bykov scanned the shop through its plate-glass window. It was large and had dozens of customers milling around. On an impulse, he followed her inside.

The bookstore had something he found odd and exotic—a café and bar. She stopped at a little marble table, leaving her groceries on a chair but keeping the pictures in her hand, and then walked to the counter and bought a mug of coffee.

Silently, he cursed. He'd had enough of waiting and following. Moreover, he realized, the longer he hung around, following her, the more conspicuous he would become. He stayed carefully on the opposite side of the store, behind a shelf of travel books, and continued to observe her.

Her back to him, she sipped the coffee, opened the envelope, and began slowly examining the photographs inside.

Bykov gravitated toward the bar. He looked around and decided to sit down when he realized that he could keep his hat and jacket on and look just like everyone else.

He squeezed in next to a pair of men who were talking over beers. The Americans paid no attention, and he decided that no one had particularly noticed him. They had a small pile of currency and coins in front of them.

Bykov pulled the wad of bills he had gotten at the clothing store out of his pocket and placed it on the bar. The bartender, a Negro, approached him and asked, "What'll you have?"

Bykov understood the man's intent, if not the words. Frantically, he searched his tiny English vocabulary for an appropriate response.

"Scotch," he said.

"What kind and how?"

Not quite understanding the question, Bykov shrugged, hoping the bartender would mistake his silence for indifference and just give him something.

To his relief, the bartender did. He poured an ounce of Dewar's into a shot glass and placed it in front of Bykov. Then he added a short glass full of ice. He counted four singles from Bykov's small pile of currency and stuffed them into the register. Bykov shoved another dollar across the counter and smiled at the man. Equally wordlessly, the bartender smiled and put the money in an apron pocket.

Bykov picked up the shot glass and almost drained it. But he remembered, with the glass an inch from his lips, that Americans sipped their whiskey. He poured it into the glass with ice, then took a sip.

The scotch trickled, slow, half warm and half chilled, over his tongue and down his throat. He relaxed slightly and looked around.

The pub was crowded and noisy. Nearly every table was full, and the drinkers at the bar were nearly shoulder-to-shoulder. He forced himself to let his gaze roam slowly over the premises, rather than remaining fixed on Jennifer Morelli.

When he did look at her, he saw that she was still poring over the photos. He stifled the urge to go over and snatch them from her hand. But what if someone joined her, and she showed them the photos?

He took another sip of scotch and felt a little light-headed. He knew his body well, and knew that such a small amount of alcohol could not affect him unless it was combined with a great deal of adrenaline. He felt loose, limber and ready, much as he had years ago before wrestling an opponent he knew he could not only defeat, but dominate, and hurt.

He let his eyes wander around the room again. The women in the store and the café looked elegant, inaccessible. That was their clothing, of course, and their cosmetics. They would look much different if they were naked. They would look much like Russian women. He wondered if American women, once he had them naked and squirming, would react to him the same as Russian women did. He thought so, but soon he would not need to speculate.

Bykov smiled into his shot glass. This was not so hard. He was more than clever enough. He pushed a ten-dollar bill halfway across the bar, caught the bartender's eye, and gestured for a refill. When it came, he left the change where it was and downed half the shot before remembering to take his time with it.

His eyes fell on another table, occupied by two men. As he watched, one of the men caressed the hand of the other. Bykov scowled.

Queers, he thought. He had heard they were open about their perversions in America. He felt a quick burst of pride that in Russia such things were still not tolerated.

Jennifer Morelli stood up then, and he could see the curve of her breasts against her sweater.

Bykov downed the rest of his scotch and strode swiftly to the exit. He wanted to be outside before she was, and he made it easily. He hurried across the street and down half a block. When she emerged from the café, he was already walking slowly in her direction, back toward the town house, on the opposite side of the street. She did not notice when he crossed and fell in behind her.

Bykov looked at his watch. It was six-thirty. She looked, now, as if she were in a hurry, and that might mean someone was coming to eat with her. He would have to act quickly, decisively. But he still was not worried. He felt more than quick and decisive enough.

He kept his distance behind her, and when she entered her building, he hung back. A moment later the lights flicked on in the second-floor windows. He checked his watch again. It was six-forty. He would give her three minutes.

In the darkness, the smells of the building sorted themselves out. He could tell that the first-floor tenant was cooking meat. Some drunk had vomited near the front steps not long ago, and whoever cleaned it up had done a sloppy job. Standing in the hallway, Bykov could hear the clanking of pipes and the murmur of voices from television sets inside. He could almost make out what people were saying. All of his senses, he realized, had become exquisitely acute. The adrenaline was seeping rapidly now into his bloodstream. He felt the same sense of enormous strength and implacable will that he had had in his wrestling days, just as he stepped onto the mat. But when he wrestled, his extraneous senses had shut down. He had never heard the crowd, smelled the sweat on an opponent's body, or saw the colors of the arena the way he heard, smelled, and saw now.

Quickly and quietly, he used his key collection until he found one that opened the front door. Then he climbed the stairs. On the second floor, he found her door at the end of a small landing. A thin line of light was visible between the floor and the bottom of the door, and he could hear music from within. It was something classical. He patted his coat pocket over his right hip. The knife was there. So were the gloves. He took the gloves out and slowly rolled the cool latex over his fingers. Surgeons' hands, he guessed, were thinner and bonier than his thick, fleshy hands, because the gloves were hard to put on. Laboriously and carefully, he rolled the latex down to his wrists and flexed his fingers until the gloves felt comfortable.

From his left pocket, he extracted the keys again. The door had two locks, but they seemed standard. Quietly, he tried his keys until one of them turned the lower lock. He waited until he could feel the bolt move. It made a sound that seemed quite loud to him. But there was no sign from within the apartment that she had heard the bolt slide over the sound of the music she was playing.

Bykov tried four keys on the top lock until he found one that fit. He was beginning to sweat, even though it was cool on the landing. The bolt in this lock was more stubborn, and he had to pull the door tightly into its frame and jiggle the key several times before he could move it. It slid open with a tinny clunk. Bykov turned the knob and pushed. There was a final impediment, a chain fastened from inside. Contemptuously, he pushed against the door and felt the screws tear out of the wood that held them.

This time she heard something, because as the door swung open wide, he heard her voice.

"Who's there?" she called out. He didn't know whether this was a name or a word, but her tone of voice told him she did not yet know what had happened.

Quickly, he shut the door behind him; the useless chain clanked against the wood.

"What . . . ?"

She had emerged from the kitchen and was standing in a narrow corridor to his left. She opened her mouth again, this time to scream. He could see the sinews in her neck bulge.

"You—" she said.

But before another sound could emerge from her throat, he was on her. With one quick, efficient movement of his right arm, he brought the butt of the knife handle down on her skull. Her eyes rolled upward and she crumpled instantly to the floor.

Bykov worked quickly. The apartment, he could see, had three rooms. He picked up her limp body under his right arm and carried her into the room that served as an office and bedroom. Over the desk hung something he hadn't seen in years, an old Party propaganda poster. There was a double bed along one wall, covered in a white down comforter and strewn with a few pillows. He stretched her out on it, tossing the pillows aside. He looked around for a chest of drawers, found it, and pulled out her panty hose. Tearing two pair apart, he used the nylon to tie her hands and feet to the corners of the bed, leaving her still unconscious body faceup. He took a third pair of panty hose, tore off a leg, and used it to make a shroud that he slipped over her head. He knew he wouldn't want to look into her eyes; that might spoil everything. He fashioned the remaining panty hose leg into a gag, which he tied tightly around her mouth. With an index finger, he probed the place toward the back of her skull where the butt of the knife had struck. The nylon was sticky with blood, but she wasn't hemorrhaging. She was still unconscious, taking shallow, fluttery breaths.

He started his search in the sitting room, where the table was half set for dinner. He found immediately what he was looking for. The envelopes with the pictures and a few rolls of undeveloped slide film were lying next to a knife and soup spoon. He pulled them out and looked at them. It was just as he'd feared. She had recorded everything. He stuffed them into his coat pocket.

Then he turned to the briefcase he'd seen in the hallway. There was a notebook inside, made somewhere outside of Russia, with brown covers and a spiral wire binder. He flipped through it for a moment, but could understand nothing written on its pages. He put the notebook in his pocket as well, then took any other scrap of paper that looked like it might hold notes. He turned to the black satchel next to the briefcase and pulled the zipper open. It contained a laptop computer, a Toshiba.

Bykov did not know how to use a computer himself, but he'd sold a fair number of them and knew that the information was recorded on loose, removable disks, and on disks that stayed in the computer. He searched the satchel and found one floppy disk. It went into his pocket. Then he took his knife, loosened all the screws he could find on the computer, and tugged at the casing for the hard drive. It wiggled but didn't move. He wedged his knife in between the hard drive and the plastic case and pressed down. The case yielded slightly, and he was able to yank the hard drive out. There were a couple of loose wires. He yanked them out as well. This went into the other pocket.

A faint moan from the bedroom told him Jennifer Morelli was regaining consciousness. Bykov ignored her for a few moments in order to search the rest of the apartment. He could find nothing that looked remotely like it contained information she had brought back from St. Petersburg.

When he turned back to her, she was beginning to strain against her nylon bonds. Behind the gag, she tried to cry out, but the sound was well muffled.

With the knife in his right hand, Bykov pressed the blade into the space just between the bottom of her sweater and the waist-band of her black jeans. When she felt the steel on her belly, Jennifer Morelli's body grew rigid. He pressed upward with the knife, catching the material against the sharpened blade. It parted easily. He barely had to exert pressure. As he did, the pale, smooth skin of her belly was revealed in a triangular form. She tried again to scream, and when she realized how muffled the sound was, she began to whimper. He reached down to his own pants with his free hand. He was starting to get hard.

Bykov flicked the blade upward when it came to her brassiere, and the white cups parted. Her breasts were smaller than he liked, but they had girlish little nipples, shrunken from her fear. He liked that.

Slowly, he caressed her right breast with the tip of the blade. A line of blood leapt up out of the flesh. She tried once more to scream.

Bykov checked his penis again. It was fully hard now, and he smiled as he began to stroke it.

Chapter Four

"**W**HY DON'T YOU GO HOME?" GRAVES ASKED.

Burke looked at the clock that hung on a green pillar, surrounded by ballooning shrouds of black plastic, in the foreign desk's corner of the newsroom. It said 9:33. The newsroom, with the first edition already on the press, was three-fourths empty. The rewriters and copy editors who would plug basketball scores and new developments into the later editions were still around, along with the cleaning ladies and a few reporters who, for a variety of reasons, preferred to postpone their homecomings as long as they could. They hung around, tilted back in their chairs, phones in their ears, trying to maintain the illusion of being busy. All of the energy had gone from the room. It was like a stadium after the game was over.

"I'm waiting for someone," Burke said.

"Who is she?"

Startled, Burke looked into Graves's sardonic face, smiling at him from the desk facing his.

"How'd you know she's a she?" he asked warily.

"The new tie," Graves said. "That and the fact that you hung your jacket up today instead of draping it across the back of your chair."

Burke smiled crookedly.

"Reporters don't ever give editors credit for having powers of observation," Graves said. "But we do."

Graves's tone was pleasant enough, and Burke relaxed. "Plus you have salacious minds," Burke said.

Graves's sallow, somewhat plump face suggested that he was pleased to be credited with being salacious. As far as Burke had seen, he was in fact either asexual or severely repressed. Graves was a bachelor, and he spent at least twelve hours every day, six and sometimes seven days a week, in the newsroom. It was one way to rise in the *Tribune* hierarchy, but Burke suspected that Graves, after giving all the evenings of his youth to the newspaper and becoming foreign editor, was beginning to wonder if the deal had been worth it. At least, Burke knew he would have wondered.

"So who is she?" Graves asked bluntly. Behind his wire-rimmed glasses, the editor's eyes looked conspiratorial.

"Sorry to disappoint you, but it's nothing romantic," Burke said. "A freelance writer named Jennifer Morelli. I met her six years ago, in Moscow. She was a summer intern for me on that program we had with the Harriman Institute."

"Good kid?"

"Definitely," Burke said. "Very bright. Worked hard. Too hard, even. If I asked her to do a little research on, say, the military budget for a background paragraph I needed, she'd stay up all night and turn in a dissertation."

"I know the type," Graves said.

"Well," Burke said, "I didn't hear from her again until six weeks or so ago. She'd married some guy at Columbia. He went into the Foreign Service. She followed him and spent three god-awful years in Tashkent. Then, when they came back to Washington for a new assignment, they split up."

In fact, though Burke didn't say so to Graves, Jennifer Morelli's husband had dumped her and taken with him what remained of her self-confidence after three years of trying vainly to find something professional to do in Uzbekistan. When Burke met her again, she'd barely been able to look at him when she asked him for help finding work, so strong was her fear of being rejected.

"And she called you?"

"Yeah. I took her to lunch. She told me she wanted to get back into journalism and to write freelance pieces from Russia."

"That's realistic," Graves snorted. "Start at the top."

Graves had climbed the ladder from copyboy, making all the editing stops in between, and he insisted that anyone who wanted to work overseas for the *Tribune* had to do time first covering fires and murders in a small town somewhere. It was one of the things Burke liked about him.

"Normally, I'd agree with you," Burke said. "But I wasn't going to be the latest person in her life telling her she couldn't do something. She needed to try. At least she speaks the language. So I gave her some tips about working over there and I let her copy my address book for Moscow and St. Petersburg."

"With all your Russian honeys still in it?"

Burke shrugged. His willingness to engage in macho badinage had its limits. "Anyway, she got back from St. Petersburg today. As a matter of fact, she called and told me she got some holy shit story in St. Petersburg. Maybe we can use it."

"What's the story?"

"I didn't find out. She wants me to see her pictures. She's really excited about it, though, whatever it is. Odd thing, though. She's late. She was always very punctual."

"What time did she say she'd be here?"

"About nine."

"Maybe," Graves said, "she stood you up and went to the *Post* instead."

Burke smiled. "I've been stood up for a lot of reasons, including the fact that I worked for a newspaper. But never because I worked for the wrong newspaper."

"Well, I'm going to pack it in," Graves said. He stuffed some papers into a briefcase and threw on his coat.

"Sorry about the Rogov story," Burke said.

"Sometimes you get the bear, and sometimes the bear gets you." Graves shrugged. "Don't worry about it."

"Maybe we could send Madonna over there to meet him."

Graves laughed. "Then Lifestyles would take over the story. G'night."

Burke waited until Graves had gone, then picked up the phone and dialed Jennifer Morelli's number.

The phone did nothing. There was no ring, no busy signal, just dead air. Then, abruptly, a busy signal. He dialed again. Same thing.

For half an hour Burke idly read out-of-town newspapers and worked on a memo to the Tokyo bureau asking for information on the cost of Toyotas in Egypt. At ten o'clock he called again. He got the same dead air, then an abrupt busy signal.

He felt angry, as he usually did when someone made him wait for something. Slowly, concern replaced his anger. Why should she break an appointment that she'd called from Frankfurt to set up? And why would her phone not ring?

He checked his Rolodex. He had her address.

―――――――

The revolving red lights from the police cars bounced slowly off the red brick facades of the houses on R Street, creating a kind of visual throbbing that matched the feeling of the blood pounding in Burke's head.

He wished he could cry. But he knew that he had the emotional makeup of the longtime journalist, and thus could not.

He could cry over things that did not involve him. Schmaltzy movies rarely failed to make his eyes brim. He shed tears watching aging veterans commemorate D day.

But the closer things got to involving him personally, the more detached he became. It was a professional advantage. He would not have cried if he were reviewing the schmaltzy movie or writing about the D-day commemoration, though he would have jotted a note that those around him did. He'd once seen a shell hit a schoolhouse in a village in Azerbaijan. His reaction had been to carefully count the children's bodies so his report would be as accurate as possible.

He never cried over his own wounds. He'd been stoic when his wife asked for a divorce, and had given it to her as gracefully as he could. It was only a few years later, when he stopped to count the number of women he'd subsequently seduced and abandoned, that he realized how much the divorce had angered him.

He wanted to cry now, in the naive faith that venting some of the anger and horror he felt would somehow be useful. But the detective sitting next to him in this squad car was being professional, and he would be, too.

Detective Robinson held a pencil and notebook at the ready. He was a slender, youthful, black man with a full mustache, Italian loafers with little tassels, and a trench coat that appeared to come from the Burberry store on Connecticut Avenue. He could have passed for a television reporter.

"Give me the names," he said, "of the people you were with for the past few hours."

Burke gave him the names. Dully, he watched Robinson write them down.

"Okay," the detective said. "Let's go over this again and get it down on paper."

Burke had already told his story to Robinson once, quickly, on the landing outside Jennifer Morelli's apartment. Despite his numbness, he was conscious of the fact that the detective would be comparing everything he said now to what he'd said then, looking for discrepancies.

"You arrived here when?"

"About twenty after ten."

"To have a date with Ms. Morelli?"

"No. I told you. She was supposed to meet me at the *Tribune* at nine. She didn't show up. I tried calling her, but her phone was weird. So I decided to stop by and see her."

"And your relationship with her was . . ."

Burke hesitated. He knew that Robinson's first instinct would be to suspect any males in Jennifer's life. But there would be little sense in trying to hide their relationship. It would only make it worse if Robinson found out.

"Business and a little social. We'd worked together. Six years ago in Moscow. Then she called me about a month ago and asked me to help her with a freelance reporting trip to Russia. I gave her some names and addresses. We had lunch—"

"You dated?"

Burke shook his head. "No. Just lunch."

"Was that all you wanted out of the relationship?"

Burke's eyes drifted down to the new tie he'd put on that morning.

"It was all I expected," he said.

He knew what Robinson's next question would be, and he knew it would be better to volunteer the information.

"This morning, she called me from the Frankfurt airport. She told me she'd gotten a really good story, apparently from one of the sources I gave her. So we were going to meet at the *Tribune* to talk about it. That's all."

"Do you usually go to the houses of people who don't keep business appointments?"

Burke understood why Robinson had asked the question. He would have asked it himself. But he still resented it.

"No. But I told you, she'd worked for me. She was a sweet person. She was going through a rough time, and I was a little worried about her."

Burke had enormous difficulty mixing the memory Robinson's questions evoked with the bloody body he had seen upstairs. He pushed the image out of his mind.

"You married?" Robinson asked.

Burke's smile disappeared, and he once again felt like he was on a griddle, searching for a cool place to land.

"Look," he said, "I understand what you're trying to do, but you're pissing into the wind here. You're going to get confirmation from the *Tribune* that I was in the newsroom until ten o'clock. You're going to get forensic evidence. You're going to get—"

Robinson's affable smile disappeared. "I'll tell you what," he said. "I won't tell you how to run your newspaper and you don't tell me how to run my investigation. Now, are you married?"

Burke sighed, exasperated. "No," he said.

"Ever been?"

"Yeah. I'm divorced."

"How long?"

"Twelve years."

Robinson nodded. "Long time." Then, "Mind telling me your ex-wife's name and address?"

Burke sighed. "Her name is Barbara. Now it's Barbara Burrell and she lives in Mill Valley, California. She's got a law practice there. She's in the phone book. If you call her up, she'll probably tell you I'm a mistake of her youth and not a particularly good father to our son because I moved East after we split up and then went to Moscow to be a foreign correspondent and wasn't there for him during his adolescence. But I don't think she'll tell you I ever used a knife on her."

Robinson made some notes, then looked up. "What was the cause of the divorce?"

Burke sighed again. "You want the long story or the short story?"

"On the papers."

"Irreconcilable differences."

"Okay," Robinson said, and appeared to wait for Burke to add something.

But the pain of contemplating his ruined marriage, on top of the pain from what he had just seen in Jennifer Morelli's apartment, was too much for Burke to shoulder willingly. He tried to change the subject and remind Robinson that he was the good citizen who had discovered and reported a crime, not a likely suspect.

"Let's get back to this case, huh? If I want to discuss my marital history, I'll find a shrink."

Robinson's jaw set and he nodded. "You saw no one as you came in."

"No one."

"How did you get into the apartment?"

"I rang her bell. There was no answer. But one of the tenants or someone was coming out, so I got in the front door and walked upstairs. Her door was open. It shouldn't have been. I went in."

"And what did you see inside?"

"Nothing. Not in the living room. I called out to her. I looked around in the kitchen. I went to the bedroom—" Burke stopped. He and Robinson had both seen what was in the bedroom.

"And then what did you do?"

"I picked up the phone and dialed 911."

"Did you touch anything else?"

"No."

The rest of Burke's answers were largely negative. He could not give Robinson the names of any of Jennifer Morelli's friends or family. She had an ex-husband in the Foreign Service, he offered, but didn't know the man's last name.

Robinson put the notebook back in the inside pocket of his suit. "So what do you think, Mr. Burke?" he said softly. "What kind of a person could have done that?"

"Sick," was all Burke could say.

Robinson nodded. "The FBI shrinks have a name for it. It's called '*piqueurism*.' A guy gets his rocks off from cutting a woman. Usually it's because his dick doesn't work for him in normal situations. So he gets a woman, ties her down like this victim was tied down, then lets his knife be his penis. He starts off with short strokes. And the more excited he gets, the deeper they go."

Burke realized that Robinson was still watching his reactions closely. He shook his head. Was that the right response?

"So, anyway, we'll ask the *federales* for some help," Robinson went on. "They got a computer that keeps track of this kind of pervert. They had a case like this about eight months ago, out in Alexandria, I think. Unsolved."

Burke shook his head again. "I'm not sure their computer's going to help you."

Robinson looked skeptical. "You said you think it might have something to do with this hot story of hers."

Burke nodded. "Yeah. She said she had some film that would show me what was such a big deal. I looked around a little—without touching anything. I didn't see it. Maybe it's up there somewhere, like in a briefcase or something. You ought to look for it. If you don't find it—"

"We'll still be looking for a pervert who likes to use a knife on women," Robinson said sharply.

"Yeah," Burke said, deflated. "I suppose you will."

Chapter Five

DESDEMONA MCCOY STOOD ON THE VISITORS' side of the security barrier and watched her escort wait for her. A minute before, the man had walked past her as if she weren't there. He'd approached another woman waiting ten yards behind her in the vast, white marble room and asked if she was Ms. McCoy. After the woman shook her head, he'd taken a position just in front of the security gate, hands crossed idly in front of his crotch, watching the entrance doors, blissfully unaware of his racism.

She looked at her watch. She would have liked to let the bastard stand there all afternoon, but her meeting was due to start in two minutes.

She walked up to the uniformed guard.

"Excuse me," she said loudly enough for the escort to hear. "I'm Desdemona McCoy, and I'm due in EUR-RO, Room 3422, for a two o'clock meeting. They were supposed to have an escort waiting, but he hasn't shown. Can you call and remind them?"

She got the reaction she anticipated.

The escort flushed crimson and cleared his throat. "Excuse me," he said. "Ms. McCoy? I'm Paul Howard. I'm, uh, your escort. I talked to you on the phone? I'm sorry, but I had no idea you were

47

so, uh . . ." He searched for a word that would not indict him.
"Pretty," he said, smiling weakly.

McCoy stifled the urge to tell the man bluntly what she thought.
Sometimes she wondered if keeping the anger inside for the sake
of a career was worth it. Nearly always, she decided that it was.

"That's quite all right, Mr. Howard," she said coldly. "I
know that to some people I don't sound—" She paused artfully.
"—pretty."

Howard looked truly abashed. "I'm sorry," he said.

"You're not the first," she snapped. "Let's go upstairs."

She signed two different registers, submitted her bag for a
search, then was issued a visitor's card. It was standard, if awkward, admissions procedure for a field operative returning to Langley for a special meeting. If she would be staying for more than a
few hours, she would be reissued her own identity badge and could
avoid all of this hassle.

Howard tried to make conversation as they waited for the elevator. It was a lame attempt.

"How's the weather in Russia?"

"Cold."

They stepped into the elevator.

"And how was your flight?"

"Long." That was obvious, she thought. Her gray flannel suit,
the one she only wore back at Langley, was wrinkled. Her eyes
were bloodshot.

Howard subsided into silence.

She'd heard that the agency's budget problems had forced some
maintenance cutbacks, but could see no evidence of that in the
gleaming walls and polished linoleum floors they traversed, heels
clicking and echoing, after leaving the elevator on the third floor.

Once, when she was a young recruit, the agency's headquarters
had appealed to the fondness for calm, discipline, and order that
her mother had instilled in her. Every door she passed was properly closed and locked. Every person she passed seemed to be walking briskly, purposefully, to the prompt and competent fulfillment
of an assigned task.

Now, walking those same halls, she felt that it would be comforting to see just one person with a door left open, feet on his desk,

papers strewn all over, listening to some zither music and day-dreaming. The agency, she thought, needed a few people like that. But if it had thought so, it would only have created a daydreaming bureau and written regulations about proper daydreaming music to listen to.

Paul Howard delivered her to the door of Room 3422 and retreated with an air of relief he did not quite manage to hide.

To her mild surprise, Nils Ostendijk, the National Intelligence Office for Russian Affairs, occupied the chair at the end of the long conference table.

"Des," he said, greeting her as if they were friends. At least he'd taken the trouble to learn her nickname.

Nils Ostendijk had managed, as far as she could ascertain, to forge a successful career out of being judiciously wrong about the Soviet Union and Russia.

He had risen to prominence in the 1970s as a staff assistant for Team B, the conservative outsiders' group that the Ford Administration had invited into the agency to second-guess the in-house Sovietologists. He had given them the data, skewed if necessary, to buttress their prediction that the robust Soviet economy, harnessed to the defense industry, would produce a colossal war machine by the mid-1990s.

The contacts he made then had led to a post on the National Security Council staff during the Reagan years. In the early eighties he specialized in reinforcing Reagan's inclination to believe that nothing would ever change in the Soviet Union. Then he helped persuade Reagan to keep Gorbachev at arm's length in 1986 and 1987, when there might still have been time to help him survive. Back at the agency, under Bush, he misread the signs pointing to the aborted coup of August 1991. But he had always taken what Washington perceived as the hard-headed, realistic approach, and he cultivated some of the right columnists and senators. He looked like a wise man: tall, thin, with a neatly trimmed beard that contained just enough gray to convey an impression of intelligence and gravity. On the basis of those assets, he flourished.

Whatever the subject of the meeting, she thought, it had to be important. Otherwise, Ostendijk would not have bothered.

She recognized only one of the men flanking him: Charles

Palmer, the deputy director of operations. Flanking him were two younger men in suits who looked like they had come to the agency straight from the Marines or Brigham Young or wherever it was that the agency found the cautious, unimaginative, and upright types it craved. They all seemed to wear the same baggy blue suits and striped ties. In the agency culture, suspenders were considered a sign of radical individualism.

Ostendijk introduced them: Peter Strauss and Richard Ostrovsky. He didn't tell her where they were based, so she assumed they were in Operations. As she shook their hands, she had the familiar feeling she was being evaluated. She wondered if and when that eternal evaluation would end.

"Welcome back," Ostendijk said, smiling a little too hospitably. "And thanks for coming straight from the airport."

She nodded, wondering what he wanted.

"I'm sure you're curious as to why we called you in on such short notice, and I'll get to that in a moment," Ostendijk went on. "But first let me say how highly I value the quality of the reporting you've been doing. First-rate."

"Thank you," McCoy said carefully. She knew her work was good. She had a feeling he was stroking her in order to prepare her to swallow something painful. "And of course I'm wondering."

Ostendijk pulled some papers out of a red folder on the table and put on a pair of half-lens spectacles.

"Well, what we have is the conjunction of two or three things that have suddenly given rise to a very dangerous situation," he said.

He looked at the papers in his hand, seeming to tease her a bit.

"I don't have to tell anyone here that the next six months are going to be, without doubt, the most critical period in Russia since the summer of 'ninety-one. If the country can make it to the elections this summer, there is no question that someone we can work with will win—Chernomorsk or Yablokov, most likely. There'll be a fresh start, a clean slate. The question is whether the present government can make it to the finish line."

"How do you personally read the army, Nils?" Palmer asked.

"Unhappy, humiliated over Chechnya, but still responsive to discipline. Grachenko's been badly damaged by Chechnya, but he's still in command. And his loyalty to the president is unquestioned. Some of our people have sat up with him in the wee hours at conferences and such, and they say it's quite evident that he truly believes in him," Ostendijk said.

"Touching," Palmer replied. "What about Zhezl?"

Ostendijk's eyebrows flickered. "Very dangerous man. Untainted by Chechnya. If he were to take over from Grachenko, the army would be in play. And he's obviously accumulating authority. The Baltic troop announcement shows that."

Palmer nodded.

"But we're not here today to talk about the army. We're here to talk about the second great danger to the government, a major corruption scandal."

"They have those every week," McCoy ventured.

Ostendijk shook his head with studied gravity. "Not on the scale that I'm afraid we're looking at," he said.

McCoy felt more uncomfortable than she had when she entered the building. Obviously, the problem they were talking about involved her bailiwick. But what were they talking about?

She said nothing, waiting for Ostendijk to tell them. After an awkward five seconds, he did.

"Of course, Des, you know about Fyodor Vasiliev's death."

"It happened just as I got the message to come in," McCoy said.

Ostendijk looked at her from over his eyeglass lenses. "Does it surprise you?"

She wondered what the correct response was. She knew Fyodor Vasiliev. He was an apolitical man, the scion of a family that had cared for the Hermitage art collection for four generations. And there was no doubt that the crime rate in St. Petersburg was such that anyone alone on the streets at night was likely to get robbed.

"Should it?" she asked Ostendijk. It was a weak response, and she hated to make it.

He grimaced, and she knew immediately she had somehow failed.

"Perhaps," he said. "We have a report from a very well-placed source in Moscow. This source tells us that an extremely lucrative deal has been struck for the sale of some art from the Hermitage. To a foreign buyer with a private collection."

"And you think Vasiliev was killed because he opposed the deal?"

Ostendijk nodded.

"So, would they sell stuff from the Hermitage?" he asked.

"It wouldn't be the first time," McCoy said. "Back in the thirties, Andrew Mellon founded the National Gallery of Art on the basis of several dozen Renaissance paintings he bought from the Hermitage collection, with Stalin's approval. He paid six million dollars."

Ostendijk's expression brightened. "I didn't know that," he said.

Score one for the home team, McCoy thought.

"But I assume Stalin used the money for the state treasury. Unfortunately, that's not the case here. A number of people in high positions in the government are in line to get cuts on this sale. The cuts, we're told, are each well in excess of five million dollars."

McCoy blinked. "What are they selling?"

Ostendijk clenched a fist. "First and foremost, the remaining integrity of a government. This could be a scandal of the sort that the public, the Duma, and the army might finally find intolerable. But we don't know exactly what. What do you think it could be?"

McCoy thought for a moment. Now, at least, she understood the problem and why she was here.

"They want to keep this sale secret?" she asked, trying to make certain she had all the facts before she hazarded a guess that would be used against her if wrong.

Ostendijk nodded.

"And just for letting it happen, people in Moscow are getting five million dollars apiece?"

Ostendijk nodded again.

McCoy let out a brief, sibilant exhalation. "Then whatever they're selling is worth at least two hundred million, maybe twice that."

"That's the way we calculate it," Ostendijk said.

The men around the table waited for McCoy's opinion.

"Well," she said, deciding to be frank, "I don't know offhand what it might be. The Hermitage collection is enormous, far more than they could ever exhibit. There are pictures stored in the attic by painters like Bilotto that could bring in five, ten, maybe fifteen million dollars if they sold them—not nearly as much as some of the paintings on exhibition, but still a nice piece of change. It might get up as high as a hundred million if you bundled together a dozen or so. But all the paintings in storage have been catalogued, the catalogues are public, and scholars regularly go see the important ones. If they sold enough of them to bring in the kind of money you're talking about, someone would blow the whistle."

"That's roughly the way we see it," Ostendijk said.

"Even more so," McCoy went on, "it would be impossible to sell secretly the paintings they have on exhibit. They have a couple of dozen Rembrandts, for instance, that might collectively be worth a billion dollars. But if they sold even one of them, it would be missed immediately."

"So what does that leave?" Palmer spoke for the first time to McCoy.

"Obviously, Charles, that is now one of the unsolved variables in this equation," Ostendijk broke in.

His intervention puzzled McCoy. Nils Ostendijk hardly knew her, and owed her nothing. Why did she get the sense he was defending her? There was a game going on here in which she was the only player who knew neither the stakes nor the rules.

"Couldn't it be arranged," she asked, "that word got to the president about this deal? Why not just let him stop it?"

Ostendijk shook his head. "Two reasons. One, we don't want to do anything to risk blowing our source. He'd be on any short list of possible leakers. Two, we don't know that the president isn't in on it."

McCoy nodded. Inwardly, she cursed. She should have known that without being told.

"Our first priority," Palmer said, "has to be to keep this whole thing from blowing up in a scandal. We may not be able to stop this sale. But if it stays quiet, we don't need to. We need to make sure it does. We can't have any news coverage. And there may be reporters poking into Vasiliev's death. They'll have to be diverted."

"Okay. What do we know about the buyer?" McCoy asked.

"We don't have a name," Palmer said. "All we know is that the Russians who are in on this seem confident that he's got enough money to swing the deal and that he's not going to talk about it."

"How many people fit that description?"

"Not many," Palmer said. "Couple of Japanese collectors. Couple of people in the LCN in Italy. A couple of guys in Colombia. Maybe a few people in this country. We're going to be watching as many as we can identify."

McCoy felt a low surge of excitement. After eighteen months in Moscow and St. Petersburg, tediously cultivating intellectuals and artists, she was, serendipitously, in a position to shine.

"The McCoy-Fokine galleries are at your service," she said, permitting herself a slight smile.

She was proud of the galleries. Her assignment in Russia was to monitor the thoughts and activities of artists and intellectuals. She had established the business as a cover, taking advantage of her fluent Russian and her undergraduate minor in art history. Ostensibly, it was a joint venture with a New York partner, the eponymous and fictitious Fokine, designed to discover talented Russian artists and sell their work in the West. With small branches in both St. Petersburg and Moscow, it enabled her to shuttle around the country, making contacts. And, she was proud to note, it had actually turned a small profit in the past six months.

"They'll be helpful," Palmer said. "But, uh, we think that something else is going to be needed. Not that you're not immensely capable, Des . . ."

Her temper flared. Finally, she could guess the whole agenda for the meeting.

"But what?" she said sharply.

Palmer flushed. "But, uh, we think that the direction of this operation calls for someone with a little more experience."

So that was it, she thought. The members of the club wanted to horn in. Now that the operation looked like it might be beneficial to someone's career, they were going to take it away. She felt her face get hot, and she reminded herself to keep her anger in check for the moment, saving it for when it would be useful.

"Gentlemen, I disagree," she said, as levelly as she could.

"Yes?" Ostendijk said. She glanced from Palmer to him, trying to read his face. Ostendijk looked benign, even encouraging.

"First of all, I'm the only one with the contacts. If we had anticipated and planned for this contingency, we could not have set up a more advantageous cover operation than the one I have.

"Second, I'm a known commodity in St. Petersburg. There aren't many black, female art dealers running around. When I got there I was a bit of a curiosity, but now everyone knows me. If we send in someone new, that person is only going to attract attention, and attention could lead to the kind of disclosure we're trying to avoid."

She paused for a moment, wondering whether she'd gone far enough. She decided she hadn't. Her mother had always said her inability to hold her tongue would get her into trouble, and maybe this was the day. But she couldn't keep silent about it.

"And finally," she said, looking directly at Palmer, "I have to tell you that I am disappointed that as soon as an operation of importance comes up, you look to send someone in to take over for me. I'm not sure I believe you'd be doing that if I were a different color and a different sex."

Palmer flushed, and the men with him all but stopped breathing. She realized that by bringing race and gender into the open, she had violated a taboo. She could not have discomfited these men any more if she'd reached into her briefcase and tossed a dead rat onto the table. That thought gave her a fleeting moment of satisfaction.

"Damn it Nils, that's not fair," Palmer began. "This is not a gender or a race thing. And I resent the implication. It's a matter of experience."

"As far as experience goes," McCoy snapped, "I challenge you to find someone with more experience in St. Petersburg or more background in art than I have. And I've been in the agency for eight years."

She noticed that Ostendijk didn't look as uncomfortable as Palmer. In fact, his face, if she was reading it right, suggested something like satisfaction. Why?

"We're not trying to denigrate your experience, Ms. McCoy—" Palmer said, suddenly off first-name familiarity. He was about to go on, when she interrupted.

"Then let me do the job I've been trained to do."

Nils Ostendijk made a tent with his fingers. It seemed calculated to look judicious.

"I have to say, Charles, that I'm sympathetic to Des on this one.

I'm sure race and gender had nothing to do with your desire to send someone more experienced to oversee the situation. But I think she makes good points. She has positioned herself well for precisely this sort of operation. And injecting new people into the situation does carry certain risks."

McCoy could barely keep her mouth closed, she was so surprised. As far as she knew, Nils Ostendijk had never gone out of his way to help a black agent, or a female agent. In fact, his protégés in the agency were all clones of himself—white males with tough attitudes toward Russia. Why would he be helping her now?

As soon as the question occurred to her, an answer suggested itself. It was so infuriating that she almost voiced it. She managed to restrain herself.

He wanted her to fail.

He wanted the Russian government to make the deal, and he didn't want the agency helping to keep it quiet. He had no interest in the survival of Russian reform. To the contrary, the rise of a tougher, more threatening Russia would vindicate everything he had been saying for the past ten years. It would revive the Cold War and make sure that the agency swam in money for the foreseeable future.

He had summoned her back to this meeting calculating that she would fight to preserve her turf. He must have calculated, as well, that she would play the race and gender card against Palmer, and that Palmer would not be able to counter it, because the agency, like the rest of the government, was so guilty of racial and sexual prejudice.

Palmer was, in fact, shrugging eloquently across the table. "All right, Nils. It's your call," he said.

Ostendijk allowed himself a thin, complacent smile. "Good, then," he said mildly. "Let's move on."

McCoy sat rigid. Bastard, she thought.

She would handle this operation, she told herself, and she would succeed, if for no other reason than to piss off Nils Ostendijk. Then she would find a decent place to work.

Chapter Six

Dully, burke stepped off the elevator the next morning on the fourth floor of the Tribune Building and turned toward the newsroom. He noticed that his field of vision had narrowed, and he saw only what was in front of him. His body seemed to be moving of its own accord.

He had not felt like working this morning, but he had not felt like staying home alone, either. In fact, he hadn't felt much of anything. He woke up with a slight headache, the only symptom of distress he had detected in himself. He felt numb, and came to work because he thought working would more likely preserve the numbness than sitting in his barren home, waiting until it was time to leave for Jennifer Morelli's funeral.

Before he could enter the newsroom, the security guard stopped him.

"Mr. Burke, there's someone who wants to see you," the guard said.

He gestured toward a short, tubby, redheaded man in a trench coat, who was waiting in the little reception area for people visiting the *Tribune* staff. The man was already getting up from his seat, hastily wiping his right hand on his coat before extending it toward Burke.

"Jimmy Duxbury," he said. "Glad to meet you."

Burke grunted. People who came into newsrooms, in his experience, rarely came bearing news. More often, they wanted to harangue someone, and he couldn't stand the thought of being harangued this morning.

Duxbury put his left hand on Burke's shoulder and smiled, as if they had known each other for years and had old stories to tell. He had rheumy red eyes and his skin was the color of a fish's belly. He could have been any age from thirty to fifty. Most likely, he was in his thirties but looked fifty. His breath stank of mouthwash. Burke knew the symptoms.

He edged away and into the newsroom, walking toward his desk. Duxbury followed. Burke wondered for a second if the man was trying to sell insurance.

He sat down and made an effort to be polite: "What can I do for you, Mr. Duxterman?"

"Duxbury."

The man handed him a business card. Burke let it lie on the desk.

"You're the guy that worked in Moscow, right?" Duxbury asked.

Burke blinked. He didn't want to think about working in Moscow. He pushed the memory out of his mind. "Yeah," he said.

Duxbury reached into a briefcase and pulled out a sheaf of papers.

The top sheet had been printed on an old dot matrix printer, the kind most people had consigned to their basements. The top line read: FOR IMMEDIATE RELEASE.

The next line read: AMERICAN EXECUTIVE REVEALS RUSSIAN SWINDLE.

Several pages of dense type followed. It appeared to be the work of a man who knew what press agents did, but did not have the money to hire one.

"You got screwed on a Russian business deal," Burke said.

Duxbury nodded vigorously. "That's right. You—"

"Well, you should be talking to the business editor," Burke interrupted him.

"The business editor said I should talk to you," Duxbury said. His voice rose an octave, edging toward a whine.

Burke rubbed his eyes and opened the container of coffee he'd brought in from the shop across the street. He sipped from it. It was bitter and scalding, just the way he needed it.

The newsroom was still nearly empty. A yard away, his computer cursor blinked stolidly and steadily, like the heart of a faithful beast waiting to do his bidding. He would have liked very much to lose himself in the morning's wire reports and story advisories. But there was no one else around to fob this man off on.

"So how'd you get swindled?" he asked, trying to sound interested.

Duxbury looked encouraged. "Well, I'm the president of a metals trading company, Duxbury and Sons in Philadelphia. My father started it. We originally specialized in scrapping old Navy and merchant ships from the Philadelphia yard and selling the metals."

Burke nodded. "And you noticed that the Soviet Union was breaking up, and decided it could be a big new market for you."

Duxbury nodded again. "That's right. I went over there for the first time in 1989. Made a deal to scrap a couple of old destroyers their Navy had been operating since Lend Lease. Broke even. But I liked the people. I wanted to keep doing business there. I thought it was a great opportunity. Then I heard about a deal in nickel."

"Nickels?"

"No, nickel. The metal."

Burke sipped more coffee and started to think of ways to get rid of this man.

"There were defense plants in Leningrad that had for years been consuming huge amounts of nickel. They use it in armor plating alloys. Suddenly, they weren't making tanks and APCs anymore. One of my contacts there said the Russians were anxious to find someone to help them unload the nickel. I was interested."

"And you started spending a lot of money to develop this deal."

"Right." Duxbury looked puzzled.

"And you paid a lot of bribes and kickbacks to get the right people behind it, get your export permits and all that."

"You've heard this story before, I gather." Duxbury seemed hurt.

"Never about nickel. Usually about oil or diamonds."

The man's doughy face seemed to sag into the lapels of his

jacket. "I took a highly leveraged position in nickel, anticipating the delivery of five thousand tons. Then the Russians screwed me. The mafia paid off the Ministry of Defense to control the nickel. They hung me out to dry by withholding nickel, not just from me, but from the whole spot market. I lost . . ."

He shook his head, apparently still dazed by what he had lost. "I lost a lot," he concluded.

Burke nodded. He had no sympathy for the man. His head was pulsing slowly and painfully. "Yeah, well, I'm sorry Mister, uh, Duxbury. If you want to leave this stuff with me, I'll pass it along to our Moscow correspondent to evaluate and check out, if she can."

"But I want you to do a story now!" Duxbury objected. "You can't wait that long!"

"Why not?"

"Because the Russians are having a big conference about international investment in converting the defense industry next week in St. Petersburg. This story needs to get out before that conference. So other people will know what they're getting into."

"Sorry," Burke said. "But I can't just take your word for what happened."

"Why not? You print accusations and charges all the time without knowing if they're true."

"Well, we print them if there's some authoritative source."

"Like Gennifer Flowers or Paula Jones."

He had a point, Burke knew. But the deputy foreign editor of the *Washington Tribune* was not in a position to rewrite the peculiar rules of Washington journalism. The fact of the matter was that there were no standards for deciding which allegations to print and which to ignore. Editors made ad hoc judgments every day, based on prejudice and intuition and competitive pressure as much as anything else.

Burke's prejudice and intuition told him that this man's story was undoubtedly going to be self-serving and one-sided, even if basically true. They told him that all of the competitive newspapers would have more or less the same reaction, so he didn't have to fear getting beaten on a story. They told him that aggrieved businessmen like Duxbury stood little chance of getting media attention unless the government took their side, or unless they had the means to hire a P.R. firm that knew how to attract attention.

"You should probably go see the State Department," he said, looking on his desk for something he could start to read, to let the man know that his time was up.

"I've been to the State Department. The guy there said they'd look into it, but if I wanted something done, I ought to try to get the media interested." Duxbury was almost wailing.

"Well, we're more likely to write about something if the government takes some kind of official action," Burke replied. The knowledge that he was giving Duxbury a bureaucratic runaround depressed him further. "Have you gone to see the Commerce Department?"

Duxbury's face grew purple and contorted in a scowl. "Bastards!" he hissed. "You're bigger whores than the Russians! Whatever sells papers you'll print. But when someone comes to you looking for a little justice—"

Burke's own temper snapped. "Get out of here," he snarled at the man. "You blew your inheritance. If there was any justice to begin with, you wouldn't have had one."

The businessman's rage had spent itself, like the gas coming out of a cheap balloon. His face was pasty and white again and his expression was slack. Without another word, he scooped up his papers and walked out of the newsroom.

"Asshole," Burke muttered as he watched him leave. He glanced around to see if anyone had been watching. A news clerk three desks away bent studiously toward a pile of wire copy.

Burke turned to his computer and wished he had had the good sense to stay home.

⸻

It snowed that afternoon, a wet, windy snow that blew in over the mountains from Kentucky and West Virginia into southern Pennsylvania, where Jennifer Morelli came from, and turned the brown earth around her grave to caramel-colored mud. Burke, standing ten yards away from the little green canopy that protected the immediate family, turned his collar up and shivered.

"Grant her eternal rest, O Lord," a priest in a black overcoat prayed, adding a spray of holy water to the moisture from the sky that was falling on the bronze casket.

Burke tried to match the faces under the canopy with the survivors' names that had appeared in her obituary. The slender woman with the gray hair and black veil would be her mother, whose name was Susan. The other adults would be her two sisters and two brothers, only one of whom still lived in Fairfield. Judging by their addresses, not many young people hung around a little town like Fairfield. In fact, only one of Jennifer's siblings still lived in town. The children would be her nieces and nephews, and he guessed that the rest were childhood friends or cousins, but there were no more than a dozen of them.

He looked around for anyone who looked like a District of Columbia cop and saw no one.

The priest finished his prayer, and one of the sisters nodded at a girl of about ten. The girl stepped forward and tossed a flower, a red carnation, on the coffin. One by one the rest of the family members did the same. When they had finished, one of the brothers took his mother's arm, and the other raised an umbrella over her head. The family turned and began walking slowly, heads bowed, toward a line of black limousines on an asphalt drive some fifty yards away, their engines running and spewing white vapor into the air.

As Burke picked his way between the flat headstones toward his own car, one of the sisters detached herself from the family group and approached him. He waited for her, hesitant.

Her eyes were red beneath her own black veil, and her face was grim, giving away little of what she was feeling. "Excuse me," she said. "I'm Connie, Jenny's sister. Are you Colin Burke?"

He nodded. "Yes. I'm very sorry about your sister."

The woman extended a gloved hand and he shook it.

"My mother wanted me to thank you for coming, and to ask if you wouldn't like to stop by the house. She'd like to talk to you."

For a moment, Burke's irrational guilt and fear welled up and he thought that Jennifer's mother wanted to blame him, if not for the murder, then for helping her daughter get into harm's way, or for not getting to her apartment on time, or for something. He had felt that way himself, often, during the past three days. But the look in this woman's face was devoid of reproach. Her eyes showed only grief.

He'd stifled his own grief, he realized. He had gone to work the next day and the day after that, and this was the first time he had no choice but to think about her. He needed to be with people who were thinking about the same thing, he realized now. He needed someone to pat on the shoulder and commiserate. That was why he had come.

So he got into his car, turned the lights on, and followed the limousines into Fairfield, past a war memorial, two churches, and a fire station, to a white frame house with green shutters, a basketball hoop over the garage, and a couple of spiky black elm trees dominating the snow-covered front yard. It was the kind of house and neighborhood film companies find when they want to show the wholesome side of small-town life.

Inside the house a dozen people, all of whom seemed to know each other, milled about, talking quietly and eating pieces of lasagna, cut from a platter on the dining room table. Burke stood awkwardly for a moment. Someone was pouring scotch from a bottle on the sideboard. He watched and fidgeted.

Susan Morelli saw him and made her way to him.

Like her daughter's, her eyes were red, but she was composed, her greeting restrained but cordial. Her face was heavily lined, but Burke could see the resemblance to Jennifer in her eyes and cheekbones. She invited him to follow her, and he walked behind her, through a living room where neighbors stood quietly conversing, into a small, paneled study. Books lined all of its walls, except where a desk stood under a window that looked out to the elm trees in the yard. Pictures of smiling children were on the desk, catching the light coming in from the south. Two maroon leather easy chairs stood at the opposite side of the room, and Susan Morelli gestured for Burke to sit in one of them.

"This was her father's study," she said. "It's a blessing he didn't have to see this happen. Jenny was our youngest. His favorite."

She stopped. Her eyes welled, and she took a tissue from a pocket on her hip and dabbed at them.

Burke could think of nothing to say.

"You found the—her, that is—that night," Susan Morelli began again.

"Yes," Burke said, uneasy. "Detective Robinson told you that?"

The woman nodded. When she spoke again, fear and anger grated across her voice like the blade of a dull saw. "Who—Who could have done this to her? Why?"

Burke shook his head. "I don't know. It could be just some random thing. There are lots of sick people in a place like Washington."

He paused, aware that the woman in front of him might well suspect he was one of those sick people.

Susan Morelli broke the silence. "I wanted to thank you for trying to help Jenny. She wrote us from Moscow years ago about how much she learned from you. She wrote me last month and told me you'd helped her prepare to go to Russia and maybe you'd help her get some articles published in the *Tribune*. She liked you."

Burke closed his eyes and felt his headache resume pulsing. He thanked her and tried to think of something he could say in return.

"I guess I ought to tell you that I didn't know her very much or very long," he said. "But she was always quiet and smart and diligent and—sweet, I guess. I . . ."

"Yes?"

"I wish I had had a chance to get to know her more."

He sounded lame to himself, but Susan Morelli's eyes brimmed and she patted him on the arm.

"Thank you for saying that," she said. "So do we all."

"Did Jenny talk to you at all about the story she brought back?" he asked. "The one that was so hot?" He felt almost ghoulish probing for information, but the habit was so ingrained that he could not stop himself. It showed up under stress.

Susan Morelli shook her head. "The last time I spoke to her, she was still in St. Petersburg, about a week ago. She said the trip was going all right, but she didn't say anything about something really spectacular."

"Do you remember anything else she said?"

"Just that she was going to see the director of the Hermitage the next day. Is that important?"

Burke didn't want to cause the woman any more distress than she was already feeling. "Probably not," he said. "Did you tell Detective Robinson about it?"

"No," Susan Morelli replied. "He called me, but he was only interested in Jenny's old yearbooks and address books. I mailed what I could find to him yesterday. I guess he thinks that maybe somebody she knew . . ." Her voice trailed away.

"Probably," Burke said. Then he shuddered at the thought that someone who knew her could have inflicted the wounds he had seen when he walked into her bedroom that night.

"You haven't got anything to drink," Mrs. Morelli said. "Would you like a scotch?"

Burke swallowed. "No," he said. "I really have to get back to Washington."

Burke called up the communications program in the computer next to his desk.

        LO SOVSET, he typed.

The machine dialed a computer in suburban Virginia. He heard a simulation of a ringing telephone, the sound of static, and then a beep as the two machines connected. Words flashed on the screen:

        WELCOME TO SOVSET, MANAGED BY COMTEX AND
        THE CENTER FOR STRATEGIC AND INTERNATIONAL
        STUDIES.
        SOVSET'S OBJECTIVE IS TO FACILITATE RE-
        SEARCH, ANALYSIS, AND DISCUSSION ON RUSSIAN
        AND EURASIAN AFFAIRS AMONG SCHOLARS, POLICY-
        MAKERS, BUSINESS EXECUTIVES, JOURNALISTS,
        AND OTHER SPECIALISTS.
        PLEASE ENTER YOUR FIRST NAME . . .

Burke typed COLIN.

AND YOUR LAST NAME . . .
BURKE.
YOUR NAME IS COLIN BURKE. PLEASE ENTER YOUR
PASSWORD . . .
SAM.
LAST LOG ON 6 JANUARY AT 11:07.12.
YOU HAVE LOGGED ON 18 TIMES.
THE LAST MESSAGE YOU READ WAS 756.
CURRENT LAST MESSAGE IS 1242.
YOU ARE USER NUMBER 833.
YOU HAVE DOWNLOADED 47 FILES.
THERE ARE TWO BULLETINS TODAY.

SOVSET MAIN MENU

(D)ATA LIBRARIES

(B)ULLETINS   (P)RIVATE MESSAGES TO
                             OPERATOR
(E)NTER MESSAGE   (R)ETRIEVE MESSAGE
(F)ILE TRANSFER   (S)CAN MESSAGES
(G)OODBYE   (U)SER LOG

COMMAND?

D, Burke typed.

THE FOLLOWING DOWNLOAD AREAS ARE AVAILABLE:
WS - WIRE SERVICES   DA - DAILIES
-----------------   -----------
PE - PERIODICALS   RE - RESEARCH
----------------   ------------
ENTER AREA OF INTEREST?

Burke entered WS, DA, PE, and RE. The machine took a moment to digest the command.

NO FILE SYSOP BULLETIN TODAY.

    ENTER NAME OF FILE TO DOWNLOAD, L FOR LIST,
S TO SEARCH.

S, Burke typed.
KEYWORD TO SEARCH FOR?
HEMRITAGE, he typed.
The machine paused, then replied:

    NOTHING FOUND FOR KEYWORD HEMRITAGE.

"Shit," Burke muttered.
S, he typed again.

    KEYWORD TO SEARCH FOR?
    HERMITAGE

The screen went idle while the computer searched. Then it spit out the results.

    ITAR1394.1207   7DECEMBER   2K HERMITAGE TO
EXHIBIT IMPERIAL COACHES
    STPKP1425.1215   15DECEMBER   1K   HERMITAGE
VISITORS DOWN THIS YEAR AS TOURISM DROPS
    ITAR1633.0107   7JANUARY 2K HERMITAGE DI-
RECTOR FOUND DEAD IN CANAL
    ENTER NAME OF FILE TO DOWNLOAD, L FOR LOST
OR S TO SEARCH OR <CR> TO EXIT.

Burke exhaled sharply.
ITAR.1633.0107, he typed. The story appeared about five seconds later.

    ITAR.1633
HERMITAGE DIRECTOR F.P. VASILIEV DEAD IN
ROBBERY
    ST. PETERSBURG, JANUARY 7 (ITAR-TASS)—
FYODOR PAVLOVICH VASILIEV, DIRECTOR OF THE
STATE HERMITAGE MUSEUM, WAS FOUND DEAD IN THE
GRIBOYEDOV CANAL TODAY, AN APPARENT ROBBERY
VICTIM.

A MILITSIA SPOKESMAN SAID THAT VASILIEV WAS
PRESUMED TO HAVE ENCOUNTERED A ROBBER OR ROB-
BERS YESTERDAY EVENING AFTER HE LEFT THE MU-
SEUM AT AROUND 9:00 P.M. HIS BODY WAS FOUND
WITH WALLET AND PAPERS, BUT THE WALLET WAS
EMPTY, SUGGESTING A THEFT.

VASILIEV, WHO WAS 55, SUCCEEDED HIS FATHER,
ACADEMICIAN PAVEL VASILIEV, AS DIRECTOR OF
THE HERMITAGE IN 1989.

ST. PETERSBURG MAYOR ARKADY KURYAGIN
CALLED VASILIEV'S DEATH A GREAT LOSS TO THE
CITY. HE SAID HE HAD TELEPHONED THE MINISTER
OF THE INTERIOR IN MOSCOW TO ASK FOR MORE
HELP IN KEEPING THE STREETS OF ST. PETERS-
BURG SAFE.

TOURISM DROPPED 30 PERCENT LAST YEAR AFTER
A SPATE OF ROBBERIES AND ASSAULTS ON FOREIGN-
ERS IN THE FORMER IMPERIAL CAPITAL.

ENDS

ITAR-TASS

Burke downloaded the file. Then he rummaged on his desk until
he found the card he'd been given by Detective Robinson. As he
dialed the number, he noticed that his headache felt a little better.

Chapter Seven

THE G-44 BUS FROM SIENA TO COLLE DI VAL d'Elsa was the first thing in Italy that felt even vaguely like home to Andrusha Karpov. Squeezed into a hard, narrow seat next to a window, Karpov could almost smell the dirt under the shoes and fingernails of the people around him. They were peasants, like the peasants in Russian buses. The woman sitting next to him was balancing a sack, made of paper reinforced with plastic, between her knees. It was full of vegetables. He guessed she was taking them to a market to sell. The flesh on the inside of her legs jiggled when the bus bounced, and both movements reminded him of the buses he sometimes rode in the countryside around St. Petersburg. Between the woman's ample rear end and his own, nearly as broad, there was very little room on the seat. And this, too, reminded him of home.

The land they were riding through, though, looked very little like Russia. There were vineyards, with the winter skeletons of grapevines propped up by wooden posts, and if that was all he looked at, he could for a moment think that they were like the vineyards he used to pass in southern Russia, near the Black Sea, on the way to the Sanitarium of the Union of Scientific Workers.

But then the bus would pass a stout brick cottage with a red

69

terra-cotta roof and a Fiat outside, or a checkerboard of small
fields and pastures, some of them still implausibly green and lush
in January, and he would be reminded that he was indeed *za
rubezhom*, out in the world, on a difficult mission in a strange land.
At such moments he could feel his bowels tighten with fear.

The bus rounded a curve and he saw, for the first time, a river,
gray and narrow, winding its way down toward the Mediterranean.
He guessed that it must be the Elsa, the river that gave its name
to the place he was going. It meant he was getting close. The bus
was ascending, heading in the opposite direction from the river's
current, and the hillsides were growing gradually steeper, until they
could almost be called mountains.

Then he saw the town, and he blinked in amazement. It was
like nothing he'd ever seen before. Colle di Val d'Elsa rose like a
mushroom from the summit of a green hillside, almost a cliff. High
walls of brown, weathered stone surrounded the town, and inside
the walls, houses of the same weathered stone were jammed hap-
hazardly together, with tiny windows that attested to their age. An
angular Tuscan bell tower, perhaps fifty meters high, was the tallest
structure. It was a town built to be easily defended. He wondered
from whom. Maybe the French? He grimaced. European history,
the history of his own continent, was just one of the things that his
Soviet education had deprived him of, filling his head instead with
useless garbage about class struggle.

The gears in the bus's transmission ground noisily as the driver
shifted down to gain traction for the ascent. The motion, coupled
with the excessive warmth from the heater, made Karpov feel
slightly nauseous. But that feeling disappeared as soon as he
stepped out at the terminal, which was built outside the walls of
the old city, at the edge of a newer quarter that sprawled down the
slope of the hill toward the river. The temperature was perhaps
five or ten degrees above freezing, and the Italians around him
looked as if they were dressed for Siberia. But to Karpov, two days
out of St. Petersburg, the air seemed balmy and pure, and he stood
motionless for a moment, taking deep breaths.

He appeared, he knew, very foreign. His shoes looked like they
were made of plastic, in comparison to the leather boots he had
seen on Italians, even on the peasants in the bus. His suit was

made of polyester and his hat was a fur *shapka*. Self-consciously, he took it off and stuffed it into a pocket on his blue parka. Then he picked up his suitcase. There was a gateway flanked by cylindrical towers built into the fortifications of the old part of the town, and he headed for it.

A taxi, a nearly new Fiat, pulled up next to him. The driver pushed a button and the window smoothly and silently descended into the door on the passenger side. Karpov appreciated such things. He knew that the best Russian car, the Zhiguli, was an imitation Fiat, built with technology imported from Italy in the 1960s, but he had never seen a Zhiguli quite this shiny, not to speak of one with electric windows.

"Dove?" the driver asked.

Karpov shook his head. He did not speak Italian, and he had no hard currency to spare for taxicabs.

He walked through the gateway and entered a small, cobblestone plaza filled with parked cars. The museum, he thought, was probably close to the tall, rectangular tower, the top of which he could see farther up the hillside. On the opposite side of the plaza was something he had never seen in flat St. Petersburg: a street in the form of a staircase, narrow and steep, leading up toward the center of town. Houses lined the staircase like walls, each with the same tile roof and the same green shutters framing its small windows. But he noticed that none was quite the same as its neighbor. One had a garret, and the next one was three stories instead of two, and the next had a little awning and a greengrocer on the first floor.

Karpov began to walk, and before he got halfway up the hill, he was puffing and beginning to sweat. His body was shaped like a pear, and he moved slowly and ponderously, with steps shorter than they should have been for a man of his height. He pulled down the zipper of his parka.

Two doors farther on he saw a small bakery. The odors wafting from it were irresistibly sweet. He stopped and looked through the shop window. He saw breads and pastries adorned with chocolate and cream. They were like nothing he had ever seen in St. Petersburg, but the sights and smells reminded him of things he had read about in Tolstoy. He saw a price tag. One of the pastries, a small one coated with chocolate and brown sugar, cost two thousand lire, which he knew to be about a dollar. The lira, he had found to his pleasure, was almost precisely twice the value of the ruble, which made his calculations of his purchasing power much easier. He did not have much purchasing power, and what he had he must carefully conserve until he bought what he had come for.

On the other hand, he hadn't had anything to eat since leaving the international train in Rome, and he was beginning to feel a little fluttery. Probably that was a sign that his body truly needed food.

He walked into the shop and gestured toward the pastry. An old woman in an apron wrapped it for him in a piece of wax paper, and he paid her with two of the thousand-lire notes he'd bought in Rome.

He tried to eat it slowly, but discovered a sweet custard filling that mingled on his tongue with the sugar and the chocolate in a way he had never before experienced. In a second the pastry was gone, stuffed into his mouth by thick fingers that seemed to act independently of his will, and Karpov was remonstrating with himself for being piggish, which altogether spoiled the pleasure of the pastry. He was, he told himself, a fat pig of a Russian and he would always be a fat pig of a Russian unless he learned to discipline himself.

He loosened the collar of his shirt, which was too tight to begin with and was becoming unbearable as he struggled up the hill.

Ahead he could see that the staircase widened and then spilled into another cobblestone plaza. But before he got to it, a café caught his eye. It had three outdoor tables, all empty, their red umbrellas furled tightly like flowers closed against the cold. But through the doorway he could see a few more tables, and a waiter in a white apron that reached nearly to the floor, and he stepped inside. His watch told him it was after noon in Italy, which meant it was well past two in St. Petersburg, and he hadn't had lunch and perhaps could afford a little soup.

He did not have to count the remains of the hard currency that Nadyezhda Petrovna had given him; he knew exactly what it contained. In his wallet he had the lira equivalent of $198, less the dollar he'd spent for the pastry a few minutes before. Neither he nor she knew how much pigments cost in Italy, but he could not imagine they would cost the whole sum, small though it was, even if he wound up having to hire a taxi.

The café was warm and inviting, and the waiter smiled cordially and called him *Signor* as he seated him. He could make out a few words on the menu: *zuppa* and *pizza* and *vino*. The prices were higher than he expected, but he'd never had pizza except for the ersatz kind they sold in St. Petersburg from street kiosks, and the wine looked local. He wound up with a bowl of minestrone soup, some cheese pizza, and a glass of Chianti.

They were superb. They were a revelation. Now he knew why Italian cuisine was famous.

A single man was sitting at the table next to him, and Karpov stared, as he sipped the last of his wine, at the plate the waiter set before him. It was full of macaroni of some kind, but in a white, creamy sauce, flecked with pepper. The man attacked it with great relish, and Karpov's appetite kicked up immediately.

He calculated he had just spent about twenty of Nadyezhda Petrovna's dollars. It was more than he had intended to spend on food for the entire journey, but he was suddenly ravenous. Before he could stop himself, he motioned to the waiter, and by pointing discreetly at the plate on his neighbor's table, and watching where the waiter pointed on the menu, discerned that it was fettucine Alfredo.

It looked marvelous, but Karpov's appetite was spoiled by his conscience and the price: 28,000 lire. He'd already spent an unconscionable amount of money before even finding the pigment, and he swore to himself that he would eat no more until he returned to Russia. He would fast in expiation of his gluttony.

Or at least, he thought, he would eat no more purchased food. He sadly shook his head at the waiter, who responded with a look of unveiled contempt. Karpov rose and slipped the remaining pieces of bread from the table into the pocket of his parka.

With his bankroll diminished by some fifty thousand lire, Karpov resumed his ascent to the center of the ancient city, trying to calculate mentally what that sum represented in dollars. For someone of his scientific prowess, Karpov was not good at mental calculations, but it came, as closely as he could tell, to about twenty-three dollars.

Then he was in a plaza more beautiful than anything he had yet seen in Italy, or in his lifetime. It was small and intimate, and every stone looked as if time had carefully shaped and fitted it for its role. To his left a cathedral with a rose window and ornately carved doors, flanked by the rectangular tower he had seen from the bus, dominated one side of the square. To each side were shops and cafés, and in the middle was a fountain. Karpov guessed that the palazzo on his right was the building he was looking for. It was an ornate building, with eight columns forming an arcade that shaded the ground floor, topped by a row of windows with alternating triangular and arched lintels, which in turn were crowned by a loggia with a small balustrade. Somehow, the pieces all worked together and made for a harmonious facade. None of it mattered as much to Andrusha Karpov, however, as the sign that he saw next to the door: MUSEO CIVICO.

He entered and confronted an ugly wood and glass kiosk, planted in the middle of a graceful foyer with vaulted ceilings and frescoed walls. He tried to walk past it, but a thin, gray-haired woman with a nose like the blade of a hatchet stepped out through a side door in the kiosk and grabbed his arm.

Karpov resorted to English. He had studied the language in school, and occasionally used it with visitors. But he had never had to speak it in a foreign country before, and he knew that his first sentences would sound ugly and stilted and ignorant. "I have letter," he said. "For director."

He pulled the letter from Nadyezhda Petrovna out of the inside breast pocket of his suit and showed it to the kiosk woman. She only shrugged, uncomprehending, and pointed to a sign that said the admission fee was ten thousand lire.

Karpov pointed to the letter. "Director," he said.

The kiosk woman pointed to the sign and demanded money.

A guard, in a fading blue uniform with one shirttail hanging out, got wearily off his chair and walked heavily to the kiosk to lend his authority to the situation.

Karpov showed the guard the letter. He glanced at it and

handed it back, shaking his head. Then he, too, pointed to the sign that said ten thousand lire. His demeanor carried the message that he had already heard all the arguments a tourist could invent to avoid paying the admissions fee.

Sighing, Karpov pulled yet another bill from his wallet and paid. With a grim smirk of satisfaction, the woman took his money and pointed to the left.

Karpov was not formally schooled in art, though he had picked up a great deal informally. He could not quite tell whether the paintings and frescoes he was seeing as he walked down a long and narrow corridor were first-class or mediocre. But he could tell immediately and surely that this was an impoverished museum, almost as impoverished as the Hermitage.

The ductwork showing in the floors and walls suggested a system installed decades ago, and he estimated that the humidity in the building was at least twenty percent higher than it should have been. The frescoes were fading badly, scaling and peeling, and in places they looked almost on the verge of mildew.

At the end of the corridor was a staircase, which led only down. He hesitated, then took it. The basement, he soon found, had been converted into office space. A woman was sitting at a desk in what he took to be a common reception area, typing at a computer terminal. He decided it would be best if he simply handed her his letter.

The letter, typed with a faded ribbon on plain, flimsy paper, read:

> The State Hermitage
> St. Petersburg
> 11th January

> Doctor Luigi Galvano
> Director, Civic Museum
> Colle di Val d'Elsa
> Italy

> Esteemed Doctor Luigi!

> I have the honor of presenting to you, by means of this letter, my colleague, Andrei Borisovich Karpov, First Deputy

Director, Department of Technology and Maintenance, State Hermitage.

We beg your assistance in the finding of pigment for Florentine ocher in Renaissance style as Cennini described. This we urgently need for our restoration work.

I will be most grateful of your help.

Yours very truly,

Nadyezhda Petrovna Naryshkina
Director of Conservation

An embossed seal, a rendering of the old czarist double-headed eagle, covered the signature.

The woman read the letter, nodded pleasantly, got up and disappeared into a room behind the middle of three doors that opened onto the reception room. Karpov looked around, shifting from one foot to the other, hesitant to sit down.

In a moment the woman reappeared, smiling more broadly this time. She held the door open and beckoned to him.

Karpov entered a small room with a working fireplace. Logs were burning merrily. A carved desk of a light, fluted wood dominated the left half of the room, and standing behind it was a thin, bald man of about sixty, wearing a double-breasted blue suit and a maroon tie. He had the smooth and polished skin that Karpov associated with an aristocrat. He extended his hand and Karpov took it.

"Welcome to Colle di Val d'Elsa, *Signor* Karpov. I am Luigi Galvano and I would be delighted to be of service." A thin mustache danced above Galvano's thin lips.

He gestured toward a wooden chair that looked to be about a thousand years old, and Karpov gratefully sat down, listening carefully for the sound of cracking wood. But the chair was sturdy.

Galvano sat down and picked up the letter. "And how is Dr. Naryshkina? Such a gallant lady!"

"She is good," Karpov replied. He was having trouble understanding the Italian's accented English, but it was the only common language they had.

"We have met several times at the Hermitage. And how is the museum?"

"Good, also," Karpov replied, not quite certain that the reply was appropriate. But Galvano's face suggested no incongruity. Karpov felt slightly more confident that he could pull this off.

"But, please tell me. Our Ministry of Culture has cooperation with the Russian Ministry of Culture. You could have sent for the pigments. Why make the trip?"

Karpov leaned toward the man, puzzled. "Excuse me?"

"Why not ask the Ministry of Culture?" Galvano repeated. "Why come here in January, when the weather is so unpleasant?"

"I don't understand," Karpov said.

"It must be an urgent matter. Too urgent to wait for red tape, eh?" Galvano said.

Karpov nodded. "Yes. Urgent."

"An exhibition opening?"

Karpov nodded again. There were always exhibitions opening. Let the man think what he wanted.

Galvano nodded sagely. "Of course. Well, I wish I could help you personally. But we are a small museum and we do not customarily keep this paint. There are modern substitutes that do quite well, as you know. Florentine ocher as Cennini described it! It is not used much anymore. But I can tell you where it is produced. It is at the Convento San Lorenzo. The brothers there make paints as they have always been made. Do you know where it is?"

Karpov shook his head again.

"Well, then, I will take you there."

Karpov understood that. And he did not want to spend any more time with anyone on this trip than he had to. The less he talked, the better off he would be.

"Please, no," he said. "You can write a map?"

Galvano shrugged, palms up. "Of course," he said.

―――――――――

Karpov found the monastery, as Luigi Galvano had promised, a kilometer from the town walls on a promontory overlooking a valley full of vineyards. It was in a newer part of the town, where the buildings were utilitarian and ugly and where it looked sadly lost and out of place. Like the buildings within the walls, the monastery was made of weathered brown stone, and it had its own high wall protecting it from the rest of the town. Karpov imagined that in Renaissance times it had been out in the country.

He rang a bell next to the wooden gate and waited for several minutes. He rang again.

He heard a bolt being thrown and the gentle groaning of hinges as someone inside swung the gate open a few feet. He found himself looking at a man of about fifty, with gray streaks among the black hairs of his beard. Contrary to Karpov's expectations, the man was not wearing a brown robe or a white rope cincture. He had on jeans, paint-mottled work boots, and a denim shirt.

"*Sì,*" he said.

"*Parla inglese?*" Karpov asked. It was the only Italian he knew.

The man inside bowed slightly. "*Momento.*"

Karpov stepped inside and watched the man in jeans walk into a building fronted by a graceful arcade. In a few minutes he emerged, accompanied by an older man. This one was wearing a black cassock, over which he had slipped a blue ski vest. His hair was white and wispy.

"May I help you?" the older man said.

"Dr. Galvano sent me to you," Karpov said, passing him the letter.

The old man nodded and read the letter carefully. "I see," he said. He spoke a few words in Italian to the man in jeans, who said "Ah" and nodded.

"Come inside," the older man said to Karpov. "I am Father Dominic."

They walked under the arcade, through another brown oaken door, and into a small reception area. The musty smell of mildew assailed Karpov's nostrils. One dim bulb in a wall sconce lighted the room, and there was total silence within. The floors beneath him were of smooth stone, and the walls were plaster. Dimly, he could discern the outlines of faded frescoes on the walls.

They proceeded down a hallway into a spacious room with two large windows that caught the light from the south.

"Our refectory," Father Dominic said.

Karpov looked puzzled.

"Eating room," the old man explained.

It did not look as if anyone had eaten there in some time. There were two long tables, but they were covered with an assortment of paints and drop cloths and a bucket with a pinkish liquid in it. One wall was covered with a peeling fresco of the Annunciation which someone obviously was trying to restore. A third of the way along the wall there was a sharp dividing line. To the right, the colors were dim, shrouded by centuries of black smoke and dust. To the left, where two lesser angels knelt, bearing witness to the conversation between Mary and Gabriel, the entire wall was brighter, but there were splotches of white in their golden hair where the paint had disappeared entirely.

Father Dominic noticed the attention Karpov was paying to the fresco. "It is by Vasari. We are trying to clean and restore it, but it is a difficult process. We have little money and we cannot hire professionals."

"What do you use to clean it?" Karpov asked. His English was starting to come more freely.

"Water, mixed with a little wine."

Karpov wrinkled his nose. It was the same traditional monastic cleanser that had destroyed da Vinci's *Last Supper*. It had destroyed icons throughout Russia, as well. Before he left, he would try to help them.

They passed through the refectory, down another silent, empty hallway, and into a small chamber with a desk and several chairs. Like the reception area, it was lit by a single bulb in a sconce on the wall. The lamp on the desk was off.

"Please, sit," Father Dominic said. "May I offer you some of our wine?"

Karpov, who was by now quite thirsty, gratefully assented.

"Vino," the priest said to the bearded man, who nodded and disappeared back in the direction of the refectory.

"Unfortunately, we do not have an immediate supply of the pigment you are looking for," Father Dominic said. "But we can get it."

"It is urgent," Karpov said.

"May I ask why?"

Karpov tried not to squirm visibly. "Um, an exhibition of Renaissance art. We are in the process of several restorations, and we want to be as authentic as possible."

The priest seemed to believe it. He smiled and nodded. "I congratulate you. Most museums nowadays use whatever ocher comes to hand. That is why we have none at the moment. The demand is slight."

"Where is it?" Karpov asked.

"You will see," the priest said.

The man with the beard returned with a green, unlabeled bottle, half full of red wine, and two wineglasses. Father Dominic poured for Karpov.

The wine, Karpov decided, was complex and delicious, assailing his tongue and nose with a dozen different sensations. He let it rest on his palate for a moment, savoring it, before he swallowed. He could not remember having wine like it.

"It is good," he said.

The priest smiled again. "From a vineyard we used to have in San Gimignano. Fifteen years old."

The wine finished, the priest led Karpov and the bearded man out into a courtyard flanked by arcaded wings that housed, Karpov assumed, the friars' chambers. To the south, away from the main buildings, stretched several acres of orchard land he had not seen from the street. But he saw no one. Save for a statue of the Madonna, the courtyard was empty.

"Where are," he said, pausing to search for the right word, "your colleagues?"

The old priest smiled. "There are few left. A couple work for the city, as teachers. A couple are here, but they are old and they stay in their cells. And there is Brother Francis, whom you met."

Karpov nodded. "In Russia, monasteries getting bigger. Very popular."

Father Dominic nodded again. "Russia is a fortunate country."

The three men passed through the courtyard and into the orchard. Interspersed with the trees, which Karpov guessed bore olives, were marble pillars with crucifixion scenes carved into them.

At the other end of the orchard the land began to rise again, until it reached the monastery's stone wall. Beyond the wall he could see that the land rose sharply, almost clifflike. And there was a wooden door in the wall.

Brother Francis pulled a large key ring from his pocket and used it to open an enormous padlock that held the door closed. With a grunt he pulled at it and swung it open.

They were at the entrance to a tunnel, but two feet beyond the entrance it was completely dark. Brother Francis reached to one side and flipped a switch. Two bulbs came on.

The tunnel, Karpov could see, stretched perhaps fifty feet into the cliff, and along its gray rock walls he could see a seam of yellow.

"The only source of Florentine ocher in the world," said Father Dominic, a bit of pride evident in his voice. "This is why this monastery was established here. The church bought the land when the pigment was discovered."

"And used its monopoly to help control what people painted?" Karpov said. He was familiar with that type of control.

Father Dominic took no offense. He moved his head sideways and down in a motion of partial assent. "Perhaps." He smiled.

Brother Francis grabbed a pickax from the wall near the entrance and walked a few meters ahead of them into the tunnel. He turned and slammed the pick into the wall, dislodging a sizable chunk of yellow rock.

"*Quanto?*" he asked.

"How much do you need?" Father Dominic translated.

Karpov pondered. They needed some margin for error. He had calculated that two hundred grams would be sufficient, but half a kilogram would be safer.

"Um, how much is it?"

Father Dominic did not reply directly. "It is of course quite rare, and there is not much of it left," he said.

"But how much?"

"A thousand dollars a kilogram," Father Dominic said.

Karpov was undeterred. If Russians knew anything, they knew about using barter to overcome shortages of cash. And the Vasari fresco would make it easy.

"I have a suggestion," he said to the priest. "If I can solve your problem cleaning the fresco in the refectory, will you give me pigment?"

The priest looked skeptical. "You know about this?"

Karpov nodded. "My work at Hermitage includes mixing formula for cleaning paintings and icons. Icons present similar problem to your fresco. Russian churches full of smoke for centuries."

Father Dominic spoke in Italian to Brother Francis. Brother Francis shrugged in elaborate indifference.

"All right," the priest said. "Let's have a look."

In the refectory, Karpov went straight to the worktable and found the bucket containing Brother Francis's solvent.

"Wine," he said, "is for drinking only."

Father Dominic smiled and nodded. Brother Francis looked skeptical.

"I am going to show you how in Hermitage we duplicated AB-57 cleansing agent used in Sistine Chapel restoration. Okay?"

Father Dominic translated. Brother Francis remained skeptical.

"You have in kitchen baking soda? Ammonia? Bathroom cleaner?"

"Of course," Father Dominic said. He whispered to Brother Francis, who turned and went off in search of the requested ingredients.

"We go to kitchen, too," Karpov said.

In the kitchen he turned on one of the stove burners and found a clean pot.

"Gelatin?" he asked Father Dominic. "Springwater?"

Father Dominic wrinkled his nose. "Unfortunately, yes, we have gelatin. Our cook inflicts it on us once a week, at least."

He disappeared into a pantry and came out with some cooking gelatin in a cardboard box. From the refrigerator he pulled a liter bottle of mineral water. Brother Francis, at that moment, came back with the cleansers.

Karpov put the water into the pot until it was half full and turned the flame up to medium.

He added a half cup of baking soda, a quarter cup of ammonia, and poured out a tablespoon of the bathroom tile cleaner.

Brother Francis pointed to the tile cleaner and asked Father

Dominic a question. Karpov did not need to wait for a translation.

"For killing fungus," he said as he added the last ingredient.

He had a noxious white liquid which soon began to simmer. Karpov stirred in the contents of the gelatin box, then went to the refrigerator and removed all the ice cubes. He turned off the heat and added the ice to the pot, stirring with a wooden spoon. In two minutes' time he had a thickened, gelatinous white mess.

He took the pot back to the refectory, trailed by Father Dominic and Brother Francis.

Karpov felt confident. The mixture he had concocted was his own invention, a weak, nonacidic cleanser, a bastardized version of the expensive AB-57 that had cleaned the Sistine Chapel, which the Hermitage could not afford. It had worked marvelously on icons. He saw no reason to think it would not work on frescoes. Just to be on the safe side, he would reduce the time he left it on the wall, making certain that it did not have time to work its way down to the paint layer. He knew what would happen when he washed it off, and he knew that they would be impressed.

Karpov took the mixture and applied it, with a clean brush, to a six-centimeter-square corner of the fresco, a section of the Virgin's robe. He looked at his watch and let it run for two minutes.

Then he sponged the solution off the wall with the bottled water.

It was like pulling up a shade in a dark room. The Virgin's robe, which had appeared nearly black, became a bright, cerulean-blue, so rich in shading that Father Dominic could almost feel the texture of its folds.

The priest gasped and smiled broadly. *"Magnifico!"* he said.

Even the indifferent Brother Francis seemed impressed.

Karpov struggled, half successfully, to retain an appearance of modesty. "I am glad I could help you," he said.

Father Dominic wrung his hand. Then he wrapped the chunk of ocher in an old copy of *Corriere della Serra* and handed it to Karpov.

"With our blessing," the priest said. "For free."

Karpov bowed. Nadyezhda Petrovna would be pleased with him. Even Lyubov might be impressed. And with luck, he thought, he could make it back to Siena before the restaurants closed.

Chapter Eight

ATHALF PAST SIX IN THE MORNING, ELEVENTH
Street NW was wrapped in a dark chill. Just a few people, hands
stuffed in their pockets and shoulders hunched against the cold,
shuffled along the sidewalks as Burke drove north. Ahead of him,
at a stoplight, he saw the Florida Avenue Grill's neon sign, glowing
on the facade of an old row house. He vaguely remembered that
the lot next door had once housed a hardware store. But it was vacant now, paved over for parking, and he realized he was relieved
that he wouldn't have to park his car on the street, or walk very
far to the restaurant, and that he was relieved as well that Edgar
Robinson had suggested they meet for breakfast, not a late supper.

He'd been to the Florida Avenue Grill a couple of times in the
late seventies, when Washington was going through a brief, transi-
tory period between the segregation of Jim Crow and the segregation of fear. When he pushed open the aluminum door, he saw
that little had changed in the ensuing years. The Grill was a long,
shoebox-shaped room with a counter down one side and a row of
cramped booths down the other. It was filling up with black men
in sweatshirts and baseball hats and coveralls. They were the taxi
drivers and furnace repairmen and ditch diggers of Washington,
and since they never won elections, or recorded rap music, or

killed people, they had little chance of appearing in the *Tribune*. Perhaps, Burke thought, that was why Robinson had picked the place. He sat down at a booth decorated with a couple of spiky green plants and autographed pictures of celebrity patrons: Lee Elder, the golfer; Clyde Wilson, a saxophone player; and a city councilman named Kwame Smith.

A waitress in an immaculate, starched white dress and a purple and white cap with the restaurant's name on it sidled over from the counter.

"What'll you have, darlin'?" she asked.

"Just coffee, please," Burke said. His head and his stomach both felt tender.

"Try the grits." Edgar Robinson's voice came from behind him. "Emma, a couple of plates of eggs with some sausage and some grits, okay?"

The waitress's face creased into a smile. "Good morning, Detective! How are you this morning? Right away, sugar."

Robinson slid into the booth across from Burke. "Two things you always gotta have in the Florida Avenue Grill," he said. "Grits in the morning, collard greens at night." He paused. "I take it you're not a regular here."

Burke's was the only white face in the place.

"Well, now I know why everyone says you're a brilliant detective," Burke said.

He knew he should be cultivating this man instead of being sarcastic, but he couldn't help himself. Under pressure, he always resorted to wisecracks. It was one of his weaknesses.

Robinson's eyebrows flickered and his lips unfurled quickly in a mirthless smile, but he said nothing. He tore open a little container of half-and-half and poured it into the coffee mug that Emma, unbidden, had set in front of him.

"So how are we talking here, Mr. Burke?" he asked without looking up. "Are you a reporter looking for an interview, a witness, or a concerned citizen? I gotta tell you that if you want an interview about the Moretti case, you have to go through the Office of Public Affairs and get their permission. And even if you do, I don't talk to the press about active cases."

"It's Morelli," Burke said.

"Morelli." Robinson nodded. "Anyway, I don't talk to the press about investigations."

"Unless you need some publicity," Burke said.

Robinson looked up at him and his face hardened a little more, until there was no softness in it at all. Again Burke wondered why he was acting like a kid unable to resist flaunting his sarcasm.

"Yeah. Unless I need some publicity," Robinson said.

"Well, I don't have any problem with being off-the-record," Burke said. "So how's the case coming?"

Robinson looked very obviously and closely at Burke's face. Burke tried to look innocent, but he'd never been very good at it.

"Well, your story checks out," the detective said. "You were still at the *Tribune* at the time of death."

Involuntarily, Burke felt relieved. He tried not to show it. Instead he nodded.

"We're still running checks on sex offenders. The computers are working on it. We're looking for cases that match the pattern in this murder and the one in Alexandria."

Burke stifled the urge to tell Robinson that computers would not help him.

"I was wondering if you had found her film or notes."

Robinson's face remained impassive. "Can't tell you."

"Why not? We're off-the-record."

" 'Cause you're a potential witness."

"Oh, come on, Detective. You tell witnesses things all the time when it suits your purposes."

"Sorry," Robinson said. He did not sound sorry. He sounded like the type of person who enjoys having a reason to say no. Burke had run into that type so often in Russia that he had almost developed an allergy to them.

Burke tried a different approach. "I was hoping you might want to exchange a little information."

Robinson's face sharpened. "If you have some pertinent information, Mr. Burke, you had better just give it to me."

"Sorry," Burke said. "If you don't want to swap, then you'll have to talk to the *Tribune*'s counsel and get permission to talk to me."

Robinson smiled thinly. "All right. Point taken. Maybe we can swap. What do you have?"

"Well," Burke said, "did you know that the director of the Hermitage in St. Petersburg was found murdered three days ago?"

"The Hermitage?"

"Big museum."

"So what about it?"

"First, did you find any notes or film?"

Robinson shook his head. "No notes. No film. And the hard disk had been taken from her computer."

"That must be it, then," Burke said.

"What?"

"Well, her mother told me that the day before she left St. Petersburg, Jennifer talked to her on the phone. She had an appointment the next day with the director of the Hermitage."

"The guy who was killed?"

Burke nodded.

"And you figure this has something to do with that hot story she said she had."

Burke nodded vigorously. "Yeah. Her mother said Jennifer didn't say anything about a big story when they talked on the phone. So it follows that she got the story the next day when she talked to the museum director. Now she and the director are both dead, and her notes and film are gone."

Emma arrived with their breakfasts. Robinson forked up a piece of sausage and chewed rapidly. He looked like the type who bolted his meals.

"What do you think the story was?"

Burke shrugged. "I don't know."

"A hot story coming from a museum?" Robinson looked skeptical.

"I don't know," Burke repeated. "I have the same problem imagining it."

The detective shook his head. "Doesn't add up," he said. "First, what could she have found out in an art museum that was so damn dangerous? And second, why does the killer cut her the way he did?"

"Why does he take the film and notes?"

"You only say she had film and notes." Robinson seemed determined to find a way to ignore what Burke was telling him.

"What about the hard drive?"

"Maybe she took it out herself to get it repaired," Robinson said. "Maybe someone stole it in Russia."

"Or maybe the tooth fairy took it and left a quarter," Burke said. "But I doubt it."

They fell silent for a while. Burke tried his eggs. To his surprise, they were scrambled badly, with the white separated from the yolk.

Robinson was halfway through the puddle of grits on his plate and his eggs were a memory.

"I know someone in the city government in St. Petersburg," Burke said.

"Congratulations," Robinson replied. He looked studiously disinterested.

"Well, I meant that maybe you'd like a political contact there."

"To help me check out your theory." Robinson's voice was tinged with sarcasm.

"Well, uh, yeah. Why not?"

Robinson put down his fork.

"Because there's a procedure to follow. I fill out a form advising the FBI of my investigative needs. They decide whether to make a liaison request with the authorities in the country involved. If they do, I get a report back."

The tone of Robinson's voice told Burke everything he needed to know.

"How long does it take?"

Robinson shrugged. "Hard to say."

"Are you going to file a request?"

There was a hint of anger in Robinson's reply. "When I find time."

"No chance of going over there?"

Robinson snorted. "Sure. I'll just stop by the petty cash drawer, pull out the money for the air fare, and go. Ain't got nothing else to do."

"Well, I know you have other cases—" Burke began.

"I got a little girl, 'round the corner from here, seven years old. Shot two days ago by a dude driving by in a Lexus. Just playin' on the porch in front of her house. I got a woman, with three kids, shot on the corner by some gang last week. I know who did it, but up till now I haven't been able to get anyone to testify. I got seventeen unsolved murders on my list right now. You know how many murders the District had last year?"

"Lots," Burke said.

"Four hundred and seventeen. Know how many we closed?"

"Less than that."

"Two hundred and forty-seven."

"I'm not saying you're not busy," Burke objected, trying to keep both his white guilt and his temper in check. "I'm just saying—"

"That this case should get a higher priority?"

"No. That there's a good lead you could check out."

Robinson's eyes were flat and cold. "And I'm telling you thank you very much, sir, and it will be checked out."

The air over the Formica table was carrying a heavy burden of tacit hostility. Burke could sense, without being told, the black man's resentment that in a city where his family and friends were at risk of being killed every day, a reporter from the *Tribune* only got interested when a white woman died. He knew Robinson could sense his own feelings about city employees who talked of filling out forms. There was nothing he could do about either opinion.

He stood up and tossed a twenty on the table.

"Thanks for the breakfast," he said.

Robinson pushed the money back across the table. "It's taken care of here," he said.

Burke couldn't resist striking out at the man. "This time, let it be on the paper. We've got a special expense account for cops' meals."

"Martini," Graves said. "With a twist."

"Yes sir," the waiter said. "And you, sir?"

"Ice tea," Burke replied, grimacing.

The waiter's supercilious eyebrow flickered momentarily, but in the dining room of the Jefferson Hotel, the staff was too well trained to comment on a change in the habits of one of the customers.

"Damn," Graves said, "I thought you were one guy I could count on not to make me feel guilty about having a drink at lunch."

Burke smiled wanly. If he had not invited Graves to lunch for a reason, he would have told him the truth. But the truth would not put Graves in a mellow and receptive mood.

"I'm taking some antibiotics," Burke said. "Not supposed to mix them with alcohol."

Graves nodded.

The truth was that a week ago, Burke had had three Jack Daniel's at lunch, alone. He had returned to the office unsteady. No one noticed. He had always promised himself that he would quit if he saw those symptoms in himself. So he had quit. So far, it had only been hard a couple of dozen times.

The waiter returned and set their glasses down. They made only the most muted of sounds as they came to rest on the thick white linen covering the table.

With no enthusiasm, Burke squeezed lemon into his ice tea and watched Graves take the first sip of his martini. At least he hadn't ordered Jack Daniel's.

He told Graves about what he had learned from Mrs. Morelli, Detective Robinson, and his computer. Graves listened, sipping his drink slowly.

"So you think someone killed her because of what she found out in St. Petersburg?"

"There's a good chance."

"I thought the police were saying it was tied to that Alexandria case."

"They do," Burke said. "I think they're wrong."

Graves set his martini glass down and ran his fingers up and down the stem. "So?"

"So I want to go to St. Petersburg and find out for certain."

"I was afraid you were going to say that," Graves said.

"Well, why not? She said she had a holy shit story. And the killing gives it a local angle."

Graves shook his head the way an adult shakes his head at the naiveté of a child. "Let me acquaint you with a few facts of life. Maybe you didn't hear about some of them because you were out of the country for the last decade." He paused. "Or was it the last century?"

"Okay," Burke replied. He folded his arms in front of him.

"Fact number one." Graves held up an index finger like a referee showing the count to a groggy boxer. "We already have a Moscow bureau. This bureau has a very good correspondent. You should know. You've been editing her copy. If we want to look into something in Russia, she's the one to look into it. And as I recall, you were fairly jealous of your territory when you were in Moscow."

Burke stared past Graves's shoulder at one of the English hunt pictures that decorated the Jefferson dining room. "She's up to her ears in Moscow stuff. She couldn't get away to do this even if she wanted to."

Graves shrugged, declining to contest Burke's assertion or capitulate to it.

"Fact two," he continued, plucking at his middle finger. "I hired you to be an editor, not a reporter. And it wasn't that easy, let me tell you. The way you quit *America Weekly* didn't impress anybody."

"I got a good story and they wouldn't print it," Burke interrupted.

"If every reporter who had a good story spiked left in a huff, we'd have janitors covering the White House," Graves said.

"Look, Colin, don't get me wrong. You were a good reporter. But now you're on the wrong side of forty and you're trying to quit drinking. There's a lot of guys like that."

Burke blushed and scowled.

"You don't think I've used the old medicine dodge?" Graves said, a small smile on his lips.

"I'm not drinking," Burke said.

"And good for you. But I'm saying it's time to make a graceful transition. Use the expertise you picked up in Russia. Help guide the paper."

Burke sighed. "I understand what you're saying. But I feel responsible for this woman's death. I encouraged her to go to Russia. I gave her contacts."

"So how will you going to Russia change that?"

"Well," Burke said tentatively, "maybe I could find out what the story was, and that way have an idea of who killed her."

Graves responded by throwing a hand up in front of his eyes and turning his face away, as if from a bright light.

"Oh, please," he said. "The glare from your shining armor is hurting my eyes."

The waiter returned at that moment, pad in hand. "Do you two gentlemen need a little more time to decide?"

Graves chortled. "To decide on lunch? Or if he should be committed?"

The waiter's professional aplomb wilted for a moment and his pad and pencil sagged.

"No," Graves said. "Just kidding. I'll have the clam chowder and a house salad."

"Broiled trout," Burke said.

"See," Graves said. "You know what's sensible for your body. How come you don't know what's sensible for your career?"

"Well, Ken, this is just something I think I have to do."

Graves made a vomiting motion with his mouth and hand. "Jesus!" he said. "What drivel! Where do you keep your white horse?"

Burke grinned. "Well, actually, I just rent one when I need to."

Graves snorted. "Sorry, Colin."

"Well, then, I'd like to take a week off."

Graves shook his head. "You haven't been back with us long enough to accumulate any vacation."

"Okay. Then I've got bad news."

"What's that?"

"My mother in California has taken ill. I'm going to need about a week's compassionate leave."

Graves snorted again and allowed himself a faint hint of a smile. "You won't give up, will you?"

Burke stared dispassionately back at him. "I don't know what you mean."

"Okay, take off," Graves said. "But if you should happen to take the wrong plane, let me advise you of a couple of things. One, don't expect me to back you up if you get in trouble. You're strictly on your own. And if you wind up with Jill Smithfield in Moscow bitching to her friends here—and she has them—that you're horning in on her turf, or any other complaints, I'm going to be on her side."

"Fair enough," Burke said.

"Use your own damn money," Graves said. "And dress warm. I understand California is really cold this time of year."

Chapter Nine

Burke waited in his seat until nearly all the other Moscow passengers, all the oil riggers and economists and evangelists and salesmen, had disappeared up the aisle. He wanted to walk off the plane alone. He found, somewhat to his own amusement, that he resented the crowds arriving at Sheremetyevo, the way he might resent the customers at a newly fashionable restaurant that had been quiet and easy when he first discovered it.

A decade earlier, before glasnost and perestroika, his first flight into Moscow had been that way, quiet and empty. And filled with foreboding. Russia in those days cultivated an image of state paranoia, and even experienced visitors on legitimate business had felt at least a twinge of dread. Now, he knew, the once-feared state had become a slatternly beggar, and the highway from the airport was lined not with Leninist slogans, but with billboards from Sony and Samsung and Snickers candy bars.

But the smell as he stepped out of the plane was much the same, a smell of acrid diesel fumes carried by cold, wet air that swept through the joints in the jetway and chilled the platform.

There was, as always, a young soldier from the Pogranichniye Voiska, the border troops, the black bill of his campaign cap pulled down low over his eyes, and he was, as always, holding a counter that clicked as he checked off each foreigner seeking to enter the Motherland. But the soldier was a kid with pimples and a goofy little half grin. He would never have been admitted to the border troops in the old days, when the soldiers who presented foreigners with their first impression of the Soviet Union all had, by regulation, dour and unsmiling faces.

Sheremetyevo Airport was still the gloomiest terminal in the world. The Germans had built it for the Soviets prior to the 1980 Olympics, but the Soviets had removed nine-tenths of the lightbulbs the designers had intended. The ones that remained emitted a dingy gray light.

Burke had a twenty-minute wait in a crowd of people at the passport control booth, before a more properly surly member of the border troops inspected his visa and passport and stamped the visa with a heavy thunk. Another thirty minutes elapsed waiting for his luggage, which appeared on a carousel that was marked as if it were reserved for an incoming flight from Delhi. He wondered whether the Delhi luggage would show up on a carousel marked Frankfurt.

He peered through the gloom to see if the customs sign designating red and green corridors was unchanged. It was, and he laughed. Sometime during the height of perestroika, some reformer had ordered the customs bureaucracy to emulate the Western practice of green customs corridors for people with nothing to declare, enabling them to avoid the slow, methodical, and often enervating luggage search that was the traditional lot of every traveler to the Soviet Union. For a couple of weeks the reform had worked, and the lines at the customs barrier disappeared. Then some resourceful bureaucrat had appended a new regulation to the sign: no one with more than fifty dollars could use the green corridor. Since everyone arriving at Sheremetyevo had at least fifty dollars, the green corridors were effectively rendered useless. They remained in place, unused. The lines at the remaining red corridors got longer than they ever had been. It seemed to Burke to epitomize the way the Russian bureaucracy had stifled perestroika, just as it had stifled the reforms of Alexander II, and Stolypin, and might well continue to stifle reforms until the next Ivan the Terrible or Peter the Great or Stalin came along and, through terror, forced the people to change.

The queues, the smells, and the dim light somehow melded in Burke's mind to produce a feeling of fond exasperation. For the better part of ten years, he had lived in Russia, watching the country struggle to overcome its own history, hoping, under his veneer of journalistic detachment, that it would. He had, of course, always been set apart from the Russians by his passport; in some important respects, he'd been like a man in a bathyscaphe going underwater to observe the fish. But he'd suffered along with the Russians under the old regime, as much as a foreigner might. And he had exulted, as much as a foreigner could, in the Russians' triumphs. He had very nearly cried, alone in his office, sitting at a window and watching the tanks rumbling out of the city in August of '91. And now he had taken the first opportunity that presented itself to come back, nine months after leaving Moscow for what he thought was the last time, nine months after ostensibly going home. He would have had to hesitate if the border guard had asked him whether he'd returned to Russia to find out more about Jennifer Morelli's death or to find out more about Russia.

Sometimes he wondered what his life would have been like if he'd studied Japanese or French instead of Russian. More comfortable, no doubt, but less interesting. Russia, Burke thought, was a hopeless affair that he couldn't quite break off.

He looked at his watch. It was ten o'clock. Between flight delays and the red tape at Sheremetyevo, he'd lost four hours. There would be no time to stop and see anyone in Moscow this evening. He would have to go straight to the station to catch the train.

He wondered if the airport taxi drivers' mafia was as greedy and rapacious as it had been since perestroika let slip the dogs of capitalism.

A member of that cartel sidled up to him as he left the customs enclosure.

"Taxi?" the man asked.

"To Leningrad Station?" Burke asked.

"Eighty dollars," the driver said confidently.

"You're out of your mind," Burke countered. "Twenty."

The driver nodded his assent.

"But thanks for asking," Burke said.

The *Krasnaya Strelka*, the Red Arrow midnight express from Moscow to St. Petersburg, stood huffing and trembling by the platform. As Burke lugged his bags along the dark macadam platform toward the first-class car at the front of the train, he felt a pleasant sense of anticipation. He would be alone for eight hours with no telephone, no messages from the Cairo bureau, nothing but his thoughts.

Trains, as far as he was concerned, were the only way to travel in Russia. In contrast to Aeroflot's planes, the trains generally left on time. In first class, at least, they were comfortable enough. There was a certain efficiency to overnight train travel. He could put in a full day in one city, sleep on the train, and arrive somewhere else with a full day ahead of him. They didn't derail as often as Aeroflot's planes crashed, and when they did, the passengers had a shorter fall.

He handed his ticket to the conductor, a stout woman of uncertain origins, with red hair and wearing a white blouse puffed out below the hem of her green uniform jacket.

"Tea, as soon as you can," he said. She nodded an affirmation.

This would be a first, he thought. A Russian train ride on tea.

He wrestled his bags around her and up the iron steps into the train. His compartment, the one next to the conductor's, was empty. He put his bags away, sat on his bunk, propped his feet on the opposite bunk and hoped it would remain empty. The culture of the rails would require a traveling companion to offer to share his vodka, and he did not want the temptation. This evening it would have been nice to get drunk, quietly and privately. He hadn't allowed himself to think so since her death.

Burke was a drinker of catholic tastes. He drank beer on hot summer days and cognac on cold winter nights. He drank wine with dinner and a Bloody Mary, on occasion, with breakfast. In Russia he'd been a vodka drinker, and he learned to throw back his head and pour the stuff down his throat the way the Russians did. In America he preferred Tennessee whiskey.

The conductor arrived with his tea, served, in the Russian style, in a thin, brittle glass with red stripes around the brim, housed in a filigreed metal container with a handle. Burke gave her a couple of dollars.

"Please bring it every half hour or so," he said. He did not want to be without something to sip on. He tasted the tea. It reminded him of hot, rusty water.

He pulled out his paperback copy of *The Brothers Karamazov*, in Russian, which had never failed to put him to sleep in the ten weeks he'd been reading it.

Burke read Dostoyevsky in Russian the way he did push-ups in the morning, not because he enjoyed it, but because he felt he had to. He had managed only two pages on the flight over before succumbing to the temptation of the in-flight movie.

He had been wading through this chapter, on the Elder Zosima's admonitions to Alyosha, for at least a month. He knew that completing the book was likely to join an infinitely long list of promises he'd made to himself and had broken. Dostoyevsky was the only Russian writer he knew who was just as turgid in his native tongue as he was in translation.

But he began his assault.

"Proclaimed the world freedom, particularly in the most recent time, but what do we see in this their freedom? Only slavery and suicide! For the world says, 'You have desires and therefore satisfy them, for you have the same rights as the most knowledgeable and powerful. Fear not to satisfy them but even multiply them.' This is the latest teaching of the world. In this they even see freedom. And what comes from this right of multiplication of desires? In the rich, *uyedinyeniye* . . ."

He didn't know the word *uyedinyeniye*, and he looked it up in his pocket dictionary. "Solitude," the dictionary said. It wasn't a term much needed in contemporary Russia, at least not in the physical sense. He continued translating.

". . . in the rich, solitude and spiritual suicide; in the poor, envy and murder; for they gave them rights, but they have not shown them the means of satisfying their desires."

The syntax was as tortuous as the layers of freeways and interchanges outside the Pentagon that commuters in Washington called the Mixing Bowl. Burke's mind wandered. He noticed the train was moving, and he took another sip of tea, thinking it might have gotten stronger. It had not.

"Ah, Brat'ya Karamazov. Ochen vnushitel'no," a woman's voice said from the corridor outside the compartment.

Burke looked up. The woman standing in the frame of the compartment's door was maybe only an inch less than six feet, with loosely curled black hair that fell to the collar of an Irish fisherman's sweater. She wore jeans, polished brown boots, and long, silver earrings that dangled when she cocked her head, as she was doing at the moment. She was wearing some kind of perfume that smelled sweet and flowery, but subtly so. Her skin was deep, cocoa-brown. He had never heard a black woman speak Russian.

He moved his feet off the opposite bunk—her bunk, evidently.

"Vnushitel'no is a very useful word, I've found," he said. "It means impressive, but leaves open the question of whether it's favorably impressive or just—impressive."

The woman smiled broadly. "Well," she said, switching to English, "I've heard that only a native speaker can read *The Brothers Karamazov* in Russian."

"I've heard the same thing," Burke said. "I think it's true."

She laughed from down in her throat, a sound that almost made him forgive her intrusion on his solitude. She stepped into the compartment, tossed a green nylon duffel bag onto the bunk, and extended her hand.

"Desdemona McCoy," she said. "I hope you don't mind, but it looks like this is the designated foreigners' compartment on this train, and I'm sharing it with you."

She moved, he thought, with an elegant economy.

Burke stood up and took the hand. It was cool and dry. Her nails were painted a deep red, almost brown.

"Not at all. Colin Burke."

She cocked her head. "Aren't you with *America Weekly*?"

"Used to be," Burke said. "I work in Washington for the *Tribune* now."

She nodded. "I remember your byline. I used to read your articles about perestroika and glasnost when I was in graduate school. For a journalist, you seemed to know Russia pretty well. You were in Moscow a long time."

"Thanks," Burke said. "But you should've read my stuff on Stalin and Trotsky. That was my prime."

She gave him a slow smile that told him she was glad to have him to talk to, and she sat down. There was a small Formica table cantilevered under the window of the compartment, extending about eighteen inches out into the narrow space between the two bunks. They were sitting on their respective bunks, knees all but touching, facing one another. She reached into her bag and pulled out a bottle, which she set on the table. It was red wine, Chateau Margaux.

"I can never sleep on a train without a glass of wine," she said. "Care to join me?"

Burke hesitated. Then he gestured toward brown remnants left in the tea glass. "Can't sleep on wine," he said. "I'm having tea. Care to join me?"

She shook her head. "I thought reporters had a union rule that prohibited passing up a free drink."

"That's true," Burke said. "But unfortunately, I'm in management now."

"Well, I'm glad to hear that," she said. She rummaged deeper in the bag and came out with a clear plastic cup and a Swiss army knife, from which she pulled a corkscrew. She had long, slender hands, with no rings on them.

He took the corkscrew when she proffered it, thanked her, and opened the bottle. When he'd poured her glass half full, he raised his tea toward her and proposed a toast.

"To strangers on a train," he said. "With apologies to Hitchcock."

"Strangers on a train." She smiled back. "But relax. I'm not going to ask you to kill anyone."

She touched the rim of her glass to his. He could smell the wine in the compartment now, and it smelled excellent, mellow and dry with a lot of fruit in it. He savored the aroma, suddenly very conscious of the enforced intimacy of the space they would be sharing for the next eight hours.

It was odd, Burke thought, how meeting in Russia seemed to narrow the differences that would normally have existed between them. Amtrak would probably never put a man and a woman, strangers to each other, together in a sleeping compartment on an overnight train from New York to Chicago. But if it did, the upshot would no doubt be an awkward and embarrassed moment, then an effort to change the arrangement.

The American social barriers between blacks and whites were subtler, though no less real. But he'd noticed, on the few occasions when he ran into black Americans in Russia, how the Russian context made them both aware of how much culture united them, rather than how much color divided them. It was a pleasant fringe benefit of working in an alien land.

The train began to pick up speed, and they both watched silently for a moment as the platform disappeared behind them, replaced by a series of dark building silhouettes and the occasional streetlight. Not many lights burned in Moscow after midnight. Few could afford to keep them on. She shifted on her bunk to be able to peer out the window more easily, and her knees brushed lightly against his.

After a while he asked her where she'd been to graduate school, and she told him Columbia.

"Did you know Jennifer Morelli?" he asked her, almost involuntarily.

"I don't think so," the woman said. Burke was relieved. "Friend of yours?"

"Yeah," Burke said. "Worked as my intern in Moscow one summer. Went to Columbia, but I guess it's a big place."

They talked for a moment about Russian scholars they both knew. He finished his tea and hesitated, wishing the conductor would come in with a fresh glass, afraid that if he had nothing to sip, he might start watching her with the sad eyes of a dog begging under a dinner table.

Then he asked her what she was doing in Russia, and she told him about the McCoy-Fokine galleries, and handed him her business card.

"Maybe you knew Fyodor Vasiliev," Burke said.

"The director of the Hermitage?"

Burke nodded.

Her brown eyes got heavier and sadder. "I met him a few times. Openings, receptions. We had friends in common, but we weren't friends. But I thought he was a sweet man, and my Russian friends all said he was."

She shuddered. "It was a horrible thing that happened to him."

Burke nodded and poured her another glass of wine.

She took the smallest possible sip and laid the glass down again.

"Hear anything about what happened to him?" he asked.

She answered casually. "Is that what you're going to Peter to write about?" Like the natives, she used a short form of the city's name.

Burke nodded.

She paused for a moment, reflecting. "I'm not sure I should tell you. . . ."

There was a knock on the door. Their conductor, wearing carpet slippers now instead of boots, was bringing tea and demanding fifteen hundred rubles each as a laundry fee for the linen they would spread on their bunks. Burke, who had a pocket full of old ruble notes, paid for both of them.

He turned back to her and gratefully sipped some tea. "What shouldn't you tell me?"

"It's just gossip," she said, evidently reluctant.

"Well, you know men," he said. "We're incorrigible gossips."

She smiled, though evidently still not ready to tell him what she'd heard.

"Why do you want to know?" she asked. "Why does the *Washington Tribune* care about a museum director getting killed in St. Petersburg?"

Burke gulped a little more tea and tried to think of a plausible lie.

"Our publisher," he said. "She met him a few years ago when he was visiting the National Gallery in Washington, because she's on the gallery board. She liked him. She thinks . . . she just—wants to take notice, I guess. Maybe it'll make a good feature."

McCoy leaned back against the cushion behind her and folded her arms across her chest.

"So you're going to exploit him for the sake of a story."

The undertone of disdain in her voice startled Burke. "Pardon me?"

"Nothing personal," McCoy said. "But you know—I see your

type on CNN. Once in a while I see 'em in Moscow. I've seen 'em in New York. You're out to get yours. That's all you're out for."

"Well, that would make us fit in well in Russia, wouldn't it? But I guess I have to admit that's part of it," Burke said. "I want to see my name on the front page one more time before I hang up my ego and retire permanently to editing."

McCoy laughed. "Burke, you're going to make me like you in spite of my better judgment about the press."

"Well, self-deprecation has always been my best interview technique."

She laughed again, but shook her head. "You're not going to talk me into it."

Now Burke was intrigued. "All right," he said, "let's talk about something else. How'd you get the name Desdemona?"

She rolled her eyes in mock horror. "Anything but that! I'll tell you anything else you want to know."

"Tell me about Vasiliev."

She hesitated. Streetlights in a rapidly passing village caused some shadows to flit across her dark face.

"I shouldn't."

She was the type who wanted to tell what she knew, he decided, but not under pressure. His best chance of hearing what it was lay with feigning indifference.

"Okay," he said. "I give up." He looked at his watch. It was past one. "I guess I'll turn in."

She finished her wine, rummaged in her bag and pulled out a blue warm-up suit, the kind of clothes she might have worn for jogging or going to the gym. In Russian trains, though, they were the equivalent of pajamas.

Under the etiquette of Russian train travel, Burke's obligation now was to leave her in the compartment and go out to the platform between cars for a cigarette. He excused himself, closing the door behind him, and spent ten minutes in the narrow corridor of the car, watching the silhouettes of telephone poles flash by.

He wondered, as he watched, what gossip she had heard. He wondered whether she had been offended by the way he had refused her wine. He wondered whether it had occurred to her, as it had to him, that they could indulge in a quick, passionate coupling on this train. He wondered when he would be old enough to count on his brain doing his thinking for him instead of his testicles.

He returned to the compartment and found that the lights were out and she'd gone to bed. In the dim light filtering in from the outside, he could see she'd pulled the combination of top sheet and blanket that the Russians called an *odeyalo* up to her neck. Her eyes were closed.

Quickly, he tossed the sheets and the blanket onto his own bunk, slipped off his shoes, and lay down in his clothes. He was wearing his usual Russian traveling outfit, jeans and a turtleneck, and sleeping in them could not make them any more rumpled than they already were. He listened for a while to the sound of the wheels clicking over the rails, waiting for it to lull him to sleep.

Her voice, throaty and seemingly half asleep, came from her side of the compartment.

" 'Night, Burke," she said.

"G'night," he replied.

But she was not through talking. "Tell me something about yourself," she said. "Here in the dark. It's so confessional."

He turned his head and peered over the flat surface of the Formica table. As best he could make out, her eyes were still closed.

"What would you like to know?"

"Well, are you married? Have a family?"

"Was married," he said. "Have a son."

"What's your son's name?"

"Sam."

"What's your ex-wife's name?"

"Barbara."

"Why'd you get divorced?"

Her eyes were still closed, and he wondered why she'd suddenly developed a curiosity about these things. Maybe, he thought, she was wondering about the prospect that he had wondered about. Maybe she was just nosy. Then again, maybe this was her way of leading up to spilling what she'd heard about Vasiliev.

"I was hard to live with," he said.

"I'll bet," she said. She shifted on the bunk, turning her back to him.

"It was the sort of thing that happens," he said, staring at the ceiling. "We met in college. We had a good time together. We were both a little counterculturish. We lived together in a group house. We worked on the *Daily Californian*, wrote editorials against the war."

He wondered if she understood which war, then decided she probably did.

"Then, after graduation, she taught school and I worked for a paper called the *Berkeley Barb*. We had a kid; we got married when she was pregnant. Somewhere in there, we decided we needed careers. I went to work for the *Oakland Tribune*. She went to law school. She complained that I wasn't there enough to help with Sam. I was working days and nights sometimes. I complained that she was the one who wanted a kid and law school both. Finally, she moved out. I was angry, so I got a job in Washington, at the *Tribune*. Then I went overseas. She's remarried, to another lawyer, and they have matching BMWs. I see my son for a few weeks in the summer, and I send him checks."

He had told her, he realized, a lot more than she had asked to hear. He wondered why.

"So ever since, you've been living the carefree bachelor life? Different girl every night?"

There had been a lot of women, he thought, fewer than he wanted, more than he needed. There had been a lot more nights alone.

"Something like that," he replied.

"I'm sorry your marriage didn't work out," she said.

"My own damn fault," he said.

"I think you're too hard on yourself," she replied from the darkness.

"Thanks."

"But you probably were hard to live with," she appended.

He smiled to himself. "Now tell me why they call you Desdemona," he said.

Her voice was muffled slightly by the wall of the compartment. "My mother taught English literature."

"Oh," he said.

"I guess I'm just lucky," she went on, "that it's not Ophelia."

Burke smiled to himself. "If I promise not to call you Ophelia," he said into the darkness, "will you tell me what you heard about Vasiliev?"

She was silent for a moment. When she replied, she did not turn back toward him.

"Well," she said, "the gossip is that Vasiliev was gay. And that it was another gay man who killed him."

"Why?"

"I don't know. Some kind of lovers' quarrel is what I heard."

"And did you hear who did the killing?"

"No."

He sat silently, weighing what she'd told him. It was hard to connect to Jennifer Morelli's death in Washington.

"Can I ask who told you this?"

She turned and raised a hand, palm toward him, as if to fend him off. He could see its outline in the moonlight filtering in from outside. "Sorry. That I won't do, even if you stick bamboo shoots under my fingernails. You're a hotshot reporter. I'm sure you can track it down."

He could sense that she meant it.

Then the pale light from the moon and the stars was cut off and the quality of the sound from the wheels and the rushing wind changed and began to reverberate.

She twisted her head toward the window and looked out. "What's that?" she asked.

"A tunnel," he replied.

She turned her face once more toward the wall.

"It just goes to show," he said.

"Show what?" She sounded sleepy.

He sighed quietly. "Sometimes a train going into a tunnel is just a train going into a tunnel."

She laughed.

Chapter Ten

CHARLES HAMILTON MERRILL GAZED AT THE vast, unfenced expanse of green, rolling pastures visible from his bedroom window and marveled yet again that one of the ten best private art collections in the world could have made its way to such a place.

He was, he knew, somewhere in the hinterlands of Colombia, an hour's flight southwest from Bogota via small, private jet. But the people who had deposited him here had not felt a need to give him precise coordinates. Nor had he felt it politic to ask.

Merrill sipped from the cup of coffee set before him on a damask tablecloth so rich it was almost moist to the touch. The coffee was delicious, and he smiled. Good coffee, at least, was something he would have expected to find in this part of the world.

The movement of some buffalo about a mile away caught his eye, and he stared again at the hacienda spread before him. Paintings, he had learned, were not the only exotica collected by his host and client. The hacienda, he had been informed politely when he inquired, had seventeen African, Asian, and North American wildlife species running wild over its 300,000 acres. He had seen zebras, giraffes, and several kinds of smaller, horned deer that he could not name.

There was a knock on the door, and a servant, a squat woman wearing a homespun dress and white blouse, entered.

"Don Rafa," she said, and pointed downward. Then she pointed at Merrill. He understood that his presence was required, and he nodded and put on his jacket. She responded with a wide smile that showed mostly blackened stumps where the teeth should have been.

He followed her out into a vast internal courtyard. Rafael Santera Calderon's country home resembled a hybrid of the traditional Spanish-American hacienda, a pillbox fortification, and one of those atrium hotels the Americans were littering all over Europe and Asia. The building was an enormous open rectangle with at least forty rooms; the walls were concrete, about a foot thick, plastered over with stucco and capped with a red tile roof. The inner courtyard had a garden the size of a small rain forest, with a fountain and a half-dozen macaws. Wooden verandas had been tacked onto the outer perimeter, and men in camouflage suits armed with oily black submachine guns with banana-shaped magazines slept on them at night, in hammocks strung between the pillars.

Merrill found his host seated alone at the head of the long glass table in the dining room, reading the appraisal report. The decor in the house was a mélange of colonial antiques, glass, chrome, and Renaissance paintings. The one in the dining room was Tintoretto's *Adoration of the Magi*, painted in 1552 and notable for its play of light and shadow; Rembrandt later adopted the technique and, in the view of some critics, but not all of them, improved it. Merrill had arranged its sale to Santera in 1991 for seven million dollars. In the report that his patron was reading as he breakfasted, the painting was appraised at ten million. He loved telling clients their paintings had appreciated, even if the acquisition price and the current evaluation both flowed from the same vaporous source, which is to say Charles Hamilton Merrill's renowned expertise.

He found he especially liked it when a client was about to make another major purchase, though neither he nor anyone else he knew had ever arranged a purchase of the magnitude that Rafael Santera had agreed to make. If Santera had any misgivings about Merrill's appraisals, he kept them well hidden.

Today, Santera was wearing a cream-colored suit with a splashy gray and red tie. A short, stocky man with gray hair brushed straight back from his forehead, his pale, washed-out face would have been handsome but for the way his bright brown eyes seemed a few millimeters too close together. His teeth, which he flashed in a brilliant smile, were too uniform and white for Merrill to believe they were his own. The work of a top-flight Miami dentist, he imagined.

Santera rose and bowed as Merrill entered the room. He picked up the report and gestured toward it with his forehead.

"Fine work, my friend," he said. "I am well pleased. Today there are things you must see in Cali."

Merrill nodded modestly. Santera had reason to be pleased. His collection had been appraised at $175 million.

Merrill nodded again and yet again when his host inquired whether he had breakfasted and whether he was ready to travel to Cali for a meeting.

In another minute Merrill found himself seated in the back of a vast, boxy black limousine, air-conditioned to a chill 68 degrees, politely declining Santera's offer of a club soda. The driver, shielded from them by a glass partition, let the big car idle while four more cars, which appeared to Merrill to be Jeeps or Land Rovers of some kind, pulled up in front and behind them. The men inside, he noted, all wore camouflage fatigues and had the same kind of weapon carried by the guards on the veranda, the kind with the curved bullet clip. He did not know its name.

"Interesting car," Merrill said. "What kind is it?"

Santera smiled indulgently. "It is a ZIL. Soviet. Modified for our climate, of course."

He leaned closer, conspiratorially, with a pleased, tight smile.

"It was Gorbachev's last car."

Merrill blinked. It was truly amazing what could be bought from Russia these days.

"Congratulations," he said. "The Button has been taken out, I assume?"

Santera smiled blankly. Maybe he didn't understand the colloquial use of "Button."

At a signal Merrill did not see or hear, the caravan sped off.

"How far is it from the hacienda to Cali?" Merrill asked.

Santera smiled imperiously, not bothering to show again those impossibly even white teeth. "Do you mean from the front gate or from the house?"

He spoke English with only a slight accent, but there were gaps in his vocabulary. Merrill had heard that he had spent a couple of years, decades ago, at an American college. Presumably, he had only learned the words he needed for business.

"Both."

"From the house, forty miles. From the front gate, twenty."

Merrill simply lifted an eyebrow slightly. In his experience, clients reacted better when he showed himself to be unimpressed by their displays of wealth, particularly new wealth.

They drove down a hill and past the airstrip, where the jet, a Gulfstream IV, stood gleaming white in the sun. Next to it was a helicopter of some kind, much larger and bulkier than the sleek little birds some of Merrill's other clients had. This one had metal missile tubes on the bottom. Merrill considered why his host had chosen not to use it for the trip to Cali. Perhaps he had something he wanted to say, or to show off.

Beyond the airstrip, they entered a dense woodland that extended for a mile or so, and Merrill amused himself by looking for birds in the shadows, not that he would have recognized any he might have seen. Ornithology had never interested him, but he assumed that in South America, one tried to appreciate the wildlife. The road was smooth and black and, as far as Merrill could tell, empty apart from this convoy.

They left the woodland, entering again an expanse of rolling green plain, rounded a curve, and stopped abruptly. Merrill peered forward through the chauffeur's partition and immediately lost his panache. His mouth dropped open.

A small herd of elephants, perhaps a dozen altogether, stood blocking the road. Some were grazing. Some were ambling along. One of the largest, no less than fourteen feet from ear to ground, with mottled tusks that appeared to be at least two feet long, had turned and was eyeing the caravan with what appeared to Merrill to be wary suspicion.

"Elephants?" he said to Santera.

His host shrugged. "My wife wanted some."

The driver of the lead car jumped out and ran to the rear of his vehicle. He opened the back hatch and pulled out a long tube of matte-green metal with a brass protrusion at one end that looked like a stylized, sharpened pineapple with a point. Then Merrill saw that the tube had a shoulder stock, a trigger, and a sight. It was some kind of grenade launcher.

The man turned toward their car, and Santera, who'd opened his window, nodded at him. He scurried to a position ten yards from the shoulder of the road, about fifty yards from the bull elephant, and dropped one knee to the ground.

At the man's signal, the remaining three men from the lead car, each with rifles, began firing in the air and waving their arms at the bull. The big animal looked puzzled and did not move.

There was a sound like a firecracker going off, a kind of whoosh, and Merrill could see the man with the grenade launcher recoil. An instant later the bull elephant was engulfed in a bright, explosive flash and a cloud of smoke.

When the smoke cleared, the beast lay still on the pavement, a gaping hole, scorched at the edges, under its neck, its massive feet splayed at oblique angles from its body. The asphalt around him was covered with a spreading pool of purplish blood. The rest of the herd had scattered in panic to the east.

Merrill felt nauseous. With an effort, he stifled the urge to vomit.

"Why?" he asked Santera. His voice sounded dry and raspy.

Santera shrugged again. "It can be replaced."

An hour later the little caravan descended through the outskirts of Cali, a series of slum barrios full of concrete huts with tin roofs, open gutters that ran brown with raw sewage, and knots of men and women in light cotton clothing gathered on street corners and sitting under palm trees. Children ran everywhere, all dressed in shorts and T-shirts and rubber bath sandals, all dirty and skinny and brown, it seemed to Merrill.

Santera pointed to the left, where light towers on stanchions ringed a large stadium. "My football team plays there," he said. "Do you like football?"

"Take it or leave it, actually," Merrill said. Although the car was still cool, the air had grown much more humid as they descended toward the city, and he could feel the dampness of sweat along his spine.

Santera's face clouded. "I love football," he said flatly.

Merrill decided that Santera wanted to be humored. "Well, a fine game, of course. I loved playing it when I was younger. But our fans—not pleasant to be around."

Santera nodded gravely. "I have read of this. My fans are perfectly well-behaved."

Merrill resisted the urge to say that he could imagine why. He smiled.

The driver turned right, and they passed a long, low building made of white brick, surrounded by a fence and gate.

"My shoe factory—the best shoes in the Western Hemisphere," Santera said. He paused. "I hope you don't mind if I show you a bit of my city and my business."

"Not at all," Merrill said. "It's fascinating."

Gratefully, he noticed that the car showed no signs of slowing and actually visiting the cobblers.

"You've seen my city, after all," Merrill added.

Santera had visited London to inspect the two previous paintings he'd bought through Merrill, a Titian and a Velazquez. Prior to that, he had bought through intermediaries.

They passed a broadcast complex—Santera's radio and television stations. They passed a white office tower that housed an oil exploration company—Santera's.

After a while this tour of Santera's legitimate businesses began to puzzle the Englishman. Surely Santera could have no illusions about his knowledge of the real foundation of his fortune, whatever other businesses he might have invested in. The *Financial Times*, for God's sake, had even published Santera's picture, identifying him as the leader of the Cali cartel. Santera had ample reason to have concluded long ago that the only thing that mattered to his art dealer, Merrill thought, was whether his checks cleared, not the source of the money. And his checks, of course, had always cleared.

So why did Santera care what he thought?

The car slowed and halted, prompting Merrill to focus on the surroundings. They had entered a neighborhood of neat, white-washed stucco bungalows with red-tiled roofs and small, scraggly lawns. Here and there Toyotas and Fords sparkled in driveways. Neither the buildings, the cars, nor the asphalt beneath the tires appeared to be more than a year old. He could see that the high rises of central Cali were no more than a mile away.

Immediately in front of him the men in the lead cars were spilling out and deploying in a circular formation. It reminded Merrill of war films he'd seen, of American soldiers, perhaps, entering a village in Vietnam.

Santera said nothing until the armed man seated next to the driver had hopped out and opened his door. The chauffeur scurried out and opened Merrill's.

"I thought you might be interested to see where I come from," Santera said.

Merrill nodded, but his unease was growing. "Of course," he said, and stepped out of the car.

The hot, humid summer air enveloped him like a steam bath, and he could feel the sweat start to seep from his forehead within seconds. His suit, he thought, would soon be stained and his hair would be matted to his head.

He joined Santera at the front of the car. The Colombian pointed to a small bungalow across the street.

"I was born there," he said. "Of course, it was just a shack. No plumbing. A dirt floor. In the winter, the wind came through the holes in the wall. Some of my family thought I should preserve it as a museum of sorts." Santera smiled. "But I am not so immodest."

Merrill nodded, working hard to keep his face blandly approving and credulous.

"I tore it down a few years ago, when I built this development. Some of my employees live here. They get interest-free loans after they have been with me for three years."

"That's very good of you," Merrill said.

Santera looked pleased.

Two dozen children had gathered around, attracted at first by the limousine, then by the face of its owner. They were dressed, as far as Merrill could see, exactly the same as the children in the poorer developments, but they were cleaner. They stood a respectful distance away, outside the perimeter created by the bodyguards.

"Don Rafa," a boy in a Dallas Cowboys T-shirt called out, and then said something in Spanish.

One of the bodyguards looked at his chief, and Santera nodded benevolently. At a signal Merrill did not perceive, the children surged forward and flocked around their benefactor like little birds around a feeder.

Another bodyguard handed Santera a cloth sack. He reached into it and pulled out a fistful of silver coins, then handed them out, smiling broadly, until all of the children had one. Still smiling, he handed one to Merrill.

"A souvenir of Cali," he said. Merrill looked at the coin. It was a silver dollar.

Merrill studied the coin and its obverse carefully, grateful for an excuse to keep his face down.

Human nature, he thought, was endlessly, pathetically funny. Here was a man with an art collection already worth at least a hundred million dollars—his appraisal had not been all that much exaggerated—and the wherewithal to spend four times that much to make it the preeminent private collection in the world. He was a man with enough weapons and soldiers to conquer a small country, a man who had probably caused, directly or indirectly, the deaths of more people than AIDS.

And yet he apparently had an urgent, neurotic need for the approval of his art broker. And he thought this little tour might win it for him.

Merrill knew he would have to be very careful to keep the sneer off his face.

In the car again, the air-conditioning slowly evaporated the perspiration from Merrill's brow, and this time he accepted a club soda when Santera offered it. His host, he observed, showed no sign that he had ever left the car. His hair and his face were still dry. Merrill wondered for a moment about his ancestry. The Spaniards he knew sweated, or at least they did on Majorca. This man must have Indian blood.

"I understand you went to Cambridge," Santera suddenly

said, and Merrill snapped into a state of higher alertness. He had never mentioned the fact that he'd gone to Cambridge. It had never come up. Santera had clearly had some research done, and Merrill reminded himself that he was dealing with a clever man, whatever insecurities he might have.

"Yes, why?"

"Did you know Nigel Hamilton, the historian?"

Merrill could not have been more startled if Santera had asked whether he knew Boy George.

"Actually, yes. But only vaguely. Nod in the library, that sort of thing. Different college, you see."

Santera nodded. "I know."

Merrill's curiosity overwhelmed his reserve. "Why do you ask?"

Santera shifted in his seat, his torso quite hard and rigid. "I wish to know what his reputation is now."

Merrill was perplexed. He vaguely remembered a successful book about President Kennedy's youth. Politics bored him, and he hadn't read it.

"Rather good I should think. His book on young Kennedy was quite successful as I recall."

"It was well-received?" Santera looked grave and worried.

"As I recall, yes," Merrill said, wondering where this was leading. Instinctively, he temporized. "But I could be wrong. It's not my field. What did you think of it?"

Santera scowled. "Trash!"

"Why so?"

"Vicious gossip, both about the son and the father. And it was so evident. He keeps saying the father is a bad parent, yet he quotes from letter after letter the father wrote to the boy's school! Would a bad parent write so many letters?"

Merrill began to see. Yes, that must be it.

"Well," he said, with a smile that said he was gracefully willing to accept a little culpability, "I'm afraid we British never quite got over Ambassador Kennedy's role in keeping the States out of the war in thirty-nine and forty. So we're prejudiced. As far as I know, Ambassador Kennedy is held in high esteem in the States, and this book is generally seen as a potty Brit's effort to throw mud at a great man."

It was exactly the right thing to say. Santera's face softened and he settled back in his seat.

Merrill silently congratulated himself for being an astute judge of character. That was important in the art business, as important as being an astute judge of art. No doubt it helped explain the success of the Merrill Gallery.

Of course Santera would be offended at Hamilton's attack on Joseph Kennedy. That was how he saw himself: the founding father of a dynasty, amassing his family's fortune by means both fair and not so fair, but emerging in the end respected and admired. And Santera had a son who, Merrill recalled, had gone to Harvard. That was it precisely.

The caravan had by now entered central Cali, and Merrill turned to his window. The passing scene pleasantly surprised him. He had not expected chickens pecking on a dirt road, but he hadn't expected to see a Mercedes dealership, either. And yet there was one, along with Acura and Lexus, and Hermes and Gucci, restaurants and cafés with bright red umbrellas on the sidewalk. Clearly, Cali had some significant money to spend. Someone would make a fortune opening a decent gallery and catering to the desire to buy a refined veneer.

But it would not be him, Merrill thought with satisfaction. After this deal, he would be able to pay off his multitude of debts and still have what he'd always thought of as "be gone money." As in, "You're a Philistine, madam, and I don't need your business, so be gone." He would deal only with people and pictures that pleased him.

The caravan turned right, onto a street called Avenida de Colombia, and slowed to a crawl next to a high concrete wall with a gatehouse that resembled a pillbox. Immediately the gate slowly began to swing open, propelled by an unseen motor. As it did, three concrete pillars, jutting from the middle of the driveway like stalagmites, receded silently into the ground. The caravan sped inside and stopped at a low-slung concrete building, perhaps three stories high, with a small veranda and glass doors. The men in the front of the limo hopped out and scurried back to open the doors.

"My office," Santera said, smiling with what seemed to be anticipation.

They made their way inside, past a trio of doormen distinguishable from the men in the escort cars only because they all wore gray business suits. A few women sat typing in offices, but the building seemed largely cool and quiet. Merrill was only mildly surprised when they got into an elevator and one of the gray suits pushed the down button. They descended for a while; Merrill had no idea how deep they were going, but he realized he was entering a bunker.

They descended to a floor that he surmised was the real working headquarters of Santera's operation. In windowless offices he could hear men chatting, cajoling, and barking in Spanish. Santera led him into a paneled room dominated by a long, mahogany conference table. Upon it was a white architect's model of a building in the manner of Edward Durrell Stone, whose work, thanks to the efforts of His Royal Highness Prince Charles, had long since gone out of style in Britain. It was low, verging on squat, with a flat roof seemingly held up by picket lines of emaciated bronze pillars that surrounded the perimeter.

"You are an expert on art and museums, my friend," Santera said proudly. "So I wanted you to see what I am going to build."

The coffee in Merrill's stomach turned to bile and began to burn.

Warily, he circled the model and noticed a small card that said *Calderon Museum of Art.*

"Named for my late mother," Santera said. He was only a step behind him.

"Very impressive," Merrill said, employing the word he habitually used to describe ugly pictures owned by clients he could not afford to offend. It was a word, he reminded himself, that he would soon be able to expunge from his vocabulary.

Santera said something in Spanish, and two of the gray suits carefully lifted the roof off the model, revealing the interior design. Santera, with evident pride, pointed out the rooms designated for galleries, restoration work, and art classes. Then he pointed to the largest gallery room, at the left end of the building.

"And this," he said with a flourish of his hand, "will be reserved for one painting only: Leonardo's beautiful naked lady."

Merrill felt faint and nauseous. "But you said—I mean—I

thought—that is, I told the Russians it would be held in a private collection, never displayed." His voice sounded squeaky.

Santera smiled broadly, showing off all of his impossibly even white teeth.

"You were wrong," he said.

Chapter Eleven

ICY CRYSTALS OF SNOW, FIRED LIKE SHOTGUN pellets by a storm hanging over the Gulf of Finland, stung Burke's face. Judging by the speed with which moisture froze in his nostrils, he guessed the temperature was a few degrees below zero. He hunched his shoulders, drew his head as far as he could into the warmth of his scarf, stuck his hands deep in his pockets, and wondered why he had ever felt nostalgia for Russia.

His feet reverted quickly to the Russian shuffle, a slow, halting stride designed for slippery sidewalks and deflated spirits. His eyes stayed fixed on the stained gray pants and worn brown heels of the person shuffling miserably in front of him, heading down Griboyedovsky Street toward the massive granite building that housed the St. Petersburg *militsia*.

The building's door, he discovered, had smoked gray glass that enabled the policemen inside to observe the pedestrians on the street without being seen themselves. To Burke, who liked to read buildings, it seemed an appropriate choice.

He pushed the door open and walked past the two memorials in the lobby: one to the *militsioneri* who fell in the siege of Leningrad, and the second to those fallen in the war on crime. The criminals, he could see by comparing the honor rolls on each side, had recently outstripped the Nazis.

To the left, as in all the Russian *militsia* stations he had ever seen, was a small citizens' waiting room. This one had paint peeling in large, bileous green shards from the walls, and the floor was grimy with the droppings of slushy boots and cheap cigarettes. But it had the requisite small table with a bored *militsioner* behind it; he had corporal's stripes on his epaulets.

Burke handed the corporal his press card and told him he wanted to speak to the chief of the homicide division. The *militsioner* straightened up and dialed a three-digit internal code. He had a clipped conversation with someone at the other end, then gestured toward the bench on the far wall.

"Please wait a few minutes," he said.

The denizens of the bench looked like the queue for the last bus to hell. It was hard to tell who they were: informants, perhaps, stopping by to pick up their envelopes. Or poor innocents who still believed that a person who was robbed should report it to the police.

Burke sat down next to an old woman with her stockings drooping over her chubby calves. She promptly and loudly released a cloud of methane. The man on his left shyly fingered the fabric of Burke's overcoat, then grinned toothlessly when Burke, feeling the fingers, turned to look at him.

"Nice coat," the man said, a small dribble of spit curling out of the left side of his mouth.

"You might be able to pick it up cheap," Burke said. "A few more minutes in here and I'll never be able to wear it again."

Before bargaining could commence, a fat *militsioner*, the bottom button of his gray shirt undone, stepped into the room and nodded at Burke.

"General Kornilov will see you," the man said.

Burke followed him underneath a digital clock and up a marble staircase, illuminated by a stained-glass window portrait of a *militsioner*, jaw jutting and weapon at the ready, standing guard in front of a ruby-red seal with a golden hammer and sickle.

General Kornilov's office had a framed photo of the president hanging over his desk in the spot once reserved for portraits of gen-

eral secretaries, and a pale outline next to it that presumably had
once also been covered with a portrait, presumably of Lenin. Technology covered half his desk, with a computer on one side and a
VCR and television screen on the other. It was obviously not a
simple detective's office, nor the office of the chief detective in the
homicide squad. Burke assumed General Kornilov was the head of
the oblast *militsia*. This did not please him.

Kornilov himself was short, squat, and bald, with a goiter the
size of a walnut protruding from his neck, just above the epaulets
with the single golden star woven into them.

"So," he said, when Burke had taken a seat at the conference table that adjoined his desk. "You want to write about our murders?"

The expression on his face was hard for Burke to read. There
were still cops, he knew, who looked at any effort by the Western
press to write about crime as part of a capitalist plot. But Kornilov
did not seem to be one of them.

A secretary entered and set teacups on the table in front of
them. Burke waited for her to pour.

"A particular murder," he said. "Fyodor Vasiliev."

"Ah, yes," Kornilov said, as if that explained a great deal. "He
was well-known around the world, wasn't he?"

Burke nodded.

"Well, I can understand your interest now." Kornilov beamed.

"So, may I speak to the detective in charge of the case?" Burke
preferred, whenever possible, to deal with the source closest to the
event.

An expression of sadness settled on Kornilov's round face. "Ah,
you see, he's very busy right now."

Burke had an idea where the conversation was going, but he
had a perverse curiosity about how blatant the touch was going to
be. So he played along.

"Well, how soon do you think he might be able to see me?"

Kornilov made a judicious steeple of his hands. "Part of the
problem, you see, is that unlike your American police departments,
we have no money in our budget for an office of public relations."

"That certainly is a tragedy," Burke said sympathetically. "A
shortage of P.R. men."

Kornilov nodded lugubriously. "So it's our practice when journalists come to ask us for cooperation to ask in return that they help defray the expenses of cooperating with them."

"That seems like elementary justice."

Kornilov smiled. "Yes. We use the money to pay overtime to the officers involved and also to help us acquire the technology we need."

"Like your VCR," Burke said.

Kornilov nodded.

"An essential tool in modern law enforcement," Burke agreed, and waited for Kornilov to continue.

Kornilov cleared his throat. "The VCR, for example, came from Nippon Television. They sent a correspondent and crew here from Moscow to work on a report about smuggling. They gave us ten thousand dollars in addition to the VCR."

"Ah, those Japanese television correspondents." Burke sighed. "They have more dollars than they know what to do with. Everywhere they go in the world they leave cab drivers and prostitutes charging higher prices."

Kornilov's face clouded as he thought for a moment, then decided that the insult was sufficiently oblique to allow him to continue bargaining.

"Since you're an American, and we like Americans, maybe for you it could be a little less."

Burke had nothing in principle against paying for news. He regarded the rules against it in the more respectable American media as less a matter of ethics than of profit. But since this was his own investigation, the money would have to come out of his own pocket. Even after he bargained Kornilov down from his opening bid, it would be substantial money. And probably for nothing more than the story Tass had published.

If he was going to bribe a cop, he'd try to get directly to the detectives involved. They'd be cheaper and more informative.

"I'll check with my editors and see what they say," Burke said.

Kornilov looked disappointed, and Burke wondered if he would make a counteroffer. But he only shrugged in elaborate indifference.

"As you wish," he said.

Burke got up to leave.

"And, *Gospodin* Burke," Kornilov called after him. "Be careful. Our streets are not safe."

Burke nodded. Most likely, he thought, Kornilov had a body-guard business on the side.

———————

Elderly tourists, lined up to board a bus, blocked the entrance to the Hotel Yevropeiskaya. They shuffled stiffly forward, hobbled by the many layers of clothes they had swaddled themselves in. The wind was still blowing the snow hard from the river up Nevsky Prospekt, and though it was nearly noon, the sky was almost as dark and gray as it had been when Burke checked into the hotel that morning.

There was a jostling in the line. Suddenly the feet flew out from under a gray-haired man dressed in an incongruous combination of Burberry scarf and moon boots. With a dull thud, his rear end hit the pavement. His head followed an instant later. A rabbit's-fur *shapka* of the kind Russians sold to tourists flew off his head. His blue shoulder bag, bearing the logo of a travel agency in Rotterdam, careened in the opposite direction.

A fine spray of snow, kicked up by the moon boots, spattered Burke's pants. Almost immediately, a woman wearing the same moon boots, *shapka,* and scarf, sank to her knees in the snow and cradled the man's head. His eyes were open, and he could hear her murmur something to him in a language that he assumed was Dutch. Then the old man smiled and nodded. The woman patted his cheek. She looked up. Burke met her eyes, read the request for help, and squatted down. He got his arms under the old man's; he could feel the bones inside, knobby and thin. He stood up, helping the man to his feet, feeling a twinge of pain in his own shoulder in a place that had never hurt him before.

"You all right?" he asked in English.

The old man nodded, vigorously.

"Thank you, young man," the old woman said.

"Well, I'm glad he's in good hands," Burke said. The old woman smiled.

Burke felt a little jealous. There would be no one to tend to his own twinges.

He walked into the hotel, past the Russian doorman whose job description, apparently, did not include shoveling snow.

The Yevropeiskaya was one of the oldest hotels in Russia. It predated the Bolshevik Revolution, and there had once been a plaque outside indicating the dates when Lenin had graced its banquet hall. The plaque had been removed in 1992, when a German firm bought an interest in the hotel and renovated it. Now it had yards of gleaming brass and glass, plush new carpets, but judging by the doorman, the same old staff. Had Lenin reappeared in St. Petersburg now, however, he would no doubt have lacked the hard currency to enter.

The telephones, also new and German, had attracted Burke to the Yevropeiskaya. The hotel had been equipped with some kind of satellite system that bypassed the Russian switching stations. And that was what Burke intended to take advantage of.

The hotel lobby had changed during his morning's absence. A large blue banner with white lettering, in Russian, German, Japanese, and English, was now hanging from the roof: WELCOME TO THE PARTICIPANTS OF THE INTERNATIONAL CONFERENCE ON CONVERSION OF DEFENSE INDUSTRIES.

Russians, whether Soviet or post-Soviet, loved hosting international conferences, which they imagined was the way the world did business. They loved designing banners and mascots and logos for them. This conference's logo, predictably enough, was a pair of curved swords that transmogrified themselves, with the aid of a few swoosh lines, into a flywheel.

Someone had evidently been watching for him, because when Burke stepped into the lobby, a bald, pear-shaped man in a badly cut frock coat stepped from behind the concierge's desk and called out his name.

Burke shook the snow off his collar and suppressed a moan. He doubted that the concierge wished to inquire whether he would like a fruit basket.

"*Gospodin* Burke, my apologies. I must speak with you."

"I'm really busy this morning."

The man—Nikolai, according to a tag on his lapel—smiled and half bowed. "I am sorry. It is necessary. Would you follow me?"

Grimacing, Burke followed him to the front desk. There, Nikolai paused and looked through a large red ledger book. Then he raised his moon-shaped face to Burke.

"We are so sorry, Mr. Burke, but there has been a mistake in your booking."

"I booked for a week," Burke objected.

Nikolai shook his head, sadly and solemnly. "I am afraid that was not possible. You see, the hotel was booked in advance for the defense industry conversion conference that begins tomorrow."

Burke crossed his arms, scowled, and expelled some air upward, from his lower lip.

"We apologize for the misunderstanding. We would be very happy to book a room for you at the Pribaltiskaya," Nikolai said, smiling unctuously.

Burke sighed. He had stayed once in the Pribaltiskaya. It was stuck in a remote corner of the city, an hour from everything he needed to visit, and the phones wouldn't make a call across the street.

He looked at Nikolai, who suddenly bore a striking resemblance to General Kornilov.

"How about if I became a special friend of the hotel?" he asked.

Nikolai looked expectantly, waiting to hear more.

"For instance, I see you don't get my favorite newspaper, the *Washington Tribune*. I could endow a subscription so your guests could read it. I think two hundred dollars should cover it."

Nikolai looked dubious.

"Three hundred."

Nikolai smiled.

"And we'll forget about the Pribaltiskaya."

Nikolai nodded. "Yes, *Gospodin*. Just between you and me, it's a terrible hotel."

Burke handed over the money and resumed the trek to his room. He thought for a second of the old Dutch couple on the sidewalk outside the hotel. He hoped Nikolai wasn't shaking everyone down.

He entered his room thinking of telephones, but then his eyes fell on a second German improvement, the little brown refrigerator humming beside the desk. He opened it, doing his best to ignore the little liquor bottles, and pulled out a Diet Coke.

It tasted too sweet.

Then he thought of Kornilov and grimaced. The lowest Romanian customs inspector would do a better job soliciting a bribe. Even the concierge at the hotel had.

He checked his watch. He had four hours until his appointment at the Hermitage. It was too long to spend alone with the refrigerator.

He got up, went to the desk, turned his computer on, booted up his address book program, and called up the St. Petersburg file. It had about seventy-five names, compiled during a half-dozen reporting trips over the past decade. But there was only one artist, a man named Sasha Vinogradov. They had met years ago, when Burke was compiling material for a piece on fresh voices set free by glasnost. In the end, he'd not mentioned Vinogradov, concentrating instead on a couple of rock and roll bands and a cinematographer. He wondered whether Vinogradov bore a grudge.

He dialed the number and got no answer. He tried again, just in case the new satellite system was going through some shakedown problems. Still no answer.

He finished off the Coke and tried to keep his eyes from wandering to the refrigerator.

There was one other lead, the one he had gotten from Desdemona McCoy on the train, and it looked as if he might as well pursue it. It was that or watch CNN on the hotel television until somebody answered the phone at Sasha Vinogradov's.

He closed the St. Petersburg file in the computer and opened the Moscow file until he came to the entry for Kieran Gilbride.

Russia was crawling with Americans on missions. Most came to baptize the heathens. Some came to help Russian lawyers learn about contingency fees, hourly rates, malpractice suits, and similar flowers of American jurisprudence. Some came to enlighten the women of Russia about feminism, putting them on the path to the same ideal relations between the sexes that the United States enjoyed. Some came to spread the gospels of business consulting, advertising, and other adornments of American civilization that the Russians, in their backwardness, lacked.

Kieran Gilbride had taken a look at post–Soviet Russia and decided that what it most needed was a gay rights movement. He had moved from New York to Moscow to organize one, and Burke had met him six months previously while covering the All-Russian Union of Gays and Lesbians first national assembly.

Burke dialed the code for Moscow and the number. The satellite, to his relief, was working.

"Union," Gilbride answered.

"Kieran, it's Colin Burke, from the *Washington Tribune*. How are you?"

Gilbride was fine.

"And how's the organization doing?"

Fine, too.

"Glad to hear it. I'm in St. Petersburg on a special assignment, about crime actually, and I wanted to look into a case of gay-bashing I got a tip on."

Gilbride asked whom it involved.

"Can't tell you that, unfortunately. Source made me promise not to until it checks out," Burke lied. He did not want to mention Vasiliev's name over the telephone. "But I need the names of some gay activists here to help me look into it."

Gilbride was eager to help promote a story on gay bashing. "The person to talk to in St. Petersburg is Larisa Damba," he said. "Hold on while I get her number."

Burke held for a moment.

"Her number is 137-29-82. Her office address is Budyennovsky 13."

"Who is she? What does she do?" Burke asked as he wrote the numbers down.

Gilbride chuckled. "I'll let you find that out for yourself. I'll just tell you her nickname. Mamochka Golubykh."

It meant, roughly translated, "The Fairies' Mommy."

When he found Budyennovsky 13, Burke was confused. It was an old, three-story brick building in one of the dark factory quarters across the Neva from the splendor of the Winter Palace. A sign on the front said "City Hospital Number 46." He could smell disinfectant and formaldehyde from the street.

He poked his head inside the door and found a small anteroom with a clerk behind a glass partition. He asked her for Larisa Damba, and she directed him down the hall and to the left, to Room 14.

In the corridor, a woman was lounging on a leather chair with upholstery dropping from the seat. She had hair bleached lighter than blond, thick mascara, red high-heeled pumps, and when Burke looked a little more closely, the shadow of a beard.

He blinked and went in.

The office he entered was small and cluttered, with a scuffed brown desk in the middle. Signs on the walls seemed to be copies of statutes from the Russian criminal code. One of them, he could see, required citizens to report cases of venereal disease. In one corner, a large Afghan hound with stringy white hair dangling from its body looked up indifferently, then dropped his head back to the floor.

Two women sat at the desk—or at least they appeared to be women. The one facing Burke could have been any age from forty to sixty. She was short and stocky, with hennaed hair cropped close to her head and a monocle in one bloodshot eye. She wore a plain white T-shirt and jeans. Her nails were painted a deep purple, almost black.

The person with her back turned to Burke had a fall of straight, chestnut-colored hair running down nearly to her waist, which was wrapped in a skirt. Hearing Burke's footstep, this one turned. She was in fact a woman, he decided, young and fair-skinned, with a faint dusting of freckles on her nose and cheeks.

Seeing Burke, the older woman leaped to her feet and pointed a finger at him.

"And just who do you think you are?" she demanded. Her tone and demeanor were those of the Inquisitor.

"A usually honest reporter struggling to make his way in a dishonest world," Burke said. "How about you?"

"You're a foreigner!" the woman harrumphed.

Burke knew he spoke Russian with an accent. He nodded. "American?"

He nodded again.

"So what are you interested in? Girls? Boys? Men? Both?"

Burke laughed. "At the moment, some information."

The woman exploded. "Information! You liar! Lying American! I saw the way you looked at this girl. Do you think it wasn't obvious?"

The woman seemed intent on whatever it took to keep him uncomfortable and off balance. Burke could barely imagine what growing up in the Soviet Union must have been like for her, but he could see where the experience might produce some deficient social skills. So he smiled.

"She is very pretty," he said.

With that, the woman's voice softened slightly. "You like her. Her name is Galina. She's a nurse. She's here for treatment of syphilis. She says she got it from an operation at the hospital. No gloves. Cut on her finger. She says. Hah!"

The girl with the freckles blushed, which made her freckles seem darker.

"It was that wretched boyfriend of yours, wasn't it, Galya?"

The girl smiled sheepishly, but shook her head.

"Well, she's had enough shots to be clean. You can fuck her if you like. Be the first since her treatment! Make her forget that damn boyfriend! You'd like to fuck a handsome American, wouldn't you, darling Galochka?"

Darling Galochka flushed crimson and said nothing.

"She'll do it if I tell her to!" the woman said, addressing Burke. "I'm her counselor. She'll do whatever I tell her to!"

"Well, it's tempting, but I'm on duty," Burke said.

"Oh, a clever one!" the woman said, nearly cackling. Her demeanor seemed to fluctuate between imperious and faintly hysterical, with nothing much in between.

She turned to Galya. "Fetch us some cookies and tea," she demanded.

Galya got up and left, brushing demurely past Burke as she did. She was wearing faded bedroom slippers with little embroidered bunnies on them.

"Sit down," the woman said, gesturing toward the chair just vacated by the patient. Gingerly, Burke sat down.

"You can't get V.D. from a chair!" she hooted. She laughed until her monocle fell out. She caught it as it did and kept laughing.

Then her round face hardened in a scowl. "You didn't know, did you, that the cure for venereal disease in this wretched country takes nineteen days."

Burke admitted his ignorance.

"Our drugs." She spat on the floor in the direction of the dog, which perked up his head, stood up slowly, and then licked the saliva from the floor.

"In America it takes, what, one injection?"

Burke nodded.

"Galochka has been here for seventeen days. She gets an injection twice a day."

Burke winced. "And you're her counselor?"

"I'm a lawyer. Larisa Konstantinovna Damba. Member of the St. Petersburg College of Jurists and Advocates." She snorted and handed Burke a business card from a drawer in her desk. Burke handed her his own card.

Galya returned with a tray of cookies and two cups of tea, which she set on the desk between them.

Larisa Damba took a cookie, broke it in half, and held the fragment in the air, waving it in the dog's direction.

"Zherebyets," she called to the dog.

Zherebyets leapt to his mistress's lap, rolled over and lay on his back, paws in the air. She cooed to him and then buried her head in his crotch, smooching noisily for a moment. Then she fed the dog the cookie.

Burke watched incredulously. To his relief, the hound did not get an erection.

"So," he said, anxious to find out what he could before this woman decided to display any more unusual proclivities. "Kieran Gilbride tells me you're called Mamochka Golubykh."

Damba turned her head up from the Afghan, which continued to loll in her lap. "You know Kieran?"

"He gave me your name."

"He's our friend! Our defender!" She thumped a fist on her chest. She seemed to approve.

"Yes."

The woman smiled. She had small, crooked teeth. "Yes, I am Mamochka Golubykh. I defend the fairies and protect them. Like Kieran. They get disease. They come here. The law says they have to disclose their sexual contacts. The cops come and try to scare them to disclose much more. All of their gay friends and acquaintances. So the cops can go and catch more and send more to jail.

"I can't stop the cops from asking for the names of their sex partners. But I can try to make sure that's all the information they get. I tell these poor boys what their rights are."

"And you're employed by?"

"By the procurator's office."

She was, then, a kind of public defender.

"So you must know a lot about the gay community here."

She nodded emphatically. "I know them all. Except for the very young ones. The chickens!" She haw-hawed.

"I'm looking into the death of an older man. Fyodor Vasiliev."

Mamochka Golubykh frowned. "Vasiliev?"

"He was director of the Hermitage. He was killed a week ago. The report said it was a robbery, but I heard that it might have been gay-bashing."

"Oh, *that* Vasiliev," Damba said. She pondered for a moment, sticking one dark fingernail into the corner of her mouth and gnawing on it.

"No," she announced abruptly. "I don't think so. I don't think he was gay."

"Why not?"

She snorted. "Believe me, I would know. I am friends with four people on the staff of the Hermitage who are gay. I have been to parties at their apartments. I advised one here as a client. I know their circle. I have never heard that this Vasiliev was in it."

Burke sighed. Given the way things had gone thus far, he was not surprised. "Can you possibly help me contact your friends at the Hermitage so I can check it further?"

He expected Mamochka Golubykh to be shocked that he would even ask. Instead she nodded and rose from her chair. She opened the desk drawer and pulled out a ring of large metal keys.

"Follow me," she commanded.

They walked down the corridor toward the front door, but before they reached it, they entered a claustrophobically narrow stairwell and climbed two flights up stairs with grooves worn in them by the impact of countless feet. At a third-floor landing she halted in front of a steel door with a small window of thick glass. She pulled out a four-inch key with teeth the size of small fingers and put it in the lock.

"The isolation ward for venereal diseases," she said.

There were two rooms, each with about forty beds, the first for men and the second for women. Some of the men in the first beds seemed to be soldiers, with pimples on their faces. They lounged in T-shirts and bathrobes, apparently enjoying the respite from their army duties. Farther down, Damba stopped.

"This is where my *golubiye* are," she announced. Burke nodded at half a dozen men, two of whom were apparently transvestites. One of them, with long bleached hair, dangling earrings, and a pink robe, walked up to Damba and whispered, with exaggerated shyness, in her ear.

"She wants to know if it's true that they do sex change operations for free in America," Damba said, turning to Burke.

"Afraid that's just more capitalist propaganda," Burke replied.

The transvestite tittered.

Damba unlocked another steel door, this one separating the men from the women. The inmates of this ward included a fair number of the lowest class of Russian prostitutes, train station alcoholics with thick, battered bodies and bloodshot eyes. There were two mothers playing with small children.

Toward the end of this ward they confronted a steel partition, its

paint a few shades brighter and newer than the paint on the surrounding walls.

"This is where our AIDS patients come to die," Damba said as
she turned the key in the lock.

The air inside was close and hot, suffused with the nauseating
smell of disinfectants and excrement. There were perhaps ten beds,
all filled with men. In the first two, the patients had soiled their bed
linen. Burke saw neither an orderly nor a nurse to clean it up.

They stopped at the third bed. Larisa Damba sat on its edge
and cradled the occupant's head in her arms, nuzzled his neck, and
whispered something in his ear.

He was a gaunt man with sunken, feverish brown eyes and the
purple blotches of Kaposi's sarcoma scattered over his papery yellow skin. The cords on his neck stood out like ropes. Burke could
not guess at his age, but it was evident he did not have long to live.

Damba plumped the pillow behind him, and the man struggled
and failed for a second to raise his head and torso.

"This is Gennady," she said. "He works at the Hermitage, in the
porcelain collection."

The man extended his hand and Burke took it. It felt both hot
and lifeless.

"I'm trying," Burke said, "to find out who killed Fyodor
Vasiliev."

"He's dead?" Gennady's voice was a raspy whisper, and Burke
had to lean closer to hear it.

"Killed last week. Police say it was a robbery. I've heard it was
because he was gay."

Gennady grimaced. "Why do you care?"

Burke cleared his throat. He could lie and say the *Tribune* cared
enough about the Hermitage to be interested in how its director
died. Gennady would probably believe it.

But he found it hard to lie to a dying man.

"Because a woman I cared about was killed after she talked to
Vasiliev," he said. "Or at least said she was going to talk to him.
And I thought the deaths might be related." The memory of
Jennifer's body as he had seen it that night flashed through his
mind and he shuddered.

"But I also heard a rumor that Vasiliev was killed because he was gay. I don't know what's true."

Gennady seemed to recede from him, back into the pillow.

"So," Burke asked, as gently as he could, "was Vasiliev gay?"

Gennady almost smiled, but it would have been a cold, mirthless smile had he been able to pull it off. "No," he rasped.

"How do you know for sure?"

Gennady struggled again to raise his head. "I didn't always look like this. Ten years ago, I was quite . . . attractive. I went to work in the museum. I was passed from man to man there. They do that with new boys. I got to know them all. All the gays. One of them gave me this disease."

"And he wasn't one of them."

The head sank away again. "No."

"Enough!" Damba hissed. "He's exhausted."

Wearily, Burke nodded. He had run into another dead end. But it was hard to worry about it when his mind was awash in the compulsion to walk through the steel doors and out of this building, and comforted by the knowledge that he, unlike Gennady, could do so.

Chapter Twelve

THERE HAD BEEN A TIME, WHEN IT WAS STILL called Leningrad and the prospects for glasnost and perestroika were infinitely brighter, when Burke had visited St. Petersburg in winter and thought the city beautiful. The snow then, he thought, had covered the grime and the dust. But now it seemed only to soak them up, becoming charcoal gray or black as soon as it fell from a sky so leaden that no single clouds were distinguishable.

Eager to get out of the wind that funneled down Nevsky Prospekt, he crossed the humpbacked bridge over the Moika, an urban canal that drained some of the marshland on which Peter the Great had decreed his capital would be built, and turned right along the canal's embankment. It was slightly out of his way, but the mustard-yellow buildings along the canal gave him a bit of shelter from the wind.

He would have looked in the store windows as he passed by, to see what was available and what the prices were. But they were covered with a glaze of frost that trailed away to lacy filigrees in the corners.

He turned into a covered arcade, a tunnel perhaps twenty-five yards long that passed through the old Ministry of Defense building and linked the canal with the Palace Square. The arcade was dark and cold, but it offered some respite from the wind and the snow. Old women, wrapped up in black overcoats and woolen scarves, their faces lined with wrinkles like pink prunes, lined the tunnel walls, huddled on stools, too stoic to shiver. On little tables, each had laid out possessions for sale. One had a few odd bits of silver, two spoons and a salt shaker. Another had some crystal, four matching wineglasses. A third offered a lace tablecloth and a bottle of Georgian wine. They looked, Burke thought, old enough to have survived the siege of Leningrad by the Germans. He could imagine their present lives, alone in one-room apartments, their pensions no longer able to buy bread, wondering whether their possessions or their lives would run out first.

Then there was a boy playing a saxophone, though Burke could not imagine how his hands stayed warm enough. Their eyes met, and Burke could tell that the boy had recognized him for a foreigner. He broke into a smooth, well-schooled rendition of "All of Me." Burke dropped a couple of dollars into his instrument case. One of the old women saw the dollars and scurried in front of him, blocking his path to the exit. He gave her a dollar. She shrieked something in Russian that he could not quite understand.

In a second the rest of the old women had surrounded him, hands out. Some wailed. One opened her mouth and formed a silent, toothless circle; tears dropped from her eyes.

"*Milosti prosim, milosti prosim,*" another chanted, plucking at his sleeve.

Yet another, heftier and more desperate, got a hand on his wallet.

He jerked the wallet away and held it high over his head, like a basketball center holding a ball out of reach of the pesky smaller players. He pulled a handful of dollars from it and stuffed them into the hand of the hefty woman.

"For all of you," he said loudly.

The women, shrieking and groaning, dropped away from him and surrounded their hefty comrade. Burke sprinted around the cluster and out to the slippery cobblestones of Palace Square. His boots thudded on the dry snow, his legs were fluttery underneath him, and he felt a sheen of perspiration on his forehead, despite the cold. Casting a look over his shoulder, he saw that no one was following him, but he kept running, circling around an obelisk that commemorated Alexander I's triumph over Napoleon in 1812.

The Winter Palace stood before him. It occurred to him that his flight from the old women in the arcade had reenacted the pell-mell run of the crowd of hungry soldiers and Bolshevik agitators on the night they seized power in November 1917. Bearing red banners with the slogan "All Power to the Soviets!" they had stormed into the palace and arrested the provisional government. An image flashed through his mind of the old women in the arcade storming into the palace again, this time behind a banner saying "We Made a Mistake!"

He smiled to himself and slowed to a walk.

In his childhood the word "palace" had been indelibly infused with the televised image of the pseudo-Bavarian Disney fantasy, a multiturreted and towered affair, floating lightly atop an ethereal mountaintop. The Winter Palace was nothing like that, and whenever he saw it, Burke recoiled at its mass and weight. The building spoke eloquently of greed and extravagance.

It hunkered on the banks of the broad, frozen white expanse of the Neva, four stories high and longer than a football field. The outer walls were painted a pastel green, and they were awash in windows and columns and pediments, thousands of them, so many that the passerby's eyes glazed and they became just a pattern of white paint against the green backdrop. Seeing it always aroused in Burke a bit of sympathy for the Bolsheviks, or at least for the idea that Russian society had needed leveling.

Leveled the society had been, and now the old palace was starting to disintegrate at the edges. As he approached, he saw that the green paint was peeling away from the corners, exposing chunks of old gray stone. The gilt around the edges of the columns which had once blazed in the sun had been replaced by a muddy gold paint that was itself beginning to flake away. Turning the corner to the front of the building, he saw that even the *militsioneri* on guard at the tourists' entrance, who once had carried themselves stiffly and proudly, had turned their backs to the wind and dropped into a slouch.

Even on this frozen day in the middle of a frozen winter, a line had formed and stretched toward him about fifty yards from the door, so great was the attraction of the art collection housed inside.

The collection had begun with Peter the Great, but its true founder was the German princess Sophie of Anhalt-Zerbst, who had married Peter's grandson, Peter III. Renamed Catherine, she conspired with a lover to stage a coup that had killed her husband. Once on the throne, she washed the blood from her hands and determined that her adopted country must shed its image of Asiatic barbarism and take its place among the respected nations of Europe.

To that end, she bought art. She bought it avariciously and copiously, like an Arab prince buying yearling horses. Her agents in France and Germany had standing orders to pounce on any and all significant collections that came up for sale. Often they presented themselves to an art collector's widow at her husband's funeral, making an extravagant offer for the entire collection, which they then packed up and shipped to St. Petersburg. Soon, Catherine had so many paintings that she had a separate structure added to the palace to contain them. Infatuated with French culture, if not by the egalitarian ideas of French political philosophy, she called this building her Hermitage. When she died, the Hermitage contained nearly four thousand paintings by European masters.

The czars who succeeded her expanded the collection and added to it the spoils of empire. Gold came from the ruins of kingdoms and civilizations that had flowered on the Eurasian plain, been conquered by Russia, and disappeared into history. Gems arrived from new Siberian mines. Conquering generals brought back looted Mongol, Persian, and Ottoman treasures. It all flowed into the Winter Palace. The Bolsheviks, after seizing power, added to the hoard by confiscating the Monets, Picassos, and Cezannes collected by plutocratic Russian merchants in the years before the Revolution. The Winter Palace became one of the great art repositories in the world, with more than two million items, including ten Monets, fifteen Gauguins, thirty Picassos, thirty-seven Matisses, thirty-eight Rubenses, twenty-four Van Dycks, and twenty-four Rembrandts. It had more art stored in its attics than most of the world's museums had on display.

Burke trudged into the wind, past the line of tourists, thinking about all that wealth amid all this poverty. The disparity might explain the connection between the deaths of Jennifer Morelli and Fyodor Vasiliev. The wealth contained in the Winter Palace would inevitably be a target for thieves, as inevitably as sugar would attract ants. He could imagine museum guards smuggling small things—cameos, jewels, old coins—out in their pockets or their mouths and selling them on the black market. But something important enough and valuable enough to cause Jennifer Morelli to think she had a major story would be hard to steal quietly. Everything in the museum had been catalogued. All of the famous items were on display. They would immediately be missed.

Still, it was the best working hypothesis he could come up with for the interview he had scheduled.

Burke laughed inwardly at himself. One day into the renewal of his reporting career and he was already in danger of falling into the worst habit of the truly bad journalist: letting his supposition prejudice his inquiry. Suppositions and hypotheses were fine, but he would try to let the people in the Hermitage tell their own story. He sometimes wondered what would happen if he had the nerve to try a psychoanalytic approach to an interview: to sit and say nothing, not letting his questions influence the interviewee, compelling the interviewee to begin talking. He had never tried it on anyone.

A hundred yards past the tourist entrance, he came to a door marked *Administratwny Otdyel*. He paused. A canal was just ahead of him, slushy and gray and still flowing, presumably because of the warmer waters discharged into it from the St. Petersburg sewers before it joined the Neva a few meters away.

He turned to an old man with a cane, who was shuffling slowly and deliberately, hunched against the wind, in the direction from which Burke had come.

"Excuse me," he said, pointing. "Is that the Griboyedov Canal?"

The old man barely looked up, nodded quickly, and passed by. *"Da,"* he said through his muffler. "Griboyedov."

Burke nodded. Vasiliev would have had to leave the building, presumably, through the door to the administration section. A robber would have had to jump him as soon as he stepped out of the museum, kill him, and dump the body in the canal, ten yards from the door. Burke looked around. Even in this weather, he could count a dozen people walking on either the river side or the palace side of the street. Vasiliev had died at night, but not so late at night that the sidewalks would have likely been deserted. Either his killers had been terribly brazen, or there was something about his death that the official account had not disclosed.

He opened the door and showed his old press pass to a tired and disinterested *militsioner*, who waved him down the hall. For a second he waited for the warmth of the corridor to envelop him. It was one of the small pleasures he remembered from Russian winters, the feeling of stepping into light, shelter, and heat. Then he realized that it was not as warm inside as it should have been. He exhaled slowly. He thought he saw a trace of vapor.

The administrative section of the museum was housed in a wing that had been added to the palace in the eighteenth century. It might originally have been a servants' wing, he thought, or a space for courtiers, because it had none of the marble, crystal, and gilt that seemed to flow from the walls in the public areas. He was looking down a straight, narrow hallway, lit only by the weak light shining through the windows. The electric lights hanging from the ceiling inside plain white globes were either switched off or not working. A faded red runner covered the plain parquet floor.

Burke knocked on the high brown double doors marked "International Relations." He heard the shuffling of feet inside.

An old woman with a knitted shawl draped over her stooped shoulders opened the door, and he stepped into an anteroom. There were a couple of old, delicate desks of deep brown wood, highly polished and trimmed with a lighter inlay. They stood out incongruously against the scuffed, dirty parquet floor, the clunky plastic telephones, and the dented old kettle that sat on the windowsill. Three paintings, with heavy, carved frames, hung on the walls. They looked old and valuable, but Burke could recognize neither the scenes nor the artists. The old woman sat down at the closer of the two desks, next to an electric space heater.

"I have an appointment with Gennady Gavril'ich," he said. "I'm Colin Burke from the *Washington Tribune*."

"He's not here," the old woman said.

Burke looked at his watch. It was four o'clock. He was right on time.

"I called two days ago from Washington and made an appointment."

The woman shrugged indifferently, a gesture she had perhaps perfected during the Brezhnev era, probably while working in a housing bureau.

"He's not here," she repeated, a rising undertone of implacability noticeable in her voice.

"Do you expect him?"

The woman shrugged again and turned to some papers on her desk. With a pencil, she started filling in blanks.

"I'll wait," Burke said, exasperated.

The woman stonily continued to fill in blanks. Burke found that his tolerance for this kind of recherché Soviet obduracy had worn thin. Maybe it was the effect of a few months in the West. Maybe it was the effect of a fruitless morning. Maybe he was just getting old. Had he known the Russian word for either obduracy or recherché, he would have told the old woman what he thought, but he did not, so he sat fuming quietly until his watch said a quarter past four.

He got up, gave the woman his card, thanked her, and walked out into the corridor again. He had, he considered, done his duty by Russian rules of procedure, had made an appointment with the head of the international relations department, the way foreign journalists were supposed to do. Now that he had been stood up, he considered himself free to poke around.

He walked farther down the corridor until he came to a larger double door with a sign that said "Director." He went inside without knocking.

This anteroom was much larger, and its antique furnishings fit better with the Oriental rug on the floor and the sleek fax machine on a side table. The receptionist, too, was different. She was young, maybe nineteen, with hair the color the Russians called *ryzhy*, a shiny mix between red and brown. She wore a beige cashmere sweater that outlined two sleekly prominent breasts. She would have been very pretty had she known how to use makeup, but she wore far too much, beginning with her lips, which were painted a precise and very bright red.

When he introduced himself, she smiled and leaned toward him, slightly swiveling in her chair and crossing her legs. Her skirt was very short and her heels were very high.

"Foreign journalists have to talk to Gennady Gavril'ich," she said. She managed to make it sound as if she would like to talk to him herself.

"But he's not here."

She shrugged. That was not her concern.

"All I'm interested in, really, is finding out whether anyone else was present when a colleague of mine named Jennifer Morelli talked to Fyodor Pav'lich a week or so ago," Burke said.

The woman's face seemed to contract, and the bright red lips hardened into a firm line.

"You remember seeing her, don't you?" Burke persisted.

"Foreign journalists have to talk to Gennady Gavril'ich," she repeated. This time her voice had a hardened edge to it, as if reciting orders she'd memorized.

"She was tall, with red hair, blue eyes, American . . ."

His voice trailed away, perhaps because the act of describing Jennifer brought him too close to remembering the way she looked in death, perhaps because he already knew that this woman was not going to answer any questions.

His eye fell on the leather-covered door behind her, which was slightly ajar. Fyodor Vasiliev's name was still on it, on a little plastic sign.

He gave her a bright smile. "I guess it won't hurt if I take a look in his office," he said, and before she could react, he strode into the room. Maybe Vasiliev kept an appointment book, and maybe that book would indicate who else, if anyone, had sat in on his meeting with Jennifer Morelli.

The director's office resembled the study of an aristocratic, eighteenth century French intellectual. Though he knew almost nothing about furniture, he could tell that the pieces in this room were very old, very well made, and very expensive. They were of a burnished red wood, perhaps cherry, and the flat surfaces were all inlaid with a lighter, fine-grained wood that he guessed was poplar.

The floor, similarly, was unlike any he'd seen thus far. It was a fine parquet, with an inlaid geometric pattern that resembled a zodiac diagram. The paintings on the walls were of the sort that the museum, in the old days, had been forbidden to display because they represented decadent Western modernism. One was a landscape that looked like a Cezanne. Two more depicted Polynesian women, lush and nude, in a forest of fat fruits and broad, green leaves. He knew little about painting and cared less, but he'd seen enough calendars and wall posters to know they were Gauguins. A credenza occupied the space between paintings, and mixed in with the leather-bound books were small treasures—primitive sculptures of gold and ivory, and an icon framed in gold and jewels. Matching gueridons flanked the credenza, each holding a lamp and some books of painting reproductions. Laid carelessly atop one of the book piles was a dented old battle helmet—of gold. There were museums, he realized, that would gladly trade their entire collections for the contents of this office.

But he took all these things in peripherally, his eye fixed on something much more modern, the calendar on the director's desk. He strode toward it and turned it around. It was open to January 31, five days ago. Vasiliev, Burke calculated, would have seen Jennifer on January 30.

He began turning the pages backward, looking for names. Vasiliev's handwriting was tight and sloppy, and he had to go slowly to make it out. There was someone named Gorbunov written in for January 29. A Platonova and either Vaskanyan or Baskanyan for January 30; it was hard to be certain. . . .

Something strong, something hard, something like a vise attached itself to his right shoulder and squeezed. In an instant it felt like his collarbone was about to be ripped free of his body and splintered. Burke grunted in pain and spun around like a fox in a trap, trying to break free. He could not.

As he twisted he saw that he was being held in the right hand of a man six inches shorter than himself, a man in a gray suit with a white shirt and maroon tie. The man's legs were almost those of a dwarf, stubby and bowed, but from the waist up he had the body of a linebacker, massive and solid, with long, thick arms. His head rose from his shoulders without visible aid from a neck, round as a bowling ball, topped with curly black hair that had thinned out to leave him with a pronounced widow's peak. Anger had etched some wrinkles in his forehead. His brown eyes were wide open but curiously expressionless.

Frightened and furious, Burke grabbed at the man's forearm and pushed. He broke free of the grip on his shoulder, but sensed that the man could have held him indefinitely had he not chosen to let go. Pain leapt from his shoulder like lightning bolts, down his arm and up to his head, until he felt dizzy and a little faint. He was trembling.

"Who are you?" the man demanded, his voice low and harsh. "What are you doing in here?"

Burke flexed his shoulders until the pain subsided and the trembling stopped.

"Thanks," he said to the man. "Had a crick in my neck ever since the flight over. You may have a future as a chiropractor."

The man glowered and his face turned a darker shade of red. He took a small but threatening half step forward. "Who are you?" he demanded again.

Burke reached into his pocket and handed him a business card. The Russian studied it intently, clearly trying hard to sound out words written in an alphabet he only dimly remembered from grade school.

"Vashing-tone Tree-boon," he said.

Burke nodded. "And you are?"

The man glowered again and pushed his face up close to Burke's chin. "What are you doing here?"

"Just came for the massage," Burke said.

"Maybe you don't realize you're not in Washington now, asshole," the man said. His voice was low, with a hard edge to it. "You are trespassing. Breaking the law. I could have the *militsia* throw you in jail."

Burke considered his options. Whoever this man was, he seemed to be in a position of authority. Even if he wasn't, he seemed eminently capable of breaking Burke's neck.

"Well, I came in to see what I could find out about an interview a colleague had with Vasiliev before his, uh—" Burke paused, searching for the right word. "—misfortune."

The man's face assumed a blank, innocent look, and he exhaled sharply enough to give Burke a whiff of garlic and onions.

Burke noticed the receptionist standing in the doorway, mouth ajar. The guard from the entrance scurried up behind her, saw what was happening and stopped, hesitant.

"Which colleague?"

"Jennifer Morelli."

The man stared into Burke's eyes for a moment, then scowled. Burke took a deep breath.

"No such interview took place," the man said.

"Well, that can't be—"

"No such interview took place," the man said, louder. He half grinned at Burke, sardonically, as if saying, I know you don't believe this, but tough shit.

"How do you know?"

"I am director of security for the museum. I know of all journalists who come here for interviews. She did not come here."

"And your name is?"

The man grinned, the same sardonic grin. "Bykov," he said. "Ivan Bykov."

Ten minutes later Bykov shut the door to his office, across the reception room from the director's. He sat down at his desk and called for his receptionist.

In a moment she walked in. He reminded himself that this was his sister's child and that he was the closest approximation to a father in her life. She was, for that matter, the closest approximation to a daughter in his. Though the urge to raise a bruise on her pretty face was strong, he suppressed it.

"Marina, why did you let that man into the office?"

The girl shrugged, and her bright red lips swelled into a pout. "I came and got you as soon as I could," she whined.

"This is not some rich American in a hard currency bar!" he said, straining to keep his voice down.

The girl's face contorted with anger of her own. "Fuck you!" she hissed. "I told you I came and got you as soon as I could."

He nodded. Perhaps she had. And she was family, and that entitled her to the benefit of the doubt. Besides, if she got angry
enough, she could contradict his denial that Jennifer Morelli had
ever visited Fyodor Vasiliev.

"All right," he said, trying to be conciliatory. "Call Merrill in
London. Tell him he needs to get here as soon as possible. You
have the number."

Marina nodded and walked out. Among her talents was an ability to speak English, an ability she had begun to polish at sixteen,
picking up johns in the tourist hotels.

Bykov picked up the phone, dialed a number, and waited for an
answer.

"Sasha," he said. "I have a job for you. It's an American journalist." He picked up the business card Burke had left and carefully
spelled out the name. "I don't know what hotel. One of the tourist
hotels. Find him. Follow him. Tell me where he goes."

He listened to Sasha's reply.

"No, Sasha. Don't do anything like that to him. You might not
know when to stop."

He hung up the phone and permitted himself a small and fleeting smile. He liked Sasha. Sasha was one of the few people who
could make him laugh.

Chapter Thirteen

D
ESDEMONA MCCOY TOOK HER NEW COMMUNI-
cations module from its container, a canvas briefcase that looked as
if it had come out of the Lands' End catalogue. She laid it on the
seat next to her and plugged it into the cigarette lighter socket. Silently, she reviewed the instructions she'd memorized on how to
operate it.

The module itself looked like a Compaq laptop computer. In
fact, it was a Compaq laptop, and no airport security device would
ever be able to show otherwise. Anyone running the software on
the hard disk would find only files that reflected the McCoy-Fokine
Gallery's financial records, letters, and other routine data. Only a
computer engineer, examining its interior carefully, would be able
to detect the hardware that made it more than a computer.

She turned the machine on and checked to make sure that the
lights over the keyboard lit up in the prescribed order. Num Lock
flashed red. Caps Lock flashed white and went off. Scroll Lock
flashed white and went off.

She checked outside her Volvo to make certain the antenna was
up. It was. She was parked next to the Summer Gardens, the largest park in the center of the city. She'd picked it because it was sufficiently distant from any tall buildings that might interfere with the

signals she intended to receive and send. She took a quick look
around and saw no one. The snow had stopped, but the wind was
still blowing wispy curls of it around the trees. The daylight was
almost gone and it was bitter cold. Not a time for strolling in
the park.

Despite herself, despite her growing disdain for her employer,
she liked having this device. Previously, she had gathered her material on the Russian intelligentsia and waited for a chance to
travel to Helsinki or New York, where she filed it with the local station. Now she needed instant communications, and she was impressed and gratified by what the technical people in the agency
could do. If only the policymakers were as competent.

She checked her watch. It was three P.M. The satellite should be
coming into range.

The Caps-Lock light flashed red. She was in range. She pressed
F1 and sent her report up into space. The Scroll-Lock light flashed
red. Report received. By now it was safely inside a computer in
Fort Meade, Maryland, awaiting retransmission, via dedicated line,
to Langley.

She could hear the hard disk whir briefly inside the computer,
and she knew it was automatically erasing all traces of the message
she'd just transmitted. The most remarkable thing about this device, though, was its encryption capability. Any surveillance satellite or ground station that happened to monitor the transmission
would record a mundane conversation between a woman in Brigh-
ton Beach, Brooklyn, and her elderly mother in St. Petersburg.
McCoy did not know how the machine did this. She just knew that
it did.

She thought, briefly, of her own mother, and the strained tenor
of all their recent conversations. No matter what subject she started
on, her mother always managed to change it to her desire that
Desdemona return to the United States, to a place where she could
have, if not a man, at least friends. The last couple of times, Mc-
Coy had felt herself starting to agree with her. Eight years in the
field was a long time. Like many Americans who had learned the
language and lived for a while amongst the Russians, she felt an
exasperated fondness for Russia. She had hundreds of Russian ac-

quaintances, and she liked many of them. But the gulfs of culture
and race, to say nothing of her work, were too wide to permit intimacy with any of them.

If she were a man, she could have found herself the kind of innocuous and innocent foreign woman that agents often married,
with the full approbation of the personnel people at Langley. But
let a female agent get involved with someone, and the immediate
assumption was that she was being seduced—"penetrated" was the
word they used to use—by an enemy agent. So for many women,
joining the agency was like joining a convent.

She pressed F2 and waited. The Scroll Lock flashed green, then
red again. She had received a message, encrypted in the same way
her transmission was.

Then she hesitated. From the moment she received a transmission until she read it and erased it, the system was at its most vulnerable. The machine would not display the message unless it was
fed her numerical code, followed by F4. The odds on anyone entering exactly that sequence of numbers were high. But the recom-
mended procedure, nevertheless, was to read and absorb the
message immediately.

That was fine, McCoy thought, for some guy sitting in a warm
hotel room in Paris. But she was past the point of scrupulously following all procedures; she didn't have enough faith in the people
who wrote them. She closed the computer, started the car and
drove to the gallery.

The McCoy-Fokine Gallery occupied a converted basement at
80 Nevsky Prospekt, about two miles southeast of the Admiralty
and the Winter Palace. She hated the space; it was cold and damp
and the ceilings were too low. But the basement had been renovated for gallery space in the late eighties by an artists' cooperative
that had gone bankrupt. She'd been able to lease the place cheaply
and avoid wasting time on supervising renovations in a more comfortable building. So she'd taken it.

She drove slowly through the alley connecting the boulevard
with the building's inner courtyard. Someone had stolen the
lightbulb again. She parked and looked around. The courtyard,
under its cover of new snow, seemed cleaner and more inviting.

The snow hid the piles of trash and old pipe that seemed to spring from the asphalt no matter how many times she hired someone to clean it.

The gallery, to her relief, was dark. In the summer, during the height of the tourist season, she employed a Russian, Volodya, as sales help. But at this time of year, tourists were scarcer, and no one noticed if the gallery occasionally stayed closed during business hours.

She locked the door behind her and walked past the white pedestals and cubes on which she displayed the objects for sale: bronze sculptures, decorated glassware, malachite chess sets. On the walls, she showed fabrics, textiles, miniatures, Soviet-era propaganda posters, and some large canvases by an artist named Seryozha, each of which depicted one swollen part of Stalin's anatomy: a gnarled hand, a bristly mustache, a piggish eye. She refused to sell only two things: lacquered boxes and *matryoshka* dolls.

She opened her office, locked the door behind her again, and set up the computer on her desk. The message came up as soon as she pressed her identification number and F4. It glowed a yellowish orange on the screen: TSEODI.

It stood for "Top Secret, Eyes Only, Destroy Immediately." Mc-Coy would have been more impressed if she hadn't once seen the same six letters atop a message telling her she should change her travel plans and return to Washington two days ahead of schedule.

The rest of the message read:

    EX OSTENDIJK
    BUYER FOR HERMITAGE ART IDENTIFIED AS
    RAFAEL SANTERA CALDERON. HIS AGENT CHARLES
    MERRILL EX LONDON.
    SALE PRICE EXPECTED TO BE $400 MILLION.
    SALE ART HAS BEEN REFERRED TO AS A FEMALE
    NUDE BY LEONARDO. OUR RESEARCH SUGGESTS THIS
    IS THE MADONNA LITTA.
    MAJOR CHANGE: CALDERON NOW INTENDS TO CROSS
    UP RUSGOV AND DISPLAY PICTURE IN COLOMBIA.
    SCANDAL WOULD BE VERY DAMAGING TO INTERESTS
    RUSGOV AND USGOV.

> STILL UNWILLING TO JEOPARDIZE ORIGINAL
> SOURCE. COUNTING ON YOU TO STOP SALE. SUGGEST
> USING WASHINGTON TRIBUNE CORRESPONDENT NOW
> IN ST. PETERSBURG TO PUBLICIZE PLAN. THAT
> SHOULD END IT BEFORE INCRIMINATING MONEY
> CHANGES HANDS. IMPERATIVE CONTAIN SCANDAL AT
> LOCAL LEVEL.
>
> SANTERA CALDERON AND MERRILL BELIEVED AR-
> RIVING SOON ST. PETERSBURG.
>
> VP THIS DATA IS NINETY PERCENT. RESPOND
> SOONEST WITH PLAN.

McCoy inhaled sharply and involuntarily. She read the message until she memorized its essentials, then pressed the buttons that transformed it into random electrons.

She pressed her palms together in a prayerful position, propped her elbows on the desk and lowered her forehead to her hands, resting her cheekbones on her thumbs. But her mind, instead of focusing on the information at hand, flashed back to a picture of her mother, sitting at the kitchen table, her hands and head arranged in precisely the same way. That was the position her mother used to ponder things. McCoy wondered how long she had been unconsciously copying the mannerism.

She knew vaguely who Rafael Santera Calderon was. His picture appeared occasionally in newsmagazine stories about Colombia's drug barons. She had not known he collected art, but it was not surprising. He had to find something to do with his money.

"VP" stood for "veracity probability," the latest agency jargon for the classification of the likely truthfulness of information it received.

A VP score of 90 was very high. It generally meant either that the information had been gleaned from an unsuspecting subject by electronic surveillance, or, if it came from a human source, that it had been corroborated by at least one other tested source. She assumed the technogeniuses at the National Security Agency had figured out a way to wire Rafael Santera, his agent Merrill, or both.

If Santera in fact planned to put whatever he was buying on display, she could only believe that Ostendijk was understating the consequences. The Russian people would tolerate an enormous amount of suffering and hardship inflicted by their government, as long as they believed that the government's mistakes were the product of honest incompetence. They would tolerate enormous corruption and graft if they believed that the government had some basic patriotism and was prodding Russia in the right direction. But the corrupt sale of a major piece of the Russian patrimony, if it became public knowledge, would irrevocably damn this government. She shuddered to think what might replace it.

She snorted quietly, however, when she reflected on the "veracity probability" attached to the speculation that Santera planned to buy the *Madonna Litta*. The agency knew a great deal about subjects ranging from the sex lives of Italian politicians to the migration habits of Siberian elk. But it knew next to nothing about art. She could imagine some flunky in Ostendijk's office running out to the Library of Congress to find a coffee table book on the Hermitage collection, leafing through it, then announcing proudly:

"Here it is, boss. Got to be this *Madonna Litta*. Only two Leonardos in the collection, and the other one's got all her clothes on. The *Litta*'s got a tit showing."

She could think of four or five reasons why that theory didn't make sense.

To begin with, the *Madonna Litta* was not even an undisputed Leonardo. Some experts regarded it as almost wholly the work of some apprentices who toiled in Leonardo's studio.

McCoy had studied the picture carefully on her visits to the Hermitage. There were fewer than a dozen genuine Leonardos in the world, and whenever she got the chance, she looked at them. She knew that the head of the Virgin, a three-quarter profile, corresponded closely to an undisputed Leonardo drawing in the Louvre. The case that the painting was a genuine Leonardo rested heavily on the theory that the drawing was a study done by Leonardo preparatory to executing the painting. And she bought that argument, as far as it went. The head and neck of the Virgin in the *Madonna Litta* shared too many characteristics of the best Leonardos, beginning with its angle to the body and ending with the delicacy of its lines, for her to believe it was by another, inferior artist.

But the Virgin in the *Madonna Litta* would hardly be called a nude. She was nursing her infant discreetly. Her breast protruded through an opening in a Renaissance version of a nursing blouse, its laces neatly and precisely loosened.

The rest of the painting, she thought, might have been done by someone else. The infant's head, in particular, was grotesque: out of proportion to the body and disfigured by a facial expression that she could only describe as an arrogant leer. McCoy could not imagine Leonardo, with his intense interest in the proper proportion of body parts, painting it. She could readily see it as the work of some mildly talented nineteen-year-old apprentice with a breast fixation.

Then there was the painting's condition. It had been clumsily "restored" on at least two occasions, once by a Milanese artist fifteen years after it was first painted, and again in the nineteenth century when the Winter Palace curators transferred it from wood to canvas.

As a result of these efforts, whatever subtlety Leonardo had originally painted had vanished. The colors were flat and dull. On the Madonna's left sleeve, the final layer of blue glaze that would have given life and texture to the fabric was almost entirely gone.

Altogether, McCoy thought, it was a painting of uncertain provenance, uneven quality, and wretched condition. Were it not for the fact that the world contained so few paintings by Leonardo, this Madonna would have been long since relegated to the Hermitage's massive attic, the home of thousands of lesser works bought wholesale by Catherine's agents.

And there was no way, she thought, even in an art market inflated by Colombian drug dollars, that the painting was worth anything close to $400 million.

Still, the *Madonna Litta* made more sense as the painting Rafael Santera wanted than the other Leonardo in the Hermitage collection, the *Benois Madonna*. Of the two Hermitage Leonardos, McCoy much preferred the *Benois*, if only because it depicted a happy Virgin, smiling and showing her babe a flower. But the *Benois Madonna* was fully clothed. In fact, as she flashed through her recollection of the other women she had seen in Leonardo's paintings, she could think of none who were not clothed. Most of them, in fact, were either the Virgin or saints. She had seen nearly all of Leonardo's paintings, except for *Lady with the Weasel* in the Czartoryski Museum in Cracow. And she had seen a photograph of that. She could remember no adult nudes. The *Madonna Litta* came closest.

But how could they sell it secretly? Thousands of people looked at it every day.

She thought of forgery. The Hermitage had a legendary art school that taught, among other things, painting restoration and copying. But it was all but inconceivable that the Russian government could think it would be able to fob a forgery off on a buyer represented by Charles Merrill. A hundred years ago, perhaps. But ever since the invention of the X-ray machine, technology had given art buyers more and more tools to detect fakes. Merrill, if not his patron, would know what technology to use in spotting a forgery.

She thought, briefly, of what was likely to happen to anyone foolish enough to be caught trying to sell a forgery to Rafael Santera Calderon. Justice would be swift and brutal.

She would have to learn more. And she would have to protect her cover as she did so. The obvious solution was to feed information to the reporter, Burke, and let him ask the questions. Then let him break the story that would blow the sale.

As she thought of Burke, she scowled. It was so like the idiots at Langley to fail to plan more than one move at a time. Forty-eight hours ago they had told her to meet him on the train and divert him with a false lead. Sending him off to chase a false rumor that Vasiliev had been gay had seemed a good idea at the time. She had yet to meet a straight white male who didn't believe that at least half the men in the art world were gay.

But now they wanted her to get his trust and put him on the right track. She could only hope that Burke hadn't yet gotten around to checking out her tip. If she was going to induce him to play the role she needed him to play, she would need unquestioned credibility.

It occurred to her that if she was right about Ostendijk's ulterior motives, everything was still going according to his plan. If Burke had successfully checked out her false tip, he would be in no mood to cooperate with her.

During her training, McCoy had heard numerous stories about drunken and ignorant reporters who stayed in their hotel rooms and filed whatever disinformation the agency chose to feed them.

Burke fit the agency's stereotypes only superficially. He was divorced, rumpled, and red-eyed, and she could tell from the way he had looked at her wine that he was no stranger to alcohol. But throughout their train ride together, he drank tea. He spoke Russian. He knew what questions to ask. Under other circumstances, she would have felt they had things in common.

Maybe Ostendijk had figured that as well, had calculated that she would be unable to influence Burke.

Well, she was damned if Ostendijk would outmaneuver her. She was damned if she would let this scandal erupt and blow away the slim chance that Russia had to make it till the next election. She would just have to work with the circumstances at hand. Somehow, she would have to enlist Burke's help, despite his distrust and without his knowledge.

At least he had made her laugh, she remembered. On a winter's night in Russia, that was something. She picked up the phone and called the Hotel Yevropeiskaya.

Chapter Fourteen

BURKE STRODE PAST THE DOORMAN AND THE small queue of taxi racketeers outside the Hotel Yevropeiskaya and headed for the Metro station at Gostiny Dvor. He always hated paying the inflated prices the drivers demanded. He knew they enforced their little monopolies by slashing the tires and faces of anyone who dared try to undercut their prices. That offended his sense of fair play. While he often ignored this when he was in a hurry and on an expense account, he was spending his own money on this trip, and now he was out an unexpected three hundred dollars.

He shuffled rather than walked. The snow had stopped, leaving another two-inch layer packed on the snow and ice deposited by previous storms. It was slippery. He wondered whether in fact, when he first came to Russia, the sidewalks had always been cleared of snow almost as soon as it fell. He thought they had.

He stopped at a liquor kiosk near the Metro entrance and tried to decide what to bring for Sasha Vinogradov. Sasha would expect something with alcohol, and something imported. But the thought of carrying a bottle to someone made him faintly queasy. He stepped to the next kiosk and bought a box of chocolates. He didn't particularly like chocolates, and at least he wouldn't have to sit on the train fighting the temptation to open the gift and sample some.

Then he descended, via escalator, into the Metro. Burke liked the Metro in St. Petersburg. It was the only one he had ever seen where doors divided the platforms from the tracks. Each train pulled up to a precise location. The train doors and the platform doors lined up precisely. They opened simultaneously, and the passengers stepped into or out of the train. Passengers waiting on the platform were insulated from the cacophony of passing trains in clean, well-lit, tiled rooms. Burke wondered if someday archaeologists would dig up these stations and wonder how the Russians who built them could fail at so many other endeavors.

His train pulled in and he wedged himself between two elderly men, each of them reading *Rossiskaya Gazeta*. Burke peered over the shoulder of the man on his left and started to read a story about the Duma's determination to exceed the president's agricultural subsidy budget by forty percent. The old man noticed what Burke was doing, gave him an irritated look, and noisily turned the page.

Embarrassed, Burke rummaged in his shoulder bag for his copy of *The Brothers Karamazov*. He wondered whether he could skip the rest of Elder Zosima's exhortations and still tell himself he had read the novel. He decided he could not. It would violate some inner sense of integrity. Glumly, he opened the book and found his place.

"The people believe in our religion," the monk was saying. "And an unbelieving politician here in Russia will never do anything, even if he is sincere in heart and a genius in his mind. Remember that. The people will confront an atheist and struggle with him and will rise up a united, Orthodox Russia!"

Burke couldn't argue, based on the history of the last decade. Or the last century for that matter. A lot of atheist politicians had passed under the bridge.

He looked up at the Metro map on the car wall. Vinogradov's station was next. With a bit of reluctance this time, he shut the book.

Sasha Vinogradov lived across the Neva in a quarter still called Krasnogvardeysky, or Red Guard. As Burke ascended to the street level, he heard music. A man and a woman, bundled in scarves and wool hats, were playing something on a pair of violins. It sounded like a truncated arrangement of one of Beethoven's string quartets. He wondered how they kept their fingers from freezing, and dropped a dollar in their instrument case.

Vinogradov's building, he had been told, was within a few hundred meters of the Metro. The wind had picked up until it was a tangible force, beating against his clothes and sucking the heat from his body as he walked, shoulders slumped, straining to read the letters on the street signs. He found the street, Prospekt Energetikov, and walked the wrong way for a block until he found a building with its number visible and got oriented. He had passed it. Cursing, he turned and retraced his steps and finally, thoroughly chilled, pushed through the wooden doors and into the dark stairwell of number 42.

Burke groped at the air, wondering why no light penetrated. He shuffled slowly forward until his hand encountered something smooth and wooden, which he took for the end of the banister. It was, and he began to walk up, hoping that one of the landings, at least, would have a surviving lightbulb that would enable him to find apartment 11. He could tell it was an old building, possibly even pre-Revolutionary. The stairs were wider than those in Soviet-era buildings, and the stone treads had deep grooves worn into them from the plodding feet of generations.

A small bulb was burning on the fourth floor. Puffing slightly, he looked at the numbers on the four doors clustered at the landing. Fifteen through eighteen. He had overshot by a floor.

Clinging to the banister, he returned to the third floor and made a good guess at which door was number 11. Sasha Vinogradov opened the door.

Burke blinked. When last he had seen him, in 1988, Vinogradov had been wearing jeans and an old flannel shirt. A thick red beard had obscured his chin and neck.

Now he was clean shaven. His red hair, which had receded during the intervening years, was clipped short. Vinogradov wore a gray frock coat and a black bow tie, and his white shirt had a starched, wing collar. Burke had seen nothing like it outside of a theater, and for a moment he thought Vinogradov was moonlighting as an actor. It was the kind of clothes actors doing

Chekhov wore. There was a steel lapel pin in the coat. Burke peered at it. It was the double-headed eagle, emblem of the czars.

"*Gospodin* Burke," the artist said, bowing and beckoning him inside.

"Thanks," Burke said. "So how have you been and when did you become a monarchist?"

Vinogradov reddened slightly. "I always was."

"You did a good job hiding it," Burke said.

The artist gestured toward a chair, and Burke sat down.

"A lot of things had to be hidden then," Vinogradov said. He had developed a pretentious, clipped sort of diction that sounded odd in a city of so many dropped Russian vowels and consonants.

Yelena Vinogradova appeared from the kitchen. When Burke first met her, she was a newlywed, a status to which she had graduated after a few years of off-again, on-again modeling for her husband. Seven years had also changed her. She had been the possessor of a voluptuous body. As Burke recalled—and he knew he had a good memory for this sort of thing—she'd worn clothes that displayed it. But now she wore a high-necked white cotton blouse with long sleeves, and the body beneath looked stocky. A silver cross, inlaid with lapis, dangled from her neck. When he extended his hand, she hesitated for a moment before taking it in a weak, delicate grasp. She took the box of chocolates with a murmured phrase of gratitude and returned to the kitchen.

Vinogradov excused himself and followed her, and Burke looked around. The paintings on the walls were in keeping with the changes in the Vinogradovs' dress and manner. In the late eighties Sasha had practiced a kind of flamboyant eclecticism, painting big, colorful canvases with clashing motifs. Burke remembered in particular one that incorporated Yuri Andropov, Jesus Christ, and Yelena as Mary Magadalen. It had gotten Vinogradov expelled from the Artists Union.

The paintings on the wall now were all pictures of a village somewhere, with a ruined Orthodox Church and people who dressed, like the Vinogradovs, in clothes from the last century. In one, a family had a picnic under a linden tree, with the church in the background, jagged patches of sky showing through the holes in its bulbous domes. In another, two men in long-sleeve white shirts and neckties fished with bamboo poles in a blue pond. A third showed a funeral procession walking, on foot, to the graveyard next to the church. The pictures all had a soft, almost elegiac focus.

Yelena Vinogradova came out of the kitchen with a tray that bore a frosted bottle of vodka, slices of brown bread, butter, and a small dish of caviar. Silently, she placed it on the table next to the day bed where Burke was sitting. She smeared some butter on a piece of bread and spread some caviar on top of it with a kitchen knife and placed it on a small plate in front of Burke. She did the same for her husband. To Burke's mild surprise, she then retreated to the kitchen. As he recalled, she had sat with them during the 1988 interview, smiling occasionally and offering a comment. He wondered when she had changed.

Vinogradov poured the vodka into two shot glasses, then offered a toast.

"To your return," he said.

Burke nodded. He watched Vinogradov toss the vodka down his throat in a single motion. He put the glass to his lips and put it down again.

Vinogradov sat still for a second, feeling the vodka work its way down to his stomach. Then he noted that Burke's glass was still full.

"You didn't drink," he said.

"You've always had a brilliant eye for human behavior, Sasha," Burke replied.

"But you must," Vinogradov said. "For—" He stopped, thinking of a good reason. "For friendship," he said.

"I mustn't," Burke said. "For my liver."

Vinogradov frowned and looked hurt. "Yelena," he called out. She emerged immediately from the kitchen.

"Make Mr. Burke some tea," he said. He sounded as if he were asking her to loan Burke a pair of her stockings.

There were probably harder circumstances in which to quit drinking than working in Russia, Burke thought. Working in a distillery leapt to mind.

Vinogradov poured himself another shot, tossed it back, and shuddered.

"Just the thought of doing what you're doing makes me uncomfortable," he said, then smiled. "And it's good vodka, too. It has some pepper in it. We make it ourselves at our dacha in the summer."

Burke swallowed. "I'm sure it's delicious."

Yelena came back with a teapot and poured some for Burke. He watched the leaves swirl in the bottom of the cup.

It was his turn to make a toast. He thought about offering one to the health of the czar, but he decided Vinogradov's sense of humor might have changed along with his sense of style over the past years.

"To your brilliant art," he said, raising his cup. When he couldn't think of anything intelligent to say, Burke found that flattery worked with most of the people he interviewed.

Vinogradov beamed modestly and they downed their respective drinks. For an instant Burke's upper lip began to go numb. He realized it must be a sympathetic reaction to the liquor Vinogradov was drinking.

"Would you like to see what I'm working on now?"

Burke had as much interest in Sasha Vinogradov's latest paintings as he had in viewing the average stamp collection. But he nodded as amiably as he could; there was a ritual to the interview, and the first part required getting the interviewee to feel comfortable and in control.

Vinogradov stood up and opened a French door that had been obscured by a curtain. It led to an adjoining room that smelled of paint.

Burke smiled. "So you got your studio after all." Vinogradov's expulsion from the Artists Union in 1988 had been painful largely because in the old Soviet system, members of the cultural unions were entitled, after a suitable period of groveling, to an apartment with an extra room for writing or painting or whatever they did to contribute to the glory of the state. Vinogradov had been just about to receive one when he was expelled. It meant he would be sentenced to continue living in a one-room apartment, sleeping, eating, and painting in the same space.

"I was reinstated in the union," Vinogradov explained, "in 1992."

"The union still controls the studios?"

"Yes, of course. Why not?"

He was tempted to ask how Vinogradov reconciled being a monarchist with living in space furnished by the Artists Union, but thought better of it. The question, he knew, would strike Vinogradov as ignorant or inane. To most Russians, there was no conflict.

Vinogradov flipped a switch and lit the room. His new paintings extended the village theme of the ones in the sitting room. The village church, judging by the paintings, had just been restored, because in the newest pictures its domes were whole and gilded. They gleamed brightly in the winter sun.

If anything, Burke thought, Vinogradov was growing insipid as he painted his idealized village and country life. At the rate he was going, he would be doing landscapes for the Russian branches of Holiday Inn by the time he was an old man.

"They're marvelous," Burke lied.

The artist coughed modestly. "They're for sale," he said.

"Oh, I'm sure I couldn't afford them," Burke said hastily. "You'll starve trying to sell paintings to reporters. But I'm sure you could sell them in New York."

Vinogradov shrugged indifferently. "Not really," he said. "The New York art market is controlled by Jews."

Burke let that one go past, for the same reason he had refrained from asking about the scruples of a monarchist in the Artists Union.

"I have met one person who sells paintings in New York," he said. "And she has a gallery of some kind here, too. Her name is Desdemona McCoy."

"The Negro?" Vinogradov asked.

The odds on two black women being in the art business in St. Petersburg were long enough to cause Burke to nod.

"What kind of connections could she have with people who can buy paintings?" Vinogradov asked. "Who would trust her taste?"

"I gather she's quite good at what she does," Burke said sharply. "I'd give you her card, but obviously you don't want it."

Vinogradov, recognizing dimly that he had offended someone

with hard currency, but not quite certain why, suggested they return to the sitting room.

This time Burke did not bother to propose a toast. He watched Vinogradov pour the alcohol down his throat and waited. He felt almost like a clinical experimenter standing behind a two-way mirror, watching some witless subject do something foolish.

He decided to find out what he could before Vinogradov's conversational ability deteriorated further.

"What have you heard about Fyodor Vasiliev's death?"

Vinogradov refilled his glass and Burke's cup. Burke began to marvel at the casual way he had once knocked off four or five of these shots in the course of an interview.

"Is that why you've come to St. Petersburg?" Vinogradov asked. His voice was losing its monarchist accent and reverting to what Burke remembered.

Burke nodded. A partial truth was close enough.

"Well, if you want my opinion, it wasn't robbery," Vinogradov said. "Not the way the *militsia* had it, anyway."

"Why not?"

Vinogradov shrugged. "I heard that the robbers didn't take his car. It was parked nearby. This is a city where they steal the wiper blades off cars."

"So who do you think killed him?"

Vinogradov emptied his glass.

"Mafia," he said.

Russians blamed everything on the "mafia." It could mean anything from a gang of racketeers to a network of law-abiding businessmen who happened to be making a profit.

"Who? Why?"

Vinogradov shook his head. "I don't know who. But I can guess who, ultimately."

He paused. Evidently, he wanted to be prodded. Or else he expected that Burke would know.

"Who?"

"Slema Chavchavadze, of course."

"I've heard of him," Burke said, only slightly lying. "He's the top guy in the St. Petersburg mafia?"

Vinogradov shook his head. "Not only in Peterburg," he said, using the old French pronunciation. "Slema has operations in Moscow, in Kiev, in Riga, in Perm. Slema is all over."

Burke caught the use of the first name. "You know him?"

Vinogradov nodded.

"How?"

The artist's eyes narrowed. "Five or six years ago," he said quietly, "Slema was getting his start. He controlled the illegal export of icons to the West. When I was expelled from the Artists Union, he gave me work restoring icons that had been damaged. He paid well."

"You liked him?"

Vinogradov shook his head. "He is an Ossetian. He paid well."

"What else do you know about him?"

The artist shrugged, then smiled conspiratorially. "I know what Slema means."

"What?"

"It stands for Stalin, Lenin, and Marx."

Soviets of a certain age, Burke knew, often had been given names like Vladlen or Proletaria, concocted from the names and slogans of the Bolsheviks by parents who either fervently believed in the Revolution or fervently wished to stay on the good side of those who did.

"So he was born before 1953, I guess."

Vinogradov nodded. "His father was an Ossetian, an oblast first secretary somewhere in the mountains in Georgia. His mother was Russian, though. From Peterburg. They sent him to school here."

"Where could I find him?"

Vinogradov laughed. "Oh, I wouldn't go looking for Slema," he said. "He might not be very happy if you did. If you want to see him, he attends the ballet almost every night. He's their big patron now, you see. Without him, the Marinsky would fold."

"He likes the dance?"

Vinogradov snorted. "He likes the dancers. Especially the young ones."

Burke wondered how much his friend Nikolai the concierge would charge him to get ballet tickets.

"Why would he want Vasiliev killed?"

Vinogradov shrugged. "It could be one of two things. Most likely it's his people who are taking things from the museum."

The baldness of the assertion surprised Burke. "Taking things?"

Vinogradov laughed in a way calculated to express his scorn both for the thieves and for Burke's American naiveté.

"Of course."

"Like what?"

"Anything small enough to hide! Coins. Jewels. Miniature paintings. Silverware. The Hermitage says it has two million items in its collection, but they're just guessing. It's stashed away in closets and attics and basements. A lot of it could disappear and never be missed."

"Who takes it? Employees?"

Vinogradov nodded. "And then they sell it to the mafia, to Chavchavadze, and he exports it. That's one reason Vasiliev may have been killed. He may have been doing something to stop it."

Burke thought of the director of security he had met so memorably that morning. "What do you know about Ivan Bykov?"

Vinogradov stiffened. "Why do you ask?"

"I met him this morning. At the Hermitage. He's the director of security."

Vinogradov's face showed genuine pain. "God forbid! The director of security at the Hermitage is an old apparatchik named Kirillov. Has been for years."

Burke shook his head. "Well, this guy said he was the director, and he pushed me around like he was in charge. Why do you say 'God forbid'?"

"The Bykov I know about is a guy who was kicked off the Soviet Olympic team in wrestling or boxing or something because he was caught taking icons out of the country on team trips," Vinogradov said. "That was ten or so years ago. Now he works for Slema."

"Guy about five-eight, very broad shoulders, thinning black hair?"

Vinogradov shrugged. "I've never seen him or met him. I've just heard about him."

"How could a guy like that, if it is that guy, be appointed director of security?"

Vinogradov rubbed his thumb and forefinger together, the universal sign language for a bribe. "You'd have to ask the Ministry of Culture in Moscow."

Vinogradov poured himself another vodka, tossed it down, and shuddered. "It's a scandal! A disgrace! It could never have happened under the czar!"

"No," Burke agreed. "Under the czar, Bykov would probably have become a police officer long ago."

Vinogradov was by this time too drunk and too exercised to take offense on the czar's behalf.

"This is what your democracy brings!" he growled. He spit dramatically, barely missing the caviar.

Burke quickly spooned some of it onto a slice of bread and placed it out of expectoration range.

"Well, actually, no," he said. "In our democracy, people do their stealing in the market and then they *give* things to museums. It's an advanced stage of development Russia can still look forward to."

Vinogradov suddenly looked older and sadder, rather than angry. "It's not a joke," he said weakly.

"I'm sorry," Burke said, and he meant it. "So how do you know that things are being stolen?"

Vinogradov shrugged listlessly. "You hear about it."

Burke scowled. "Have you ever seen things for sale?"

Vinogradov snorted. "Of course not! It all goes abroad."

Burke tried again to get something more concrete than gossip. "Ever hear of anyone being convicted or arrested?"

Vinogradov shook his head.

Burke shook his head. "If I had a dollar for every time I've heard a hot rumor like this that can't be checked out, I'd be able to buy all of your paintings."

Vinogradov did not rise to the bait. He was slumping into a studied passivity, a mannerism he had probably picked up from reading *Oblomov*.

"You said it could be one of two things. What's your other theory?"

"Well, the Hermitage has a joint venture with some Jews in the United States. Emigrants. They arrange touring exhibitions of things that go to Western museums. A year ago, they sent Catherine the Great's coronation coach to California and Texas, I think. The museums pay them. There's a good deal of money in it."

"So?"

"So, Vasiliev refused to allow the really great things—the Leonardos, the Rembrandts, or the Matisses, for instance—to go abroad. If he had, they would have made a lot more money, obviously."

Burke nodded. "How do you know Vasiliev refused?"

Vinogradov just shrugged.

"Well, while we're talking about gossip," Burke said, "have you ever heard anything to the effect that Vasiliev was—"

He stopped. There was no Russian equivalent of "gay," the word he had been conditioned to use in English. There were lots of Russian equivalents for "faggot," like *golyboi*, but he wanted to avoid them.

"—a homosexual," he finished, remembering the word, which was *gomoseks*.

Vinogradov laughed out loud. "You mean a faggot?"

Burke nodded.

"God, no. He has a wife. Kids, I think. Two years ago he had an affair with one of the assistant curators. A woman. Everyone in the city knew about it."

Burke nodded. More gossip that didn't check out.

"Okay," he said. "Thanks very much. You wouldn't happen to have the name or address of Vasiliev's wife, would you?"

Vinogradov chuckled. "I don't know whether she'd talk to an American. I don't know if she can, half the time." But he called for Yelena to get the address book and write it down.

"She doesn't like Americans?"

Vinogradov chuckled again. "I should let Galina Vladimirovna explain herself."

Burke took the piece of paper from Yelena, thanked her, and walked to the hallway, where he had left his shoes.

There was one more thing.

"Did an American journalist named Jennifer Morelli ever talk to you?"

Vinogradov's face brightened. "Yes, she did. Is she a friend of yours?"

Burke nodded numbly. "I gave her your number."

"She was charming. She called about three weeks ago, came by, and we talked. A lot about the Hermitage. In fact, I gave her Vasiliev's number."

Burke nodded again, unable to speak.

"How is she?" Vinogradov asked pleasantly. "Have you seen her lately?"

"No," Burke said, his voice scratchy. "Not lately."

Maybe, Burke thought, the cold air would make him feel better. He could think of no logical reason why it should, except that sometimes it did. Maybe, when the temperature dropped below minus twenty, the brain becomes so preoccupied with maintaining some body heat that it forgets to register pain.

It was past rush hour, and the city had subsided into its night-time stillness. People were in their homes. Burke stepped outside Vinogradov's building and tested the temperature in his usual way, by inhaling through his nose. If nothing froze with the first inhalation, it would be warm enough to walk and take the air.

Galina Vasilieva's address was on the Red Fleet Embankment, an extension of the same riverside street the Winter Palace occupied. He did not know how far it was, but there figured to be a tram running along that street, in case it proved too far to walk.

The snow, dry and cold, scrunched under his old boots as he set out. The wind blew down the Neva as he crossed it on a bridge, orienting himself by the dark, Romanesque dome of St. Isaac's Cathedral. As he'd hoped, the cold air seemed to numb his whole body.

He was lonely, and he thought for a moment of Graves, and wondered if he'd been right. He could be sitting in a warm office, drinking coffee and checking on the price of Toyotas. Maybe that was where he belonged.

He shook his head and trudged on.

The building turned out to be closer than he expected, just a couple of blocks from the cathedral. It was a hulking, six-story pile of gray limestone, grimy with the exhaust of the aging trucks that rumbled along the riverbank from the harbor, a kilometer or two downstream.

Only when he'd walked over a snowbank and made his way to the rear of the building did he understand the type of place it was. Built for the ruling class in a classless society, it hid its affluence from passersby on the street. In the back, where the entrance was, there were only three stairwells. A normal building of this size would have six or eight, but the apartments in this building were two or three times larger than average. And he could see it was still getting favored treatment, at least by Russian standards. The parking area had been plowed. The little playground had fresh new equipment, a miniature log hut, and three carved wooden deer.

The plain door of the entrance opened on an actual lobby, with bulbs burning in the light fixtures. An old man sat by the door, snoring quietly, wrapped in a scarf and a dirty old *shapka*. Burke did not wake him.

He had not called ahead because of the warning Sasha Vinogradov had given him that she might not want to talk to an American. It would have been easy for her to put him off over the phone. In his experience, though, even the most xenophobic Russians were too hospitable to shut the door in his face.

The elevator rose through a shaft, jerry-built of wire fencing, near the stairwell. The sound of the door clanking shut woke the concierge, but by the time he could react, Burke had already ascended to the second floor.

He saw the apartment he was looking for on the third floor, jabbed the button for four, and walked down the staircase. He could hear the sound of chimes when he pressed the button.

An old woman, far too old to be the wife of Fyodor Vasiliev, opened the door. She was tiny and stooped, with hair he would have called snow-white except for the fact that snow which made it through the haze and reached the ground in St. Petersburg tended to be tinged with more gray than this woman had. She looked frail enough to blow away in a strong wind.

She let him step inside. When he told her he had come to see Galina Vasilieva and handed her his business card, she croaked something in a voice he could barely make out, motioned for him to wait in the hall, and scurried off.

Burke stepped through the hallway in the opposite direction and found himself in the only Russian sitting room he'd ever been in that was big enough to hold a grand piano. Two large windows afforded a view of the white expanse of the Neva, perhaps half a mile wide. There were pictures on the wall, family pictures, all of them featuring a man whose face he had almost forgotten, though it had once hung on the wall of his office in Moscow, in the composite photo he kept of the members of the Politburo: Vladimir Nachalnik, boss of the Leningrad Communist Party under Brezhnev and, briefly, a rival for power to Mikhail Gorbachev. He had been a round-faced, stubby man with piggish little eyes and a luxuriant gray pompadour.

In these pictures he looked a trace more human than in his official portrait. There was one of him, Brezhnev, and a girl of about twelve. The men were wearing straw hats and long-sleeve dress shirts with open collars, awkwardly at ease in some summer resort. The girl had on shorts and the red neckerchief of the Young Pioneers. Judging from the reasonably alert look on Brezhnev's face, the picture must have been taken sometime in the early seventies, before Brezhnev's face and brain began increasingly to resemble a potato.

And this must be his old apartment, Burke thought. He glanced at the piece of paper Sasha Vinogradov had given him. "Galina Vladimirovna Vasilieva," it said. He hadn't paid attention to the middle name, always derived, in Russian, from a person's father's name. She was Vladimir Nachalnik's daughter.

"I thought in the West people at least knew enough to arrange an appointment before they barged in on someone."

It was a deep, gravelly woman's voice, and Burke spun around to find its owner. She was standing in the entrance to the living room, wearing a black dress and black stockings whose severity was set off by sky-blue house slippers. She had black hair pulled back in a severe bun and a gaunt face with more lines than the body seemed old enough to merit. Her eyes were bloodshot.

"Most do," Burke said. "But reporters are required to be *nyekulturny.*"

The Russian word meant "uncultured," but it covered a multitude of small sins, ranging from failure to have a loop inside one's topcoat, so the old women in the *garderob* at the theater could hang it up easily, to letting one's dog relieve himself on the sidewalk.

The woman's countenance softened slightly, as Burke had expected. Russians were usually disarmed by foreigners who admitted to being *nyekulturny*.

"This is not a good time for receiving visitors," she said, still sullen and stern, and still apparently far from willing to talk.

"I know it isn't, Galina Vladimirovna, but I'm working on a story that might reveal who killed your husband," he said.

The woman's bleary eyes widened a little.

"And I think you can help me," he went on, hoping she would take the bait.

She did. She nodded and asked him to sit down on a sofa next to the piano. Then she told the old woman to bring tea.

"So you're Vladimir Nachalnik's daughter," Burke said. "I remember watching your father up on the mausoleum on November seventh."

She seemed to be waiting for him to add something, and he tried to think of something nice to say about a man whose cruelty, by all accounts, had been exceeded only by his waistline.

"He was an impressive man," was all he could come up with.

Galina Vladimirovna actually smiled, showing brown teeth.

Once again Burke breathed a silent prayer of gratitude to the forgotten Russian who had taught him the word for "impressive."

"Russia does not have such men anymore. Or she keeps them in jail. It is the tragedy of our country," she said.

"Yes." Burke nodded. He had an urge to ask how the old man was doing, but had a vague recollection that Vladimir Nachalnik had died, widely unmourned, sometime around 1992.

"He was a very impressive man," he said.

This time there was no smile, and Burke was relieved when the old woman brought in the tea tray.

He could read some engraving on it: "To Vladimir Nachalnik from the friendly people of Finland. November 17, 1979."

Enough of the silver plating had worn away from the handle, showing tin underneath, to make it clear that the friendly people of

Finland had not been friendly enough to buy sterling for their honored guest from Leningrad.

The old woman set a cup of tea in front of Burke. He noticed that the liquid in Galina Vladimirovna's cup was clear, which suggested she was an advanced alcoholic. Russian alcoholics at the middling stages, in his experience, still mixed tea with their vodka to give it some color. When they drank it clear, they no longer cared much about appearances. In another six months, he guessed, she would do away with the teacup altogether.

There was one saving grace about people at this stage of alcoholism, Burke thought. They had no inclination to share.

"No American reporter is going to write the truth about my husband," she said suddenly, her voice a trifle blurry around the edges.

"Why not?" Burke asked, sipping his tea.

"Because the CIA killed him, of course," she said, as if explaining that water ran downhill.

"The CIA? How do you know?"

She shrugged and took a big slug out of the teacup. "Who else benefits?"

"Benefits?"

"Of course," she said, blinking. "The CIA's mission is to destroy Russia. First, they destroyed the Communist Party and the Soviet Union. Now they are destroying men who might have given Russia new pride."

"That darn CIA," Burke said, somberly shaking his head. "Once in a while, we let them take over a little country, like Guatemala. But do you think they're satisfied with Guatemala? Nooo." He drew the last word out.

Galina Vladimirovna peered at him for a moment, stupefied, then extended her arm toward the corridor, the empty teacup in her hand. The old woman, clucking softly, came forward and took the cup. Then she shuffled back to the corridor and the kitchen, where, Burke assumed, she would refill it.

"They're bastards," she said, voice slurred now. She was giving new meaning to the old phrase, "in her cups."

Burke clucked sympathetically.

The old woman came back to the room with a teacup, which

she placed, contemptuously, on the table between Burke and Galina Vladimirovna. A little vodka spilled over the rim and onto the table. When Galina Vladimirovna picked it up, Burke noticed that her hands were shaking.

"You know," he said, "how the American press likes to expose the CIA's misdeeds."

She frowned.

"It's because of factional disputes within the ruling class," he assured her.

She nodded.

"Well, if I'm going to do that, I need documents, information, that sort of thing."

Galina Vladimirovna simply stared, with vacant eyes, into the middle distance.

"Was your husband working on something unusual before he was killed?"

Her eyes glazed over and she started to cry. Within seconds mascara was running down her cheeks.

Burke ground his teeth together, then got up and patted the woman on the shoulder. "I'm sorry," he said, "I know this is painful for you."

"The bastard," she sobbed. "He died and left me no hard currency. He spent it all on his sluts! Do you know how much pension I'm going to get?"

"Not as much as you deserve," Burke said, as sincerely as he could.

"Fifty thousand rubles!"

It was the equivalent of about fifteen dollars. But he had a hard time feeling sorry for her. If she wanted to, she could sell the apartment her father had left her for hundreds of thousands of dollars. It was a lot more than the Party had bequeathed to most Russians.

"That's terrible," he said, and she sobbed harder for a moment until, with a visible effort, she partially composed herself, snuffling loudly.

"So, uh, you didn't know about anything unusual he was working on?"

She shook her head.

"Did he, maybe, leave any papers? Did he have a study here?"

The sobbing stopped. Her eyes were by now flaming red. "Yes. He had a study. His desk is full of papers."

"Would you mind if I took a look at them?"

Her eyes narrowed. "What will you pay?"

Burke could not resist snorting at her. The whole damned country was for sale. "I'll pay tribute to him in my story."

She scowled. "I mean money."

"I knew what you meant."

"Ten thousand dollars," she said.

"Ten thousand dollars!" he said. "I could buy a U.S. congressman for ten thousand dollars!"

Her jaw set firmly. Drunks, he knew, could be quite stubborn. Only people who trust their own judgment can be flexible. He'd been stubborn himself when he was drunk.

Since any payment was going to come out of his own pocket, he was going to have to bargain. First, he had to establish the right context.

"I thought you wanted to help me expose the CIA for killing your husband."

"You want to sell newspapers and make a big profit," she said thickly. "I want a piece of the profit."

Burke considered giving her the journalism school explanation of why no single story made a profit for a newspaper. But he didn't really believe it. How much money had Watergate made for the *Washington Post*?

"Look," he said. "I don't even know what's in the papers. How about if I look at them and if I find something I want to take, then we'll discuss what it's worth."

She wavered. "Five thousand dollars. Take it all."

It was time to put an offer on the table.

"Well," he said. "I can see you're in difficult circumstances, but the most I can give you is fifty dollars."

"A thousand," she said, and folded her hands in front of her spindly chest.

Burke stood up, remembering a rug merchant he had once dealt with in the souk in Damascus. The man had very artfully used the toilet as a tool in a negotiation over a rug. "I can go as high as seventy-five, but no further. If you'll excuse me, I have to use the bathroom."

He walked into the hall, found the bathroom, locked the door behind him, and waited.

Soon enough, he heard what he was hoping to hear, footsteps going down the hall to the kitchen and returning, no doubt with a full teacup.

The Syrian rug merchant, he recalled, had given him his final offer, gone to the toilet, and left him long enough to get antsy, but not so long that he walked away. He flushed the toilet and walked to the hook where his coat was hanging. Then he walked back into the living room. She was finishing off another cup.

"A hundred dollars," she said, voice scratchy.

"Deal," Burke said. "And may I say it's great to do business with a true Party loyalist."

She scowled. "You taught this to us," she said.

What, he wondered, would Elder Zosima reply to that?

Fyodor Vasiliev, Burke decided quickly, had been a meticulous man.

His papers were stacked in cubbyholes in an ancient desk that Burke had half expected to be a Winter Palace antique. It was not, as best he could tell. It was an old oak desk, scarred and scratched, with a cracked, black leather writing surface. It had perhaps at one time been a rolltop. It spoke of an honest family that had endured for many generations in St. Petersburg.

Nothing in the first few bunches of paper gave him a clue. They were letters, and they appeared to be from relatives in Saratov who needed money. He spent an hour going through each of them, reading plaintive accounts of broken legs, fevers, layoffs, and funeral expenses.

The next stack was more interesting. They were letters from someone in Connecticut who signed himself "Volodya," and they apparently had to do with the Hermitage's joint venture, the one Sasha Vinogradov had mentioned. The letters, written over the

preceding three years, were apparently intended to supplement official correspondence, which Burke assumed was sent to the office
at the Hermitage. Volodya described negotiations with museum directors in Dallas, San Francisco, and Kansas City, all of whom
wanted to exhibit works from the Hermitage collection, though
none wanted to pay as much as Volodya thought they should.
There were a couple of letters about a disputed debt the joint venture owed to an art catalogue publisher in London. There was one
about setting up a fund-raising event for the Hermitage in New
York. But there was no evidence that their relationship, despite the
debt, was approaching a violent end.

The final cubbyhole held just a sheet of graph paper, torn from
a notebook. The writing was in pencil, and Burke had to shift toward the window to read it in Vasiliev's small, precise handwriting.

Sovyeshchaniye Lida the first line read. *Sovyeshchaniye* was an aca-
demic conference. *Lida* made no sense to Burke. It wasn't a Russian name.

Underneath that Vasiliev had written *Iyun*. June, but of what
year? Was this the date for the conference?

The next line read *Glavniye dokladchiki*: the main speakers, presumably for the conference, presumably about Lida, presumably
in June.

Then came a list of four names:

> Martin Arnold, Oksford, proiskhozhdyeniye
> David Bull, Vashington, udostovereniye
> Augusto Donatelli, Firenze, znacheniye
> Nadyezhda Petrovna, vozobnovlyeniye

Burke recognized none of the names, and the words next to
each gave him no clue. *Proiskhozhdyeniye* meant descent, or ancestry.
Udostovereniye was a credential. His old press pass, issued by the Foreign Ministry, was called his *udostovereniye*. *Znacheniye* meant significance, and *vozobnovlyeniye* meant renewal. Was this supposed to be
a conference about the ancestry, credentials, significance, and renewal of someone or something named Lida?

The place names were the Russian spelling for Oxford, Washington, and Florence. Presumably, that was where these people

lived. Nadyezhda Petrovna, the only name without a city attached, was also the only Russian name. That probably meant she lived in St. Petersburg. But Petrovna was a middle name, not a surname. The usage suggested that Vasiliev knew her and respected her.

He folded the paper and stuffed it into his shoulder bag, pondering how to follow up. Maybe, he thought, his hostess would know Nadyezhda Petrovna.

He walked back to the living room. She was stretched out on the sofa, asleep, snoring quietly. Her skirt had fallen away and the top of one stocking was visible over a spindly thigh marbled with purple veins. He thought about waking her, then thought again.

He was not quite that desperate yet.

Chapter Fifteen

NADYEZHDA PETROVNA NARYSHKINA LOOKED fretfully at her wristwatch, which said 6:37. She looked at the odd, black oven standing on the other side of the studio, half expecting to see smoke seeping out of the edges of its door. She looked back at her watch: 6:38.

She sat, in a wheelchair, in a room under the eaves of the Winter Palace. The room had once been part of the living quarters of some minor member of the royal entourage. It had a parquet floor, two small windows overlooking the Neva, and a plaster frieze around the intersection of the pale yellow walls and the white ceiling. Reddish-brown and black stains, made by dripping water, disfigured the ceiling and walls. There had been no money for roof repairs in many years.

"Andrusha," she said, "are you sure it hasn't been in there too long? It's not an old pair of galoshes you're trying to dry out, you know. It's fragile."

Andrusha Karpov instantly stopped typing something into a computer. Some of Nadyezhda Petrovna's anxiety spread to him, like a cough in a theater audience. His lips pursed and his pudgy cheeks wrinkled into a nervous frown.

"Nadyezhda Petrovna, please don't worry," he said.

Her ears took in the words, but she was a person who relied on her eyes, and her eyes, scanning Andrusha's face, told her that she had good reason to be nervous.

He walked over to where she was sitting, carrying a brown envelope. "You know we tested it," he said.

She patted his hand. "I know, Andrusha. I'm sure it will work fine."

"Look," he said, and he handed her the envelope. She opened the flap and pulled out two pieces of black X-ray film. They glistened dully in the light from overhead.

She looked at the top one. It was a gray, ghostly image, the kind produced when a painting is X-rayed. Behind the image she could see the dark shape of a wooden cross, the wooden support that undergirded a canvas. She peered at it. The image was not immediately clear. Different paints reflected the X rays differently, and therefore showed up differently. It was as if she was seeing the picture through various thicknesses of gray gauze.

Then she recognized a line, a curve, and with that the image became instantly clear. It was the *Madonna Litta*.

"Look," Andrusha said. He put a stubby finger on the film and traced the line of the Virgin's forehead. "Do you see the dots?"

"Where are my glasses?" she demanded, annoyed. Andrusha probably knew exactly what her vision was, but she still hated for anyone to see that it was less than perfect. Her eyes and her hands were almost the only parts of her body that worked at all, and she was vain about them.

"Lyuba," she called out. "My glasses!"

She could feel Andrusha stiffen slightly at the sound of her daughter's name.

She pitied him for that. Andrusha had loved her daughter without reservation since they were both sixteen. Lyubov Naryshkina had recognized the love, appreciated it, but could not return it. The best she could do was try not to hurt Andrusha, not to tease him, nor to raise his expectations. That much Nadyezhda Petrovna had insisted on, and that much Lyubov had done. Willingly, her mother had been pleased to observe.

Lyubov Naryshkina entered from the larger, adjacent studio, where the lesser experts on the Hermitage restoration staff worked,

at least when there was money to pay them. She closed the door
carefully behind her.

"Lock it," Nadyezhda Petrovna instructed her, and Lyubov
quickly did so.

She stepped under the bare fluorescent bulb that illuminated
the room, and as she did, Nadyezhda noticed how the light
bleached almost all the color from her face. Her skin, fair when she
was a child, was starting to slip toward pallid. Her face, normally
thin, was edging toward gauntness. Lyubov was still a beautiful
woman, tall, erect, with ash-blond hair and blue eyes. But at
twenty-seven, she was no longer a beautiful, young woman, and
Nadyezhda Petrovna wondered how many more St. Petersburg
winters—winters without enough food and without any sunlight—it would take before she was no longer beautiful at all. Nadyezhda Petrovna's condition had robbed her of her own youth, and
she remembered dreaming that her daughter would be spared that.

"Your glasses, Mama, are probably right under your nose,"
Lyubov said, but there was no harshness in her voice.

She looked over her mother's shoulder and spotted a pile of
papers—letters, apparently—on her desk. Lyubov picked them up
and found the glasses underneath. She put them on her mother
and kissed her on the cheek.

Nadyezhda Petrovna scowled, not at the kiss, but at her own
weakness. She should have simply turned around and found the
glasses herself. She could have done so. She normally prided herself in doing as much as she possibly could. When had she allowed
herself to get so helpless and dependent?

The ache in her bones told her that fatigue was making her
weak, fatigue brought on understandably enough by the hours she
had been working. But this ache was so profound and so disabling
that she was beginning to feel that sleep would not restore her, that
some essential strength was ebbing away.

She scowled again, pushed the glasses up to the top of her nose
and stared at the X ray, determined to see whatever it was that
Andrusha wanted to show her.

Carefully standing a meter away from Lyubov, Andrusha
pointed to the profile line again. "See the dots?" he said.

Now she could see them, tiny specks, white in the X-ray film, black in reality, that underlay Leonardo's line. They came, of course, from his method, the one all Florentine apprentices learned in the late fifteenth century. He made a drawing for each of the figures in a picture, sketching over and over until he had the proportions and expressions and postures exactly as he wanted them. Then he used a pin, carefully puncturing each line in the drawing, putting tiny holes a few millimeters apart. He pinned the punctured drawing to the surface to be painted: a plastered wall, if he was doing a fresco, or a board coated with gesso for a painting. Then he took a porous bag full of ground charcoal and swatted the drawing with it. The outline of the figure appeared, in charcoal, on wall or the gesso. He would fill it in with a sketching charcoal, and only then begin to paint.

It was the same method she had just used.

"Now look at this one," Andrusha said. He showed her the second X ray. It was a close-up of her Leda's shoulder. The dots were visible in the underdrawing, just as they were in the underdrawing of the *Madonna Litta.*

"It looks very authentic," Nadyezhda Petrovna told Andrusha. Her voice was hopeful, but tinged with doubt.

"Oh, Andrusha, how can you be sure this is going to work?" Lyubov broke in "I just know it can't! These people are no fools. They'll have instruments you don't even know about. They'll find out, and they'll kill my mother!"

Andrusha's plump face clouded with pain. Other people might doubt him, but he could dismiss their doubts as ignorance. Lyubov's lack of confidence pierced him.

"We may not have all the technology, Lyuba," he replied as calmly as he could. "But I know what the technology is and what it can do. I know all the tests they can run. We have an answer for every one.

"They can test the composition and age of the panel. Our panel is Italian poplar, Leonardo's favorite. Carbon dating will place it in the late fourteenth or early fifteenth century. It even came into the museum with the same shipment of pictures that the real Leonardo came in.

"They might use our gas chromatograph and persuade Bykov to let them have a paint sample. If they do, they can analyze the pigment. All of our pigments are the same as Leonardo used.

"Our painting's structure is the same as Leonardo used—gesso, size, underdrawing, paints, varnish.

"They can X-ray the painting, even use an infrared reflectography camera, if they have an airplane big enough to bring one. They will find nothing that Leonardo would not have done.

"They can examine the brushwork, the techniques, the sfumato. Your mother has executed them just as Leonardo did. You saw the painting. Could you detect a difference?"

"No," Lyubov said, chastened.

But, of course, she had to say that. She believed firmly that her mother was the best in the world at what she did. Nadyezhda Petrovna was the ultimate product of two centuries of schooling at the Hermitage in the art of copying the masters of the Renaissance, an art that was developed and used for the restoration of the great paintings acquired by Catherine II and her successors. Of all the generations of restorers who had come out of that school, no one had equaled Nadyezhda Petrovna's talent for exact reproduction.

"The painting is flawless," Andrusha agreed.

"But her fingerprints are on it! She had to use her hands to manipulate the paint. What if they compare fingerprints?"

Nadyezhda Petrovna hadn't thought of this. She leaned forward in her chair.

"No problem," Andrusha insisted. "Even if they had access to microscopic photographs of the Leonardo paintings, which I doubt, the fingerprints and palm prints on his pictures are too blurry to make out."

"And the *craquelure*?" Lyubov's list of objections was far from exhausted. "How can you be certain of it?"

Andrusha shrugged. Even for her, his patience was wearing thin. She was a good assistant for her mother, but she simply did not know what he did about painting and science.

"How can they be certain?" he replied. "No one has ever photographed this painting. All we have to do is make certain that the *craquelure* is consistent with a painting that is nearly five hundred years old. And we will."

"How much longer, Andrusha?" Nadyezhda Petrovna asked.

He looked at his watch. "Another forty minutes."

Nadyezhda Petrovna glanced nervously around the room. Her eye fell on the computer monitor Andrusha had hooked up to the security system's surveillance cameras. A bulky body was moving along the corridor leading to her studio. He was about thirty seconds away.

"Bykov!" she hissed.

Immediately, Andrusha hopped to the computer, pressed the escape button on the keyboard, and watched to make certain that the screen dissolved into a computerized infrared reflectograph, in blocky chunks, of the *Madonna Litta.*

Lyuba wheeled Nadyezhda Petrovna to an easel in the center of the room, set her up in front of it. She flicked away a dustcloth from the painting on the easel. Andrusha lunged for Nadyezhda Petrovna's worktable and grabbed a palette and a scarred, old badger-hair brush. He thrust them at Lyuba, who in turn passed them gently into her mother's hands. Andrusha slid into the chair in front of the computer monitor.

"The oven!" Lyuba hissed. Nadyezhda Petrovna's eyes widened in alarm.

"He won't know what it is," Andrusha assured them. "It's only 105 degrees in there, and the whole room already smells of paint. Don't worry."

There was a rap on the door. Lyuba stood up, took a deep breath, walked to the door and unlocked it, wiping the sweat from her palms onto her smock as she did so.

Ivan Bykov walked in, Andrusha thought, like a great bull entered a corral, massive chest out front, nostrils flared, eyes small and suspicious. His bandy legs, slightly bowed, seemed to follow the ensemble rather than carry it. He was wearing a brown suit that Andrusha guessed might have been expensive. But it would have taken more than expensive tailoring to make clothing draped on that body look elegant.

Bykov was making a show of being pleasant. He smiled at Nadyezhda Petrovna, nodded at Andrusha, and half bowed to Lyuba. For a disconcerting instant Andrusha thought he was going to lean over and kiss Lyuba's hand.

But he focused his attention, instead, on the painting on the easel. A broad smile creased his face.

"It's finished!" he exclaimed, his voice throaty.

"Not quite," Nadyezhda Petrovna corrected him. "It still needs some glaze."

This was a lie. The minor restoration the painting had required was indeed finished and had been for days. But it was a simple matter for Nadyezhda Petrovna to flatten the finish on one section or another, then brighten it again with a coat of clear glaze. Bykov was not equipped to tell the difference.

"How long will it take?" His high, raspy voice had a slightly aggravated, slightly plaintive tone.

"A day or two, I think," Nadyezhda Petrovna replied. She looked sideways at Andrusha. He nodded in affirmation. "Yes. A day or two," she repeated.

Bykov leaned over to examine the painting more closely. As he did, his elbow brushed against Lyubov's breast. She shuddered involuntarily, but if he noticed this, he gave no sign.

"It is beautiful art," Bykov said. "It's a shame we must sell it. But, you know, otherwise the museum has no funds. After this sale, you will have an endowment! Several million dollars in hard currency. You will have what you need to maintain the collection."

"We will be grateful, of course," Nadyezhda Petrovna said. Sincerity hung from every syllable. She was well-practiced at lying to powerful men. She had been forced to do it all of her life.

Bykov's face crinkled into an approximation of a smile. Nadyezhda Petrovna thought his mouth looked like a steel trap.

"And there will be bonuses for you, of course," he said. "Big bonuses."

"I'm sure we'll donate them to the museum fund," Nadyezhda Petrovna replied immediately. It was, she sensed, the answer that Bykov would want. It suggested extreme idealism, which he would be unable to distinguish from naiveté.

Bykov smiled benevolently. Then he looked again at the painting on Nadyezhda Petrovna's easel.

He shifted his weight from one foot to another and seemed to Nadyezda Petrovna suddenly timid. Then he cleared his throat.

"Tomorrow night," he said, "our buyer arrives in St. Petersburg.

We will be hosting a small banquet for him. Would, um, would you like to attend?"

Nadyezhda Petrovna blinked. The idea that this man could earnestly invite her to dine with him filled her with anger and loathing. She struggled to keep it off her face.

"Thank you, but I don't think that I can," she said quietly. She lowered her eyes quickly to the blanket that covered her legs. "For reasons of health."

Bykov nodded sympathetically. "I understand."

He turned his thick face to Nadyezhda Petrovna's daughter.

"But, um, would you come, Lyubov Andreyevna?" His voice had suddenly gotten raspy with tension.

Now Nadyezhda Petrovna's anger boiled over. She could not abide the idea of Lyubov with Bykov, even in a room full of other people.

"She has to—" she began. But she could not finish the sentence.

"I'm afraid I can't," Lyubov said to Bykov. Her face was pale and her lips taut.

Bykov flushed with embarrassment, then forced himself to smile, showing two golden teeth.

"I'm sure," Bykov said, "that your mother needs you with her."

Ivan Bykov walked back to his office five minutes later still feeling humiliated.

His quick visit to the conservation and restoration studio had been, he decided, a complete fiasco. The painting was all but ready for its buyers. But what had possessed him to ask Lyubov Naryshkina to go to the banquet for the Colombian? Two years ago, he thought, he would have known better.

Times had changed. Most everything in St. Petersburg was available to someone with money, and in a few days he would have lots of money.

But there would still be things he could not buy, he thought. There would still be things he would have to take if he wanted them.

He buzzed for Marina on the intercom. She did not reply.

He walked out into the anteroom. She was not there.

Bykov's feeling of humiliation turned instantly to anger. Damn the bitch! She was supposed to stay until he told her the workday was over. Instead she took off when she felt like it, doubtless to spend some of the hard currency he was foolishly paying her. Or, he thought, to go to a tourist bar, find a john, and earn some more. Sometimes she enraged him.

Before he could decide whether to go look for her, the telephone on his desk rang. He returned to his office and picked it up.

"Yes," he said.

"Ivan Dmitrievich? It's Sasha."

"I'm listening, Sasha."

"I caught up with the American. He's staying at the Yevropeiskaya. He went to two places just now. You want the addresses?"

"Yes."

"The first was on Prospekt Energetikov, number 42."

The address meant nothing to Bykov. He carefully wrote it down. "The second?"

"The second was on Naberehzhnaya Krasnogo Flota. Number 16."

Bykov's grip on the telephone tightened. That was Fyodor Vasiliev's address. He thought for a moment. "Sasha?"

"I'm here."

"I want you to find him out on the street somewhere and show him a little Leningrad hospitality. Get his money but leave him his passport. Touch him up enough so that he'll want to go see a doctor. In Helsinki. I don't want him poking around anymore."

"Okay," Sasha said. "No problem."

Bykov hung up the phone, wondering whether he could trust Sasha not to get too enthusiastic and kill the American.

Normally, in order to make sure the job was done right, he would have done it himself. But he had too many other things to take care of in the next two or three days.

Chapter Sixteen

A PALE GRAY VOLVO, THE COLOR OF A GIN bottle, ran a red light and sped within a foot of Burke as he crossed Nevsky Prospekt and turned toward the Literary Café. A thick, cold wave of slush spattered against him, drenching him from his knees down to his shoes. Burke wheeled and yelled at the driver of the Volvo, but the car was already a hundred meters away, careening down a street that ran along the River Moika, a creek that fed the Neva. Burke flipped a middle finger at the taillights, then made his way, stomping to shake off the slush, to the other side of the street.

There, he stood for a moment, muttering and cursing under his breath.

"It was better under the old bosses," an old woman standing next to him observed. "They stopped for red lights."

In fact, Burke knew, the commissars of the old system had always arranged to have the *militsia* keep the stoplights ahead of them green when their limousines were on the road. But he was not inclined to argue with his elders.

Cold dampness was seeping along his shins and into his socks. The wool of his trousers was starting to scratch. He peered down, trying to visually assess how bad he looked. In the feeble light from the surrounding buildings, he couldn't tell.

Burke thought about slogging back to the hotel and changing clothes. But it was six long blocks. The clothes he had back in the hotel had been wrinkled when he packed them. And he was already five minutes late for the meeting that Desdemona McCoy had called and asked for. After chasing down her false rumor about Vasiliev being gay, he didn't much care what impression his clothes made on her.

He could think of only two explanations for the falsehood she had sent him chasing after. It could have been a rumor she had innocently passed along. Or she might have lied. If she had lied, he wanted to know why and for whom. If she was just a gossip, talking to her would still beat sitting in his room, staring at the little refrigerator.

He would not have chosen a place with a name as pretentious as the Literary Café. He preferred to eat in places that bore the owner's name; his favorite restaurants in Washington were Germaine's and Nora's. Failing that, he liked places named for the streets they were on, like the Florida Avenue Grill. At the opposite end of his list were places with phony British names, like the Frog and Nightgown, unless they were in Britain. And at the very bottom were places that tried to define themselves as hangouts for writers and journalists by calling themselves something like the Pen and Pencil. Or the Literary Café.

But there it was, complete with a drawing of Pushkin in the window. There was probably a bust of Dostoyevsky in the john.

He pushed through the doors, handed his damp overcoat to the old woman in the wardrobe, and went into the dining room.

It was a low room with rough, whitewashed plaster walls, vaulted ceilings, and linen napery. A smattering of Scandinavian tourists and a few Russians were dining, but at least half of the room was empty. In one corner, a young violinist played something quiet and pastoral.

McCoy stood up in the shadows at the far end of the room, smiled and waved at him. Involuntarily, he waved back. No matter how badly she had misled him, and how much he resented it, it was nice to enter a restaurant and see a woman stand up and wave at him.

She was dressed differently this time, in a black cashmere sweater over an ivory silk blouse, a few strands of gold necklace, beige pants, and a pair of gleaming, calf-length boots. She looked carefully casual. She was easily the most attractive woman in the place.

He walked to the table, and as he neared her, he could see her gaze drop down to his knees. He looked down at his shins. His trousers hung, limp and dark, like damp dishrags.

"When you've got great legs, dress to call attention to them," he said. "But you know that already."

She smiled again, and the light from the candle on the table gleamed in her dark eyes. Burke reminded himself that he had good reason to dislike her.

"Thank you," she said. "I'll take that as a compliment."

"It was," he replied.

She was drinking white wine and had a carafe and two glasses on the table. Her eyes widened when he declined her offer to pour him some.

"Do you never drink, or just not with me?" she asked.

For some reason, Burke had no more interest in pretense about antibiotics or sleep. "It's not you," he said. "You know how boxers wind up with cauliflower ears?"

She nodded.

"Well, reporters get cauliflower livers."

She blinked, startled. Then she smiled, tentatively. "So I can't ply you with liquor?"

"Just your presence will ply me enough," he said.

She smiled again, and he sensed that he had somehow disconcerted her. If he was going to be a teetotaling journalist, he thought, he would have to get used to that.

The waiter came, and he ordered some Georgian mineral water.

"So how goes the Dostoyevsky?" she asked him, breaking a short silence.

"Slowly," he replied. "But it seems remarkably current. Just before I came over here, I was reading the Elder Zosima's assessment of politics in the 1870s. 'The flame of corruption is multiplying visibly, even hourly. It spreads from above downward.' "

She nodded. "Lot of that going around," she said.

He noticed, over her shoulder, that a middle-aged couple with dirty blond hair and blue eyes were staring quite openly at her. He wondered what it must be like to own a dark face in a Baltic country. He decided that he wouldn't want to find out.

The waiter arrived with the mineral water and two more glasses. They ordered *osetrina*, Russian sturgeon. Burke offered her some mineral water. She accepted.

"To strangers on a train again," she said, raising the glass.

He clinked his against hers.

"So," she said. "How's your story coming?"

He was tempted to tell her that her tip about Vasiliev being gay had been a bum steer, deliberate or not. But he decided not to let her know he knew that. There was nothing to gain by it.

"About as fast as *The Brothers Karamazov*," he said.

She bit her lip for just a second. "Well, that's one of the reasons I wanted to get together with you."

"One of the reasons?"

"Apart from your worldly charm," she replied, smiling.

"And my wet socks."

She laughed. "Them, too."

He said nothing. This seemed like a good opportunity to try the psychoanalytic approach.

"Well," she said, "you got me curious. I've been talking to a lot of my artist friends in the last two days. And what I hear is that Vasiliev was opposing some kind of major sale from the museum collection."

"A sale?"

She nodded. "Museums do it a lot. They call it 'deaccessioning'. And it's happened before at the Hermitage. Back in the thirties, Stalin was desperate for money and Andrew Mellon was trying to start an art museum in Washington. A broker arranged for a six-million-dollar sale of more than a dozen paintings from the Hermitage collection. Several Rembrandts, a Van Eyck, two Raphaels. It became the foundation for the National Gallery of Art. Before that, Nicholas the First auctioned off dozens of Catherine the Great's paintings in the 1850s."

He had not expected her to suggest another lead, this one much closer to what he had been starting to think. The sale idea intrigued Burke, but he could see huge flaws in the theory.

"Stalin and Nicholas could do whatever they wanted and no one would complain," he said. "If the government tried to sell off something important nowadays, wouldn't people notice and complain? Wouldn't it be a scandal?"

She pursed her lips. "It would if people found out about it."

"How could they keep it secret?"

"Two possible ways," McCoy said. "One, they could be selling stuff out of the attic."

He remembered that Sasha Vinogradov, in his stupor, had mentioned the attic.

"The attic?" he asked.

"The attic. You have no idea how big the Hermitage collection is, do you? It's millions of items. And no more than a fraction of it is on display. They're trying to take over old Ministry of Defense buildings and renovate them just to let people see some of the treasures they have to keep in storage."

"But presumably," Burke said, "the best stuff, the stuff that would command big money, is already on display, and if they sold it, people would notice it was gone."

She nodded. "They would, unless they intend to do some forging."

"Forging? You mean make copies of the real paintings and hang them in the museum?"

She nodded.

"And you figure Vasiliev refused to go along with something like this, so he was killed."

"I can see," she said, "why you're a good reporter. You catch on quickly."

It was the kind of compliment bad P.R. men handed out. It told him she was conning him. He decided to let her know it.

"And I can see why you're so successful in your business," Burke said. "You bullshit so well."

She laughed, but her laugh sounded forced and the smile fell quickly from her face.

"Okay, now answer one question," he said.

"What?" she asked. Her face took on a studied impassivity.

"Why are you trying to manipulate me?"

"Manipulate you?"

He normally refused to let someone answer a question with a question, but this time he made an exception. "Yeah. First you get on the train and very carefully manage to drop the suggestion that Vasiliev was gay, which you knew he wasn't. Now you find me and invite me here and tell me to chase the idea that they're selling art."

Her eyebrows furrowed and her posture became rigid. "What do you mean I knew he wasn't gay?"

"I checked it out today. He wasn't. I know how gossipy Russians are. If he had been, you'd have known it."

"You checked it out?"

"With his wife. And with a gay Hermitage staffer who's dying of AIDS and had no reason to lie."

She blinked once and said nothing.

"So why shouldn't I think you're misleading me again?"

"I'm not," she said.

The waiter arrived with the sturgeon, and his bustling around the table filled the awkward space into which he would have inserted something sarcastic.

"I'm telling you something I have good reason to believe is true," she said.

He bit into the sturgeon. It was covered with a crusty layer of fried bread, and the fish inside tasted slightly of motor oil.

"Why tell me?" he pressed her. "Apart from the fact you're enthralled by my charm and damp trouser legs."

She laughed then, a drier, more contemplative laugh. "Actually, Burke, strangely enough, I do like you. I'm not sure I could say why."

"I'm thrilled. But you're avoiding the question."

"I'd hate to see the Hermitage collection pillaged," she answered, seeming to weigh her words. "If you can find out why

Vasiliev was killed and who killed him, you can blow the whistle and stop it."

"So why give me a bum steer on the train?"

"I could explain that," she said. "But if I did, I'm afraid you'd stop talking with me, and I want to help you. Just take my word for it that the situation has changed in the past day or so."

He started to understand, but some things were still not clear.

"Why would I stop talking to you?"

She played with the potato on her plate, thinking of her reply. "Because I think you have some integrity. And if certain things were stated explicitly, you would have to react in a certain way. But if they remain vague, I think we can work together."

Then Burke understood. She was an intelligence agent, and the relationship between an American journalist and an employee of the CIA was full of ethical dilemmas.

The ethics of journalism, with good reason, had built a high wall between reporters and the intelligence agencies. Before that wall existed, the CIA had frequently given its agents journalistic cover. As a result, any American journalist abroad was suspected of espionage. In a lot of countries the suspicion alone could be fatal. And for that reason, a strictly ethical American correspondent abroad did not knowingly cooperate with intelligence agents.

The longer Burke had been a reporter, though, the less absolute his ethics had become. There were only a few things he always insisted on. He picked up his own checks. He protected the confidentiality of sources who asked for it. And he never wrote something he knew was false. Everything else was negotiable.

When it came to intelligence agents, he had long since decided that the purely ethical approach was impractical. Intelligence agents knew too much to be ruled out of his list of sources.

So when he talked with someone whom he suspected of posing as a diplomat, or a businessman, or a traveling scholar, but who happened to know a great deal about, say, the sources of the weapons used by Abkhaz rebels in the Caucasus, Burke let the pose stand. He asked his questions, traded his gossip, and behaved just as he did with genuine diplomats, businessmen, and traveling scholars. He chose not to know.

He knew this was hypocritical, as hypocritical as a politician's choice not to ask whether a hundred-thousand-dollar contribution from the Exxon Employees Political Action Committee really came from the individual decisions of a hundred donors who each gave a thousand dollars.

The politician needed the money. He needed the information.

"I can live with that," Burke said, "but I need to know why you switched signals on me."

"I can't tell you precisely," she said. "I can tell you that I've heard that the buyer is a man named Rafael Santera."

"The drug guy?"

She nodded. "Until a couple of days ago, I heard he was going to keep this purchase a secret. Then I heard that he wasn't."

"So at first you didn't want publicity because you didn't want a scandal. And now you think a story might prevent a bad scandal from getting really huge."

She nodded. "That's not an illogical conclusion."

"Ah," he said, "The classic nonconfirming confirmation. You handle this sort of thing quite well."

"Is that a compliment?"

"Should it be?"

"Burke," she said, "why do I sometimes get the feeling that deep down inside your mean, cynical exterior there's a mean and cynical heart?"

"Well," he said, "when I'm being manipulated by someone, it tends to suppress my normal kind and gentle instincts."

Her face showed a little hurt. He wasn't sure what she felt.

"Normally," she said, "I'm very forthright."

He had a feeling she meant it, or at least wished it were true.

"All right," he said, "let's stipulate that under other circumstances, I'd be kind and gentle and you'd be forthright. And you won't take it personally if I get a little cynical."

She smiled. "And you won't take it personally if you feel you're being manipulated?"

"As long as it's done competently," he said, "and for a good cause."

She reached across the table and offered her hand. "The best," she said.

He took her hand and shook it. "Okay. Now that that's established, what are your sources for this?"

She shook her head. "I really couldn't let you jeopardize them. If you get this story, there's going to be a major stink."

"But you promise that normally you'd be forthright?"

She smiled demurely and nodded.

"Well, okay," he said, "as long as normally you'd be forthright."

She laughed softly.

"There's no story until I know what they're trying to sell," he said. "Any ideas?"

She nodded. "I don't know, but I was thinking it might be one of the Leonardos."

"I won't ask why that thought just occurred to you," he said.

"Good," she replied.

What she said made some sense. The Hermitage had Leonardos. And she obviously knew more about them than he did. He decided to show her what he had found that afternoon at Vasiliev's house, and he pulled his notebook from his bag.

"The grieving Widow Vasiliev, for considerations I won't go into, let me rummage around in her late husband's desk," he told her.

She looked very interested. "And?"

He opened the notebook and extracted the piece of graph paper. She pulled her chair to the side of the table so she could read it with him.

"The Lida Conference," he said. "What could that be about?"

"The Hermitage has a Leonardo called the *Madonna Litta*. Maybe he misspelled that name? Or maybe that's how it's rendered in Russian?"

Burke shrugged. "And this list of names? The main speakers?"

"Martin Arnold, Oxford, *proiskhozhdyeniye*. David Bull, Washington, *udostovereniye*. Augusto Donatelli, Florence, *znacheniye*. Nadyezhda Petrovna, *vozobnovlyeniye*," she read. Her voice took on an undertone of urgency.

"Any ideas?"

"Well, it's obviously a list of art experts," she said. "I recognize two names. Martin Arnold is one of the foremost experts in the world on Renaissance art. David Bull is very well known. He's from the National Gallery in Washington. I'm not sure about Donatelli. And I have no idea who Nadyezhda Petrovna is."

"Nadyezhda Petrovna Naryshkina," Burke said, "is the name of the director of conservation and restoration at the Hermitage."

She looked at him with slightly wider eyes. "How did you know that?"

"I didn't. An artist friend told me." He had called Sasha Vinogradov from his room at the Yevropeiskaya just before dinner. He could tell that his possession of this knowledge impressed her, and that gratified him.

"What," he asked, "do you make of these words: 'ancestry,' 'accreditation,' 'significance,' and 'renewal'?" He gave the standard English translations for the Russian terms after each name. "I guess *vozobnovlyeniye*, next to Nadyezhda Petrovna's name, could mean 'restoration.' instead of 'renewal.' "

She nodded. "In art, *proiskhozhdyeniye* has a special meaning. It's usually translated as 'provenance,' not 'ancestry.' It means the history and ownership of a certain picture. And *udostovereniye*, in an art context, is usually translated as 'authenticity,' not 'accreditation.' "

"So he was planning a conference about the *Madonna Litta*, with speakers on its provenance, authenticity, significance, and restoration?"

She shook her head. "Maybe, but it doesn't make an enormous amount of sense. The *Madonna Litta* has been studied for more than a century. There's a pretty strong consensus about its merits and how much of it Leonardo painted. I can't see a good reason to have an international experts' conference about it now. . . ." Her voice trailed off.

"And there's the spelling."

She nodded. "And there's the spelling."

He reached for the carafe and poured her another glass of wine. She sipped, then stopped.

"Damn, Burke," she said. "You're making me feel guilty. Like a lush or something."

He sipped some water. "Well," he said, "we who are pure of heart have to learn to live with that reaction."

She laughed. "I suspect it's something you haven't had much practice at."

"You don't think I'm pure of heart?"

"Burke," she said, "I think you're conniving and morally corrupt. But don't worry. I like that in a man."

"Well," he said, "I've always been partial to women with that kind of good taste."

Abruptly, she got serious again and the chimera of intimacy that seemed to have arisen between them vanished.

"I think tomorrow I can help you find out how to contact Nadyezhda Petrovna at home."

"I got her address and phone number," Burke said.

"Colin," she replied in mock seriousness, "if you're not careful, you're going to force me to reconsider all my prejudices against journalists."

"Well," he said, "I wouldn't jump to any hasty conclusions."

Clearing the air seemed to unburden her. As they ate, she became almost loquacious. She told him about her childhood. Her father had been a professional football player for a while, a tackle for the New York Giants. After football, he sold insurance. Her mother was a frail, scholarly type who loved Shakespeare. Des had been a tomboy growing up, because she wanted more of her father's attention. She had a sister named Juliet who lived, like their parents, on Long Island.

McCoy liked baseball better than basketball. She preferred Anne Klein to Calvin. She liked Turgenyev better than Tolstoy, and Rita Dove better than either of them. She thought Reagan was dumb and Clinton a hypocrite. And she knew better than to try to draw Burke into a conversation about contemporary art. She laughed when he asked the violinist to play "Take the A Train."

Burke enjoyed just letting the sound of her voice wash over him. He insisted on paying the tab, despite her objection that she had invited him and ought to pay at least half.

"How about a walk?" she asked as they left the restaurant.

"Sure. Clear my head from the mineral water," he answered.

She laughed again.

The night air had turned frigid. Using the nostrils test, he fig-

ured that it was about ten degrees. As they walked he was conscious of the space between them. Somehow, the appropriate gap
had become narrower. It was not quite touching, but close enough
so she could speak to him and no one else would hear.

They walked down toward the silent, white Neva. They passed
between the spire of the Admiralty and the vast, dark hulk of the
Winter Palace, and turned along the deserted embankment prom-
enade. Across the river the building lights were softened by a cold
haze that somehow made the cityscape look glowing and a little
warmer.

"So," she asked, "did this Jennifer Morelli do you wrong?"

He was startled. "No. Why do you ask?"

She patted him on the arm.

"On the train," she said. "As soon as I told you I went to Columbia, you asked me if I knew her."

He was surprised that she remembered that. "You're very ob-
servant," he said.

She didn't argue the point. "So is she the reason you've got a
cauliflower liver?"

He started to laugh, but the laughter was cut short by the memory of her death. "No. She was my intern in Moscow one summer.
You're about her age. I thought you might remember her."

"Is that all?"

"No," Burke said.

"What else?"

"She was killed in Washington about a week ago, just after she
came back from St. Petersburg. I encouraged her to come, and
loaned her my list of contacts here. When she came back, she said
she had a hot story. She died before she told me what it was."

"So you're here to find out what it was. And who killed her."

"Yeah."

He didn't want to think about that anymore, and before she
could press him any further on the subject, he changed it.

"You must have a tough life here," he said.

She seemed surprised. "What makes you say that?"

"Well, I mean, what you do. Who you are. Foreign country.
All that."

"You mean that I'm black in the whitest corner of the world?" She didn't seem offended.

"Partly," he said. "Partly that you're a foreigner in a strange country. Partly that your work gives you secrets to keep."

"It's not as bad as all that." She laughed, but the laugh sounded forced.

"If it were me," he said, "I'd be lonely. I was lonely in Moscow, and I had lots of colleagues."

"It happens," she said.

"Ever been married?" he asked.

"Sorry, Burke. No personal questions," she said, sounding as if she meant it.

He recalled that she hadn't minded talking about some personal matters over dinner, but they were childhood things.

"You got to ask personal questions in the train," he said.

"Well, I'm not going to tell you if I am married or have been married. It's irrelevant."

"But you're not going to deny you're hard to live with," he said. "I didn't."

"I remember you said that," she said, laughing lightly. "All right. I'm hard to live—"

Burke heard footsteps behind him, muffled by the snow, and he started to look over his shoulder an instant before he felt the blow. Had he not half turned to see who was approaching, he probably would have taken the hit on the back of his head.

As it was, he took it on the shoulder. The force of the blow sent a shower of pain rushing down his arm and up his neck to his brain.

He felt strangely as if his knees were made of mercury, liquid and wiggling, and he fell backward to the snow. He saw a husky man in a greasy parka and a sable *shapka*, backlit in the foggy glow of a streetlamp, gripping a small club in his right hand, like a hatchet. The man's arm was going up, preparing to strike again. Burke scrambled to his knees, feeling the damp, cold snow. Raising his left arm, he grabbed the club, and for a moment they wrestled for it. Burke could sense that the man was stronger and would very quickly wrench it away and swing it again, down on his skull.

But before that could happen, McCoy stepped forward. With her hands, she caught the man's arm just below the wrist. Simultaneously, her right foot swung up and caught the attacker in the crotch. Even in his dazed state, Burke could hear the thud of the contact, and he winced involuntarily when his attacker half groaned, half shrieked in pain. Shocked, they both let go of the club, and it flew ten feet away, into a snowbank. The attacker fell to his knees, clutching his testicles with one hand.

McCoy's left foot slipped on the packed snow as she kicked, and she went down, sprawling on her back. For a moment the three of them formed a static tableau, Burke and the attacker on their knees, in pain, and McCoy on her back.

McCoy got to her feet first, but the attacker was only an instant behind. With an enraged bellow he lurched toward her.

This time she had better purchase in the snow. Again she got her hands up to the attacker's forearm. She bent one knee for leverage and neatly flipped him over her shoulder. He landed on his back and head, his skull crunching into the snow.

McCoy wasn't finished. Making it seem like a single motion, she stepped around to his side and delivered a quick, vicious kick to the prostrate man's head, just above the ear. His fur *shapka* absorbed some of the blow, but not all. His fingers went limp. Burke crawled to the snowbank where the club—actually a foot-long length of pipe—had made an indentation. He got it and rose, wobbly, to his feet.

McCoy stood above the attacker for a second, her breath a trifle ragged, her knees bent, ready. When she was satisfied he wouldn't move, she turned to Burke. He was lurching toward the prone figure in the snow, the club in his left hand raised above his head like an ax.

"Let it go! We have to get out of here!" she hissed.

She put a hand on his arm until she was sure he wouldn't kill the man. Awkwardly, with his left hand, Burke tossed the club over the wall and onto the ice-covered river. It made a soft thunk as it landed. His right arm and shoulder were starting to throb.

"Let's go!" she said. "He might have friends."

Slowly at first, Burke put one leg in front of the other and began to walk. She kept a supporting hand on his elbow for a few strides as they hobbled across the embankment drive. Then they were on Nevsky Prospekt, and he managed to pick up the pace to a slow jog.

They covered the next block and a half like that, until McCoy slowed down to a walk and looked back over her shoulder as they reached the top of a bridge that arched gracefully over a canal. She saw no sign of anyone following them. The sidewalks were nearly deserted. Only a hunchbacked old man, gaping toothlessly at the sight of a black and a white foreigner jogging on the snow, seemed to have noticed them.

Burke took advantage of the respite to walk over to the railing of the bridge and empty his dinner onto the frozen canal below. It made a dull, yellow splotch on the snow. He spat the bile from his mouth, then turned around. Tentatively, he tried to raise his right arm. Halfway up, the pain forced him to drop it back to his side.

"Anything broken?" she asked him.

"I don't know," he said. "But this may really hurt my chances at Wimbledon this summer."

She smiled tightly and pressed down on the shoulder. The pain shot out to his neck and down to his hand. He yelped and lurched away from her.

"Probably just a bruise," she said. "If it was broken, you'd have gone down. Not had much experience as a street fighter, have you?"

"The last time was when I was twelve, I think," Burke said. "I lost then, too."

"Well, you're rusty," she said.

It galled him to thank a woman for protecting him, but he realized he had to. "Anyway, thanks for your timely intervention," he said. "You were very impressive."

"Ah, that word again," she replied.

They walked on until they were under the marquee of the Yevropeiskaya.

"I don't think you should spend the night here," she said. "I think you ought to get some things together and stay at my place. I've got a couch that should fit you. Then, tomorrow, I can help you find Nadyezhda Naryshkina."

He weighed her offer. He wanted very much to accept it, and

not only because he probably would be safer spending the night elsewhere. But something held him back. He told himself that he had to limit this to an alliance of convenience, not a partnership.

"It's a nice offer," he said. "But if I let you take me home on the first date, you might think I was easy."

She cocked a hand on her left hip and her voice rose slightly. "Burke, are you trying to be offensive, or are you just groggy?"

"Do I have any other choices?"

"Someone just tried to hurt you—maybe kill you."

"Probably just a mugger," he said.

"Or maybe it's someone who doesn't like what you've been sticking your nose into!" she snapped. "If I'm trying to keep your ass out of trouble, the least you can do is let me."

Burke shook his head. "Sorry, Des," he said. "You're just going to have to allow me to delude myself into believing that I'm in control here."

"But you—" She caught herself, shrugged and smiled. "Okay," she said. "Have it your way."

"Thanks for a lovely evening," he said, sticking out his hand. She laughed, and kissed him quickly, first on the right cheek, then on the left.

———————

The smell of her lingered in his consciousness for all of ten seconds. His shoulder claimed his full attention as he entered the lobby of the Yevropeiskaya. The initial shock was wearing off, and he knew he faced a painful night.

He needed ice.

In a corner of the lobby bar an excellent string quartet was playing something lively and vaguely Mozartian. The tables around the bar, Burke noticed, were packed. He remembered that the conference on converting defense industries was due to begin tomorrow. Over the strings, he heard the sound of ice clinking behind the bar.

He walked up, wedging himself between two Japanese salarymen who were drinking scotch. He was trying to catch the bartender's attention when he felt a tap on his sore shoulder. Wincing, he turned around.

"Well, if it isn't Mr. Big Shot Fuckin' Media."

It was Jimmy Duxbury, the pasty-faced, red-haired, and bankrupt metals broker from Philadelphia. Duxbury was plainly drunk. His eyes were a bright, glowing red, his body listed slightly to the left, and his speech was slurred. A drop of spittle ran down his chin from the left side of his mouth. He wiped it away with the back of his hand.

"Yeah, I'm drunk," he said, reacting to Burke's silent appraisal. "But in the morning I'll be sober, and you'll still be an arrogant asshole."

"So you're a Churchillian scholar as well as a canny, successful international businessman," Burke said.

"Fuck you," Duxbury said.

"Churchill could not have put it more eloquently," Burke said.

"You here for the conference?" Duxbury abruptly changed from a tone of hatred to a tone of plaintive solicitation.

"No," Burke said. "Something else. You?"

"I'm going to raise as much of a stink as I can," Duxbury said. "Before they throw me out. Or before fuckin' Slema Chavchavadze kills me."

A young woman scurried up to Duxbury, a look of alarm on her face. She was dressed in a form-fitting, black knit sheath that dropped low to show off the tops of her breasts and rode halfway up her thighs. She had shoulder-length, *ryzhy* hair and too much lipstick. After a second Burke remembered where he had seen her. She was the receptionist outside Vasiliev's office at the Hermitage.

She put her arm through Duxbury's and leaned over close to his ear. "*Jeemochka,*" she said. "Why you leave me?"

Duxbury grinned at Burke.

"*Jeemochka?*" Burke asked.

Had Duxbury's face not already been reddened by drink and high blood pressure, he might have blushed. "Her little nickname for me," he explained.

The woman leaned over again—she was a couple of inches taller than Duxbury—and whispered in his ear.

He smiled and patted her hand. She took it and began to pull. "Okay, honey," he said. He turned to Burke. "Gotta go. She says she's got a friend and they're having a two-for-the-price-of-one sale."

"Lucky guy," Burke said, and watched them make their way slowly across the lobby toward the exit, the Russian girl propping up the little American.

He wondered for a moment at the coincidence of seeing this woman at the Hermitage and then with Jimmy Duxbury. For a moment he had the sense that he was walking, innocent and ignorant, in the middle of a play. Everyone but him knew his or her role.

But lots of young Russian women moonlighted as hookers.

Jimmy Duxbury, he thought, had better hold on to his wallet.

Then his shoulder started to throb more heavily, and he caught the bartender's attention, only to learn that a bucket of ice was five dollars. Angrily, he shoved a bill across the bar and collected a small paper container half full of watery ice.

He rode the elevator upstairs, put the key card into the slot outside his room and waited for the light to blink green. It did not. He tried again. Nothing. Cursing under his breath, he rode the elevator down to the lobby again.

The night concierge urged Burke to try the key card again, but Burke refused. McCoy's warning about the danger of staying in the hotel was reverberating in his mind. Maybe someone had tampered with the lock. He insisted that a bellman come up and open the door. The concierge reluctantly agreed to send one.

Burke took the elevator back up to the room and waited. In a few moments, a bellman, a thin, towheaded kid who looked about nineteen, ambled down the hallway. Barely bothering to disguise his disdain for anyone who couldn't cope with the lock technology, the boy slipped a passcard into the lock. The light turned green, and he pushed the door open.

"Check the heat for me," Burke said. The kid nodded, flipped on the lights, and walked inside. Burke stayed three wary paces behind him.

The room was empty. Feeling foolish, Burke watched the boy flick the switches on the heater and tipped him three dollars. He wondered how long he was going to feel skittish.

He fell asleep wondering what would have happened if he had taken McCoy up on her offer.

Chapter Seventeen

THE MAN SAID HIS NAME WAS VLADIMIR, BUT even before he opened his mouth, Bykov could tell he was not Russian. He was tall enough, but it was the way his brown eyes were set close together over a long, sharp, curving nose that came to a point over his mouth. The man had a fox's face, a face full of guile. Bykov had never met a Russian with a face like that. Russian eyes tended to be set wider. A Russian face might have bovine simplicity, it might reflect canine loyalty and friendship, or lupine ferocity, or it might glitter with intelligence.

But he knew faces, and Russian faces never showed the wary, calculating cruelty of this man. He looked capable of charming a man, befriending him, benignly observing his wife and his children, and then tearing all of their throats out without the slightest emotion. Russians could kill as well, but not as dispassionately.

As soon as the man spoke, Bykov placed him. He had the accent of someone from one of the old fraternal countries, someone who had learned his Russian in a classroom, and someone who had no native familiarity with Slavic vowels and consonant clusters. That made him either a German or a Romanian, and he was too dark for a German.

Probably, Bykov decided, a veteran of the Securitate fallen on hard times. Chavchavadze knew dozens like him, and he was adept at finding them when he needed them.

Fortunately, Bykov observed, the man was dressed well for his role, in a camel-hair overcoat and a charcoal-gray, double-breasted suit that might have come from a good tailor in London, or Frankfurt. And he carried an inconspicuous but expensive attaché case of well-tooled cordovan leather. Russians, Bykov knew, still tended to judge people by the clothes they wore and the things they carried. It was part of their inheritance from the Soviet era, when clothing and accessories of a certain quality were unavailable to the masses and indiscreet for Party members who needed to honor the fiction that they were part of the masses.

The car, a Mercedes, rolled to a halt in front of the main entrance to the Hotel Yevropeiskaya. Bykov started to open his door, but the Romanian put a gentle restraining hand on his forearm.

"Wait," he said.

After ten seconds the doorman, looking less than pleased, trundled out through the light dusting of snow that had fallen since midnight. He opened the car's rear door. Vladimir stepped out. Bykov followed. He wondered if it was wise to force the doorman out into the cold. Wouldn't it just enhance the possibility that their faces would be remembered? Or was this the way a real German businessman would act? He could only guess that Vladimir was an experienced man and knew what he was doing.

They attracted no attention, as far as he could tell, as they entered the lobby. Though it was nearly one o'clock, the lobby bar was still full. Visiting Westerners, he remembered, came from time zones where it was still evening or late afternoon. He scanned the bar quickly. He saw neither Marina nor Duxbury. He had not expected to. But he had to make certain.

They boarded the elevator and went to the sixth floor. According to Marina, Duxbury's room was number 614. It was ten doors down the hall on the left. Bykov pulled out the universal entry card that he had secured for the Yevropeiskaya months before, just as he had cards and passkeys for all the tourist hotels in St. Petersburg.

The little light over the lock turned green, and they entered the room. The two double beds were freshly made, with the spreads turned down and a chocolate on each pillow. Duxbury's luggage was stacked neatly in the closet and his toilet articles arrayed around the sink. He had clearly not spent much time within these walls this evening.

Vladimir immediately set his attaché case down on the desk next to the television set and flipped open the locks. He extracted two pair of rubber gloves, put one pair on, and handed the second pair to Bykov. Then he pulled a handkerchief from his breast pocket and wiped down the handle of the door. Bykov watched him, beguiled, as he pulled on his own gloves. The latex was surprisingly soft and powdery. It felt like skin.

Then Vladimir went to the window, drew open the curtains and looked out. Bykov walked over and peered past his shoulder. The line of sight to the hotel entrance was unobstructed.

"Okay," Vladimir said. He grinned crookedly. "Time for sleep."

Bykov watched, mute with surprise, as the Romanian carefully removed his topcoat, his suit, his shirt and tie, his shoes and socks. In a moment he was down to his underwear, which was dark blue and cut high on the thighs. He had a wiry, athletic body, and Bykov wondered, for a moment, what it would be like to wrestle with him. It would be interesting to learn what the Securitate had taught him.

Vladimir walked over to the bed and carefully rumpled the covers, still wearing his latex gloves. Then he removed a square of thin polyethylene from his attaché case. Bykov could see the scope and stock of his rifle. He peeled the polyethylene apart and handed what appeared to be half to Bykov. "You'll have to use the floor, I'm afraid," he said, smiling at Bykov's evident wonder.

Then he carefully and precisely unfolded the plastic until he had a thin sheet as big as the bed. He spread it out, lay down on it and closed his eyes. Within a minute he appeared to be asleep.

Bykov spread the second sheet on the floor, understanding that it would not do to rumple two beds. Then a thought occurred to him.

He grabbed Vladimir's foot and pinched it. Instantly, the man sat up, but Bykov noticed that his body remained loose and relaxed, the way a good athlete's body would be.

"Should we set an alarm?"

Vladimir smiled, not bothering to disguise the condescension on his face. "No," he said. "I'll wake up."

He closed his eyes again and resumed the posture and appearance of sleep.

Bykov took off his clothes and watched the man for ten minutes. He appeared to be sleeping soundly. Bykov himself could not imagine sleeping. He was too tight.

Restless, he turned his attention to the brochure atop the television set. In English, German, Japanese, and Russian, it described the pay-per-view movies available. Two of them, he noticed, were adult films. Duxbury, he reasoned, was just the kind of person who would watch one.

Carefully, he reached up to the television, turned the volume down to zero, and dialed up a film called *Burning at Both Ends*.

The screen filled with an image of a woman sandwiched between two men. One of them had his penis up her vagina. The second was slowly entering her anus. Bykov could readily imagine the sounds she was making.

He glanced backward at Vladimir. His eyes were still closed. His posture had not changed. He was still asleep.

Furtively, Bykov masturbated.

═══════════

Bykov awakened, feeling stiff and sore. He rolled over and heard plastic crinkle underneath him. He hit his head against the base of the television pedestal. It raised a small bruise.

"Shit," he muttered, and looked around. In an instant he remembered where he was, and why. He looked at his watch. It was seven-twelve. They had about forty-five minutes left to wait.

Vladimir, already dressed, sat on the edge of the bed, which was still covered in the thin sheet of polyethylene. His attaché case was open in front of him and he was practicing assembling and disassembling his rifle. For a few moments Bykov watched him.

He moved with practiced grace, never hurried, highly efficient. He could break the rifle down and place each component in its fitted slot in the attaché case in a matter of about twenty seconds.

The rifle, in its assembled state, had a long, steel-blue bore, a scope, and a wooden stock of a kind that Bykov did not recognize. He knew all the weapons that circulated in the old Soviet Bloc; this was not one of them.

"What kind is it?" he asked Vladimir.

The Romanian, if in fact that was what he was, gave him the same small and condescending smile he had used the previous evening. "It's a mixture," he said.

Bykov began to dislike him. He wished he had not agreed to do this job. He felt like Petya, the moronic aide-de-camp in a thousand Russian jokes about a dashing if slightly stupid military hero named Chapayev. He was too experienced, too important, to be assigned a flunky's role. But that's what he had been ordered to do.

He put a hand under himself and got up, carefully keeping his feet on the polyethylene. He wondered for a moment about the toilet paper he'd used the night before to catch his semen. He had flushed it away. It should be safe. When they left this room, they would leave no fluids, no fingerprints, and no fibers behind them.

He dressed, put on his shoes, and carefully folded his sheet of polyethylene.

He tried to make small talk. "So what's your real name?"

"Vladimir," the man answered. He seemed neither offended nor amused by Bykov's question. His answer was so matter-of-fact that Bykov half believed it.

They lapsed into silence. Vladimir stopped disassembling the rifle. He checked the bullet clip, making sure it was full. Then he slipped it into place.

The hotel had installed a modern variant of the traditional Russian windows. The main pane of glass was locked in place. But there was a small corner section, the *fortochka*, that could be opened separately. The idea was to create a small opening for ventilation, keeping a room from getting too dry and stuffy during the winter, when the heat was on constantly.

Vladimir opened the *fortochka* and experimented for a while with different postures and positions, until he found one that would give him a steady stance and allow him to extend the rifle barrel down the line of fire.

They waited some more.

"You know Grachenko," Bykov asked. The question seemed

silly, but he could think of nothing else to say, and the silence between them had stretched his nerves taut.

"The one with the big gold star on his epaulets," Vladimir said.

"Well, there might be another marshal."

Vladimir laughed derisively. "Of course I know him. I've seen pictures. I've seen film. I know what he looks like and how he walks and how he bends his neck when he gets out of a car. I know him."

Bykov flushed and said nothing.

"Look," Vladimir said. "I assume you know your job, getting me in here and getting me out of here. Why don't you assume I know my job?"

There was a sharpness in his voice for the first time, and Bykov realized that this man, too, was becoming a little tight as the time approached. Briefly, he thought about the possibility of strangling the man as soon as he had pulled the trigger, and leaving the body in the room for the *militsia* to find.

It was a pleasant idea, but it would have too many unforeseen consequences.

Vladimir looked at his watch and resumed his firing posture. Bykov walked to the other side of the window and watched from there.

Precisely at eight o'clock a yellow and blue *militsia* car, its blue lights flashing, appeared on Nevsky Prospekt. A long, black ZIL limousine followed.

Bykov took a deep breath. Vladimir raised the rifle to the edge of the open *fortochka* and sighted on the curb in front of the hotel's main entrance.

Ten seconds later the little motorcade arrived. Bykov watched it slow to a halt.

His perception of time was completely distorted. Things seemed to be happening in slow motion.

An aide in a soldier's fawn-colored greatcoat opened the right-side door in the front and in one stride reached for the rear door. It seemed to take him a full five seconds to do so, even though Bykov realized he must be moving smartly.

After what seemed like ten minutes, a leg emerged from the car, clad in a muddy-olive pair of pants with a thin red stripe. Slowly, almost like a child being born, a torso emerged, then the other leg.

There was no mistaking the burly figure and the big yellow star on his shoulder. It was Grachenko.

Vladimir extended the rifle barrel out the *fortochka* for the first time. His finger went around the trigger, and he squeezed off a shot.

Bykov could see Grachenko's head jerk forward as if someone had crept up behind him and hit him with a sledgehammer. He saw a pink spray erupt from the other side of Grachenko's skull and stain the snow beyond. The defense minister's body crumpled slowly.

The shooter withdrew the rifle part of the way back into the room, until the muzzle rested on the sill of the *fortochka*. Then he fired again, leaving a noticeable powder burn on the white paint.

"Okay, let's go," Vladimir said. He had the scope off the rifle barrel and the clip snapped shut before Bykov could respond.

Five minutes later they were walking slowly but purposefully away from the hotel, toward the docks. Fifteen minutes later Vladimir was safely hidden away in a freighter beginning its semiweekly voyage across the Gulf of Finland to Helsinki.

Chapter Eighteen

BURKE WOKE UP, SITTING UPRIGHT IN BED, thinking that he had somehow fallen on the street chasing a bus that backfired. An instant later he heard another sound, and he knew it was too close and pitched too high to come from a bus. It sounded like gunfire.

As if paralyzed, he remained in the sitting position, shaking his head and trying to separate what had happened in his dreams from what had happened in reality.

Slowly, his memory separated the sounds from the rest of the dream. The sound, or at least the last one, seemed to have come from somewhere above him.

He got up and strode to the window, where his own *fortochka* was cracked slightly open.

He looked down at Nevsky Prospekt. He saw a long, boxy ZIL limousine, the type that conveyed only the president and cabinet ministers. He saw a huddle of officers in army greatcoats, bent over something in the street, and saw other soldiers and *militsia* men, pistols drawn, scanning the facade of the hotel.

He knew what he was seeing, and what he'd heard.

Hastily, Burke threw on some clothes and checked to make sure his old press credential was in his wallet. His shoulder felt stiff and sore, but the pain was not sharp. It appeared nothing had been broken.

In the corridor, he pressed the down button next to the elevator and waited. Ten seconds later his patience ran out. He bolted through the door to the stairwell and began descending two steps at a time, grabbing the railing at the end of every flight and spinning himself around.

He emerged into a lobby in chaos. Somewhere, glass shattered. Men shouted. A woman screamed. In a few minutes, he knew, someone would take charge and the *militsia* and army would jointly seal the area and start interrogating everyone in the hotel. A spokesman would be designated to refuse to answer questions from the press. Information would be hard to come by.

But for the next few minutes he could take advantage of the confusion and shock he could see on the faces of the people coming in from Nevsky Prospekt.

He grabbed the elbow of a passing bellman and asked him what had happened.

"Someone's been shot!" the bellman said, barely breaking stride.

I knew that, Burke thought. He strode toward the front door, seemed to be moving against a tide of people coming in the opposite direction.

He bumped into an officer in his greatcoat.

"Who was shot?" he asked, putting a hand on the man's shoulder.

"Grachenko," the officer replied. "Where's a phone?"

"Manager's office," Burke said, gesturing backward with his thumb. The officer sprinted away.

Burke stopped and checked his watch. It was half past eight in St. Petersburg, twelve-thirty in the morning in Washington. In the *Tribune* newsroom a few late copy editors were finishing up the final edition, a job that consisted mainly of adding basketball and hockey scores from the West Coast to the sports pages. He had perhaps half an hour before the final closed irrevocably.

He would need about fifteen minutes to compose and dictate a brief story for the front page. That left fifteen minutes to answer two fundamental questions.

Was it really Grachenko?

How badly was he hurt?

He pressed forward through what was now a surging crowd of people seeking shelter inside the hotel. Some of them still had snow on their shoes and fright was evident in their eyes. Burke surmised that they were worried about a sniper. Outside, he could hear sirens.

Beside the front door he saw an older officer, potbellied and gray-haired, trying to direct some subordinates to close the front door.

"Secure the hotel!" he roared. "Where the fuck is the doctor?"

But securing hotels was apparently not something they had learned in officer candidates' school. The men milled around, confused. In their midst he could see a body prone on the floor.

Burke elbowed his way up to the gray-haired officer and flashed his press card.

The officer, distracted and confused himself, wheeled toward Burke. "Doctor?" he shouted.

Burke said nothing.

The officer said nothing, but took a tentative step to one side.

Burke squatted down and took a look at the body. Someone had removed the greatcoat and laid it underneath the body, and a great stain of purplish blood was seeping into the wool. Burke could see the marshal's star on the dead man's epaulets. Half the skull on the side facing Burke had been blown away. Gingerly, he craned his neck to get a look at the face.

It was Pyotr Grachenko. There was no mistaking his pumpkin-shaped head. And there was no doubt that he was dead. The bullet had opened up the back of his skull like a carving knife opening up a jack-o'-lantern. Burke felt faintly nauseous, but he was aware as well of an undercurrent of adrenaline.

"Sniper?" Burke said, turning to the gray-haired officer.

"Yes," the officer said.

"How many shots and from where?"

"Two. From the hotel."

The officer suddenly realized that these were not questions a surgeon would need to ask. He looked at Burke again. "You a doctor?" he demanded angrily.

"No. Journalist. I showed you my press card," Burke said.

The man's face went from red to purple. Burke rose and scurried away before anyone could think to arrest him.

———————

Back in his room, he opened his laptop and started to type. But before he had gotten three words on the screen, he forced himself to sit quietly for thirty seconds and consider the ramifications of what he had seen.

He felt a kind of guilty exhilaration. The knowledge that he would be breaking a story that would make people in Washington choke on their bagels in a few hours exhilarated him. The knowledge that he was exhilarated by the death of another human being made him feel guilty, but the exhilaration overwhelmed the guilt.

He wondered, occasionally, why he should feel this way, why being an observer of cataclysm and disaster should make him happy. Partly, he knew, it was the fact that very few people were capable of witnessing something like a coup in a foreign country, sorting out the facts, and composing a coherent story ahead of a deadline. He had this skill, and using it gave him pleasure.

And he knew that in some limited ways, the presence of journalists could affect events for the better. He believed, for instance, that the coup plotters of 1991 might well have bombed the Russian White House and blown it away were it not for the presence of the press.

And he knew that he had not felt this exhilaration in the months he had worked as an editor. He doubted that he ever would.

He was old enough to allow himself a brief moment to savor it—about five seconds. Then he turned his thoughts back to the story he was about to write.

What could he add to the simple facts of Grachenko's assassination?

He could not and would not speculate about who might have done the killing, or who might have been behind it. Given the turmoil in Russia, there were too many candidates. And the killer was not necessarily Russian. He could be an Iraqi, exacting vengeance for Russia's support of the United States in the Gulf War. He could be an Afghan settling a score from Grachenko's participation in the

Soviet invasion. He could be an angry Chechen. He could be anyone.

Regardless of who was responsible, though, the assassination threatened to alter the balance of power in Russian politics. The bond between Grachenko and President Yelichev had been the glue holding Russia together for four years. Thanks to Grachenko, the army had refused to support the attempted coup in 1991. Thanks to Grachenko's control of the army, the president had triumphed over the old communists again in 1993. Thanks to Grachenko, the defense establishment had gone along with all of the cutbacks in budget and prestige that the president had imposed on them.

Thanks to Grachenko, Yelichev had gotten involved in Chechnya, but that had only bound the two more closely.

With Grachenko gone, the next candidate in line to become Minister of Defense was Marshal Vladimir Rogov. Burke thought back to the press conference in Riga a week ago. He could certainly cite that as evidence indicating that Rogov would be much less likely to line the army up on the side of reform and cooperation with the West.

Burke had heard other things about Rogov. He had heard that he had wanted to keep fighting in Afghanistan and opposed the withdrawal of Russian troops from the Baltic states. He'd heard that Rogov chafed at the diminishing pay and prestige of the officer corps, and that he led a faction of younger officers who wanted the restoration of the old pay, the old perquisites, and the old empire. He'd heard that had Rogov commanded the army in 1991, it would have supported the coup. He'd heard that Rogov had opposed the misbegotten plan to assert control in Chechnya.

But Rogov had not been in Moscow at that time. He was commanding the southern military district, from which armed Russian "volunteers" had gone out to fight in Tadjikistan and sow enough chaos that the central Asian governments had had to turn to Moscow for protection.

And he had heard rumors of corruption, rumors that tied Rogov to the sale of T-72 tanks, MiG fighters, and SS-20 missiles to Libya.

But it was nearly all gossip. Burke had never recovered from the influence of an old, night city editor named Carl Bell. "Don't write the truth, write facts," Bell had told him. Facts were what you could support with quotes or direct observation. The truth was merely what you thought you knew. Carl Bell had long since died, his lungs riddled with cancer, and lots of reporters these days believed their job was to write the truth. Burke was not one of them. The Moscow bureau would have to check out the rumors as best it could. He would stick to what he knew in what would have to be a terse little story.

"ST. PETERSBURG," he typed. "February 7."

> Marshal Pyotr Grachenko, Russian Minister of Defense, was shot and killed in front of a St. Petersburg hotel this morning. His death removed one of the key pillars of the present Russian government.
>
> An unknown gunman or gunmen fired at Grachenko as he was arriving for a conference on the conversion of Russian defense factories to consumer production. An army officer at the scene reported hearing two shots, which he believed came from inside the Hotel Yevropeiskaya.
>
> Grachenko suffered a massive wound to the head and appeared to have been killed instantly.
>
> Chaos reigned in the hotel lobby in the immediate aftermath of the shooting. There was no indication that the assassin or assassins were arrested.

He paused. He could have added something about himself, some "this correspondent was on the scene" crap, but that was best left to television and tabloid reporters. He would do without it.

He added six more tight paragraphs about the importance of Grachenko's support for Yelichev over the past five years and what he could remember about Rogov's press conference in Riga the previous week.

Then he plugged the modem jack into the telephone and transmitted the story to Washington. He was glad again that he'd gotten a room with good phones. Even better, he thought: Now he'd be able to bill the three hundred dollars and a piece of the whole trip to the *Tribune*.

When the story had been transmitted, he pulled the modem cord out and dialed the *Tribune* foreign desk.

He got a junior copy editor, a young woman named Sandra McInerney, the last person working on the foreign desk that night.

"You've seen the piece I just sent?"

McInerney sounded both excited and skeptical, as if suspicious that this might be some trick the old boys were playing on her to see whether she'd fall for it and try to put the story in the paper.

"Yes," she said, drawing out the syllable.

"Why don't you set up a conference call with Graves," he suggested. "You're going to have to call him anyway. I might as well be in on it."

She dialed Graves's home number. He was awake. His voice sounded slightly slurred. Burke could imagine him sitting alone, watching Letterman, unable to sleep, sloshing a fourth shot of bourbon around in a glass full of cracked ice.

Graves, like all the *Tribune*'s editors, had a computer at home that was hooked up to the mainframe downtown. McInerney gave him the story number the computer had assigned to Burke's report. He called it up, and for a few minutes there was silence, at about ten dollars a minute.

"No shit," Graves said finally.

It was his penultimate compliment. He reserved "Holy shit" for obvious Pulitzer candidates.

"You were there?"

"I'm staying in the hotel. The shots woke me up. I saw the body. Talked to a witness," Burke said.

Graves grunted. "Nice work for a guy tending to a sick grandmother."

"Mother," Burke corrected him.

"Whatever. Nice work."

Burke listened while Graves gave McInerney instructions for redoing the front page. He felt his mood rising from cheerful to exultant. This felt good.

McInerney got off the phone.

"Ah, Burke," Graves said. There was a slight hint of inebriated sentimentality in his voice. "You're like an old fire horse." He paused. "Scent of smoke, you're ready to go."

"Oh, okay," Burke said. "I thought you were going to say gray, lame, and ready for the pasture."

"Maybe I made a mistake making you an editor," Graves went on. "Maybe I should've left you out there."

Abruptly, his tone changed. "So, what're we gonna do for tomorrow?"

The thought of the next day's paper pricked a small hole through which Burke's exultation began to seep slowly away. It always did.

"Well, the obvious," he replied. "Who did it. Why. What happens with the army now."

"There's a Moscow angle and a St. Petersburg angle," Graves said. "I wonder if I shouldn't have Smithfield switch places with you. That'll give her the lead story, but you'll be able to use your contacts in Moscow to get the political repercussions better than she would."

Burke had no intention of leaving St. Petersburg. "Well, I don't know, Ken," he said, trying to think of a plausible reason. "The planes are really unreliable. One of us might get stuck in an airport somewhere."

"Yeah," Graves said. "You're right. I'll tell Jill to cover the Moscow angle. But give her a call and give her some help. Contacts and stuff."

Burke promised that he would. He hung up and looked out the window. The street was filled with police cars, their blue lights flashing. That was as good as any place to start piecing together tomorrow's story.

———————

Desdemona McCoy's computer began to blink as she was taking off her coat in her office at the McCoy-Fokine Gallery. It startled her. In the week she'd had the machine, she had received messages only during her regular communications window, at hours that varied with the passage of the satellite. She'd been told that transmissions outside the window period would be very rare. Involuntarily, she put a finger in her mouth and gnawed on a fingernail. This show of weakness angered her.

"Calm down, girl," she whispered to herself.

She took off her coat and tossed it hastily over a bulbous plaster sculpture that she had liked, bought six months ago, and been unable to sell. The piece was smooth, white, and rounded, with a vague cleft. The coat settled over it like a shroud.

She punched in her identification number, then F4. The message burst onto the screen.

```
TSEODI
EX OSTENDIJK
THIS MORNING'S EDITIONS OF WASHINGTON
TRIBUNE WILL CARRY BULLETIN NEWS OF GRACHENKO
ASSASSINATION IN FRONT OF HOTEL YEVROPEIS-
KAYA, EX COLIN BURKE. ACCORDING TO STORY,
THIS OCCURRED AROUND 0800 LOCAL TIME.
    NEED URGENTLY AVAILABLE DETAILS ON THE AS-
SASSIN AND MOTIVE, OTHER RELEVANT INFORMA-
TION. FILE BY 1445.
    THIS IS HIGHEST PRIORITY.
```

Burke, she thought. She calculated the amount of time he must have had between the shooting and the last deadline for the *Washington Tribune.*

The man was very fast. The journalistic pack back in Moscow would think he was lucky to have been in the right spot at the right time. That's what she would have thought if she hadn't known him.

Chapter Nineteen

B Y THE TIME BURKE GOT TO GRIBOYEDOVSKY Street, a Finnish television crew, down from Helsinki, had already set up a broadcast truck across the street from the St. Petersburg *militsia* headquarters. The clouds had abruptly cleared away, and the top of the transmitter was bathed in cool yellow light.

He pushed quickly through the doors with the one-way mirror glass. He strode past the Board of Honor with the pictures of the casualties in the wars against crime and fascism. Instead of the corporal who had manned the reception desk two days before, he found a couple of officers, a major and a colonel. Burke showed his press pass and tried to catch his breath. He had jogged the last three blocks.

"Where's this press conference?" he asked. "Has it started?"

He could see cables snaking up the marble central staircase from the television truck outside, so it was not hard to guess where the press conference would be. The staircase led to General Kornilov's office.

The colonel looked at the pass and shrugged. He beckoned to a sergeant standing nearby, and the sergeant politely escorted Burke up the stairs, underneath the stern, mosaic visage of the *militsioner*, on guard in front of the gleaming hammer and sickle.

Burke looked at his watch. It was two-ten. The press conference, he'd heard on the radio, was supposed to start at two P.M. He pushed up the stairs ahead of his escort.

The trail of cables led directly to the reception room outside Kornilov's office and curled inside. As he reached the top of the stairs, he could hear the hubbub of a couple dozen voices, and he relaxed. It was the sound of reporters killing time, waiting for a press conference to start.

They had gathered in General Kornilov's conference room, adjacent to his office. It was a hall perhaps fifty feet long, dominated by a massive, polished birch table with seats for forty. The early arrivals had grabbed the seats around the table. The latecomers stood against the walls, under maps of various towns in the St. Petersburg *oblast.*

Elliott Lantz of the ABC News Moscow bureau had a spot in the back of the room, in front of a map of the village of Pavlovsk. In a blue, double-breasted suit and shiny black loafers, he was the only well-dressed man in the room. He bought his clothes in Rome.

When he saw Burke, he shook his head

"One thing I thought I could count on in life," Lantz said, "was that I'd gotten my last fucking call from New York telling me to match a story by Colin Burke. You son of a bitch. Did you shoot him yourself just to get the damn byline?"

"I was trying to do you a favor," Burke said. "I saw the big black limo and I figured it must be Barbara Walters coming to Russia to big-foot you again."

Lantz grimaced. He was still angry over the way Walters had flown into Moscow on a Learjet the year before to appropriate an interview with the president he had worked six months to arrange.

"Salt in my wounds. Thanks," he said sourly. "So how come you were here?"

"Well, I just came over on my own to take a look at the Hermitage," Burke said. "Never really got a chance when I was stationed in Moscow."

"Working on a piece?"

"Yeah," Burke said. "He offered no details. Instead, he

diverted the conversation. "So how'd you get up here so fast?"

"CBS chartered a plane right away when your story broke," Lantz said. "Made seats available."

Burke nodded, turned around and looked at the array of waiting reporters; boredom was beginning to show on the edges of their faces.

"So what's holding up the show?"

"CNN," Lantz replied. "Atlanta made 'em buy tickets on an Aeroflot flight. They're scraping bottom, budgetwise."

"They'll be scraping bottom, asswise, if they have to fly Aeroflot commercial very often," Burke said. "The only decent planes they have are being chartered for dollars."

Neil Fenno, the burly, gray-haired correspondent of the *Guardian*, walked over from the other side of the room.

"Ah, the man of the hour," he said. "Nice to see you, Colin. So were you staying at the Yevropeiskaya when all this happened?"

"Yeah, but I didn't see much," Burke said. "Shots woke me up a little before eight." Fenno took out his notebook and started jotting things down.

"I saw the body before they carted it away. The soldiers on the street said they thought the shots came from the fifth floor of the hotel, but they weren't sure. I know the police have sealed that floor off. They're looking at something there, but won't say what it is. I assume they'll be talking about it here."

"No idea who did the shooting?"

"No," Burke said, "but I'd like to get my hands on him. I was planning to sleep till ten."

"I know Yelichev would like to get his hands on him," Fenno replied. "If Rogov takes over the army, I'd say Yelichev's no better than even money to last till the election."

"Can't Yelichev appoint someone else?"

Fenno shook his head. "Not bloody likely. The officer corps will want Rogov. The Screw Yelichev people in the Duma will, too. He won't be able to make them back off."

"Unless he can prove that one of them gave the nine grams to Grachenko," Lantz said. Nine grams of lead had comprised a bullet in the Stalin era.

There was a bustling at the door, and Stu Jorgenson, Moscow correspondent of CNN, walked in. A woman, loaded down like a Sherpa with a camera and sound equipment, followed him.

"Hail, hail, the gang's all here," Fenno said. "Maybe we could play a few hands of poker for old times' sake while we're waiting on the *militsia* to enlighten us."

"You still play every Thursday night?" Burke asked.

"Yes, and I've been doing significantly better since you left." Fenno grinned.

At the other end of the room, Jorgenson and his sound woman completed plugging in their lights and clipping their mike into the mult box set up by the earlier arrivals. As if on cue, General Kornilov and a second man, also a general dressed in olive, but with the light blue epaulets of the Ministry of Security, emerged from Kornilov's office.

"Ah, now that CNN's here, we can proceed," Fenno said. "These two obviously know what's on the television in the Kremlin."

Behind the two generals came two junior officers, who set up a movie screen and a small slide projector.

General Kornilov's goiter seemed to have gotten redder in the past twenty-four hours. It gleamed in the television lights. Burke assumed it was due to stress. No doubt, he thought, the general had had to reshuffle his shakedown collection schedule because of the Grachenko assassination.

Kornilov cleared his throat and picked up a paper.

"Good afternoon, ladies and gentlemen," he read in a stilted monotone that suggested his unfamiliarity with talking to a roomful of people who were not obliged to salute him. "This is a sad time for us all. We mourn the untimely death of Marshal Grachenko. He fought for peace, for the Russian Motherland, and for democracy. His memory will live with us forever.

"Under the laws of the Russian Federation, investigation of his murder is the joint responsibility of the Ministry of the Interior and the Ministry of Security. May I introduce General Pavlenko, V.I., commander of the St. Petersburg oblast division of the ministry."

General Pavlenko nodded silently.

"As soon as word was received of the attack on Marshal Grachenko, the Ministry of Internal Affairs deployed two hundred men to the case. They included fourteen specialists in forensic science from the Department of Criminal Apprehension."

"Who no doubt trampled on the evidence and bollixed it all up," Fenno whispered to Burke.

"I can now announce that we have made an arrest in this case," Kornilov said. He paused for dramatic emphasis.

"Maybe not," Burke whispered back to Fenno.

"The accused is Dooksboory, Dzhems B., citizen of the United States, resident of the city of Philadelphia."

One of the general's subalterns flipped a switch, and a mug shot of Jimmy Duxbury appeared on the movie screen. He looked hung over and, Burke thought, bewildered.

"Jesus Christ," Fenno said. "An American!"

An involuntary murmur of surprise rose from the table. An AP reporter popped up from her chair and bolted out of the room. She was, Burke knew, looking for a phone. This would be a news bulletin that could not wait for the end of the news conference.

Half a dozen reporters started to shout questions, but Kornilov recognized Jorgenson of CNN.

"What evidence do you have for your accusation against this Dooksboory?" Jorgenson asked.

Kornilov shuffled his papers, apparently looking for the one that contained an approved answer to this question.

"I can say that our specialists have determined that the shots which killed Marshal Grachenko came from his room at the Hotel Yevropeiskaya," Kornilov said.

"Follow up!" Jorgenson said. "How do you know that?"

Kornilov's chest seemed to swell slightly. He was obviously pleased with this investigation. "There is forensic evidence. And bullet casings."

"Eyewitnesses?" Jorgenson demanded.

"I cannot give more details on this," Kornilov replied.

A German woman in thick eyeglasses, a reporter for *Bild*, was recognized next.

"Do you know of a motive?"

Kornilov shuffled his papers again. "Dooksboory was apparently dissatisfied with the results of a joint venture he had undertaken involving the Ministry of Defense," he read.

"Joint venture? What joint venture?"

"I have no more details. Our investigation is continuing."

Burke shouted a question. "Where was Duxbury arrested and was the murder weapon found?"

Kornilov recognized Burke and glowered. "He was arrested in the hotel lobby. The weapon has not yet been found. We think he had left the hotel to dispose of it," he replied.

Before Burke could follow up, Timothy Crater of the BBC jumped in.

"What effect, if any, do you think this will have on Russian relations with the United States and the West, General Pavlenko?"

Pavlenko remained impassive as he considered his reply. At least ten seconds went by.

"You will have to ask the politicians that question," he said.

There were more questions. The reporters in the room all took cracks at Kornilov and Pavlenko, repeating themselves.

"When you said 'No comment' to the question about having further forensic evidence, were you saying no comment in the sense of not being allowed to talk about the evidence you do have, or in the sense that there is no further evidence?" a Swede asked.

"No comment," Kornilov replied, his fat cheeks now gleaming with sweat.

Pavlenko rose. "Thank you all," he said. Kornilov, taking his cue, stood up as well. The reporters gave up.

Neil Fenno tapped Burke on the shoulder as he walked out. "You knew how to pronounce this man Duxbury's name," he said. "Do you know him?"

Burke hesitated, weighing three conflicting considerations. He knew things about Duxbury that were suddenly very hot. If no one else knew them, they might distinguish the *Tribune*'s story about the arrest and keep it ahead of the pack on the story he had broken.

On the other hand, he had always shared background information with his competitors, on the theory that he would someday need the favor returned. That theory had always proven true. Not only that, but Duxbury had probably gone to other papers besides the *Tribune*, seeking publicity for his grievance. Burke probably was not the only journalist with the information.

And then there were his doubts about Duxbury's arrest. He had not struck Burke as a man likely to murder. Last night, he had not even struck Burke as a man likely to be awake at eight A.M. If he had been planning to murder Grachenko, why would he have been trying to peddle his story to the press? And why would Duxbury have called his attention to his presence in the hotel?

"Do you know how to spell it?" Fenno prodded him.

"D-U-X-B-U-R-Y," Burke replied.

"So you do know him."

Burke nodded.

"What was that spelling?" It was Catherine Morrison of the *New York Times*, who had overheard the last bit of his conversation with Fenno.

When she stopped, Elliott Lantz stopped as well. Within seconds a small cluster of reporters had surrounded Burke, and he was holding his own informal news conference in the corridor outside Kornilov's office.

"He's a metals broker," Burke said. "He came to see me a week or so ago in Washington, trying to get the paper interested in a story about how he'd gotten screwed in a joint venture. Something to do with selling nickel that used to go into armor plating."

"So why'd that make him pissed at Grachenko?" Morrison asked.

"He said he'd gone bankrupt because he had to fulfill a lot of spot contracts for nickel. Said he couldn't fulfill them because the mafia bribed the Ministry of Defense not to give him the nickel he'd been promised. They were keeping it off the market to jack up the price. I'm sure if you check with your foreign or business desks, you'll find someone who heard the same story."

"So he did have a motive," Lantz said.

"Yeah," Burke responded. "Or someone arranged to make it look that way."

Chapter Twenty

Burke PACED BACK AND FORTH IN HIS HOTEL room, watching CNN declare the beginning of a new Cold War.

In Moscow, the Duma was outraged. A coalition of right-wing nationalists and ex-Communists were demanding the promotion of Marshal Rogov to Minister of Defense and an immediate cessation of all cooperative exchanges and aid programs with the United States. A source in the Kremlin said Rogov's promotion would likely be approved that evening. In Washington, the National Security Council met; the White House issued a statement mourning Grachenko's death but insisting that Duxbury be afforded due process of law. The CIA issued a terse denial that Duxbury had ever been in its employ. Stu Jorgenson appeared from St. Petersburg, rehashing the information Burke had given to Fenno and attributing it to "informed sources." In Cambridge, Massachusetts, Alan Dershowitz announced that he had been in contact with Duxbury's family and would be flying to St. Petersburg to handle his defense.

Russian television conveyed both confusion and foreboding. In Moscow, Vladimir Zhirinovsky described the assassination as an act of war by the United States against Russia. He demanded the resignation of the entire government, beginning with the president, in atonement for its failed policy of rapprochement with the West. And Fidel Castro, interviewed in Havana, spent five minutes recalling his brushes with CIA assassination plots.

Burke fumbled with the remote until he found the button that turned the set off.

His computer cursor blinked remorselessly at him from the desk, like a hungry animal waiting for its master to feed him.

His story, half complete, left him feeling thoroughly dissatisfied. It had the account of Duxbury's arrest, pieced together from the press conference and a few crumbs of information he'd picked up from cops in the street and employees at the hotel. He'd wasted two hours at the Hermitage, waiting for Vasiliev's receptionist to show up. She hadn't.

So he still hadn't come close to answering the questions he considered essential to understanding who had killed Grachenko, and why. Why had Duxbury been with a woman who worked with Ivan Bykov and, perhaps, for Slema Chavchavadze? What would they gain from assassinating Grachenko and framing Duxbury for it? And what, if anything, was the connection to Jennifer Morelli and Fyodor Vasiliev?

Worse, his story didn't even have Slema Chavchavadze's name in it, and he couldn't decide whether he had a legitimate reason to put it in there.

He felt like an archaeologist trying to reconstruct a civilization from some mud walls and a few shards of pottery. He saw fragments, but not the whole picture.

Archaeologists, though, didn't have deadlines. His was just a few hours away.

He sat down at the computer and tried to think of ways he could write his way around the unanswered questions in his story. But his mind rebelled. It refused to focus.

He cracked his knuckles, ran his fingers through his hair, and gnawed on the nail of his right thumb. He flipped through a copy of *Peterburgskaya Istina*, a local tabloid published by Russian fascists, and read halfway through a story claiming that Jews and homosexuals had secretly taken over the city government. Disgusted, he

tossed that toward the trash can. It missed, the pages fluttering separately to the floor. He checked the nightstand by the bed for a Bi-
ble. Nothing. The Gideon people hadn't arrived yet.

Frustrated, Burke walked over to the window, staring out at the
lights of early evening as if they might hold some answers. They
did not.

He sat down again at the computer and rubbed his hands over
his eyes until the eyeballs blazed with red and yellow streaks.

Still, his thoughts remained a swirling jumble, like clothes being
tossed in a dryer.

Burke paced some more. He hated this part of his job. He had
only found two ways to cope with it. When he worked in an office,
around other people, he liked to schmooze. He would find someone equally frazzled and talk until his mind calmed down and his
thoughts sorted themselves out enough to enable him to write.

When he was alone and plagued by this kind of disability, he
had always found that a drink calmed him down enough to work.

He stopped in front of the small refrigerator and opened it. Inside the door was a shelf with a row of small bottles; two of them
were Jack Daniel's. He knew they were there because he had
checked when he first occupied the room. And in the tiny freezer
was the bag with the remnants of his five dollars' worth of ice from
the night before.

He pulled out a glass and filled it halfway with ice. Then he
opened the first mini-bottle and poured it.

He watched the brown liquor, marbled with streaks of orange
where it caught the light, work its way toward the bottom of the
glass, filling in the spaces between the ice cubes. Then he put the
glass to his lips.

The whiskey tasted cold and vaguely sweet, and he held it on his
tongue for a moment, letting the fumes fill his head, before he
swallowed it. He felt it work its way down his throat and into his
system.

He took a deep breath. He was amazed at how quickly he had
fallen.

Just this one time, he thought. He would start anew tomorrow.
Then he looked at the second bottle, opened it, and poured it.

He felt calm, clear-headed, and decisive. He wrote three quick paragraphs, establishing the link between Duxbury and Chavchavadze, identifying Chavchavadze, and quoting Duxbury's fear, without the epithet.

He swirled the ice around in his drink, enjoying the way the whiskey sloshed against the side of the glass. He felt no numbness in his lips, no heaviness in his eyelids, no pain in his liver. He imagined he would wake up loathing himself the next morning, but he would deal with that then. For the moment, he felt strong and exhilarated. If alcohol were always this good, he thought, he would long since have wound up living on a grate somewhere.

Now he needed just one more item to complete his story: a comment from Chavchavadze.

The phone rang. It was McCoy. She wanted to meet.

"I was just thinking that this would be a marvelous evening to take a beautiful woman to the ballet," he said. "Meet me at the theater."

Burke strode to the concierge's desk. Nikolai was on duty.

"Rough day, eh, Kolya?" he said. Using the nickname of a Russian he barely knew was mildly insulting, but he figured that for three hundred dollars, he was entitled to a little presumption.

"Very," the concierge agreed. He looked tired.

"I've decided it might be just the evening to take in a ballet at the Marinsky," Burke said. "What can you do for me?"

Nikolai managed to look sad as he shook his head. "Nothing, I'm afraid. Tickets are all sold out."

Burke nodded. "Have you got the theater's phone number?"

Nikolai's face stiffened. "I'm sure it's sold out, Mr. Burke," he said.

"Just give me the number."

He got the number and, using Nikolai's phone, called the theater. He asked to be connected to the international relations office.

He identified himself and said that since he was in St. Petersburg, it might be an opportune time to do a story for the *Tribune* on the Marinsky, a story that would certainly be of interest to people in the United States who were in a position to book a

Russian ballet company that might be looking to tour and earn a little extra hard currency. Thirty seconds later two tickets were waiting for him at the box office.

Smiling, he handed the phone back to Nikolai, who looked like a man who has just seen fifty dollars flushed down a sewer.

"Chin up. Can't get greased all the time, pal," he said in English.

If Nikolai understood the term "grease" in this context, he gave no hint. He resumed his stolid, concierge's demeanor.

There were foreigners in Russia who doted on the ballet, spending all their spare time at the Bolshoi in Moscow or the Marinsky in St. Petersburg, learning the names and life histories of the principal dancers, gossiping about spats between cultural bureaucrats and artistic directors, and arguing passionately at cocktail parties over the merits of ballerinas past and present. Burke was not one of them. He appreciated the grace and athleticism of the dancers, but half an hour of pirouettes and fluttering feet was generally enough for him.

So as he trudged up Decembrists Street to the theater, he was thinking only of two things: ways to leave early if it turned out that Slema Chavchavadze was not in attendance, and Desdemona McCoy.

The Marinsky Theater had been built as a venue of entertainment for the czars, and it reflected their opulent bad taste as fully as did the Winter Palace. Like the palace, it had fallen on hard times. Where gilt had been, Burke saw muddy gold paint. The carpets had frayed and the marble columns were chipped and scratched. The chandeliers were full of burnt-out bulbs.

The character of the audience had changed as much as the theater. Once, when it was known as the Kirov, the ballet had attracted equal measures of foreign tourists and earnest Communist balletomanes in baggy suits and clunky boots with zippers up the sides. Now, with its imperial name restored, there were fewer tourists, but the locals dressed better. They were the Russian entrepreneurial class, dressed up in new clothes and looking vaguely uncertain about them, like children dressed up for Easter.

He stomped the snow off his shoes and handed his parka to the crone in the *garderob*. Then he went to the box office and got the tickets. There was no sign of McCoy.

The lights flickered off and then on, suggesting that the performance was about to start. The stragglers filtered through the doors toward their seats. Burke checked his watch.

Then he heard her, or heard the clicking of high heels on the marble floor of the lobby. He turned and spotted her, striding quickly, her coat thrown over her arm.

She was dressed in black—loose black trousers and black boots, a black silk blouse with the top three buttons undone, black bangles dangling from her arm. Three heavy gold chains hung from her neck, dropping down toward a hint of cleavage between her breasts. She was wearing her hair up, with loose tendrils blowing in the breeze. She carried her coat slung over her arm.

She kissed him first on one cheek and then the other. "You didn't give me much time to get ready," she said.

"You mean you could look better?" he replied.

That made her smile, and he thought for a moment that she meant it. Then he reminded himself of who she was and who employed her. Everything she did would be calculated.

"Is that what I think it is on your breath?" she asked him.

Burke flushed. "What can I tell you?" he said. "The story wasn't coming."

She nodded. To his relief, she did not seem to be judging him. She seemed, if anything, sad.

"Is that when it's hardest?" she asked. "When you're writing?"

"No," he said. "It's when I'm failing to write."

The lights blinked again, and they walked into the theater. It was all white and gilt, like the bedroom of a French courtesan, with seats upholstered in threadbare gold plush. The usher was a stoop-shouldered man with a fringe of graying hair and a blue suit of the style that used to predominate at the theater in the Soviet days. He led them to seats in the seventh row, on the aisle. The theater, Burke thought, must really want a Western tour.

"By the way," Burke asked the usher, "could you tell me if Slema Chavchavadze is here tonight?"

The usher grimaced, as if Burke had asked when the strippers came on. "There," he said, and he gestured with his head toward a private box on the level above the orchestra, to their right.

It was not hard to pick out Chavchavadze. He was sitting alone in the front row of the box. Three much larger men in suits sat in the row immediately behind him, paying no attention to the stage. They looked out over the audience with the vaguely bored alertness of bodyguards. Two more of them stood at the rear of the box, by the door.

Burke sat down and looked at his program. *Swan Lake*. He scowled. He had been to the ballet perhaps ten times in Russia. Six or seven of those performances had been *Swan Lake*. He listened to the overture and watched the opening scene with most of his attention focused on Chavchavadze's box.

"Is Slema why you suddenly wanted to see the ballet?" she whispered.

He took the opportunity to turn toward her and bring his lips close to her ear. She was wearing a perfume, something subtle.

"Among other things," he whispered back.

The object of Chavchavadze's attentions became clear as soon as the princess appeared. The first time she pirouetted across the stage, Chavchavadze leapt to his feet, applauding. Like a football team taking signals from its quarterback, the men in the box rose and began applauding. And taking their cue from them, hundreds of people in the uppermost balcony also rose.

"Brava!" Chavchavadze shouted.

"Brava! Bravissima," echoed the rest of the *klakery*. Burke had seen this before in ballet theaters, and it was one of the reasons he preferred drama. All the principal dancers had their little rooting sections, their *klakery*. But this was the largest and most robotically enthusiastic he had ever seen. He assumed Chavchavadze had bought their tickets and given them a little extra to assure enthusiasm.

He checked the name of the favored ballerina in the program. "L. Fedotova," it said. There was no other information. Burke looked at her. She was blond, and her features, underneath the white feathered cap of her costume, were classically beautiful. She was blushing as she stood on point, and her breath came in shallow little gulps. She looked very young.

The rest of the dancers carried on. Soon it was time for Mademoiselle Fedotova to move again. Again Chavchavadze and the *klakery* rose in a loud and prolonged ovation.

This time the rest of the dancers seemed distracted and their movements became less certain. By the time the intermission came, they had all but given up. The ballet had degenerated into a series of disjointed fragments interspersed with Fedotova solos and wild applause from her *klakery*.

As the house lights went up and Burke rose from his seat, he felt a gentle tap on his shoulder.

He turned and found a slender, middle-aged woman with close-cropped, straight black hair, wearing a blue dress, black hose, and black pumps.

"I'm Svetlana Markovskaya, the director of international affairs," she said in English. She had an air of sad solemnity. "Are you Mr. Burke?"

Burke nodded and smiled. Wanly, she smiled back.

"Thank you for the tickets," he said. He introduced McCoy.

"We're glad you're here," Markovskaya said. "But tell me, did you come to St. Petersburg to work on this story, or are you here because of the . . ."

"The assassination?" he asked.

She nodded.

"Neither one, actually," he said. "I came principally to work on a piece about the Hermitage. But while I'm here, I couldn't miss the Marinsky."

She smiled again, slightly reassured. At least he was artistically conversant.

"Well, whom would you like to talk to?" she asked. "I believe I could arrange a meeting with our artistic director, Mr. Budryakov. He could tell you everything you want to know about the company."

"Perhaps so," Burke said. "But right now I'd be grateful for a chance to talk to Miss Fedotova. What's her first name?"

"Lyudmilla," the woman replied. Her face clouded. "But she is just a beginner. You'd be more interested in talking to Olga Bitmanova. She's been a prima ballerina for ten years. She's toured in London and New York. She speaks English. She's playing Odette tonight."

"No," Burke said. "Ms. Fedotova interests me. And I speak Russian well enough."

Svetlana Markovskaya's face registered almost physical pain. "But she really is not . . ."

"Not what?"

"Not, um, not used to giving interviews," Markovskaya improvised. "She's only seventeen."

"Ah, a phenomenal young talent, then," Burke said.

Markovskaya grimaced again. "Well, yes, but—"

"Then we'll do it after the performance. Backstage," Burke said.

Markovskaya was looking increasingly hemmed in. "Well, I don't know if we can do it then."

"It will be my only chance to work on this article," Burke said.

"Very well." Markovskaya's face reflected resignation. "I'll see you here immediately after the performance."

They made their way out to the lobby behind Ms. Markovskaya.

"Would you like a drink?" Burke asked McCoy.

McCoy looked at him dubiously. "Are you sure you know what you're doing?" she asked.

"One place I know what I'm doing is at a bar," Burke said.

He bought her a glass of champagne, then hesitated. The barman waited, expectantly.

"Juice," he said.

She smiled at him then and touched her glass to his. "Bravo," she said.

———

Burke watched the rest of the ballet only when Lyudmilla Fedotova took the stage, and he began to see why Svetlana Markovskaya had tried to steer him to an interview with another ballerina. Dancers like Olga Bitmanova, or any first-rate Russian dancer, were as precise as an industrial robot. Every movement began and ended on time. Every movement reflected exactly the vision of the choreographer. At the very summit of the art, they achieved this precision and still somehow remained individuals, contributing something of their own to the dance.

Compared to this standard, Lyudmilla Fedotova was slightly, almost imperceptibly, ragged. Occasionally, her legs quivered when they should have been still, or she rounded off a pirouette a microsecond before or after the orchestra expected her to. She had only one clear advantage over the other dancers: she was easily the most beautiful. But he wondered whether she would even make it out of the corps de ballet once Chavchavadze tired of her.

He waited impatiently through the post-performance rituals. Chavchavadze's *klakery* gave him his money's worth, all but drowning Fedotova in ovations and piling her arms high with bouquets of red flowers, neatly wrapped in cellophane.

As the lights went up, Svetlana Markovskaya appeared once again behind Burke's left shoulder. Whatever earlier misgivings she had felt about arranging an interview for Lyudmilla Fedotova seemed to have disappeared. Her face was placid and composed. Silently, she led Burke and McCoy to the rear of the theater, then down three corridors until they arrived at an unmarked door. Somewhat to Burke's surprise, there was no security guard. Markovskaya opened the door and they were backstage.

Burke had never been backstage in a theater before, and what he saw did not live up to the expectations nurtured by the movies. There was little or no bustle, no electricity. A few stagehands in grimy blue coveralls lounged by a brick wall, smoking. They passed one room, roughly the size of his hotel room, that seemed to be awash in white tulle and bathed in a cold, fluorescent light. It was the dressing room of the female members of the corps de ballet, but there was no buzz of post-performance excitement. The women he saw as he passed by the door looked listless. They reminded him of coal miners finishing a shift.

Markovskaya knocked at the door of the next dressing room. An elderly woman in a gray smock and hair to match opened it. Burke guessed she was there to help the ballerinas with their costumes.

Lyudmilla Fedotova had removed the feathered white skull cap of her costume and was sitting in front of a small mirror, brushing out her blond hair. She still wore her stage makeup. On another girl it would have looked garish in the harsh light. But on her it only served to accent the cast of her cheekbones and the pale gray beauty of her eyes. She was slender, with a body that still seemed to be growing into her bones, and she appraised Burke and McCoy in her mirror without turning around, continuing to brush her hair. He stood there for a moment, watching the muscles move in her shoulder and arm, raising and lowering the tops of her breasts. When Markovskaya introduced them, the ballerina nodded and smiled. Her teeth were small and a little yellow, marring her perfect face.

She smiled again when he told her he wanted to feature her in a story about the company in the *Washington Tribune*.

Burke took a small tape recorder and a notebook from his coat pocket, opened his mouth—and stopped, his mouth slightly ajar. He had not anticipated actually having to interview this girl. He had expected Chavchavadze to be backstage when he got there. What the hell did one ask a ballet dancer—how she did her plié? He wasn't sure he even knew how to spell *plié*, much less what one looked like.

He leaned over toward McCoy. "What do you ask a ballerina?" he whispered.

"You're supposed to be the reporter," McCoy whispered back unhelpfully.

In the corner of his eye he saw Markovskaya looking at him, puzzled.

"Uh, tell me about yourself," he said.

The ballerina shrugged. "Nothing to tell," she said.

"Well, where are you from?"

"Vologda."

"Vologda. Where's that?"

"I don't know. Three hundred kilometers away."

"Big town or small town?"

She shrugged. Burke started to sweat. Keeping this girl talking till Chavchavadze showed would be, in Nikita Khrushchev's famous phrase, like teaching pigs to whistle. He looked at the clear liquid in the glass on the dressing table, wondering suddenly if it was vodka.

"And when did you start dancing?" he tried.

"When I was four."

"Why?"

Another shrug. "Because I liked it."

"Why did you like it?"

Yet another shrug. A slight giggle. The girl was either inordinately shy or she was getting bored with him.

"And how did you get to the Marinsky Company?"

"They invited me."

Burke scratched his head. "Is *Swan Lake* your first big role?"

She nodded.

"How do you like it?"

"It's okay."

Burke was getting exasperated. "And what do you think the popularity of *Beavis and Butt-head* says about the cultural level of your American peers?"

The girl's face clouded and she cocked her ear toward him as if she were about to ask him to repeat the question.

A male voice, but one with a strangely high pitch, like a baritone singing falsetto, interrupted her.

"And what the hell is *Beavis and Butt-head*?"

Burke turned around. Slema Chavchavadze stood in the doorway to the dressing room. Two of his bodyguards were visible behind him.

He was at once more and less impressive than he had been from a distance. Up close, Burke could see that he was shorter than he had appeared while sitting; his legs were stubby and he could not have been more than five feet, seven inches. His face was faintly pockmarked with old acne scars.

But he looked sleek. His hair and eyes were of the same gleaming black. The hair was pulled straight back from his forehead, exposing the only tanned skin Burke had seen since arriving in Russia. His nose was long and curved, like a falcon's beak, but it fit his face.

He had a London tailor. His shirt was either a Turnbull & Asser or a very good copy, and his suit, a gray pinstripe, hung precisely from his broad shoulders, camouflaging the slight paunch around his waist. He could have been twenty-five, and experienced. He could have been forty-five, and well-preserved.

More than anything else, his posture impressed Burke. He carried himself like a man accustomed to deference, from both sexes.

The girl smiled, rose and walked over to Chavchavadze. She managed to make the movement seem sexy and graceful. She kissed him on the lips, mouth slightly open.

Chavchavadze ran his right hand up the back of her thigh until it cupped her tiny buttocks under the tulle and crinoline of her dress, a gesture of territoriality so obvious that it reminded Burke of a dog pissing at a fire hydrant.

Then he let the hand drop and turned his complete attention to Burke. "So what is *Beavis and Butt-head?*"

"Some American television stars. Our best and brightest," Burke said, extending his hand. "Colin Burke. The *Washington Tribune.* This is my friend, Desdemona McCoy. I was just interviewing Ms. Fedotova for a story on the Marinsky."

Chavchavadze looked at McCoy as curiously and directly as he might an animal in the zoo, and Burke wondered again what it must be like to have the only black face on this segment of the planet.

Chavchavadze took her hand and then covered it over with his left hand, pumping several times. Evidently, he had decided to be charming for the moment.

"Slema Chavchavadze," Burke said when the man shook hands with him. "I've heard that name before. Where was it?"

Chavchavadze's eyes narrowed. "Probably what you heard was not true," he said. "I find I inspire a lot of false rumors, for some reason."

"What kinds of rumors?" Burke asked.

Chavchavadze smiled, keeping his mouth closed. "There was a rumor that I like seeing my name in the newspapers, for instance."

Burke shook his head. "Nope, that's not it . . . oh, I remember. Mr. Bykov at the Hermitage suggested I talk to you. I'm doing a story about art smuggling."

Chavchavadze looked blankly at him for a moment, as if not believing the temerity of what he had just heard.

"I don't know Ivan Bykov," he said.

"But you know his first name," Burke said. "Well, maybe it came from Jimmy Duxbury. He said he'd been cheated on a nickel deal and he was afraid you were going to kill him if he complained about it."

Chavchavadze's face set into stone and he remained silent. But the two bodyguards took a step into the room, until they were at arm's length from Burke. Behind him, Burke could hear Lyudmilla Fedotova's hairbrush clatter as it fell to the vanity table in front of her mirror. Svetlana Markovskaya, he could see in the corner of his eye, had placed a hand over her chest and grown pale. McCoy alone, of the people in the room, seemed relaxed.

"I've never met him," Chavchavadze finally said, in a quiet and even voice. "Judging by what he did to Marshal Grachenko, he is obviously crazy." Chavchavadze paused. "Only a fool would believe him."

"And I'm sure General Kornilov is no fool," Burke said.

Chavchavadze showed the thin smile again. "No. He's a very wise man."

Burke nodded. "And you're not in the nickel business?"

Chavchavadze shrugged. "I'm in a lot of businesses."

"The art business?"

"I'm in a lot of businesses," he repeated.

"Including icons and paintings," Burke said, stating the question as a fact. "Know anyone at the Hermitage?"

This time Chavchavadze could not remain impassive. His mouth turned down into a scowl and his cheeks flushed. "Get out of here, fool," he commanded.

Burke smiled, trying to make the smile as irritating as possible. "Why? Have I said anything to offend you? I'm doing an interview here."

Chavchavadze flickered an eyebrow at the bodyguard to his right, and the man stepped forward. A hand like a slab of pork reached out and pulled Burke by the tie. His head lurched forward, slamming into the doorway to the dressing room. For an instant Burke saw twinkling lights. Then the man slung him into the hallway. He crashed against the wall on the opposite side and fell sprawling to the floor, one foot splayed upward and his head wedged between the wall and the floor. Burke shook his head, dizzy.

Chavchavadze's bodyguard saved him the trouble of getting to his feet. He picked Burke up as if he weighed no more than a sack of sugar and hurled him underhanded down the hallway. He landed on the same shoulder the attacker had hit the night before. Pain shot through his arm and up to his brain. The air rushed out of his lungs and he lay on the floor, stunned and breathless, unable to rise.

Slema Chavchavadze watched Burke for a few seconds, then turned to Svetlana Markovskaya.

"I'm surprised you let trash like that lie around in the theater," he said. "Better help him leave."

Markovskaya, trembling now, nodded silently and scurried out into the hall. McCoy followed her.

Chavchavadze closed the door. He turned to the remaining bodyguard and spoke in Ossetian, a Caucasian language that Lyudmilla Fedotova did not understand.

"Wait until he's away from the theater and alone," he said. "And do him."

Chapter Twenty-one

"**W**ELL, YOU WERE A BIG HELP," BURKE SAID to McCoy. He was limping alongside her, en route to her car, which was parked near the opposite end of the theater.

The pain in his shoulder was back, redoubled. It throbbed persistently in a region that extended from well below his shoulder blade all the way down past his elbow. And he had bruised his left knee.

"What do you mean by that?" McCoy asked sharply.

"Well, I mean where were you with the ninja stuff when I needed you?" he said. He knew he was being unfair, but his body hurt and his brain was suggesting that alcohol was the balm he needed, and he felt lousy.

"There were two of them. They no doubt had guns. And if you ask provocative questions of a man like that, you have to expect consequences."

They reached the car, a blue Volvo. She drove.

"Why'd you have to provoke him like that?" she persisted as they pulled away.

"I got what I wanted," Burke said.

"What? Getting beat up?"

She turned onto the riverside embankment, driving fast and looking in the rearview mirror.

"No. But suppose I'd asked polite questions."

"You might not have gotten your butt kicked."

"Right," Burke said. "I'd have gotten polite, plausible answers. All lies, but I'd have been obliged to quote him accurately. Readers might have believed him. This way, I write that he angrily denied the allegations and had two goons throw out the reporter who asked him about them. The readers get the picture."

"You sure you didn't do it because you were coming down from those drinks you had?"

"Coming down? Des, this isn't cocaine."

She looked at him as a streetlight flashed past overhead, briefly illuminating the inside of the car.

"I know," she said, and he saw the same sad and somehow vulnerable look in her eyes that he'd seen back in the theater lobby.

"You've passed the turn for the hotel," he said.

"We're not going there," she said.

"Whoa," he protested. "I have to."

"It's not safe for you there."

"You mean the refrigerator in the room?"

She shook her head. "No, I mean the man you just infuriated. What do you think, he's just going to forget about that?"

"No," Burke said. He sighed. "You know, I miss the old days, when the KGB ran things. They might blackmail an American reporter. They might boot him out of the country. But they generally didn't go in for corporal punishment."

"That's progress," she said.

"Thanks a lot," he said, and laughed. He felt better. His thoughts turned to the hotel.

"I've got to go up there for a few minutes so I can finish my story and file it. Then I can check into another hotel."

"I'll take your key card and get your computer," she said. "You can file from my place."

She poked a cup of coffee under his nose.

"Drink this," she said.

Burke stared at the cup. It was as inviting as old motor oil.

He looked at McCoy. She'd gone into the bedroom and changed clothes while he'd sat hunched over the computer. She was wearing the jeans and sweater she'd had on that night in the train. Her hair was down again. She still looked terrific.

"Thanks, but you sure you don't have a bottle of vodka I could go lie in the gutter with?"

"Please don't joke," she said. "It's not funny."

"Sorry. I thought it was a joke at my expense."

"Hits close to home," she answered. "My father is an alcoholic."

Burke blinked. "I'm sorry," he said.

She shook her head. "Don't be. He hasn't had a drink in ten years. That's what you're going to have to do."

"I know," he said, and at that instant he believed he would.

"He still struggles with it. Every day," she said. "It's not going to be easy."

He didn't reply, turning his head back to the computer, where his story was just about done.

Typing primarily with his left hand, he stitched the last words into the story.

He plugged the modem into her cellular phone. Fortunately for him, she was part of a network that bypassed the regular St. Petersburg switching equipment and connected directly to a satellite.

While the modem did its work, he looked around. The apartment, though clearly intended for a foreigner and luxurious by Soviet standards, was flat and impersonal. Everything was new and shiny. Its walls were white. Its furnishings looked like they had all been bought from the catalogue of Stockmann's, in Helsinki. It contained nothing of her.

"It's not exactly the kind of place I'd envisioned you living in," he said.

"Well," she replied, "when you move as much as I do, and

into places like this, you tend to leave the stuff you care about at home."

He nodded. If he'd had much of a home when he first moved to Moscow, he'd have left his good stuff there, too.

He picked up the phone, disconnected the modem, and, using a credit card, called Graves.

"Not bad," Graves said after he'd called the piece up onto his screen in Washington and scanned it. "It should be more than anyone else has got."

Burke thanked him for the compliment.

"Now I need you back here," Graves went on.

"Well, I haven't finished here," Burke said.

Graves's tone became peremptory and abrupt. "Look, Colin, I know how you feel about Jacqueline—"

"Jennifer," Burke corrected him.

"Jennifer. Sorry," Graves said, managing not to sound sorry. "And I indulged that as much as I could. But now we've got a crisis in Moscow. This guy the Zhezl looks like the second coming of Napoleon. Smithfield's working her ass off over there, and she's smart, but she needs someone on the desk to feed ideas to her, make suggestions. You know, guide her. What we hired you for."

Arguing this time, Burke realized, would do him no good. Besides, had he been in Graves's position, he would have said the same thing.

It occurred to him that he could tell Graves he realized editing didn't suit him, that he wanted to be a reporter again, and that he quit.

But after making the last tuition payment for his son at the University of Colorado, he had about twenty thousand dollars in the bank. He couldn't afford to be unemployed.

"All right, Ken," he said. "I'll take the next plane."

"I'll expect you tomorrow evening," Graves said. "Have a nice trip."

Burke hung up the phone. "They want me back in Washington," he told McCoy. "Tomorrow. I can get an extra day or so maybe by telling 'em the planes were full. But no more than that. So if I'm going to get the story I came here to get, I've got to go out and find Nadyezhda Petrovna Naryshkina. Tonight."

McCoy nodded. "Mind some company?"

He thought it over for a second. Normally, he would do this alone. But it was too late to rely on taxis. He had no car and she did.

But it was more than that. He wanted her around.

He smiled. "Best offer I've had in weeks."

She smiled back. "Before we go," she said, "let me look at that shoulder and rub some liniment in it. Take off your shirt."

"The offers just keep getting better."

Using his left hand, he unbuttoned the shirt while McCoy retreated to the medicine cabinet in the bathroom. She came back with a tube in her hand.

She stood in front of him and, with her right hand on his shoulder and her left under his elbow, slowly raised his arm until Burke winced. She raised it farther, until it was three-quarters of the way over his head.

"Ouch," he said.

"Well, you're going to have a beautiful bruise," she said. "But I think that's all."

She started with the liniment on his back. Her fingers were both strong and light. Burke felt the heat begin to work its way down to the bruised muscles. But he barely noticed that, so conscious was he of her scent and her fingers.

She moved around in front of him, still rubbing, getting the liniment down into his arm and under his collarbone.

Her movements became slower as her face came closer to his, until she was directly in front of him and her hand all but stopped. Her eyes were open, wide open.

He kissed her, brushing tentatively against her lips, uncertain how she would react. She reacted by stepping closer.

He moved his lips against hers, tasting, exploring, and she opened her mouth and the kiss became prolonged, until she drew a breath and he stepped away, surprised not by the kiss, but by its intensity.

She shook her head and smiled.

"Not the time," he said, and started to button his shirt.

"No," she agreed, her lips turned upward. "It isn't."

"Thanks for the liniment," he said. "I can feel the heat."

She looked at his trousers, where his erection was pressing against the cloth. Then she turned and walked back toward the bathroom, screwing the cap back on the liniment.

"I'll bet you can," she said over her shoulder.

He told himself to think rationally. Either she saw in him some shade of the alcoholic father she had wanted to save, or she just wanted to manipulate him. Whatever it was, he was violating prudence and journalistic ethics every minute that he allowed her to stay with him.

"Hurry up," he called out. "We need to get there before they go to sleep."

The building was one of those Soviet-era blocks of crumbling cement that stood in rows of four and five on the Vyborg road, toward the northwest end of the city. Nadyezhda Petrovna Naryshkina lived at number 46, Korpus Two, apartment 156. Four buildings shared the number 46, and it was up to the visitor to guess which one was Korpus Two. The street lights were all dark and the signs and numbers had long since been ripped off the buildings. Finally, by entering two buildings, they deduced that Korpus Two was the third building in from the street, and they slogged toward it.

Burke's feet shuffled onto a patch of ice hidden under dusty snow, and he skidded. His right arm went out instinctively and broke his fall by grabbing onto the lowest branch of a linden tree. His shoulder felt like it was tearing apart.

McCoy helped him up, and he leaned against the tree for a moment, panting and a little dizzy, until he caught his breath and his head steadied. They plodded on.

Apartment 156, to his pleasant surprise, was on the first floor. Usually, it seemed to him, the places he visited were all walk-ups, at a minimum three flights above the street.

He checked for a seam of light under the door and found one. He looked at his watch. It was almost midnight.

In Washington, calling on people at this hour of the night would be a good way to be shot or arrested. But in Russia, he had found, intellectuals stayed up late, talking and drinking. They got to work whenever it suited them.

This was particularly true in times of political upheaval, when people went out to evening meetings and then spent more hours on the phone, parsing the evening news with friends. He had gotten used to calling on Russians until one in the morning. Grachenko's death was not as momentous as perestroika, but it was no doubt the subject of a lot of kitchen debates that night.

The door to number 156 was lined in leather, to deaden sound. He pressed the button to its left and hoped the buzzer worked. It did.

Soon he heard the papery scraping sound that he knew was made by slippers scuffling across a grimy, unwaxed parquet floor.

The woman who opened the door struck him later as frightened and still later as beautiful. But for the moment, he paid her no attention. He was overwhelmed by the painting that hung on the wall behind her.

It was three feet wide and about four feet high, and it hung in a gilded, carved frame. It was a picture of a man, dressed in severe black save for a snowy white, pleated ruff around his neck. He had a quill in one hand, and he was copying something from a heavy manuscript. His face bore a perfect, open-mouthed expression of surprise, as if someone had unexpectedly entered his carrel in the library, and his head was bathed in a soft white luminescence.

Burke knew little about art, but he knew enough to tell that this was an exquisite picture. The ruff around the man's collar and the way the light surrounded his head suggested that it was by Rembrandt.

He looked at McCoy. She, too, was staring at the painting, almost as if she were appraising it.

The woman at the door reclaimed their attention. "Excuse me," she said. "Who are you and what do you want?"

Burke flushed and pulled a business card out of his shirt pocket. She took it and glanced at it.

"This is Desdemona McCoy," he said. He was about to add that she was from the McCoy-Fokine Gallery when he stopped. Let her

introduce herself. McCoy pulled a business card from the pocket of
her coat and handed it to the woman, who stood silent, examining
them warily, as if they might be contaminated.

"We're terribly sorry for coming this late," Burke said. "But it's
urgent. You're Nadyezhda Petrovna Naryshkina?"

"No," the woman said.

The apparent Rembrandt on the wall suggested that this must
be the right apartment.

"But she lives here?"

The woman pursed her lips. "Why do you want to know?"

Burke wondered what sliver of truth, if any, would get him past
the threshold and into the apartment.

"Well," he said, "I'm working on a story about the Hermitage."

She started to shut the door in his face.

"And about the death of Fyodor Vasiliev," he added.

It was the wrong thing to say. The woman's eyes widened, and
she slammed the door shut. But at the last second he heard another woman's voice.

"Lyuba!" the voice said. "Let them in."

Burke heard indistinct noises for a minute from behind the
closed door. It sounded like an argument. Then the door opened
again.

The woman was flushed and unhappy. But she gestured to her
left and invited them in.

He shrugged off his parka and turned toward the spot on the
wall where, in nearly every Russian apartment he had ever visited,
there were three or four hooks for hanging coats and a rack for the
slippers that Russians wore inside their apartments.

Instead he saw a smallish painting in a plain brown frame. It
was an exquisite portrait of a Madonna and child. The girl who
had posed for it looked about fifteen. She had a plait in her hair
and a jeweled brooch atop a rust and aquamarine gown that
looked so real, he felt he could reach out and bunch the fabrics in
his hand. The child, disproportionately large for some reason, sat
in her lap and groped toward a sprig of flowers that she held in
front of his face.

McCoy was looking closely at the painting, but he could not
read the expression on her face.

He dimly remembered seeing the picture before. He could not remember where. The Hermitage?

"Raphael?" he said, uncertain.

The woman, still looking unhappy, smiled briefly at his ignorance. "Leonardo," she said.

She gestured again toward the left. McCoy walked in. Burke followed.

He felt as if he were entering a small and very crowded museum. Everything in the apartment was the poor, threadbare, and flimsy produce of the Soviet Union, kept in service years beyond its life expectancy, save for what was on the walls. The walls were covered with paintings, starting at the level of the furniture and going up to the ceiling. The smaller paintings hung one atop the other, but there was one enormous picture that took up half the wall facing him. A gray-bearded old man, in robes of red and gold, embraced a younger, shaven-headed man in rags. Like the picture in the entrance hall, this one was bathed in a soft light, and he guessed, again, that it was a Rembrandt. But of course, he thought, it couldn't be.

Nor could it be a manufactured reproduction, because he could see the texture of the paint on the canvas.

He could not begin to guess the names of most of the artists, but he could tell they were Renaissance paintings. They depicted virgins, saints, goddesses, and burghers in somber black suits and white collars.

Then he noticed, in one corner, a row of Impressionists. There was a landscape that looked like a Cezanne. And underneath it, the same picture of Polynesian women he'd seen in the director's office at the Hermitage and decided was a Gauguin.

"They're copies," he said.

"That's right."

He turned to the source of the voice, which was in a corner behind him and to his right.

He saw a woman whose coarse, black hair was streaked with gray, pulled back from her face and captured in a severe bun. The skin around her face was the color and texture of old parchment. It looked dry, thin and finely wrinkled. But she had clear, sparkling blue eyes that picked up streaks of deeper blue from the paint stains on the old smock she wore. Her hands and forearms were blunt, square and strong, in contrast to her shoulders and torso, which looked shrunken and weak.

She was sitting in a wheelchair, a blanket thrown over her legs. "Nadyezhda Petrovna?"

She nodded. "That's right. And this is my daughter, Lyubov. I'm sorry she was rude to you."

They shook her hand.

"Please don't apologize. We're being rude by calling so late without an invitation. You painted all of these?"

She nodded affirmatively, amused at his reaction to seeing them. "This is my work," she said.

"You work at the Hermitage?"

She nodded again.

"How did you know to come to us?" It was the daughter, evidently nervous. "How did you know where we were?"

Burke cleared his throat and tried to decide where to begin.

"Please, sit down," Nadyezhda Petrovna said before he could reply. Her voice was gravelly but somehow soft and refined. She spoke the fluid, melodic Russian that marked the best of the intelligentsia, a Russian that conveyed the language's great capacity for poetry. Burke had always admired that style and accent but had never been able to imitate it.

"Some tea," she offered. "Cookies?"

Burke swallowed. He was glad she hadn't offered vodka, because it seemed that every cell in his brain was standing at attention clamoring for more alcohol.

"Yes, please," McCoy said. Without being asked, Lyubov went into the kitchen.

There was a daybed along the far wall which was the only piece of furniture in the cluttered room big enough for two people to sit down on. They took it.

Nadyezhda Petrovna turned her wheelchair toward them, but said nothing. Her presence seemed to be comprised only of four imposing elements, her bright, unblinking eyes and her strong hands.

"Nadyezhda Petrovna," McCoy began, "it's very late, so I think the thing is to come right to the point."

She looked at Burke. "Colin, this has to be off-the-record. Agreed?"

"I sure as hell wasn't planning on mentioning you in any story," he said. "You'd be very hard to explain."

She smiled for an instant, then grew serious and turned to Nadyezhda Petrovna.

"I know that the Hermitage has been drawn into a plan to sell a very valuable painting or paintings," she said. "The plan involves people at the very highest level of government in Moscow. It's supposed to be a secret sale, but I can tell you that it's not going to be secret very long. And when it comes out, there will be an enormous scandal. Now, with Grachenko dead, the government might well . . . be replaced."

Lyubov Naryshkina stepped back into the room from the kitchen, were she had obviously been listening.

"How do you know this?" she demanded. Her voice had risen half an octave, and it had an undertone of shrill fear.

McCoy looked at her impassively. "I can only tell you that it's my business to know. And I can tell you that I have contacts in the government of the United States that are in a position to help you."

"Help us? How?" Lyubov's voice cracked on the vowel sounds.

"If you give me the information needed to understand this situation completely, to stop the sale, and to prevent someone like Marshal Rogov from taking power, I can offer you safe passage out of the country and a chance to resettle in the United States, with an assurance of employment in your field and economic security."

Nadyezhda Petrovna's eyes narrowed.

"I'm sorry," she said. "We have nothing to say to you."

"But—" McCoy began to object.

"Please. It's very late," Lyubov said. "My mother is not well." McCoy's mouth tightened, but she said nothing.

"Just a minute," Burke said. "Ms. McCoy may have spoken a little too, shall we say, provocatively. But she had good intentions. I'm just a reporter. I don't have her connections in the government. But she and I both respect your love for your country and your desire to stay here and protect its patrimony."

The woman in the wheelchair looked slightly mollified. McCoy's jaw thrust forward and her mouth closed to a thin line.

"If you want us to leave, we'll leave, of course. But I suspect that you told Lyubov to let me in a couple of minutes ago because there's something you want me to know. Maybe something you want me to write because it might forestall whatever this plan is that Ms. McCoy was talking about."

Nadyezhda Petrovna smiled faintly.

"No, Mama, no! It's too dangerous!" Lyubov was as pale as the evening light in St. Petersburg.

Nadyezhda Petrovna looked fondly at her. "My daughter wants to protect me, Mr. Burke," she said. "But I'm afraid that there is no protection in this situation, without risk. I ask only one thing: that you wait until I tell you it is safe—perhaps three or four days—before you publish anything that I tell you."

"Agreed," Burke said.

McCoy cleared her throat. "I apologize for offending you, Nadyezhda Petrovna." She turned to Burke. "I'll let you handle the questions for a while."

"Don't apologize, Miss McCoy," Nadyezhda Petrovna said. "I want you to know what is happening. But, you understand, I cannot work for your, um, connections."

She smiled as she said it, but the smile had iron behind it. McCoy, Burke thought, looked like she wanted to chew nails and spit bullets. But she swallowed her pride. He respected that.

He started Nadyezhda Petrovna off with questions about herself, hoping to get her as relaxed and garrulous as possible.

"You paint copies for the Hermitage?"

The woman nodded.

"How did you come to do that?"

Nadyezhda Petrovna placed her hands on her lap and folded them. "That's a long story."

"I like long stories," Burke said.

Nadyezhda Petrovna looked pleased with the answer. "When she began to collect paintings," she said, "Catherine the Great established a small school of the arts at the Hermitage. She was determined that her collection would help to train Russian artists.

And, in turn, Russian artists would be the ones who preserved the collection. She was German, you know. But she loved Russia."

"I know," Burke said.

"You probably know that paintings deteriorate from the moment the artist finishes them. If they are shipped long distances, as Catherine's were, they suffer damages. Or time causes paint to peel, crack, and fade. To preserve and restore art, one must be able to copy everything the original artist did—the brush style, the materials, everything. So, this school began to train artists whose speciality was copying. It did so under the czars and it did so under the Bolsheviki."

"And it trained you," Burke said.

The old woman smiled faintly. "Not only me. My grandfather was the chief of restoration under Alexander the Third. My father was a restorationist who became curator of Spanish paintings. So it was a family tradition. I began to study in the school when I was eight years old."

Lyubov at that moment brought a teapot into the sitting room and set it on a small table in front of the daybed. The conversation stopped while Burke and McCoy accepted cups of steaming tea with the leaves floating around in the bottom and declined the customary offer of sugary little cookies.

"My mother is the best of them all," Lyubov said quietly. "No one in the world is as good as she is."

The old woman smiled again. "It's my talent," she said, suddenly more animated. "I've painted my own pictures, of course. But, somehow, they had no life. They had no vision of their own. When I copy a painting, it's as if the vision of the artist fills me up."

Lyubov broke in. "You never answered my question about how you found us," she said to Burke.

Burke hesitated, then decided to be honest. "I got your name from some papers in Fyodor Vasiliev's desk. I got your address from an artist who lives here in St. Petersburg."

The smile disappeared from Nadyezhda Petrovna's face. "And what were you doing in Fyodor Mikhailovich's papers?"

"It's a long story," Burke said. "And it's late."

The old woman smiled wryly. "I don't sleep much anymore, Mr. Burke," she said. "It seems I don't need to. I think it's God's compensation to me for this." She gestured toward her unmoving legs. "So I like long stories, too."

Burke found himself liking this woman very much.

He told her about Jennifer Morelli and her big story and her death, and how he came to be in St. Petersburg and how he had found her name in Vasiliev's papers.

"Jennifer," Nadyezhda Petrovna said. "What did she look like?"

"She was almost thirty years old, very tall, blue eyes, freckles, very serious. Short hair. *Ryzhy*," Burke said.

Nadyezhda Petrovna nodded sympathetically. "Well, I did see your Jennifer," she said. "She was with Fyodor Mikhailovich."

Her words jolted Burke. He leaned forward. "Do you remember what he was showing her? Was it the *Madonna Litta*?"

"Mama!" Lyubov interrupted before her mother could answer. She said nothing else, but her face was flushed, the skin drawn tightly around her cheeks and jaw. She looked badly frightened. A tear dripped out of her right eye and spread slowly down her cheek.

Nadyezhda Petrovna turned toward her daughter and caressed her under the chin, and he could see them for a moment as they might have been twenty-five years ago, when the mother consoled the little girl. Lyubov, as she might have then, stopped crying.

"It's all right," Nadyezhda Petrovna said. "This is the right thing to do.

"The painting," she said to Burke, "is by Leonardo. But it is not the *Madonna Litta*. It is called *Leda and the Swan*."

McCoy gasped and broke into the conversation. "*Leda and the Swan?*"

"You've heard of it," Nadyezhda Petrovna said.

"I'd forgotten, but now I remember. I read about it in college," McCoy said. "Raphael drew a copy of it, but the original . . ." Her brow furrowed as she tried to recollect a paragraph from an old art history text. "It was destroyed, wasn't it?"

Nadyezhda Petrovna shook her head. "Hidden."

Burke took a notebook out of his pocket. "Hidden? How? And how do you spell 'Leda'?"

Nadyezhda Petrovna, for the first time, leaned over to the table and took a sip of tea. Then she settled back into her chair.

"Leonardo," she said, "painted *Leda and the Swan* sometime around 1510. It was unique among his paintings—the only nude he ever did, and the most beautiful. You have seen the *Mona Lisa*?"

"Of course," McCoy said.

Burke said nothing. When he'd been in Paris, visiting the Louvre had not been high enough on his priority list.

"It is the equal of that painting."

"But it hasn't been seen in hundreds of years!" McCoy objected. "It was destroyed!"

Nadyezhda Petrovna shook her head. "The painting was purchased by the French court. It appears in the inventories of Fontainebleau in 1692 and 1694. Then it disappears."

"But it wasn't destroyed?"

She smiled. "No. In 1697, King Louis the Fourteenth married for a second time, to the Marquise de Maintenon. She was a very delicate, affected woman, or so she pretended."

"Delicate and affected?"

"She thought there should not be so much discussion and display of—" Nadyezhda Petrovna paused. "—sexual matters." Apparently she was a little delicate herself.

"And the painting was a nude," McCoy said.

Nadyezhda Petrovna nodded.

Burke suddenly understood. "She destroyed all the nude paintings?"

"So it has been thought," Nadyezhda Petrovna said.

"But if it wasn't destroyed," Burke said, "where did it go and how did it get here?"

"We don't know precisely," she said. "My guess is that someone, perhaps the curator at Fontainebleau, realized what a terrible loss it would be if the painting were destroyed. He looked around in the collection and found a large but thoroughly mediocre landscape by a French artist named D'Amboise. Jacques D'Amboise. He took that landscape off its original frame and stretched it around *Leda and the Swan*. This D'Amboise landscape, 150 years later, had found its way, somehow, into the collection of a French aristocrat, the Count de Bruhl.

"Catherine's agents would certainly not have selected this D'Amboise for her. But they wanted some of the other paintings in the count's collection. He had three or four Rembrandts, five Rubens, I think. Watteau. Billotto, others. He died. She had an agent go to the count's funeral, and he arranged on the spot to buy the entire collection from the countess for 180,000 gold rubles."

"A lot of money then, I guess," Burke said.

"It would have been a lot more if they had known what lay behind that D'Amboise canvas."

"So how did you find it?"

"The de Bruhl collection was evaluated and catalogued when it came to St. Petersburg. The Rembrandts and Rubens were put on display. The D'Amboise landscape, along with a lot of others, was stored in the attic. And it stayed there until three or four months ago."

"What happened then?"

Nadyezhda Petrovna grimaced. "Our museum is so poor! We have thousands of paintings in our attics, and we cannot maintain them properly. We cannot even maintain what we have on display! Great works of art are disappearing slowly!

"So, Fyodor Mikhailovich and I decided we had to conduct a kind of triage on the paintings in storage—to save the ones we might someday want to show if we get the space, and to give away the ones we cannot keep any longer. We were going to send them on indefinite loan—give them away," she said, emphasizing the last three words, "to museums in other countries that would be delighted to have them. As gifts from the people of Russia."

"And the D'Amboise . . ." Burke prompted her.

"Was one of the ones we decided to give away. But some of the canvas had frayed, and it needed repairs. When I started to work on it, I noticed what was underneath the canvas."

"Leda and the Swan," Burke said.

She nodded. "It was in very good condition. The D'Amboise canvas had protected it for all these years. Of the dozen Leonardos in the world, I would say it is in the condition closest to the way Leonardo painted it."

"My God," McCoy said. "Do you realize how much that would be worth?"

"Not precisely," Nadyezhda Petrovna said dryly. "Leonardos don't get auctioned every month at Sotheby's. Many millions of dollars."

"Hundreds of millions," McCoy corrected her.

"And Vasiliev wanted to have a conference to show the picture to the world?" Burke asked. "And you were one of the experts he wanted to speak?"

"I was going to talk about how the small imperfections in the painting were repaired."

"What happened then?"

Her voice dropped subtly, to a slower, more secretive tone.

"About a month ago, he came to me and told me that things had gone wrong. The Ministry of Culture in Moscow had been told of the discovery. But instead of putting the painting on exhibition, they wanted to sell it, secretly. This painting that was paid for by the blood and sweat of our ancestors!"

"Who, specifically, wanted to sell it?"

Nadyezhda Petrovna shook her head. "I'm not sure. But it would have to be the Minister of Culture and either the president or someone close to him. And I think that our St. Petersburg mafia is involved. A man named Ivan Bykov suddenly replaced our old director of security. He's a thug and an icon smuggler. He's supposed to keep track of the painting and make sure that nothing goes wrong during the restoration work."

"Have you ever seen Slema Chavchavadze involved?"

"No," Nadyezhda Petrovna said. "But rumor has it that Bykov works for him. So I suspect he is involved."

"I know for sure that Chavchavadze knows Bykov," Burke said.

Lyubov, who was pouring more tea, started to tremble when she heard this and spilled some on the little table.

Nadyezhda Petrovna laid a reassuring hand on her daughter's forearm.

"And then Vasiliev showed the painting to Jennifer Morelli," Burke prompted.

"Yes. He did not say why he did this, but I knew it was because he wanted her to write something in the American press. If she hadn't happened to come to St. Petersburg, I'm sure he would have tried to contact correspondents in Moscow. But then he was killed."

"Do you know who killed him?"

"No. But it seems obvious why he was killed."

"And now you've come to the same conclusion. You want something in the American press about the painting so the public will know and the sale can't go forward. I want to write it. But I'll have to see the painting, photograph it. I'll have to quote your opinion that it's a genuine Leonardo. Do you understand all that?"

Nadyezhda Petrovna nodded. "Yes, of course. Except for one thing. I don't want you to write this article until after the sale has occurred."

"After?" Burke was startled. "Why?"

The old woman smiled serenely. "Because we are going to sell them a copy."

Chapter Twenty-two

THE JET IMPRESSED IVAN BYKOV.

He liked the knifelike sharpness of its forward edges. He liked the smooth, phallic thrust of its engines. He liked the high-pitched, powerful whine it emitted as it hit the east-west runway of the Titov Air Base, fifteen kilometers north of St. Petersburg. The plane was as white as the snow surrounding the runways. The pallid rays of the dawn sun seemed to grow brighter when they bounced off it.

Next to him, his niece Marina stomped her feet against the frigid concrete floor of the small staging building where they waited. He looked down at her shoes. She was wearing flimsy black patent-leather pumps that were suitable, perhaps, for the tourist bars, but not for a foray into an unheated Russian Air Force building.

"You should have worn boots," he said.

Marina turned to him. "Fuck you," she said.

Bykov said nothing. He turned toward the window and pretended to be engrossed by the sight of the plane, nearly a kilometer away now, slowing to a halt and beginning to make its turn back toward them.

"And so what," he asked, resuming an interrupted conversation, "did Duxbury say to the journalist?"

"All I heard was that my nickname for him was *Jeemochka*," Marina said. "And that I was having two-for-one sale with Larisa."

Marina, her attention also focused on the plane, never saw the punch coming. It exploded against her solar plexus like a tank shell, blasting the air from her lungs. She blacked out and crumpled to the ground.

Thirty seconds later the yellow and black checkerboard pattern swimming before her eyes slowly dissolved. She realized that she was coughing and gasping for breath. Her cheek was pressed against the cold, hard cement and was slowly starting to freeze.

She looked up.

Her uncle stood over her, right hand still doubled into a fist. His face was almost purple, and he was shouting something at her. A small bubble of spittle formed at the corner of his thin little mouth. Then the ringing in her ears stopped and she heard him.

". . . stupid cunt! Didn't you think he'd recognize you?"

She propped an arm under her body and began the process of getting up. This put strain on her rib cage. Despite the pain, nothing seemed to be broken. But this did not surprise her. Her uncle had long since proven to her his ability to inflict shattering pain without doing shattering damage. He knew how to hit a woman in such a way that her will was broken, but nothing else.

His foot came forward, but he did not kick her. He just nudged her in the same place where his fist had landed. The pain, nevertheless, was unendurable, and she fell back to the cold, hard floor, staring up at him.

"I just want you to know. If he finds out about Duxbury, I'll tear your tits off with my bare hands," Bykov said to her.

Then he turned back to the window and resumed looking at the jet.

Marina waited until her breathing had returned to normal, then tried again to get up. She made it back onto her elbow, and then, warily, onto her knees and then to her feet. As she rose she saw, out of the corner of her eye, a young pimply-faced soldier, in his winter greatcoat, staring at them. The boy's mouth was partially open, as if he could not yet believe what he had just seen. Marina flushed. She hated being humiliated in front of another man.

"Fuck you," she said again to her uncle. "What was I supposed to do? Let them talk?"

"You should have sent Larisa to get him," Bykov said, his eyes still fixed on the runway.

Marina felt tears well in her eyes. "You asshole! You told me to make her wait at the apartment!" she screeched. "So he'd be sure to want to leave the—"

Bykov doubled a fist and she fell instantly silent.

She looked down at her clothing. Her skirt had a dusty gray smudge from the hem to her hip. Her sheer black stockings had a run in them. She began to sob.

"Go clean yourself up," Bykov said, without bothering to look at her. "You're a mess."

She wiped a hand across her eyes, smearing her makeup, then shuffled away.

Bykov resumed watching the airplane, still furious at her. He did not know why Marina provoked him so frequently to such violent rages. He only knew that there was something about her that did. His head began to hurt. Sometimes, getting angry caused him to suffer from a terrible headache, a headache so fierce that nothing he tried, from vodka to, on one occasion, cocaine, had relieved him. He hoped this would not be one of those headaches.

He wondered whether the American journalist had deduced anything from his encounter with Duxbury and Marina. According to Marina's version, he had been quite obviously drunk, so the chances were he hadn't. He had not impressed Bykov as a particularly intelligent man.

Still, he wondered whether he ought to tell Chavchavadze about it. Then he discarded the idea. Chavchavadze had often told him he wanted to know nothing about the details of what he did. He cared only for results.

The plane trundled slowly along the tarmac toward an airman waving two red flashlights. Bykov could now dimly see the pilot's head through the cockpit window.

He walked over to the corridor into which Marina had disappeared. There was a foul-smelling bathroom with no door. She was inside, groping at a trickle of cold water that ran from a rusty faucet into a small sink, then dabbing at her face with a handkerchief.

"Let's go," he said. "They're here."

She turned to him with an expression of pure loathing on her face. She did not look bad. In fact, by getting rid of some of her excess makeup without having time to apply more, she looked better.

Wordlessly, she pushed past him. They left the building through a bulky wooden door and walked toward the plane, which was just coming to a stop.

Bykov's head started to throb.

In a moment a hatch on the side of the plane's fuselage opened and swung down silently, extending a staircase to the tarmac.

Bykov reached inside his jacket and handed Marina a bouquet of red carnations wrapped in cellophane.

He recognized the first man to step down the staircase—it was Merrill, the art dealer from London. The man in the doorway behind him, though, did not match his preconception of what a Colombian would look like. He was young, emaciated, and had a scraggly head full of dirty blond hair that hung down to his shoulders. He resembled one of the German kids with backpacks who sometimes came to St. Petersburg on the ferry from Helsinki, looking for a cheap drunk and Russian girls. He had on torn jeans, a blue peacoat, and a knitted ski cap that said "Adidas." But it had to be Rafael Santera Calderon.

The man stepped forward as Merrill came off the staircase and shook Bykov's hand. The broker was wearing a camel's hair coat that was wildly impractical for St. Petersburg, and a rather elegant sable *shapka*. Marina quickly translated his greeting.

"*Gospodin* Calderon," Bykov said to the younger man behind Merrill. "Welcome to St. Petersburg." Marina gave the young man the flowers and then translated.

The kid laughed, and Bykov was shocked to see teeth that would have shamed a Karelian peasant, mottled and chipped.

"You've got the wrong man, I'm afraid," the kid said.

At that moment a third man appeared in the hatch's frame. He wore a full-length down overcoat and a sable *shapka* identical to Merrill's. He stood there for a moment, surveying the flat, white landscape around the air base and the line of thick green larch and pine trees that surrounded it.

Bykov considered taking the flowers back from the kid with scraggly hair. Taking him for Santera had been an understandable mistake. Chavchavadze had only arranged two entrance visas.

Something told him, however, that he had better make the best of it.

He waited for the third man to descend the staircase, then greeted him. Marina translated. Santera barely bothered to return Bykov's handshake.

"And where is Chavchavadze?" Santera asked.

Pain flashed from Bykov's frontal lobes to his temples, and he wondered if Santera could see the same throbbing that he felt along the side of his head. For a moment his knees felt watery and he thought he might have to double over in pain. But he steeled himself.

"He sends his apologies," Bykov said through clenched teeth. "A business matter that he had to take care of personally. He will meet you for dinner. We've arranged a banquet."

Santera nodded as Marina translated into English.

Chavchavadze's absence from the airport, as far as Bykov knew, was a calculated slight, an effort to establish a pecking order prior to the transaction. Why Chavchavadze played these games, Bykov did not know. He did not think, judging from the look on Santera's face, that it would make him any easier to deal with.

Santera's face softened suddenly and he turned to Marina. "And you are?" he asked.

Marina smiled and introduced herself. Santera smiled back and kissed her hand.

Bykov could see the appraising glint in Santera's eyes and the greedy glint in his niece's. He recognized both. He knew what they meant. She'd probably be under the table sucking hundred-dollar bills out of his trousers before lunch was over.

His headache began to pound harder at the inside of his skull. His ears felt pressured, as if he were descending in an airplane.

"Excuse me," he said to Santera, gesturing to the kid with the flowers, who had shyly receded from the gangway as Santera descended. "Who is he, and does he have a visa?"

Santera smiled again. "Excuse me. Your translator is so beautiful, I forgot my manners," he said. "This is Gerhardt Schlegel from the Alte Pinakothek in Munich. We picked him up on the way in. My friends at the Ministry of Defense in Moscow have authorized another visa for him. I've hired him as a consultant to help authenticate the painting."

The young man nodded at Bykov again.

Bykov hated complications, and now there were two more. The fact that the Colombian could call the Ministry of Defense and arrange an immediate visa suggested there were layers of influence involved in this sale that he did not understand. That bothered him. And the fact that Santera had added yet another expert to his staff would mean, at best, a delay.

"There's another plane following us," Santera said, "with Herr Schlegel's equipment and some of my men."

Bykov's head felt as if it might split open along a fault line, beginning at the ears.

Chapter Twenty-three

SLOWLY, BURKE WOKE UP.

The dim morning light, he noticed, shone on his eyelids from an unaccustomed angle. He opened his eyes. The window was not where it was supposed to be. And there was a picture on the wall, a picture of two black eyes, set close together, a couple of wrinkles on the bridge of a nose, and a set of demonically curving black eyebrows—Stalin's eyes. He saw a chest of drawers, brown, low and Scandinavian, with books and magazines piled atop hats and boxes of plastic earrings.

"Good morning," said a woman's voice to his left, barely louder than a whisper.

He turned and looked into Desdemona McCoy's brown eyes. She was lying on her side, her head propped on an upturned hand and forearm. Her hair fell in curls and ringlets around her shoulder and face, hanging almost to the top of her breast. It framed a tentative smile that conveyed pleasure and wariness about equally. She had a long, lean body—bony at the neck and in the arms, firm below—that stretched down almost to the foot of the bed.

He reached out and brushed a strand of hair away from her eyes.

Her expression softened, and she leaned over and blew, slowly and lazily, into his right ear.

"I think," he said, "that we have to talk."

She extended her left arm until it was draped over his neck, pulled his face closer to hers, and answered him with a long, slow, and lazy kiss. She tasted sweet and smelled faintly of perfume, sweat, and spent passion.

Her leg came up and rested easily on his thigh.

He ran a hand slowly from the crook of her knee upward, over the swell of her hips and along her back, then pulled it forward until it rested below her breast. He felt the nipple stiffen in his palm.

He leaned down, took the nipple of her left breast into his lips and sucked slowly.

Almost imperceptibly, she arched her back, and he could hear and feel her breathing quicken. Her index finger traced the line of his left thigh, and then her hand cupped his scrotum.

"As I recall," she said, with an aroused edge in her voice, "this is why we didn't get around to talking last night."

He dragged his lips from her nipple over the slight swell of her breast and up to the protrusion of her collarbone. Her flesh felt soft and warm, and his ears picked up an exhilarating increase in the tempo of her breathing.

"So talk to me now," she said.

She moved her hand up an inch and let his swelling penis fill it. Then she stroked it gently.

"This," he said, moving his lips up to her ear, "is impossible."

She looked down at her hand. "I don't know. Looks pretty possible to me," she said.

He moved his hand down between her legs and then ran it back slowly to the crease of her vagina. It was slick and wet, and her hips rose instantly to meet his hand.

"I mean us. We are impossible," he said as his finger penetrated her. "You shouldn't be with me. I shouldn't be with you."

Slowly, he worked the finger in and out.

"That's right," she said, timing the movement of her hand on his penis to match the movement of his finger inside her. "That's right."

"What's right?"

"I don't care," she whispered. "Right now, can't I just want you?"

She rolled on top of him, and when she kissed him, her tongue probed urgently and insistently inside his mouth. He felt her fumbling on the nightstand, and then suddenly she sat up, astride his thighs, her breasts swaying slightly, his erect penis standing in front of her. He watched her open the foil packet and sheath him in a condom.

Then slowly, deliberately, she lowered herself onto him, guiding his penis with one hand, propping herself on his ankles with the other.

He felt himself sliding into her, her internal muscles gripping him tightly, until he was completely inside and her pelvic bone ground against him.

For a long moment she sat like that, above him, quiet, eyes closed, her hair bathed in the morning light from the window.

Slowly, her head came back down toward his, and this time it was his tongue that was insistent and penetrating.

He thrust upward and she matched his slow rhythm.

"You feel even better this morning than you did last night," he whispered, and she responded by surrounding his head with both arms and hugging him tightly as they moved together.

He rolled her over without breaking the connection between them and found, when he propped himself on his elbows, that his shoulder was much improved by his night's rest.

Her rhythm quickened and then she was thrashing underneath him, dragging her fingers across his back and almost lifting him off the bed with the force of her climax. Responding to her, he finished.

They lay, almost gasping, side by side for a minute. Then she smiled and kissed him lightly.

"You're right," she said. "This is impossible. We shouldn't have done it. But I'm glad we did."

He kissed her back. "So am I." He paused. "Any chance you can quit your job?"

She laughed. "That's a possibility every morning."

He was curious. "Why'd you get into this business, anyway?"

"You want to know the real truth?"

"Only if it's entertaining."

"My mother's father. He came out of the South, worked for the post office. Raised six kids. Educated all of them. Taught 'em all that government work might not be great, but it's a better place for a black person than most others. So my mother became a public school teacher. And I . . ." Her voice trailed off.

"Yeah," he said, "but why . . . this particular branch?"

"Well, if you graduate with a degree in Russian studies, your choices are limited," she explained. "And I failed the State Department test on the oral section. I'm not the most diplomatic person in the world."

He laughed. "I hadn't noticed."

He knew, but could not say, that she had invited him into her bed for the wrong reasons. Maybe she saw in him the chance to let love redeem a drinker, the way she had no doubt wanted to redeem her father. Maybe it was just the oppressive loneliness of being a black woman, working undercover, in an alien land. Maybe it was just lust. Whatever it was, he feared it would be ephemeral. But he was grateful for it.

He wrapped his arms around her, hugged her, and looked at his watch over her shoulder. It was nearly mid-morning.

"We've got to get going," he said. "Who gets the first shower?"

"You," she answered. "I've got to check some things on the computer."

When he was dressed and drinking coffee, he turned on the radio she had in the kitchen and listened to the BBC news. The domestic news was just ending. Margaret Thatcher was hinting that she was available should the Tories wish to turn to a leader with charisma. Prince William had broken an ankle playing rugby.

The lead international news item caught his attention. In Moscow, the Duma had voted overwhelmingly to make the military answerable to the legislature, rather than the executive. President Yelichev had immediately issued a decree declaring the Duma's action unconstitutional. It was not clear who was running the Russian military anymore. The next item rehashed the previous day's

assassination story, and Burke listened until he was satisfied that
the BBC had uncovered nothing he had not already filed.

She came out of the bedroom wearing flowing black trousers
and a stark white blouse, with a loose, black leather vest over it.
Her parka was draped over one arm. She looked very fresh and
energetic.

She opened the refrigerator and produced a can of orange slices.
In Russia in midwinter, they were a great luxury. She spooned
them out into a bowl, and they moved to the small table that occupied a corner of her living room.

She handed him a couple of sheets of paper. "I downloaded
something from the Internet," she said. "I thought you might find
it helpful."

He looked it over. It appeared to be an encyclopedia article.

> LEDA: In Greek mythology, a beautiful and virginal young
> princess who was affianced to a Greek king, Tyndareos of
> Sparta. Prior to the consummation of this union, she bathed
> in a stream with her attendants. Zeus, watching from above,
> was taken with her beauty.
>
> Zeus summoned Aphrodite and enlisted her help in a ruse.
> He transmogrified himself into a swan and she into an eagle.
> They flew to the stream where Leda was bathing and pre
> tended that the eagle was attacking the swan.
>
> Leda, her sympathy aroused, ran to protect the swan.
> Once she was close, Zeus, as the swan, enfolded her in his
> wings and deflowered her. As a result of this union, she bore
> four children, hatched from eggs—Castor, Pollux, Helen, and
> Clytemnestra.
>
> According to some versions of the myth, she was later
> taken into heaven and became Nemesis, the goddess of retrib-
> utive justice.

Burke put the paper down. "Thanks," he said. "I can sort of see
Nadyezhda Petrovna as Nemesis."

"You're welcome," she replied. She paused. "Colin. There's one
thing."

"Yes?"

"Regardless of what I might have said in bed, as far as we're concerned, I'm an art gallery owner. Nothing more. Okay? It's important."

He sipped some coffee. "All you told me was that your grandfather worked for the post office."

"I shouldn't have told you that," she said. "Can I trust you?"

"I don't know," he said. "You certainly can trust me not to write that your grandfather worked for the post office. You can trust me not to write about you at all. Beyond that, I'm not sure I trust myself."

She smiled sadly. "In the end, it's business, isn't it? Business for you. Business for me."

"I don't know," Burke said. "Like I said, I can't trust anything anymore."

———————

They found Andrusha Karpov where Nadyezhda Petrovna had said he would meet them, next to the foreign tourists' ticket window on the first floor of the Hermitage.

"Perhaps you would like to hire a guide," he suggested. "I know museum very well."

"I think that would be a fine idea," Burke said. He turned to McCoy. "I seem to be very much in need of guides today."

She smiled sweetly. "Pay him," she said softly.

Burke frowned for a second, then understood. He reached into his wallet and extracted a five-dollar bill. Ostentatiously, he handed it to the pudgy Russian.

"So," Andrusha said, "what would you like to see first?"

"Italian Renaissance painting," Burke said.

"You know," Andrusha replied, "I was thinking of showing you French Impressionists."

Burke at first could not figure out whether Karpov was obtuse or merely had problems with English. Then he realized that it was neither. He simply wanted them to walk toward the French Impressionists.

They walked quickly to a staircase of white marble wide enough for a full-scale parade, half covered in a red carpet.

"This is Jordan staircase, designed by Rastrelli," Andrusha said, staying in his role as tour guide as they started to ascend. "Notice the allegorical statues representing Justice, Prosperity, and Mother Russia."

Burke looked. The staircase defined what nouveau riche had been in the eighteenth century. Mirrored windows, gilded friezes, and a ceiling mural competed for attention with the three statues Andrusha had pointed out.

"An unusual combination, those three," Burke said, but if Andrusha understood the reference, he felt no urge to reply.

They walked, then, through halls with two-ton bronze chandeliers, halls full of armor, galleries full of portraits of Russian warriors, galleries full of Rembrandts, halls full of porcelain and gold, and throne rooms edged in crimson and gilt. The sheer volume of the collection dulled Burke's observation. Nothing seemed special, and his surfeited mind stopped cataloguing the things that Andrusha duly pointed out as they passed.

Instead he started to notice the building's age: the windows with tiny cracks in them, the water stains on some of the wallpaper, the places where the parquet floors appeared to sag.

McCoy, though, seemed as fascinated by the fifteenth crucifixion painting they saw as she was by the first, and after a while Burke decided she really was. He envied her, slightly and silently. Art was one of the refinements of life he had never had the inclination to master.

They ascended another, plainer staircase, and suddenly the decor changed. The gilt and marble disappeared, and the walls were painted an austere gray.

"This is the collection of nineteenth and twentieth century paintings," Andrusha said. "For many years, when Stalin was in power and afterward, they were not allowed to be exhibited. They were very nearly destroyed." Andrusha smiled faintly. "Too decadent."

They turned a corner and confronted a large, brilliant canvas by Monet, a picture of a woman in a long white dress, with a white parasol, walking in a garden full of green grass and red flowers, flooded with sunlight.

"I see what he meant," Burke said. "Dangerously decadent."

Andrusha became serious. "It was Nadyezhda Petrovna's father who saved them," he said. "He kept stalling the bureaucrats who wanted them gotten rid of. Finally, they sent him to the camps in 1952. They say Stalin died just before he could sign the order to burn them."

"What happened to Nadyezhda Petrovna's father?"

"He was released in 1956. He very nearly died. His health was ruined."

"How did Nadyezhda Petrovna become paralyzed?" McCoy asked him.

"Polio," Andrusha said. "She got it when she was a young woman, when her father was away. About 1955 or 'fifty-six, I think."

"They didn't have vaccine, I guess," McCoy said.

Andrusha shrugged. "I don't know if they did. But certainly not for the child of an enemy of the people."

Andrusha paused by a small gray door set inconspicuously toward the end of the modern art gallery. He pulled a chain of keys from his pocket, selected one, and opened the door. He beckoned them to follow, then shut the door behind him and locked it again.

They entered a corridor much narrower than the grand hallways that linked the galleries. The walls were of plain white plaster, and the carpet on the floor was a standard Soviet runner, threadbare and grimy.

"This is the back way into the painting storage and conservation area," he said.

Burke looked around. There were half a dozen doors off this segment of corridor, all of them closed. Mounted above one of them, though, he saw a surveillance camera. A small red light glowed underneath the lens.

He stopped and grabbed Andrusha's elbow and cocked his head toward the camera. "Won't we be seen? I've already had the pleasure of meeting your director of security. I don't really want to meet him again."

Andrusha smiled proudly, like a kid showing off a particularly good science fair exhibit.

"I've diverted the transmissions from the cameras in this area," he said. "And substituted a loop of film that shows the ordinary people coming and going as they should."

Burke looked at him skeptically. "You sure?"

Andrusha nodded.

He turned to McCoy. "That possible?"

She nodded gravely, evidently impressed. They walked under the camera toward the far end of the corridor.

"The security director you met," Andrusha said. "What was his name?"

"Bykov," Burke said.

Andrusha's chubby face tightened and he nodded.

"You know him?"

"Yes," Andrusha said. "He's—I think he killed Fyodor Mikhailovich."

"He's a killer?" Burke asked.

Andrusha shrugged. "So people say. I've never asked him."

"Did he leave town for a couple of days recently?"

Andrusha looked surprised by the question. "I don't know," he said. "Why do you ask?"

"Just curious," Burke said.

Andrusha decided to accept that nonexplanation. He was intent on other things.

He stopped at the door at the end of the corridor and keyed a number into a locking device. There was a click as a bolt slid back. He pushed the door open.

The smell of oil paint filled Burke's nostrils. Then he noticed the light. They were in a studio the size of a small gymnasium, lit by four large skylights and a profusion of overhead lamps. Perhaps a dozen artists, most of them women, stood at separate workbenches. Each had a painting propped on an easel.

"This is the restoration department," Andrusha said.

McCoy stopped next to the first bench. A slight, pale woman in her mid-thirties was working on a landscape, depicting a white villa on the banks of a still, mirrorlike river. Blue-green trees surrounded the house, set against a purple and lavender sky.

"That's a Cezanne?" McCoy asked the artist.

The artist nodded. *"The Banks of the Marne."*

"It's a beautiful picture," McCoy said.

The woman dipped a tiny brush into a palette and began work-
ing on an area of trees. Her brush strokes were so small that at first
Burke was not sure she was actually applying paint to the canvas.
He stepped closer and determined that she was.

"You're painting over a Cezanne?"

The artist turned to him, a mildly amused smile cracking her
pallid face.

"Not painting over. Restoring. The paint had cracked and
chipped in this section."

McCoy was the only one who understood Burke's surprise.
"It's normal, Colin," she said. "Nadyezhda Petrovna explained it
to you."

"Yeah, but it's supposed to be a Cezanne," Burke said. "A conductor wouldn't just add a few bars of his own to the Fifth Sym-
phony and still call it Beethoven's."

McCoy smiled at his naiveté. "That's music, and this is painting.
Two different things. You can only hope that the restoration work
on a painting is very skilled."

"I can show another example," Andrusha said.

He walked over to the next bench, where another artist, this one
a woman in her sixties, was working on an enormous canvas, more
than seven feet tall and six feet wide. It showed a plump, naked
woman, leaning on a vase, confident and provocative. In front of
her a muscular Neptune, complete with trident, rose from the edge
of the sea. An angel placed a garland on each of their heads. The
painting was obviously old, but in its nonchalant sensuality, it
seemed modern. The woman was slowly retouching a conch shell
being blown by one of Neptune's entourage.

"This is *The Union of Earth and Water*, by Rubens," Andrusha
said. He turned to the restorer. "May I borrow it for a moment?"

The old woman smiled shyly and nodded. Casually, Andrusha
picked up the canvas by the wood frame on the back.

"How much do you figure that painting is worth?" Burke whispered to McCoy.

"More than you can afford," she whispered back.

"No. Really."

She shrugged. "Not many Rubens come on the market. I'd guess fifty million, but that's just speculation."

Burke shook his head. "And they just paint on it!"

McCoy shrugged. "They have to. Or it wouldn't be worth fifty million anymore."

Andrusha lugged the painting past them and said, "Follow me."

He opened a door to one side of the studio and walked in. They followed. It was a small room, barely bigger than a closet. Andrusha placed the painting on another easel.

Then he reached for a switch and flipped off the incandescent light. Another switch was flipped, and the room was bathed in the dim, purplish glow of ultraviolet light.

Andrusha gestured toward the painting. "Under this light, you can see how often the painting has been restored," he said. "The older paint is, the fainter it is under ultraviolet light."

Burke looked at the canvas. Under the ultraviolet light, nearly all the color had disappeared from the painting. The Rubens looked like some child had taken a brush wet with deep purple paint and sprayed it on the canvas. It was stippled with dots and slashes of varying shades of purple. As he looked, Burke realized that each dot or slash marked a spot where some restorer had added paint to Rubens's work. There was barely a square inch of the painting without some kind of mark on it.

Burke was appalled. "There's almost nothing left that Rubens painted," he said.

Andrusha flipped the normal light back on. McCoy responded to Burke.

"No," she said. "If there had been no restoration, the picture wouldn't now be what Rubens painted. It would have faded, cracked, deteriorated. I don't think that's what he would have wanted. He would have wanted good restorers to keep it as it was when he finished it."

She turned to Andrusha. "And the Hermitage restorers are among the best in the world."

Andrusha's chubby cheeks turned pink, and he bowed slightly.

He walked back into the main studio and returned the Rubens to the woman who was working on it.

"Now," he said, as if introducing the climactic act of a play, "follow me."

They walked straight through the rest of the studio without another stop and came to a door at the far end. Andrusha pulled a ring full of keys from his back pocket and selected a large, old-fashioned one with a long cylindrical stem and large notches at the end.

When the lock had turned, he knocked once. Lyuba opened the door.

They were in a smaller studio, with one skylight, but the same smell of oil and pigment that dominated the larger room. Nadyezhda Petrovna, in her wheelchair, sat in the middle of the room, facing two easels. Each easel held an identical version of the most beautiful painting Burke had ever seen.

"My God," McCoy said.

Whoever had posed for Leonardo had been a breathtaking young woman. She was slender, with gleaming brown hair, parted in the middle, done up partly in braids and partly left in tendrils that framed her face. Her skin was faintly flushed, her nose small and aquiline, and her lips sensuous. The artist had captured a remarkable expression on her face. Her eyes were cast down and slightly hooded, but combined with the evanescent smile on her lips, they conveyed equal and irretrievably mixed portions of innocence and passion.

She was gloriously naked, her body facing the viewer, breasts firm and high, belly rounded and fertile. She had draped her left arm behind the swan, which in turn had half enveloped her in its right wing. With her left hand she caressed the erect shaft of the swan's neck.

On the ground in front of them, four infants had just hatched from a pair of large eggs. Burke assumed they represented the four mythological characters in the encyclopedia article: Castor, Pollux, Helen, and Clytemnestra. Behind them was a rich and fertile landscape that could have been Greece but more likely was the Tuscan countryside.

Burke's eye took those details in but his brain barely registered them. He could not pull his attention away from the woman's face.

He had seen that expression, fleetingly, when he was younger, on women in love. He had never seen it captured before.

"You have a camera?" Nadyezhda Petrovna asked him abruptly.

Burke said nothing. Now he was staring at both paintings. One, he knew, was nearly five hundred years old. The other, presumably, had been painted within the past couple of months. He could see no differences between them. He thought that the aging process would be apparent in the older painting. But each had a network of fine cracks in the surface.

He walked around them, trying to detect something. But even from behind they were nearly identical. Each had been painted on a panel of aged, reddish-brown wood, and the back of each panel was marred with faded letters, in both Latin and Cyrillic characters.

"I asked if you have a camera," Nadyezhda Petrovna said again.

"Oh, um, sorry, yes," Burke said. He had a slender Nikon, which he always carried on road trips, in his coat pocket. He took it out and started trying to get the dots and needles lined up.

Then he shot the pictures, both by themselves and with Nadyezhda Petrovna sitting beside them. He changed film and shot some with another roll.

"You're going to have to tell me which is the original and which is the copy," he said, "so the picture caption can identify them."

"You cannot tell, can you?" Nadyezhda Petrovna said, sounding pleased.

"No," Burke admitted.

"But he's no expert," McCoy broke in. "The person with the money and interest to buy this picture will be. Or he'll hire experts. And they'll test it scientifically. I don't see how you expect to get away with this."

"You underestimate my mother," Lyubov responded, evidently miffed. "And Andrusha," she added.

McCoy ignored her. "Well, for example, they can test the age of the wooden panel it's painted on with carbon dating."

"We hope that they will," Andrusha said. "We took an old but almost worthless Italian painting on a panel from the same time as Leonardo. We sanded the painting off and used the panel for the copy. If they test it, they will find it is Italian poplar, just as Leonardo used, and five hundred years old."

Burke was more impressed than McCoy.

"Well, all right," she said. "But all good forgers use old canvases or wood panels. There are lots of other tests."

"And we're prepared for all of them," Andrusha said.

"But don't you think—"

McCoy's objection was cut short by an urgent whisper from Lyubov, who had drifted into the next room.

"It's Bykov," she hissed. "He's left his office. He's coming."

Nadyezhda Petrovna looked at her watch. "We have three minutes," she said to Andrusha.

She turned to Burke. "You have the photographs you need?"

He was reasonably certain. He had bracketed his exposures. He would have something publishable. He nodded.

McCoy asked, "How do you know he's coming?"

"We have a computer monitor in the next room," Andrusha said hastily. "It's hooked up to the surveillance cameras in the building."

Andrusha strode toward the paintings and looked at them carefully for a second. Then he took hold of the one on the left and looked inquiringly at Nadyezhda Petrovna. She nodded. He threw an old sheet casually over it.

"Follow me," Andrusha said.

Burke and McCoy fell in line behind him. He walked through the next room, where they saw the computer he had referred to. It was showing a black and white picture of the hall Burke remembered from outside Bykov's office. Andrusha stopped momentarily, hit a few keys on the keyboard, and the monitor abruptly switched to a screen full of text.

They exited into a narrower, darker corridor than the one that had led from the Impressionists' gallery. Burke's sense of direction was gone. He had no idea which way they were walking.

"These are supply storage rooms," Andrusha said, nodding vaguely to the closed doors that lined the hallway. "Old servants' rooms."

"How many rooms are there in this place?" Burke asked.

"More than a thousand," Andrusha answered.

He stopped by the last door in the corridor and waited for Burke to catch up. "Hold this," he said, and handed Burke the painting. "Careful."

The picture felt unexpectedly heavy in his hands. It was about four and a half feet high and three feet wide, and the wood of the panel was solid and heavy, almost oaken. As Andrusha had, he held it warily, trying to keep a firm grip without getting his fingers into the paint. He wondered, fleetingly, how much damage he could do if he dropped the painting or brushed it against a door frame. Say, a small crack or a scrape. Maybe fifteen million dollars' worth. At his present salary, he could pay that off in—

Andrusha interrupted Burke's calculations somewhere in the twenty-third century. He had produced another key and opened the door. He took the painting from Burke's hands again.

They entered a small, cluttered room that Burke imagined had been about the right size for a maid's room. It was lit, dimly, by a half window that seemed to be sliced off at the top by the palace's eaves. The ceiling sloped slightly down toward the outside wall. It was full of shelves, and the shelves contained a mélange of paints, rolled canvases, and brushes. Andrusha lugged the painting to the far end of the room and opened another door. He threw a switch. Burke and McCoy followed.

They found themselves in a tiny, steep staircase, perhaps three feet wide. Andrusha was carefully maneuvering the painting between the walls.

"This was a way for the chambermaid to get quickly downstairs to someone's bedroom," Andrusha said.

"To bring tea, no doubt," McCoy said.

"They had many duties," Andrusha replied vaguely.

They emerged what seemed like half a floor below the level of the studio into another empty corridor. This one was wider and, like the one outside the studio, had a red runner and a surveillance camera. Andrusha quickly strode to the third door on his left and again handed Burke the painting. He opened it.

"My lab," he said.

The room, about as large as Nadyezhda Petrovna's studio, was full of apparatus—microscopes, beakers, paint cans, a computer, and instruments Burke could not identify. One corner was filled by the oven that, a few days before, had been used to bake the fake picture.

Andrusha flipped a switch on the computer and tapped a few keys. In a moment the monitor showed a black and white image of the studio they had just left. Nadyezhda Petrovna and Lyubov, seen from overhead, were waiting. In a moment the door opened and Ivan Bykov walked in.

Burke watched the man go directly to the fake picture. He looked at it for a moment, said something to Nadyezhda Petrovna, and listened to a reply that, to them, was inaudible.

"Can't you get audio?" McCoy's question sounded demanding, but Burke heard a note of respect in her voice as well. Andrusha's technological skills had impressed her.

"The system doesn't have microphones or speakers," Andrusha explained, failing to catch the inflection in her voice and looking hurt. "All I can do is divert or replace what's in the system."

"I know," McCoy said. "It was a rhetorical question."

Andrusha looked puzzled by that phrase.

"Rhetorical means *nyekulturny*," Burke offered.

McCoy looked at him from under her eyelids. "Watch it," she said.

On the computer screen, Bykov seemed to finish his conversation. He left the way he came. Nadyezhda Petrovna and Lyubov stayed where they were.

In a moment two workmen entered the room, lugging an instrument the size of a coffee table, with a computer screen and a camera mounted to it.

"It's a camera for infrared reflectography," Andrusha said calmly. "It gives them a kind of Roentgen of the painting. The rays penetrate certain levels of the paint, but they do not penetrate the carbon in the underdrawing, for instance."

"What does that do?" Burke asked.

"They can see the underdrawing, and they can compare it to the underdrawings of other Leonardos," McCoy explained. "It's one of the main ways to examine a painting and detect forgeries."

"But they will find exactly what they should find," Andrusha said. "We have three Leonardos, the *Benois Madonna*, the *Madonna Litta*, and *Leda and the Swan*. We examined all of the underdrawings.

Nadyezhda Petrovna is an expert on Leonardo's method. She was able to duplicate it precisely."

He explained how they had copied Leonardo's technique of pricking holes in the preliminary drawing, then attaching it to the panel and swinging a bag full of charcoal dust against it to produce a dotted outline of the composition.

"But that's not all they'll test," McCoy objected.

"We know that," Andrusha said. "We're ready for whatever they can do. The painting that remains in the studio is, in practically every sense, a Leonardo. It is simply a Leonardo executed by Nadyezhda Petrovna."

"Forgers get caught, eventually," McCoy insisted stubbornly.

"No forger has ever worked with the resources we have," Andrusha said.

McCoy did not look convinced. She pulled the sheet away from the painting and looked at it for a long time. On the computer screen the workmen brought more instruments into Nadyezhda Petrovna's studio.

Finally, McCoy turned to Burke. "You know what really bothers me about this painting?"

"You don't like the way she's braided her hair," Burke said.

"No," she replied.

"If the thing gets sold and a scandal ensues, the Russian government would topple and Rogov would take over, meaning the end of the New World Order as we know it?"

"Don't joke about it," she said.

"Sorry," Burke replied. "I'm afflicted with terminal cynicism about the New World Order."

McCoy ignored that. "It's that this picture shows a woman who's been raped," she said. "And look at the expression on her face! It's the old male fantasy! She loved it!"

Burke shook his head sadly. "That Leonardo," he said. "He was such an insensitive brute."

Chapter Twenty-four

Charles Hamilton Merrill stood, arms folded, in a corner of Nadyezhda Petrovna's studio, nursing his anger. He was a man keenly sensitive to manifestations of status and prestige. He noticed where he was seated at dinner parties. He knew the pecking order of the Oxbridge colleges, and he used it to gauge the likely tastes of his clients. He showed due deference to those properly considered his superiors. And he expected a certain deference, in return, from those properly deemed his inferiors.

Consequently, he had not reacted well at all to Rafael Santera Calderon's detour to Munich to pick up Gerhardt Schlegel. It was not that he objected to Santera's decision to engage a technical expert to assess the picture. That was to be expected, especially when a buyer was about to invest four hundred million dollars in a picture with such an irregular provenance. He had, in fact, anticipated that Santera would want one.

He had already alerted a friend of his, the best technical consultant in Britain, a man with thirty years at the National Gallery, to stand ready to travel.

Then Santera informed him he'd already hired this German. Merrill intensely disliked Germans. It was a prejudice he'd picked up as a small child, during the bombing of London. The passage of time had only confirmed his opinion of them. Occasionally, he had German clients. They all reminded him of Hermann Goering. No doubt Herr Schlegel knew how to operate his computers and his microscopes. He was young, and young people knew about such things. And he was German, so he probably had a knack for operating machinery. But he was a boor.

That, he decided, was probably how Santera had found him. Through the International Network of Boors.

Merrill would have as little to do with him as possible. He would not participate in an inspection that could only be perceived as an insult to his own ability and integrity. He folded his arms more tightly around his chest and glowered. Preserving a grudge was a faculty he had long since developed to a high degree.

Schlegel, meanwhile, was busy with a razor. Carefully, he scraped a thin layer of wood off the back of the panel. He took it to a microscope, mounted it on a slide, and examined it. Then he opened a large catalogue he had carried into the studio with him and double-checked the image in the microscope against the images in the catalogue, which showed the grains and textures of different types of wood. This step, Merrill assumed, was purely for Santera's benefit, so Schlegel could show him that he was being meticulous. Any technician knew what the standard types of wood looked like under a microscope.

"It is Italian poplar," Schlegel said to Santera. "It might very well have come from the same grove as the panel for the *Madonna and Child* in the Alte Pinakothek. You would like to look?"

Santera was standing, as if transfixed by a vision, before the picture. He had been like that, more or less, since he entered the studio. Obviously, Merrill thought, the painting had engaged him. Enraptured might be a better word. Merrill had seen the same look, occasionally, on the faces of small boys when the queen passed by.

Bykov's sluttish niece, ostensibly a translator, stood nearby. She had not left Santera's side since he got off the airplane.

Merrill would have found more time to be appalled by Marina had he not been even more repulsed by her uncle, the hulking "director of security" for the museum. Merrill understood why Chavchavadze and his friends at the Ministry of Culture had had to install Bykov to monitor everything that happened until this painting left the country. But he found the man's presence in the Hermitage disgusting. For one thing, his body smelled. For another, he looked like a gorilla. The one percent commission he was getting on this sale, Merrill decided, was not nearly enough compensation for the kinds of people he was associating with. The room was cramped and close. Two of Santera's Colombian bodyguards lounged in a corner. Merrill sniffed. Whatever they ate in Colombia, it had lots of garlic.

Santera stepped, almost reluctantly, away from the painting and over to the table where Schlegel had set up his microscope. He peered into it. He saw what looked like elongated, translucent pieces of spaghetti.

"Ah, yes, I see," Santera said.

Merrill was not surprised that the wood matched. Schlegel would only be corroborating an authenticity that he had already determined, six weeks previously, in his own, strictly visual inspection. Merrill had encountered many forgeries in the course of his work. He had always found something clumsy in them that gave them away.

He had never encountered a machine that could take the place of an educated eye. But this was the age of high technology, and there was nothing he could do about it.

Schlegel took the slide out from the microscope, removed the plastic cover, and placed the tiny wood shaving in a metal canister about the size of a tin of caviar. He inserted the tin into the top of a gray metal apparatus that resembled a filing cabinet without handles. He hooked a plug from the back of the cabinet into his computer and flicked a switch.

"This machine will measure the carbon 14 in the sample, and that will tell us how old the wood is," Schlegel said to Santera.

"How does it work?"

"Living organisms produce an isotope of carbon called carbon 14," Schlegel explained. "Once they die, they stop producing it. It then begins to decay and turn into nitrogen at a steady, predictable rate. When you determine how much of the original carbon 14 in a sample remains, you can tell how old it is. Plus or minus fifty years."

The German began typing data and parameters into the computer.

Santera turned to Nadyezhda Petrovna. "I understand you had to make a small repair in the panel," he said.

Marina immediately began to translate the words into Russian. Merrill watched Nadyezhda Petrovna's face as she did. He suspected the old woman knew English well enough to do without a translator. He wondered why she chose to wait for Marina.

Nadyezhda Petrovna nodded as Marina finished her translation. She replied with several sentences in Russian.

"She says, yes, she did," Marina said.

Merrill snorted. Nadyezhda Petrovna probably knew more English than the translator did.

Santera pressed on, even though the information about the crack in the panel had been in his original report from Merrill. "What was the damage?"

Marina translated. Nadyezhda Petrovna replied. Marina hesitated, flustered.

"A, um . . ."

"Crack," Merrill offered.

Marina blushed slightly. "Yes, precisely. A crack about three millimeters in broad. It was in lower corner of picture on right. We sealed the back of the . . ."

She turned to Merrill again, obviously thinking that he spoke Russian.

"Panel," he suggested.

"Panel," she nodded, "and repaired paint on other side."

Merrill struggled successfully to repress another snort. Santera would get more information talking to the walls than he would through this doltish translator.

Schlegel finished tapping at his computer keys and turned to Santera. "The wood for this panel was cut between 1470 and 1530," he said.

Santera beamed. "Exactly!" he said.

Merrill sighed quietly, relieved. He knew that the dates would be right. But the eagerness in Santera's face dispelled his sole remaining fear, that the Colombian would see the painting and decide he did not want it. Clearly, he wanted it.

Schlegel beckoned to the two bodyguards, and together they moved a camera mounted on a tripodlike device to a position two feet in front of the painting. Schlegel spent a couple of minutes plugging jacks into various outlets, connecting the camera to the computer and disengaging the carbon-dating device. Then he turned to Santera.

"This is an infrared camera," he said. "It will show us the underdrawing."

He flipped some switches and the machinery began to hum quietly. An image appeared on the computer screen, and he beckoned to Santera to join him.

The picture on the screen vaguely resembled an X ray, except that black and white were not reversed. It was vague and ghostly, but it was quite evidently an outline of the figures on the painted canvas.

"You see, the infrared light penetrates the pigment layers of the painting and is reflected back by the white gesso layer at the bottom," Schlegel explained to the Colombian. "Except for substances containing carbon, which absorb the infrared waves. The computer processes what the painting reflects back, and it gives us this picture. Anything that contains carbon, such as a graphite or charcoal sketch, shows up on the screen."

He slid the camera upward along a pole attached to the tripod, and the image flickered and changed. Merrill could see that it was now focused on Leda's head.

"Do you see the dots?" Schlegel asked, and for the first time Merrill could detect a hint of excitement in his voice.

Santera leaned over and peered at the screen. "Yes, yes, I see them," he said, but his tone sounded dubious.

"You will see similar dots if you look at an infrared reflectograph of a Leonardo," Schlegel explained. "This was how he worked."

He explained Leonardo's method of attaching a drawing to the gesso-coated panel, pricking holes in the outline, and swinging a bag of charcoal dust at the drawing until the outline was transferred to the gesso.

"So this authenticates it?" Santera asked.

Schlegel shook his head. "It only means that it may be authentic," he said. "To test it some more, I am going to have to have a sample of the paint."

He picked up his razor again and approached the painting. For a moment he stood silently, trying to choose the spot where a missing fleck of paint would be most easily restored.

Nadyezhda Petrovna, watching warily from one side, began to wheel herself closer to the easel. As Schlegel extended his hand, she reached out and grabbed him by the wrist. He drew back, shocked.

"*Nyet!*" she said in a hoarse voice. Her eyes were wide with emotion. Merrill, startled by the sudden movement, thought she looked either angry, frightened, or both. He could not tell.

Schlegel froze where he was, then looked around in confusion, shocked that this frail, still woman could move so quickly.

Nadyezhda Petrovna, anger rising in her voice, snapped out a few abrupt Russian sentences to Santera.

"She says you have not bought picture and cannot take paint sample," Marina translated. She pondered for a moment. "She says sample can be taken only after picture is buyed."

Schlegel turned to Santera. "You said this would not be a problem."

Santera Calderon turned to Bykov, then to Marina. "Tell him if there is no sample, there is no deal," he said.

Marina translated.

Bykov glowered at the old woman. Then he said something to her in Russian. She cut him off, evidently before the end of a sentence.

Their argument ratcheted quickly upward, until Bykov was standing directly over the woman in the wheelchair and both were shouting. Merrill could only imagine what they were saying.

But he understood the situation perfectly when Bykov took the wheelchair, spun it around, and shoved it hard away from the painting. The old woman hurtled toward a workbench. At the last instant she managed to extend an arm and grab the edge of the bench. Otherwise, she would have plowed into it.

Merrill shuddered and swallowed and focused his attention intently on a Rubens that was being restored in the far corner of the room. It was a mediocre Rubens, he thought. But looking at it was far better than thinking about the people and the deal he had involved himself in.

Nadyezhda Petrovna sat for a moment, back turned to the rest of the room, trembling. Merrill thought she might be crying. He was considering whether to go to her and ask whether she was all right, but then she turned around. Her face was composed, her visage sterilized. She looked like someone whose emotions were being held under thorough restraint. She said nothing.

Lyubov moved quickly to her mother's side and took her hand, glaring at the men in the room with undisguised hatred.

Bykov looked at them, then dropped his eyes to the ground. He gestured to Schlegel to go ahead, and the German picked up his razor. Delicately, he removed a few flakes of paint from one of the eggshells at the bottom of the picture, then a few flakes more from some daffodils around Leda's ankles.

Chapter Twenty-Five

ANDRUSHA KARPOV STARED SILENTLY AT THE television picture on his computer monitor. Then he turned to Burke and McCoy.

"He's making test samples out of the paint flecks he took from the picture," he said.

"How long will that take?" Burke asked.

Andrusha grimaced. "I'm not sure. When I test paint samples, I embed them in a block of clear resin. It takes eight or ten hours for the resin to harden so I can use it with the instruments. But I've heard that in the West they have a new plastic that hardens much more quickly."

McCoy pointed to the monitor. "Look. Most of them are leaving."

On the screen, Burke could see Santera, his bodyguards, Bykov, and Merrill putting on coats and getting ready to leave. Only Nadyezhda Petrovna and Schlegel remained.

He looked at his watch. It was seven in the evening. The Hermitage had been officially closed for two hours.

McCoy asked, "Leaving for dinner or for the night?"

"I'll bet just for dinner," Burke said. "I suspect they're going to work straight through till this deal is done."

"I can find out," Andrusha said. "Assuming this expert doesn't speak Russian."

Andrusha left his lab and they heard his keys slapping softly against his chubby hip as he maneuvered through the storage room leading into the corridor and back to Nadyezhda Petrovna's studio. In a moment Burke and McCoy saw him on the computer monitor, entering the studio, shaking hands with Schlegel and conversing briefly with Nadyezhda Petrovna. In another minute he was back.

"They have gone three hours, for dinner," Andrusha said. "They'll return around ten. The expert is a German, from the Alte Pinakothek in Munich. His samples will be ready to test by then. Nadyezhda Petrovna sent Lyubov home, she said. She's supposed to stay there until we call to have her pick us up."

"Bykov gone to dinner, too?" Burke asked.

"As far as I know."

"That ring of keys you carry," Burke said. "Can you open any door in the building?"

Andrusha was immediately suspicious. "Why do you want to know?"

"I collect all the details I can," Burke said. "How'd you come by them?"

Andrusha hesitated, apparently deliberating whether to reveal yet another secret.

Then he said, "They belonged to Nadyezhda Petrovna's father. During the war and the siege of Leningrad, all of the paintings and the small objects were moved, to the Urals, where the fascists couldn't reach them. But many things had to remain—carriages, armor. And the Winter Palace itself had to be protected. The commissars, of course, all fled to Sverdlovsk with the paintings. But some of the staff remained. They lived in the basement. They nearly starved. At night, they would go out on the roof with buckets and put out any fires that broke out when German shells landed. And Nadyezhda Petrovna's father was the director of that staff."

"And after the war, he kept the keys?"

Andrusha nodded. "When he died, Nadyezhda Petrovna got them. And then she gave them to me."

McCoy broke in. "Wait a minute. You mean they haven't changed the locks since 1944?"

The right side of Andrusha's mouth curled upward in a half smile. "That's hard for you to understand, probably. But only the KGB could change locks. They had no reason to. Since 1991, of course, the KGB has not been here. But there was no money for proper new locks."

"So you have the run of the building?" Burke asked. "Including Bykov's office?"

"That, too," Andrusha affirmed.

"Oh, no," McCoy said. "Colin, you can't go down there. It's too dangerous."

She turned to Andrusha. "Aren't there guards moving around? Night watchmen? Alarms?"

"Yes," Andrusha said. "In the galleries. At the entrances to the building."

"But not in the administration wing," Burke said.

Andrusha shook his head.

"And you could get me down there without going through the galleries or past the entrances, couldn't you?"

"I could," Andrusha said.

"But you won't," McCoy broke in. "It's too risky. It's not necessary."

Andrusha looked dubious. "I think she's right," he said to Burke.

"Andrusha," Burke argued, "I need to look in that office. If I find what I think I might find, I could write a story that the police would have to act on. It might keep Bykov from harming others. It might keep him from harming Lyubov and Nadyezhda Petrovna. It might get him arrested. Or do you want to continue to let him run this place?"

It was the right button to push.

"All right," Andrusha said. "I'll take you."

"The hell you will!" McCoy was angry. She turned to Burke. "Just what do you think you're going to find?"

"I'm not sure," Burke said, getting up from his chair. "Airplane tickets. A passport with a visa. Something."

"And what does that do?"

He thought of the story he was going to write. "It fills in a hole," he said.

"A hole," she said. "We're sitting here with a four-hundred-million-dollar painting, the Russian government is teetering, and he talks about filling in holes."

"It's what I came here to do," Burke said.

"Don't do this, Colin," she said. "You're going to get a great story if you play it smart. Be smart."

"If I were smart," Burke said, "I would've gone to medical school."

He and Andrusha moved toward the door.

"Shit," McCoy said. "I'd better come with you."

He wondered, briefly, if she were coming along because she cared what happened to him, or because she wanted to limit any damage he might cause. He decided it was a naive question.

They moved out into the darkened corridor and headed in the opposite direction from Nadyezhda Petrovna's studio. Very soon, Burke had no idea where they were. As silently as they could, they walked on, following Andrusha's slow, waddling gait. The hallways they traversed were dark, in some cases pitch-dark. In others, a single lightbulb burned.

The Winter Palace at night, Burke realized, was not a silent place. There were the occasional creaks as their feet pressed down on a loose floorboard. The building seemed to shift and rumble quietly. Twice he heard faint thumping and scurrying that seemed to come from the walls and ceilings.

They passed a window, and he could see the Neva outside, its icy surface faintly reflecting the lights from the buildings on the opposite bank. After about five minutes they came to a door. Cautiously, Andrusha unlocked it and opened it about four inches.

"This is the Teatralnaya staircase," he whispered. "It leads to the administrative wing."

The stairs were of marble, but in the dim light it appeared to be a plainer, grayer marble than the brilliant white stone in the Jordan staircase.

Carefully, they inched down the stairs. They seemed, Burke thought, to go on interminably.

Then they heard someone else's footsteps. They were coming from the gallery to the left of the staircase. Two shoes slapping on the parquet floor, coming closer.

"Quick," McCoy hissed. "Get behind the stairs!"

She grabbed the marble banister and vaulted lightly and easily down to the floor, bypassing the last six steps. Burke followed her. He landed with an audible thud. Andrusha did not try to vault. Quickly, clumsily, he tried to step over the banister and lower himself, but he caught his toe in the space between two balustrades. For a long moment he hung there, one leg still up on the banister, wriggling frantically.

The footsteps grew closer, and Burke could see the pale light of a flashlight in the crack underneath the double doors that separated the gallery from the staircase. He heard the sound of a key in the lock.

He reached up, grabbed Andrusha around the waist and jerked backward.

All of Andrusha's heavy body toppled backward into Burke's arms, save for his right foot, which remained wedged in between the balustrades. Burke grunted and felt his knees buckle. He held his breath and tried to squat slowly, drawing Andrusha down below the level of the staircase. He put his right hand on the floor for balance, and his shoulder began to burn again.

The door opened and the beam of a flashlight poked into the staircase area. It probed up the far wall and then up the staircase, flicking quickly between the balustrades.

Burke's thighs began to tremble as he struggled to hold the load he was carrying. He could not see the door, because his head was jammed into Andrusha's fleshy back. He caught the faint whiff of fear and perspiration from above.

The flashlight beam withdrew. The door closed. A moment later they heard the sound of the lock turning again, and then the footfalls as the guard walked away.

"Jesus, get his foot out of there," he gasped, twisting his face toward McCoy.

She leapt up and quietly unlaced Andrusha's shoe. Then she helped him extricate his foot from the shoe.

Andrusha slipped backward, and his entire weight fell on Burke. Burke toppled to the floor. The back of his head slammed against the marble. Stunned, he lost consciousness.

He came to a few seconds later. McCoy was squatting over him, a cool hand pressed to his neck. He blinked his eyes. He realized she was checking for a pulse.

"I'm all right," he said. His words sounded to him like they were being spoken underwater. "I never knew this cloak and dagger stuff could be such fun."

McCoy laughed softly. "Burke," she said, patting him on the cheek. "If I'm not careful, I might start to like you."

Burke shook his head. The little dots of light stopped blinking on the back of his retinas.

She grabbed his hands and helped pull him to his feet. Together, they lifted up Andrusha, who had rolled off Burke to the right.

Burke leaned against the staircase for a moment until he was certain he had his balance again. Then Andrusha produced a key and unlocked the door on the opposite side of the staircase area from the door the guard had opened.

There was only the dimmest of light coming through some dirty windows that opened into an internal courtyard. But Burke could vaguely make out the shapes of the lamps that identified this corridor as the one he had visited three days before.

They stopped in front of a door just down the hall from the director's suite. Andrusha fumbled for yet another key. They heard the sound of footfalls on the floor above. The hair on the back of Burke's neck stood up. His head throbbed sympathetically.

The door yielded to the third key Andrusha tried, and they were inside. It was a room about two-thirds the size of Vasiliev's office. Burke pulled down the shade and turned on the light.

The desk was standard Soviet Utilitarian, made of some unpolished blond wood. It reminded Burke of the desks the teachers had in his elementary schools. There were three phones, a calendar, and one of St. Petersburg's local smut tabloids on the desk surface. A file cabinet stood in the corner.

"Okay, look quick," McCoy said. "Let's not press our luck."

Burke tried the desk drawers. They were locked.

"You wouldn't have a key to this, would you?" he asked Andrusha. Andrusha shook his head.

McCoy pulled something that looked like a small penknife from her pocket. She slid it into the space between the top of the drawer and the desktop, worked it vigorously for a few minutes, and then slid the drawer open.

Burke's eyebrows rose, suitably impressed.

"All in the wrists," she said.

Burke slowly went through the contents of the drawer. All of the papers appeared to predate Bykov's arrival at the Hermitage. There were schedules for security guards that dated back to 1993. There were bits of paper with odd letters and telephone numbers written on them. There were receipts, in Russian, for deliveries of some kind of supplies. None of it meant anything to Burke.

McCoy, meanwhile, was pawing quickly through the filing cabinets.

"Nothing," she said as she closed the last cabinet drawer. "Just museum records. Check for yourself if you like, but make it fast. We need to get out of here."

Burke shook his head. He felt strangely relieved. He had done everything he could have possibly done to find corroboration for his suspicions, to find an individual to blame for what had happened to Jennifer Morelli. His best effort had failed. But he had tried. Now he could perhaps set aside the gnawing little question that had played in the back of his mind as they descended the Teatralnaya staircase: What would he have done if they had found some evidence?

He closed the desk drawer and got up to go. McCoy fell in step next to him, but suddenly she stopped. He glanced at her and could see that something in the corner of the room had caught her eye. He followed her gaze to the coat rack that stood to the left of the door.

It was empty, save for one thing: a Washington Redskins cap.

Chapter Twenty-six

IVAN BYKOV SHUDDERED. HE HAD NOT FELT THIS sense of anticipation and danger in a long time, not since the first couple of times he smuggled icons out of the country on wrestling trips, back when there was still a Party and a KGB and getting caught was not something a bribe could fix. Before that, he remembered this same edginess in the waiting hours before a few big bouts, like the Olympic trials. He remembered the same thirst for something to happen in the dead hour as he waited, his little red singlet on, his muscles warm, his body sweating. It had always been a precursor of his best efforts, a sign that he was not only going to win, but to dominate, to punish an opponent, and then pin him when the man's will was gone and he could be turned over onto his back like a roach, wriggling weakly, helplessly.

He reveled in the feeling. For the first time in three days his head felt free of pain.

Then he turned to Marina, who was sitting on a small divan next to him, and the feeling curdled. She was avidly examining the bright red polish on her fingernails. He wondered, for a moment, whether she could ever look any different, even if he scrubbed the paint off her face and put her in quiet, modest clothing. He doubted it. The girl had slut in her genes. Her father, whoever he was, must have been an asshole.

"Go on upstairs to Santera's suite and remind him it's time to go," he growled at her.

She looked at him in silent contempt and stayed where she was.

He wanted to yank her by the hair and slap her sneering face until she ran up the stairs, weeping, to do as he told her. But he couldn't, not in a hotel lobby.

He lowered his voice but tried to put enough threat in it to get her off her ass. "Go upstairs and tell Don Rafael and the others that we are ready to take them to dinner," he said again.

"No," she said.

Bykov felt an angry flush spreading up his neck. "Do as I say," he snapped.

Lazily, she rose. "I'll use the house phone," she said.

He stepped toward her, then stopped. "The house phone?"

"Uncle," she said, laughing at him. She patted his cheek. "Any good hotel has one. It's for calling inside the hotel."

The vessels in his chest seemed to constrict, and for a moment he felt light-headed with anger and shame.

"You would know!" he hissed at her.

Marina was intelligent enough not to provoke him further with another wisecrack. She walked slowly, languidly, across the lobby and picked up the phone.

As the small caravan rolled through the streets of St. Petersburg, tires thrumming on the packed snow, Bykov tried to avoid being caught staring at the attaché case on Santera's lap. It was simple and black, with brass locks and a combination. It could have been carried by any of the middle-class Swedes and Finns who came to Russia in search of business opportunities.

But he had noticed that one of Santera's bodyguards, the one called Miguel, never strayed more than a foot from the attaché case. Miguel had carried it down to the lobby and then out to the limo, in fact, before placing it on his boss's lap and climbing into the seat beside him. Bykov was sitting on the jump seat.

The attaché case, Bykov thought, probably contained the two million dollars he insisted on being paid in cash as his share of the deal. Everyone else would be paid by wire transfers to bank accounts in Vienna and Zurich. He wanted cash. He wanted to feel his money, to be able to touch it.

And he wanted more. The more he thought about it, the less happy he was with his share. Some damned *chinovniki* sitting in Moscow offices would be getting more than he would, simply for turning a blind eye. He was the one making sure that the deal went through. He was the one taking the risks. He deserved more.

His headache blossomed forth in all its fierce intensity, and he put a stubby hand to his eyes and rubbed them.

Marina shifted on the seat in front of him, opening her legs. She was sitting between Santera and Miguel, and her skirt rose halfway to her crotch. He could see the white, glutinous flesh of her thighs above her stockings. In another two years, maybe three, he thought, she would start getting as fat as his sister. It was the only pleasant thought that had occurred to him in the past fifteen minutes, and he almost smiled.

They crossed the Neva on the Liteyny Bridge and turned right, traveling at about a hundred kilometers an hour. Bykov peered through the rear window to make certain that the trailing cars made the turn correctly. There were two of them: a Mercedes that Miguel had insisted had to be driven by one of the Colombians, which followed immediately behind Santera's car; and a Volvo, in which the broker, Merrill, and more Colombians were riding.

They entered a quarter of St. Petersburg that even Bykov, growing up, had deemed a dangerous place to walk around in alone at night. It was a neighborhood of squat, five-story apartment buildings, pre-Revolutionary homes that had been divided and subdivided into communal flats, four and five families sharing a kitchen and a bath, vomit in the hallways and no privacy, ever. Interspersed with them were the grimy brick walls of small factories, many of them abandoned now that the Ministry of Defense no longer ordered millions of bolts and gears and axles every year. Bykov watched Santera as the Colombian observed the passing scenery. If it surprised him, he gave no sign.

The driver slowed as they reached the gate to one of the old factories. Someone inside flipped a switch, and the gate swung smoothly open. Bykov had watched, a year ago, when the gate was installed. He had seen the concrete poured underground, seen the steel reinforcements. He knew that if the limo driver or, say, a driver with a truck full of dynamite, had tried to ram through the gate, he would be crushed like a fly slamming into a window. The gate would not give way to a tank.

A new sign over the gate said ALL-RUSSIA INDUSTRIES. Otherwise, the place looked like nothing new had been built since Stalin's death.

The limo slowed and stopped in the courtyard outside the administration office. Bykov peered out the window. To his surprise, Chavchavadze was waiting outside to greet them. Normally, he waited for guests inside. He enjoyed watching the reaction on their faces when they stepped into the world he had created within the dingy brick walls.

Chavchavadze, hatless, his breath frosting in the night air, stepped forward and opened the limo door. Bykov scrambled out and then waited until Marina and the two Colombians had exited.

"Welcome to St. Petersburg and my little enterprise," Chavchavadze said to Santera. They shook hands, but quickly. The Colombian appeared anxious to get inside.

Inside, after the initial, welcoming gush of warm air, the surprises were visual. Chavchavadze had decreed that his headquarters would replicate the look and tone of a discreet Zurich law firm he once had visited. And after a year of construction, with the expensive help of a Swiss contractor, it did. The walls were paneled in dark, mellow wood that the contractor had found in an old bank building in Vienna. The chairs were overstuffed leather, carefully made copies of nineteenth century originals. The lighting came from recessed wall sconces. The carpet was plush, maroon, and unostentatious. The centerpiece of the reception area was a huge marble fireplace, in which a half-dozen birch logs were crackling brightly. The decor conveyed warmth, solidity, and prosperity, an impression made all the stronger by the contrast with the surrounding streets.

Two men in uniform frock coats that looked like they'd been liberated from the costume closet of a theater somewhere acted as

butlers, one taking overcoats and the other serving crackers spread
with butter and caviar and champagne in fluted glasses. They had
straight, thick black hair and dark features. Bykov assumed they
were Ossetians, part of the small army of men from the Caucasus
who filled the ranks of Chavchavadze's organization.

Slema Chavchavadze was dressed in clothes that Bykov had not
seen before, a tweed coat, striped tie, and gray slacks. He was trying to look like a proper Englishman. Bykov thought he would
never pull it off. His face would always give him away. But he was
not going to say as much.

He took a glass of champagne and a cracker spread with caviar.
The caviar was the best—smooth, shiny, with a gray sheen—and
he gobbled it down quickly. Then, with reluctance, he sipped some
of the champagne. It tasted unexpectedly dry, so dry that at first he
was not sure it was even wine. He finished it off. It was good, but
he preferred vodka with caviar.

The room was nearly full of people. Chavchavadze's ballerina
had brought a few of her friends, and they were pairing off with
the Colombians. Only the devil knew what they would say to one
another, or in what language.

Chavchavadze had one arm around Santera's shoulder and he
was talking animatedly. Bykov sidled close enough to hear.

". . . enormous growth," Chavchavadze said. "We are going to
have new opportunities in armaments, in metals, in lumber. There is
no better place in the world for investment right now than Russia."

Marina slowly translated.

"Maybe if you're a Russian," Santera replied. "But I have a
friend in the shoe business who came here and tried to start a joint
venture. He spent three million dollars, and *phfft*." He gestured
dismissively with his right hand, imitating a balloon with a leak.

Marina looked at him quizzically. She translated for a moment,
then stopped. She asked, "*Phfft* means nothing?"

Santera nodded and smiled at her. Bykov could see he was looking down the front of her dress.

"Nice translator you have," Santera added.

Marina simpered.

Chavchavadze's smile was broad. He patted Marina on the buttocks. "Thank you. I hope she's accommodating you in every way."

Marina translated again, stepping close enough to Santera to let her breasts brush against his arm and leaning in close to his ear. Bykov's anger fed on the frustration he felt at being unable to intervene. He would never try to do her a favor by asking her to translate again.

Chavchavadze returned to business. "Your friend's problem was he didn't start the joint venture with me," he said. "Just as I would not try to go into business in Colombia without you as a partner. You shouldn't try here without me."

Santera returned a polite nod and half smile. Chavchavadze clinked his champagne glass against the one in Santera's left hand.

"To partnership," Chavchavadze said.

The Colombian nodded and took a sip. "But what about the government? Does this assassination mean a change in policy?"

Chavchavadze's answering smile said that he had a delicious secret that he would like to share but could not.

"I think it's safe to say that the government may soon change," he said. "And I think it's safe to predict that the new government will be very easy to work with."

"Rogov?"

Chavchavadze nodded. "An old friend of ours. Of course, you know his role in a lot of what you've already bought."

Santera clinked his glass against Chavchavadze's. "To export licenses," he toasted.

"To friends in government," Chavchavadze replied. "And now I see it's time for dinner."

Chavchavadze's cook had stepped into the room. Like the servants, she was also an Ossetian, a round little woman whose hair was pulled back into a tight bun. Her parents, Bykov knew, had worked for Chavchavadze's father when he was Party first secretary in the Caucasus region. She cooked Georgian style, and the occasional invitation to eat in Chavchavadze's private dining room was one of the things that made working for the man tolerable.

The dining room, Bykov saw, had been laid in with new linen, china, crystal, and flatware, imported for the occasion from England, probably. One long table had replaced the three round tables that normally occupied the room, and new art had been hung on the walls—English hunting scenes, with dogs and horses and riders in red coats. A fire flickered in the fireplace at the end of the room.

And there were place cards, another innovation. Sullenly, Bykov looked for his name. It was down toward the bottom of the table, wedged in between two of Santera's bodyguards, far from the ballerinas, far from the power at the head of the table. He sat, trying to keep his attention focused on the food, not the hierarchy. But his jaws ground rapidly together, making his pudgy cheeks almost spherical.

After the third course, and the fifth round of drinks, the Ossetians began to sing.

It began with one of the bodyguards, who sang in a high, keening tenor, a shepherd's lament that only people of the Caucasus understood. After a few bars one of the servants joined in, singing a slightly different melody, in counterpoint to the first. Then a third, and a fourth, until all the Ossetians in the room, including Slema Chavchavadze, were on their feet, singing loudly. It was not a round, it was not harmonious, but it was somehow moving, at least to the Colombians. Bykov hated it. He always called it nigger singing, though never to his employer's face. He swallowed a glass of champagne with one long pull and refilled his glass.

When the song was over, Santera said something to Miguel, who shook his head no. Santera said something else, and Miguel rose to his feet, unsteady. He began to sing. In a minute all the Colombians were singing, a song that made the Ossetians sound gifted. Bykov swallowed another glass of champagne.

When the song was over, Chavchavadze and Santera applauded loudly. The rest of the room joined in. Then Bykov saw Santera say something to Marina. He pulled out a wallet and handed her money. Bykov couldn't see the denomination, but he knew the color. Dollars.

She shook her head, and Santera pulled two more bills off a roll he carried in his pocket. This time Marina nodded. Then Santera leaned over and whispered in Miguel's ear. The bodyguard grinned and nodded.

Marina and Miguel both stood up, slightly unsteady, and started walking toward the door at the back of the dining room. The Colombians, who had seen their leader reward men in this way before, began to holler and whoop. In a second the Ossetians caught on. They added to the din.

It was more than Bykov could tolerate. He stepped in front of Marina.

"Where are you going?" he demanded, hissing.

"None of your business," she snapped.

"It is so my fucking business," he screamed at her. He slapped her, hard, and knocked her to one knee.

In the corner of his eye he could see Miguel reach inside his jacket pocket. Bykov's arm was quicker. With the back of his hand he almost stove in the Colombian's jaw, knocking him against the paneled wall. Miguel sank to a sitting position, head propped against the wall, blood dribbling from his mouth.

In an instant four guns, all small, gleaming black Uzis, were trained on Bykov, who stood, defiantly, panting slightly.

Santera, scowling furiously, stood up so abruptly from the table that he knocked his wineglass over. He was trembling, on the verge of giving an order to shoot.

"Wait!" Chavchavadze shouted at the Colombians.

With a gesture of his right hand, Santera bade his bodyguards to wait.

"Forgive us, but she's his sister's child," Chavchavadze said to Santera.

Santera's angry scowl slowly faded into a grim frown as he thought the situation over. He nodded curtly, then said something in Spanish to his men. They put their guns away and one of them went over to tend to Miguel.

Santera sat down. As he did, he stared coldly at Bykov until Bykov got a clear message. This was not over.

Bykov stared back. Fine, he thought. He would be happy to have a reckoning—after he got his money.

The dinner party, obviously, was ruined. Chavchavadze did the only thing he could.

"I suggest," he said, "that we go back to the Hermitage and watch your man finish his tests."

Marina, her left eye swelling, translated.

Grimly, Santera nodded his assent.

———————

Schlegel's equipment had spilled out of Nadyezhda Petrovna's studio and into the conservation department's main workroom. The instrument he was using now reminded Bykov of the instrument console in an airplane. It was as big as a small car, and covered with screens and dials.

"This is an electron scanning microscope," Schlegel was explaining to a small knot of people that included Santera, Chavchavadze, Merrill, and Marina, who was now translating into Russian for the benefit of Chavchavadze. None of the four had spoken to Bykov since he'd punched out Miguel. The atmosphere in the room was painfully tense.

"If you look at this image, you can see the grains of pigment from the sample I took," Schlegel said. He pointed to a computer monitor built into the console.

The four pressed around to look, leaving no room for Bykov. Scowling, he stepped to one side and peered between Merrill's and Marina's shoulders.

"This is the yellow pigment that is a main component of the paint used for the daffodils," Schlegel said.

It looked to Bykov like a badly focused picture of a head of cabbage.

"It is Florentine ocher, of the type used in Leonardo's region of Italy in the fifteenth and sixteenth centuries," Schlegel said. "I have seen it in our *Madonna and Child* as well as in other paints of the period."

Santera asked, "But not used now?"

"No," said Schlegel. "It's not made anymore."

For the first time since his bodyguard had been knocked out, Santera's face softened. "Good," he grunted. "So what other tests do you have?"

"There is one other that I could do if we had this picture in Munich," Schlegel said. "A Fourier transform microscopy would analyze the organic material in the paint and identify the medium used—linseed oil or whatever. But you didn't want to charter a second plane and we couldn't fit it into the plane we used."

"Couldn't charter one," Santera corrected him. "There wasn't another one available on short notice."

"Couldn't," Schlegel agreed.

"So what's your decision? Is it a genuine Leonardo?"

Schlegel smiled. "Well, that's a complicated question," he said.

Santera's patience evaporated. "I'm not paying you to tell me it's complicated. Is it by Leonardo?"

Schlegel swallowed and nodded like a man who already knew how he would spend the money he would get for this job.

"The tests demonstrate that this painting was produced in Italy during the period when Leonardo was alive," Schlegel said. "The underdrawing and the brushwork are consistent with Leonardo's style, as I've seen it in our *Madonna and Child* and in other established Leonardos that have been tested. While you were gone, I even found some fingerprint traces in the paint. We don't know what Leonardo's fingerprints were, but we know he manipulated wet paint with his fingers to get some of the effects he wanted."

"So. Your conclusion?"

Schlegel smiled again, trying to mollify his client. "I've seen the drawings, the preliminary sketches Leonardo did for Leda. They're in the Windsor Library in England. They match perfectly the beautiful head and shoulders of Leda in this painting."

"And?"

"And that's as far as I can go," Schlegel said. "I am an expert in the science of painting. I agreed to conduct tests on this painting. I have done them. They suggest that the painting is genuine. And I believe it is genuine."

Chavchavadze broke into a smile when he heard the final sentence. He clapped Santera on the shoulder. Bykov's lungs expelled a gush of air. He looked around to see where Santera had deposited his briefcase. The money was almost his now.

Schlegel raised a hand. "But," he said, "I am not a Leonardo expert. I'm a technician. Mr. Merrill is the Leonardo expert. Let him have the final word."

Charles Hamilton Merrill nodded at Schlegel, evidently pleased at this ultimate recognition of his own irreplaceable expertise. For

the first time since arriving in St. Petersburg, his face lost its look
of offended dignity. For the first time since his previous visit, he
deigned to approach the picture, which had been moved, on its easel, from Nadyezhda Petrovna's studio.

He would, Bykov guessed, give the client his money's worth, examining it slowly and carefully. Bykov scowled. More time would
pass before he got his money. And what was the point? Merrill had
spent a day and a half with the picture six weeks ago. If he hadn't
decided it was genuine, he wouldn't have brought the damn Colombians here to buy it.

To his surprise, Merrill walked behind the painting and began to
examine the back of the wooden panel. He stayed behind the picture for a long time. After a while Bykov noticed that he had
pulled out a small magnifying glass and was rapidly scanning.

When Merrill finally emerged from behind the painting, he
looked as if he had just been sentenced to spend the rest of his life
panhandling on a heating grate outside Buckingham Palace. His
face was pale and his jaw was slack. The magnifying glass in his
hand was visibly shaking.

"What is it?" Santera demanded.

Merrill straightened slowly, struggling to maintain some
composure.

"I regret . . ." he said, and his voice trailed away. "I regret to
say that . . ."

Santera stepped forward and grabbed Merrill's coat lapels. His
face was contorted. "What?"

"Well, my initial. I scratched my initial C on the panel in the
back. I sometimes do this with a painting I admire, with an important painting. Very small. Discreet. So, in the future, people will
know I played a role?"

"Yes?" Santera still had hold of Merrill's lapels. But now, guessing what was ahead, he dropped his arms and let Merrill go.

"It's not there," Merrill said, his voice scratchy. "It's not there.
I looked everywhere."

"So?" Santera demanded.

"So," Merrill said, swallowing. "I can only conclude that this is
not the picture I saw six weeks ago."

Chapter Twenty-seven

SLEMA CHAVCHAVADZE PRIDED HIMSELF ON having the wit to wriggle out of deteriorating situations, and this one had certainly deteriorated rapidly.

"Wait," Chavchavadze said to Santera. "I'm sure we can straighten this out."

Marina translated. Santera stopped in the act of putting on his overcoat. His tanned face remained flushed red with anger.

Chavchavadze turned to Merrill. "You're certain that you saw a different painting six weeks ago?"

Merrill nodded, too shocked to speak.

"And it was genuine?"

Merrill nodded again.

Chavchavadze turned to Bykov. "And you're certain that this original painting has not left the Winter Palace?"

"Absolutely," Bykov said. "All the exits are monitored."

"Well, then, it appears obvious that the painting is still here," Chavchavadze said. He was the soul of reason and civility.

"Bullshit," Santera said.

Marina, after a second's hesitation, translated.

Santera pointed at Chavchavadze. "You tried to screw me with a fake."

The finger moved to Bykov. "Or he did. I'm sure you've got the real painting hidden away. You probably have another buyer lined up for it."

He turned bitterly to Merrill. "If it ever existed."

"It was real," Merrill whined. "It was real."

Chavchavadze addressed Bykov. "Make sure all the exits are sealed," he said.

Bykov relayed the order to Sasha, who turned on his heel and began implementing it.

Chavchavadze turned back to Santera. "We have too much to lose by making you angry," he said. "This is not our doing. I think it's hers." He pointed to Nadyezhda Petrovna.

Santera seemed to reconsider. "Take some of my men," Santera said. He said something in Spanish, and three Colombians joined Sasha.

Chavchavadze turned to Nadyezhda Petrovna. She'd watched the events of the past few minutes with an impassive face. Only the fluttering of her blunt fingers along the wheels of her chair betrayed her anxiety. She had no way to run, of course.

Chavchavadze sidled slowly up to the wheelchair. He addressed her in a voice that was all the more menacing for being so gentle.

"Nadyezhda Petrovna," he began. "You painted that copy, didn't you?"

Nadyezhda Petrovna said nothing. She glared back defiantly.

Chavchavadze gestured to Bykov, who went to the other side of the wheelchair. With his right hand he took Nadyezhda Petrovna's left hand. Then he bent the pinky finger backward until it broke with an audible snap.

The old woman gasped with pain. Then the blood drained from her face and she passed out. Her head lolled back over her right shoulder.

Chavchavadze waited for a moment, then began slowly slapping her cheeks, first the right, then the left. A trace of blood returned to each of them.

After thirty seconds or so Nadyezhda Petrovna's eyes opened and she moaned.

"You painted that copy, didn't you?" Chavchavadze repeated.

This time, she nodded. Her broken finger remained splayed at an oblique angle from her hand.

"Why did you do this?"

She glared at him again. "You told me to," she said. Her voice was hoarse and cracked with pain and fatigue. Only the eyes remained strong.

Marina shuddered, stammered, and continued to translate for Santera.

Chavchavadze's face flushed with rage. He stepped forward and slapped her, hard, across the mouth. Her neck snapped to one side and a tooth came flying out of her mouth, followed by a spurt of blood. The blood spattered on her smock, where it mixed with the old paint stains. And a trickle oozed out of her mouth.

Nadyezhda Petrovna was still, however, conscious. Chavchavadze beckoned to Bykov again.

"The right hand this time," he said.

Bykov took the fifth finger of her right hand and began to bend it backward.

"This is the hand you paint with," Chavchavadze said to her. "We haven't touched it up until now."

Bykov bent it back farther, and Nadyezhda Petrovna began to sob.

"Now," he said, "did I tell you to paint a copy?"

Her head sagged toward her chest. "No," she mumbled. "No."

Despite this answer, Bykov kept the pressure on. Her finger snapped, with a louder sound than the first one had made. Marina shrieked. Santera folded his arms in front of him and looked impassively at the wall above the tableau being enacted before him.

Nadyezhda Petrovna moaned, and again her breathing grew labored. Her eyes rolled back and closed. Her pasty face excreted a clammy sweat. She was panting and whimpering like a tortured puppy.

Chavchavadze looked sharply at Bykov, and Bykov let her hand go. It fell against the armrest of her wheelchair, and she screamed at the new pain stabbing up her arm.

Chavchavadze bent over her and grabbed her chin in one hand. He drew her head around until her eyes were a few inches from his own.

"Who asked you to paint it?"

"Bykov," Nadyezhda Petrovna groaned. The name sounded like a curse.

Now it was Bykov's turn to become enraged. He laid a heavy hand on her right shoulder. It looked as fragile as an egg under his thick fingers. He began to squeeze.

Nadyezhda Petrovna's whimpers grew more intense and frequent, building to a painful crescendo.

"You're lying," Bykov said to her. "Say that you're lying. And tell us where the painting is."

She looked at him intently and managed to stop whimpering. She drew her head up.

"You can kill me if you want," she said. Her voice was so low that Bykov and Chavchavadze had to lean closer to hear. "But I'll never tell you. You're pigs and traitors. I won't let you have what belongs to Russia."

Then she spat in Bykov's face.

His face contorted and his grip on her shoulder tightened. Chavchavadze could hear bones cracking. Her eyes rolled back until only whites showed and she lost consciousness.

This time when Chavchavadze slapped her, she did not revive. He picked up a hand and felt for a pulse.

"She's alive," he said. "I think."

He turned to Bykov. "But we can't wait until she's ready to talk. If what you say is true, the picture is still in the Winter Palace. We'll simply search until we find it."

Chapter Twenty-eight

BURKE, TO HIS UTTER DISGUST, COULD NOT take his eyes off the beaker on Andrusha Karpov's lab table that was marked "Alcohol."

He had first noticed it an hour before. And as the waiting time dragged on, his mind had wandered more and more often away from the computer monitor that showed Nadyezhda Petrovna's studio and back to the beaker.

Once, he had gone so far as to stand up, wait until he was certain McCoy was not watching, pick up the beaker and slosh the liquid around, loosing fumes that wafted upward to his greedy nostrils.

Horrified at himself, he put the beaker down.

But he had not been able to get it out of his mind. Now, as the screen showed Bykov's torture of Nadyezhda Petrovna, as the realization dawned that something had gone terribly wrong, he found the urge to drink getting perversely more powerful.

He forced himself to look again to the monitor.

"We have to help her," Andrusha Karpov said, eyes locked on the silent picture.

But his voice conveyed no hope. It was the voice his grandparents might have used, alone in their room, whispering that Russia had to do something about Stalin.

Burke felt a stab of fear, and then an echoing spasm of guilt—fear that he might actually be asked to help rescue Nadyezhda Petrovna and guilt at the instant awareness that he would refuse, noble as the attempt might be.

"I'm afraid there's nothing we can do for her now," McCoy said. "There are too many of them."

On the screen, Bykov was breaking Nadyezhda Petrovna's second finger. Andrusha winced. Burke shuddered.

"What do you think happened?" McCoy asked Burke.

"I don't know," Burke said. "But I don't think they'd be breaking her fingers just for doing a lousy restoration. Well, Bykov might. But we have to assume that they've figured out the fake somehow."

"Which means they could be here any moment," McCoy said. "Even if she doesn't tell them where it is, they'll search for it. We're going to have to get out of here."

Grimly, Burke nodded agreement.

McCoy turned to Andrusha. "Can we get the picture out? Assuming they have people at the normal exits?"

"Screw the picture," Burke broke in. "Can we do anything for her? Can we get ourselves out?"

"We can't leave her," Andrusha insisted.

"We have to get help," Burke said to him. "As soon as we can, we'll come back for her. It's all we can do."

Andrusha looked one more time at the monitor. Bykov had his hand on Nadyezhda Petrovna's collarbone.

"All right," he said, sadly and bitterly.

McCoy grabbed his arm. "I promise we'll come back for her. Now how do we get out?"

"There's a basement exit," Andrusha said. "Down a back staircase. No one will be guarding it. I have a key."

"Let's go. You lead the way," McCoy said to Andrusha.

Andrusha picked up the phone, quickly dialed a number. Lyubov apparently answered. He spoke a few terse words to her and hung up.

"She'll be waiting," he said. "Let's go."

"Pick an end," McCoy said to Burke, gesturing toward the painting.

"In bed, of old age, is starting to look mighty attractive," Burke said.

"I mean an end of the painting. To carry," McCoy rasped.

"I knew that," Burke said. He grabbed his coat and stuffed his arms into the sleeves.

She glared at him, and then they lifted the picture, conscious still of the cost of scraping it against a wall. Trying not to leave prints, they gripped the back, unpainted side, allowing the painted surface to face up. Burke had the end nearer Leda's feet. She looked almost alive, as if she were reclining in front of him.

They canted the picture, inched their way through the door and followed Andrusha's right turn.

Somewhere in the distance, a few walls away from them, they could hear running footsteps.

"Hurry," McCoy hissed over her shoulder.

Andrusha lengthened his stride, then opened a door on the left. Slowly, Burke turned the picture on its edge and waited for McCoy to get herself square to the doorway. Then she started to back through. Her elbow banged against the doorjamb.

"Shit," she said. "My funny bone."

The running footsteps grew louder.

"No time for humor," Burke said. "Hurry up!"

She managed to get the painting through the door and let Burke follow her inside. He found the door with his foot and was about to kick it shut when he heard a door open at the far end of the corridor.

"Check all the rooms," a male voice said. "I'll check the next corridor."

"Don't slam it," McCoy whispered.

He could hear a door being opened and shut down the corridor. Then another, somewhat closer. As quietly as he could, he pushed the door shut, without letting the latch catch and make a noise. The unlocked door would be noticed, but perhaps not for a minute.

Andrusha had opened a door at the far end of the room. Behind him, Burke could see a dark stairwell. As quietly and as quickly as they could, they maneuvered the picture through the door and again canted it, this time so it fit in the stairwell. They by now had forgotten all thoughts of protecting the painting from fingertips. Burke simply held onto it and hoped he wouldn't drop it on anything sharp.

The slamming of doors drew closer. He had heard perhaps four open and shut. He thought he remembered that they had gone through the seventh door in the corridor. He shut the stairwell door behind him and they started to move down.

Two more doors had opened and shut by the time they got to the first landing below. Fuming, Burke waited while McCoy tilted the picture yet again to maneuver it around the turn.

"Let's leave the goddamn thing," he hissed.

"No!" Her tone was peremptory. He admired her tenacity. She wasn't going to be the first one shot at, either, Burke thought. His own back would be the first target.

Just as they maneuvered around the corner and onto another flight of stairs, he heard a shout. The unlocked door had been discovered.

His hands, previously clammy, started to sweat profusely. He pushed forward and nearly knocked her down the stairs.

"Not so hard," she cried out.

Above them he could hear footsteps again. It sounded as if only one man was making them. And the footsteps had slowed. Burke could imagine the man suddenly growing cautious as he realized he was getting close. He wondered if McCoy had a gun and was prepared to use it.

"Got a gun?" he whispered.

She shook her head. "I was afraid of metal detectors going into the museum," she whispered back, continuing to step down.

Burke said nothing and pushed ahead harder.

Ahead of them Andrusha opened another door. He caught a whiff of dank, cold air. It was the basement.

Behind him, Burke could hear the stairwell door slowly open, but no immediate footsteps. Their pursuer was two flights behind, treading cautiously. Maybe he would wait for reinforcements before starting down.

Then he heard a cautious step on the first tread. So much for that hope.

They tilted the picture yet again and emerged into the basement. McCoy lengthened her stride until they were half trotting and had pulled abreast of Andrusha. Burke's sweaty fingers began to ache.

They could not have been more than a hundred meters from the cold waters of the Neva. The basement atmosphere suggested that it was much closer. He could smell the algae decaying in the humid air.

The corridor they were in was arranged like a stable, and perhaps once had been a stable. Partitioned sections that looked like old stalls opened on either side. A single lightbulb hanging above them gave a shadowy illumination.

The stalls were full of the detritus of imperial life: carriages, slowly rotting in the damp air; bits and pieces of tables and chairs, long since cannibalized to preserve the patina of elegance above.

They were running now, sidestepping stools and brooms and odd bits of trash left littering the corridor. McCoy's foot connected to an old tin bucket and set it clattering against a stall door. The noise reverberated against the moldy bricks. Burke hoped it was not an omen.

Just ahead the corridor intersected with another. "To the right," Andrusha panted.

They heard the first shot just as they reached the corner. It sounded like an explosion, echoing up and down the corridor. A puff of powder erupted from the brick wall three feet to Burke's left as the bullet hit the decaying mortar.

Out of his right eye Burke could see the silhouette of a man, down on one knee, the gun pointing toward them as they vanished from his sight.

The new corridor was dimmer and narrower than the one they had just left. At its far end, perhaps fifty meters away, another single bulb burned, and Burke could see a door. He calculated the distance the man pursuing them had to travel before they'd reach the door, about ten meters away. They would be delayed as

Andrusha opened it. The man with the gun would have time to get off half a dozen shots. He would certainly hit something.

Frantically, Burke glanced around. The stall to his right held odd bits of armor—several helmets, a few chest pieces, and a couple of rusting swords.

"Andrusha," Burke said. "Take this end." He thrust it at him and the Russian grabbed it reflexively.

"Go," he hissed to McCoy. "Now!"

"No," she said. "We have to stick together!"

"Go!" he shouted at her. She looked anguished, but she had no time to argue with him. She began backpedaling furiously down the corridor. Andrusha followed, his hips twitching back and forth.

Burke lunged into the stall and grabbed the first sword he could get his hands on.

It was heavier than he'd anticipated. The handle was braided steel, long enough for him to get both hands on it. The hilt was plain steel, unadorned. If there had been any precious metals in it, he realized, he would not have found it rusting in the basement.

The edge had long since dulled. He had trouble even deciding which was the cutting side. It hardly mattered, he realized.

He took up his position, crouching in the entry to the stall, the sword cocked behind his right ear. For some reason he suddenly remembered his father, years ago, teaching him to hit baseballs before his first season in Little League.

"Always swing level," his father had said. "And step into it."

He could hear the footsteps coming, and he tried to hold his breath, fearful that the sound of a gasp would tip the man off. He gauged the man's pace by the sound of his footsteps. He was running, confident now that his quarry had no gun. Andrusha and McCoy were making slower progress toward the far end of the corridor. Burke could hear his own heart pounding.

Then he could hear the gunman's exhalations. Timing, he realized, would be everything. He decided to wait until he saw the barrel of the gun protrude into the intersection. He would simply have to trust that the gunman's momentum would carry him beyond the corner. If the man stopped short, it would be like swinging early at a change-up. He would get no torque into it, and the impact would be weak.

He saw the gun barrel, long and black, and he tried to swing just under it, stepping forward with his left foot and bringing the sword around with both hands, his right arm providing the final thrust.

The flat side of the sword made satisfying contact. It reminded him of the times he had hit a baseball solidly and all of the energy of his swing had been transmitted from the bat to the ball, with nothing left to reverberate back up to his arms. He heard a shriek of pain and saw the gun skitter away. It hit the wall on the opposite side of the corridor and went off, blasting at Burke's eardrums, deafening him.

Hands and arms shaking, Burke stepped forward, into the light. The man was lying on the ground, stunned, clutching at a red blotch seeping on both sides of his belt buckle.

Burke recognized him. It was the man who had attacked him on the riverside embankment.

Feeling anger of overwhelming intensity, he raised the sword over his head and brought it down as hard as he could toward the man's head and shoulders. He hit him with the flat side of the sword, and miscalculated slightly. Instead of the satisfying, flat feel of contact he had with the first blow, the tip of the sword hit the stone floor beyond the man's head, jarring Burke's arms clear up to the shoulders.

He looked down at the man for a second. He gave no sign of being conscious. Burke raised the sword again, then dropped it to the floor. There was no need to kill him. He turned and ran down the corridor.

Andrusha was slipping the key into the lock, holding up the painting with his left hand. McCoy was staring at him, mouth slightly open. Burke grabbed the end of the painting from Andrusha.

"Let's hurry," he said. "There'll be others."

The door creaked open and cold air blasted through. Burke sucked it in greedily. The chill quickly penetrated his coat. It didn't matter. He wanted to be outside.

They pushed through the door. They were in the vast square on the opposite side of the Winter Palace from the river. A light coating of new snow dusted the Alexander Column, the memorial to Russian victory over Napoleon in 1812. The square was deserted.

"Where to?" McCoy asked.

"Lyuba should be waiting for us with her car," Andrusha said. "Through the arch."

They trotted across the square and through the archway, retracing the steps Burke had made several days before. A few stray snowflakes fell on the painting.

They emerged on the street beside the Griboyedov Canal. Andrusha peered into the gloom.

"There." He pointed. A battered old blue Zhiguli was parked by the curb, its engine running.

They wedged the picture into the backseat and squeezed their bodies in around it. Lyuba took off.

Burke was sweating lightly, his body awash in a cocktail of adrenaline and remorse, thinking about the old woman back in the Winter Palace.

McCoy, sitting on the backseat with her knees drawn up around her chin, patted his hand consolingly.

"That was great, what you did back there," she said. "Thanks."

Burke smiled wanly at her. More than anything else at that moment, he wanted to be back in his hotel room, sipping a shot of Jack Daniel's and contemplating the schedule of flights west.

"Yeah," he said. "I may have to rethink this whole sword and pen thing."

Chapter Twenty-nine

"**W**HY DON'T YOU JUST DRIVE THEM UP TO-
ward the Finnish border," Burke demanded, "call in some kind of
stealth helicopter, and get them out of the country?"

"It's not that simple," McCoy said.

"I know it's not simple—" Burke began to reply.

"No!" Andrusha interjected sharply. "The painting will not leave
Russia! And we will not leave, either, until we have done what we
can for Nadyezhda Petrovna."

Lyubov Naryshkina appeared startled by the vehemence of
Andrusha's outburst, but she nodded.

"Andrei Borisovich is right," she said, using his proper name
and patronymic for the first time in Burke's presence. "We can't
leave my mother. Or the painting. I am sorry to say this, but you
know the experience we have had with the Germans. Once a
painting is in another country, it can be extremely difficult to get
it back."

"Well, you're not going to have it for long," Burke said. "This
is one of the first places they're going to look."

They were in the anteroom of Nadyezhda Petrovna's apartment,
their coats on, clustered in front of her copy of Rembrandt's
scholar. The scholar's mouth still hung open in surprise, as if he

were astonished at the arrival of a genuine painting—the Leonardo that Andrusha had propped on his right foot.

"He's right," McCoy said.

Burke's equanimity, never very deep, had been scraped away. If they hadn't been in a near panic, they wouldn't have come to Nadyezhda Petrovna's in the first place.

He turned on McCoy. "Des, come on," he said, trying to keep the fear out of his voice. "Can't you take them to the consulate and have them ask for protection or asylum or something?"

"I don't think so," McCoy said.

"What, you don't want to blow your cover? It's blown!"

McCoy looked sad rather than angry. "No. It's not that. There's just a lot more at play here than even this painting. This government probably couldn't survive the scandal. And you don't have to yell at me."

"Sorry," Burke said. "I've been under a little stress lately."

She patted his cheek. "I know the feeling."

Andrusha chewed nervously on a fingernail. "So we have to find a place to hide it."

"But where? Could we bury it?" Lyubov looked dubious even as she broached the possibility.

"The ground is frozen," McCoy pointed out. "Even if we could dig, we'd have to disturb the snow. It wouldn't be hard for someone to figure out where it was."

"And even if we covered it in plastic," Andrusha said, "it would be exposed to moisture and ruined in a short time."

"Don't you have a friend," Burke asked them, "who has an apartment where we could stash it?"

"Legally, it's stolen government property," Andrusha said. "I wouldn't expose a friend to that risk."

"Or that temptation," Lyubov added.

"That was cynical," Burke said. "Have you ever worked as a reporter?"

Andrusha looked puzzled and Lyubov looked mildly offended.

"Excuse him," McCoy said sharply. "He needs a drink."

"I can get you one," Lyuba said.

Despite himself, Burke laughed. "That's not what she meant," he told her.

Now Lyubov looked both puzzled and annoyed, and she opened her mouth to begin to speak.

"There's the dacha," Andrusha said abruptly.

"Whose dacha?" McCoy seized on the idea.

"Nadyezhda Petrovna's."

"Where?"

"In the country, about ten miles north of the city. It's in a village called Pashkino on an old collective farm called Legacy of Ilyich."

"Did she get it from the Hermitage?" Burke asked.

In Soviet society, dachas were usually distributed to favored workers by their employers. If the Hermitage had given the Naryshkins their dacha, it would be easy for Bykov to locate it.

"No," Lyuba said. "That dacha has been in the family almost since the Revolution. It was the overseer's cottage on the old family estate. After the Revolution, they turned the mansion into a Communist Party school. They turned the land over to the collective. But they gave us the cottage."

"So how many people at the Hermitage know that you have it?" McCoy asked.

"Not many," Lyubov said. "Since my father died, we rarely go there."

"She's got a studio out there? Supplies?"

Lyubov nodded.

"It might be safe there for a couple of days," McCoy said.

"And after that?"

"Let's get through the next forty-eight hours," McCoy said. "Then we'll worry about 'after that.'"

"What about Bykov?" Burke asked.

"What about him?"

"Is anyone going to do something about him? Are you?"

"Do what?" Lyubov's voice was raw. "And who? The police? Chavchavadze owns the police."

"The best thing you can do on that score," McCoy told Burke, "is to help make sure he doesn't get this back." She gestured toward the picture. "Then go home and write your story."

Burke nodded. She seemed to be right.

"And I need your help," she said. She pulled some keys from her pocket and handed them to Burke. "I want you to go to my gallery. Use this key to open it. Get my computer. Then use this key to bring my car out to this dacha."

"Your computer?"

"Don't ask," she said.

Burke shrugged. He would ask his questions later.

"Andrusha," McCoy said, "you and I are going to take this to the dacha and hide it."

"No," Andrusha replied firmly, still chewing on his sausage and bread. "I want to go back to the palace. I might be able to do something for Nadyezhda Petrovna."

"I don't think that's wise," McCoy said.

"It's not wise. It's duty. And thank you, Andrusha," Lyubov said. "But I'll go."

Andrusha objected. "You can't go alone!"

McCoy, fatigued, rubbed her eyes. "No, I'm sorry. Even if Nadyezhda Petrovna is . . . all right, there's too much chance you'll be caught. And if you're caught, they'll make you tell them where the painting is hidden. And then they'll kill you. We lose everything."

She turned to the other woman. "I'm sorry, Lyubov. I can see why you love and respect your mother. But it's just not an option."

"Not an option," Lyubov repeated numbly.

"It must be!" Andrusha objected.

McCoy folded her arms. "I'm sorry," she repeated.

"I think your army is deserting you on this one, commander," Burke said. "Andrusha and Lyubov are right. We owe it to Nadyezhda Petrovna to see if we can get her out of there."

"It's too dangerous!"

Burke shrugged. He gestured with his head toward Lyubov. "She's a cynic already," he told McCoy in English. "I sure don't want to be the one to make her spend the next forty years trying to forget leaving her mother over there."

McCoy looked angry, but she held her temper.

"All right. I don't think it'll do any good. But all right," she said. "But you have to go with her. I need Andrusha's help out there and we can't delay. And be careful. Wait till you're sure that they've left."

Burke turned to Lyubov. "How will we get in?"

"The same way you got out," Lyubov said.

"How will we know if they've gone?"

"Check for cars," McCoy replied. "Then, when you get into the palace, check Andrusha's monitor. And when you find her, don't bring her back here. Take her someplace else. They're going to be coming here very soon, I suspect."

"I know a doctor," Andrusha volunteered. He wrote down an address and gave it to Lyuba.

McCoy looked at her watch. "Let's get out of here now."

She kissed him, quickly and lightly. "Stay safe."

"Believe me," Burke said, "I have every intention of trying. You do the same."

Lyubov Naryshkina looked at her watch and lengthened her stride. "We've got to hurry," she said. "The last train runs at a few minutes after midnight."

Burke picked up his pace to keep up with her. "I'm sorry that we couldn't help her at the time," he said.

Lyubov looked briefly at him, then set her eyes again on the slick, icy sidewalk. "It's a risk she took," she said. "I would have taken it. Our family has cared for the art in the Winter Palace for six generations. We protected it from the Bolsheviks. We protected it from the Nazis. We will protect it from these people."

"For how long?"

"Until Russia has a government worthy of the job," she said flatly.

"I believe you," Burke said.

They descended the broad, gray granite stairs into the Lesnaya Metro station. The fluorescent fixtures above gave light but no heat. The handful of people on the platform huddled in their coats and fur hats, shivering slightly. Their exhalations hung in the air above them.

Burke looked down the tracks to the clock at the end of the station. The last train had come through six minutes ago.

He heard a rumbling from the other end of the tunnel. The blue train's stubby nose clattered into the station. They got in. Burke sank into one of the brown leather benches, opposite a bleary-eyed man with a large spittle stain on his parka.

But Lyubov was too anxious to sit. She remained on her feet as the train started slowly out of the station, biting her lip with frustration. He stood up and patted her awkwardly on the shoulder.

"We'll be there as soon as we can," he said. "Whatever can be done, we'll do."

"I still don't know why they couldn't have driven us in," she said quietly.

"Because the dacha's in the opposite direction. They needed to get out there as soon as they could," Burke said, repeating the explanation McCoy had given.

Lyubov shook her head but said nothing.

They got out at Gostinny Dvor station and found the McCoy-Fokine Gallery in the little courtyard off Nevsky Prospekt. He realized it was only a couple of blocks from her apartment.

As McCoy had instructed, he turned the key and punched in the code to disable the burglar alarm.

The place was in shadows and darkness, illuminated only by the streetlamp outside in the courtyard, and he left it that way. No sense in calling attention to their presence.

He groped his way over the gallery floor, stepping around some small pieces of sculpture until he found her office. The computer was on the desk, where she'd said it would be. He hefted it. It felt no heavier than an ordinary laptop, and for a second he wondered whether it was only that.

Her Volvo was in the parking space. He started it up and wheeled out of the courtyard as fast as he felt he could go without risking unwanted attention from a *militsioner*. Nevsky Prospekt was not entirely deserted, though it was by now after midnight. An occasional cab or private car sped by.

He saw headlights in his rearview mirror, and he slowed and pulled over to the right, waiting to see if the car would pass. It did, and he saw a man and a woman in it. They paid him no attention, and he decided he was being paranoid.

"Hurry, please," Lyubov whispered. She had said scarcely a word in the past ten minutes, and her agony was palpable.

He punched the accelerator and they sped over the humped

bridge that spanned the Griboyedov Canal and saw the Neva up ahead. He turned right and slowly approached the Winter Palace.

He had half expected to see the palace lit up inside and surrounded outside by *militsia* cars with flashing blue lights on their roofs. But it was dark and quiet. The light coming from its windows was faint, as if someone had left a few inside lamps burning.

He cruised down the long, riverside facade of the building, past the tourist entrances and the administration wing.

Three black cars stood in a line outside the door to that wing, their headlights off. Exhaust plumed from their tailpipes, and he could see the silhouettes of men inside one of them: drivers, sitting together and passing the time.

"A ZIL, a Mercedes, and a Volvo," Burke said. "I would imagine that means Chavchavadze and this buyer of his are still inside."

He sped up and went past, trying to be as inconspicuous as possible.

Lyubov twisted in her seat and stared back at the cars. "What will we do?"

"Well, I guess we'll have to use the secret tunnel from Prince Potemkin's house to Catherine the Great's bedroom," Burke said.

She looked blankly at him.

"Sorry, bad joke," he said. "When I get nervous, I make bad jokes."

She smiled faintly, distractedly. "If they're still in there," she said, "it means they're not certain whether you got out with the painting or without it. They're still searching inside."

"How long would that take?"

"It could take days," she said. "There are more than one thousand rooms. If they start checking carefully in all the painting storage areas, it could take weeks."

"My guess, they'll take a look around tonight. But they won't attract attention by continuing to search tomorrow when the museum is open. Whatever they'll do, they'll do quickly."

He drove another hundred meters, until the street had twisted out of sight of the Hermitage entrance. Then he switched the lights off and made a U-turn. He slowly nosed the car forward into the bend it had just passed through and stopped it along the curb as soon as he had a line of sight to the trio of cars parked at the Winter Palace. They were about 250 meters away. He shut off the engine.

A man got out of the Mercedes and walked around to the ZIL, sticking his head in the window, apparently talking to the limousine's driver. He gave no sign that he had noticed them. Burke exhaled slowly.

"Now what?" she asked. "Wait?"

"Wait."

He looked at her. Her fine, narrow features were contorted, anxiety evident in the tight little lines that seemed to be growing around her eyes. He looked back at the palace.

She slapped the dashboard with her open palm. The sharp crack made Burke wince.

"I don't want to wait," she groaned. The groan had a feral quality to it, like the sound of an animal in pain.

He patted her hand, wishing the gesture did not seem quite so fatuous. "You're doing everything you can," he soothed her. "Your mother would be doing exactly this."

She said nothing, but looked even more miserable.

"I know how it feels when you can't help someone you care for," he said.

She looked bitterly at him. "How can you know?"

There was a rich connotation in her pronunciation of the pronoun, an assumption that of all the peoples in the world, Americans were the least qualified to empathize with Russian suffering.

He thought for a moment, then said, "I can."

Then he saw movement out of the door to the Winter Palace. He leaned forward and used his fingers to wipe away the fog that had formed on the inside of the windshield. He peered out.

A party of about a dozen was leaving through the administrative entrance. He could barely make out their figures, and he could see no faces. But from the low, heavy bulk of one of them, he knew he was watching Bykov.

He watched the figures climb into the cars. The three cars split up. One turned up Nevsky Prospekt toward the Yevropeiskaya. Two headed across the bridge, in the direction of Nadyezhda Petrovna's apartment.

Burke waited until their taillights were out of sight and started the car. He eased around the palace and parked on the street adjacent to the Palace Square.

"Quickly," he said.

They got out and walked briskly across the square, trying not to look like burglars, but scanning the area. He heard footsteps behind them. He grabbed her arm and pulled her close.

"H—"

He wheeled her around, trying to look drunk, embraced her and peered over her shoulder. A *militsioner* was checking them out, casually, looking bored.

"*Militsia,*" he whispered in her ear, trying to look romantic.

She clung to him, breathing heavily, for a minute. She felt light and fragile, and he could feel her heart racing in a vein in her neck.

The footsteps resumed and the *militsioner* made his way out of the square, up Nevsky Prospekt. Gratefully, they ducked into the shadow of the palace wall.

She produced the key, and in a moment they were inside. The light over the door was still burning. They stood still for a moment, listening. They heard nothing except the sound of their own breathing and the faint creaks and rumbles of the old building at night.

Slowly, they walked up the corridor to the intersection where Burke had ambushed the gunman. The light was fainter here, but he saw the sword, lying where he had dropped it. The gun had been removed. So had the gunman. He could see splotches of blood in the grime that coated the brick floor.

She led the way now, since she knew the territory better. Burke was amazed at how short the corridors and the staircase were. An hour earlier they had seemed as long as the tunnel that led out of Vietnam.

They listened carefully before they opened the door to the corridor that led to Andrusha's room.

He whispered a question to her. "Why don't we hear any security guards? If Bykov and his men were searching the building, surely they'd have run into some?"

Lyubov frowned. "He can do what he wants. If he meets some-one, he tells them he's conducting a private, evening tour for a po-tential contributor. It happens."

He opened the door and poked his head out. The corridor was dim and empty. Quickly, they made their way to Andrusha's door.

The room had been ransacked. Loose papers covered the wooden floor and a bookshelf had been flipped over in the search for the painting. A broken vial of bright yellow paint was dripping slowly on the upturned spine of a blue book, a manual on artists' materials.

But the computer was still as Andrusha had left it, displaying an innocuous graph.

"Can you get it to show the cameras again?" Burke asked.

She leaned over the keyboard and tentatively began punching keys. After two failed trials she remembered the sequence properly.

The conservation studio blinked into view, flipped over a few times, and then settled onto the screen.

"There's no one there," she said. Her voice dragged with despair.

The slice of the room shown by the camera indeed was empty. The conservators' worktables stood, immobile and unchanging, in the shadowy light.

Lyubov's voice was dull with shock. "What have they done to her?"

He was afraid to answer her. "We'll go check," he said, and laid what he hoped was a comforting hand on her shoulder.

As they approached the big studio, he found that setting one foot in front of the other had become a treacherous task. Some boards creaked and others did not. He could discern no pattern. Each creak sounded to him like a train slamming on its brakes, as if metal were grating loudly against metal, and he expected to hear an answering shout and the drumbeat of footsteps. But the old building kept its composure.

They did not have to use the keys Andrusha had given to Lyubov. The door was ajar, testimony to the haste with which Bykov and his men had searched, then left, the palace.

For some reason, he felt the impulse to duck down and stay low as they entered the room, like a soldier entering a hostile environment. It would make no difference, he realized, and stood up.

The fake Leonardo was still on its easel, and for a moment he looked at it and wondered why the genuine article was worth hundreds of millions of dollars and a perfect copy was worthless.

Then Lyubov brushed past him, scanning the room. She gasped. Then she darted toward a corner of the room, a corner shielded from his view by a conservator's table. He saw what had drawn her in that direction. A single withered ankle, covered over in thick, brown, cotton lisle stocking, protruded from behind the table.

By the time he got there, she was already squatting on the floor, cradling her mother's head in her arms.

She turned to him, her eyes glistening. "She's alive!"

Nadyezhda Petrovna did not look alive to Burke. Her skin was white and waxy, and her eyes were closed. Her wheelchair was a few feet away. Evidently, she had been pushed out of it, or she had fallen.

He knelt beside her and picked up a wrist, looking for a pulse. Her skin felt cold and papery. The small finger on that hand splayed out from the palm like the digit in some child's drawing. He felt nauseated as he remembered how it got that way.

But he could feel a pulse, faint and rapid, under the skin.

"We have to get her out of here," Lyubov hissed.

He nodded, though he doubted she could survive being moved. "Let's get her into the chair."

He put his hands under her shoulder and knee and prepared to lift. Lyuba wrapped her arms around her mother's torso to help.

As soon as she applied pressure to the torso, Nadyezhda Petrovna groaned. It was a weakened, rattling groan, but the first sound they had heard from her.

Nadyezhda Petrovna's eyes opened. "Mama," Lyuba whispered. "It's me." She cradled her mother's head.

When Nadyezhda Petrovna spoke, it happened in slow motion. It seemed to Burke that he could see the thought form behind her eyes, then see her choose to make the effort to express it. Then he could see her lips open, and finally, words came out, so faintly that he could barely hear them.

"Don't touch me there," she said. Each word required a separate effort. "He kicked me."

Lyubov started to cry. She unbuttoned her mother's smock and pulled it up to show the doughy white flesh, hanging in thin little folds, above her right hip. The ribs, Burke could see, had been crushed inward, and a dark purple splotch had formed on the skin over her liver. She was bleeding internally. He shuddered with disgust at what Bykov had done, and with fear at what he might do.

He turned his eyes away.

"The broker," Nadyezhda Petrovna said.

"Yes, Mama?"

Nadyezhda Petrovna paused to summon her strength. "The broker carved the English letter C behind the real picture. Upper right corner. To identify it."

"Don't talk, Mama."

"That's how they knew."

"I understand, Mama. Don't talk. We'll get help."

Nadyezhda Petrovna's eyes slowly slipped shut again.

Lyubov turned to Burke. "There's a phone in Mama's studio. Call an ambulance."

Nadyezhda Petrovna opened her eyes again. "Do no good," she said.

"Oh, yes it would, Mama," Lyubov said. "Yes it would. It would." Tears were streaming down her cheeks.

"No," Nadyezhda Petrovna said. "I'll stay."

Her eyes closed again.

Burke hesitated.

"Yes it would, Mama. Yes, it would," Lyubov repeated.

Burke picked up the wrist he had felt before. The pulse was gone.

Lyubov started to sob, quietly whispering, "Mama."

He let her go on like that for a few moments. Then he reached behind the old woman's head, gently lifted it from her daughter's hands and lowered it to the floor.

He helped her up and held her for a while, comforting himself more than he was comforting her. Her body shuddered and heaved with silent sobs, and he waited until they subsided and she was still in his arms, her face buried against his shoulder, a faint smell of soap and perfume rising from her hair into his nostrils.

Then he asked her to help him carry the copy of Leda down through the basement and out to the car.

She looked at him as if he had lost his mind.

"Why?"

"Because," he said, "now that we know what's wrong with it, it might come in handy."

Then something remarkable happened. Almost instantaneously she shut off her tears, straightened her shoulders and nodded. It was, he thought, as if all the enormous strength of will her mother had possessed had flowed into her body, an inheritance.

The dacha, Desdemona McCoy decided, would have to do.

As a hiding place, it had some obvious advantages. It stood alone in a copse of birch trees on a forested corner of the kolkhoz, Legacy of Ilyich. But though it was on the kolkhoz, it was not of the kolkhoz. It had its own entrance, a dirt road that wound through the spruce and birch forest from the St. Petersburg–Vyborg highway. The village where the kolkhoz workers lived lay off another road, a kilometer north. It could not be seen through the dacha windows.

But as a redoubt, its wooded isolation was its disadvantage. She would not be able to see people approaching the dacha until they were on top of it.

She held the painting, now covered in a blanket and bound up in string, sideways to the wind as she waited for Andrusha Karpov to unlock the dacha's front door. She shivered. It had grown colder in the hour before dawn, and the wind had picked up again. She felt chilled past the bone, to the depths of her body.

Andrusha cursed quietly and pulled off his glove. Then he continued to work on the lock.

"I'm afraid it's frozen," he said.

He squatted down, growing bulkier as his parka flared out and settled around his ample posterior. Opening his mouth, he exhaled on the lock, looking like a grouper fish. He tried the key again. This time it turned.

The dacha had four rooms, including a veranda with large, mullioned windows, a linoleum floor, and a couple of daybeds with tattered afghans draped over them; a living room with similar furnishings, whose floor sloped toward the kitchen; and a studio, attached to the south side of the house and lit by an old skylight.

It was just as cold inside the house as out, except for the wind. They set the picture down carefully and she folded her arms in front of her chest, trying to conserve heat.

"There should be some coal outside," Andrusha said. "I'll start the stove."

The kitchen had a big old Russian *pyech*, the kind of tiled stove that formed the heart of the peasant's cottage, supplying heat, food, and a place to sleep, on a pallet set atop the stove and warmed by the embers inside.

"No."

He turned in surprise.

"It would attract too much attention," she explained. "People would see the smoke coming out of the chimney."

"But we'll freeze," Andrusha objected.

She forced herself to smile. "Probably not."

"Yes we will," Andrusha said. "You don't know Russian winters."

She hesitated.

"Besides, the wind," he said. "The wind will blow the smoke away before anyone can see it."

She let herself be persuaded. "All right," she said, and within a couple of minutes Andrusha had lit a small pile of coal. Ten minutes after that the stove began to radiate a little warmth.

McCoy stepped outside into the cold again and looked at the stovepipe. Andrusha was right. The wind dispersed the smoke before it rose to the height of the surrounding trees. As long as the breeze was blowing, no one in the village would see anything.

Reassured, she went inside and looked around the dacha a little more closely. To her surprise, the pictures on the walls were not copies of Renaissance classics, but small, abstract studies, mostly bright, geometric shapes on white backgrounds in the manner of Mondrian.

"Did Nadyezhda Petrovna do these?"

"No," Andrusha said. "She wouldn't. Lyuba did them years ago, when she was a teenager. They kept them out here, though. It wouldn't have been a good idea to have someone in the city see them."

McCoy nodded, preoccupied. Then she got the Leonardo and held it up to the wall against the largest of Lyubov's abstractions. The Leonardo panel covered the abstract and then some.

"The trouble with these," McCoy said, "is not that they're abstract. They're too small."

"Too small?"

"For what I want to do."

Andrusha looked puzzled.

"We're going to hide this with camouflage, the same way they hid it from Madame de Maintenon," she said.

Comprehension dawned in his eyes.

"Do they have some blank canvas and some paints out here?" she asked.

"They do."

"Then let's get busy."

McCoy cut a piece of canvas large enough to wrap around Leonardo's panel, and Andrusha prepared paper to cover and further protect the painting. They wrapped the canvas tightly around the panel and secured it in the back with tacks.

Then McCoy covered the canvas with white acrylic paint. As it dried, she mixed some turpentine with oil paints to thin them. Then she took a medium-sized brush and drew a dozen broad, closely spaced stripes in different colors, running from the top of the canvas to the bottom.

"Morris Louis," she said to Andrusha. He smiled.

They hung the picture on the wall, and McCoy frowned.

"Only one problem," she said. "It's bigger than the other pictures. It stands out. We need to do another big canvas."

Andrusha found some stretchers and more canvas and prepared a white surface as before. He took the brush and dipped it in some acrylic paint. Then he shook the brush, hard, in the direction of the canvas. The paint spattered and stuck to the canvas in globules.

"Jackson Pollock," he said.

Chapter Thirty

THE BLACK CHAIKA ROLLING SLOWLY THROUGH the gates of All-Russia Industries sounded as if it needed a tune-up. Its valves rattled in counterpoint to the sound of the snow crunching under its tires.

The Chaika was a slightly smaller limousine than the ZIL, the Politburo members' car that Rafael Santera Calderon owned. Originally, the Soviet Ministry of Machine Building had designed the Chaika for officials one step below the pinnacle of power. As he watched it approach, Santera wondered whether he was being trifled with yet again, by the dispatch of an officer of inferior rank. The car was even dirty. The rays of the sun, just beginning to edge above the horizon at this ungodly latitude, were absorbed in a coating of grime.

Santera sipped some of the tea that Marina had pressed into his hands and turned from the window. Chavchavadze and Bykov sat at the table that last night had been laden with food. It was stripped nearly bare now, down to a tablecloth and their teacups. He had not spoken to either of them since getting off the phone with Rogov in Moscow. The silence in the room was sullen and stifling. It suited his mood. He hoped the two Russians were unhappy and getting unhappier.

He himself was very unhappy. His picture had turned out to be either stolen or a fraud. Then Merrill had demanded to be taken to the station and put on the first train to Finland, insisting that he would be involved no further in this deal. Schlegel had asked to do the same. Santera wondered if he had done the right thing by letting the Englishman and the German go. He decided that he had had no choice. Too many people knew Merrill and Schlegel had gone to Russia with him. Killing them would have had too many unpleasant consequences. They would know better than to talk about what they had seen.

In a sense, Santera thought, his decision to let Merrill go showed his own maturity and coolness. Ten years ago he would have shot the man himself. Now he was composed in the face of adversity.

The Chaika stopped outside the front door and a tall, trim man with a thick head of graying hair, brushed back from his head in a stiff pompadour, emerged. He was wearing the ugliest gray suit Santera had ever seen. It was some kind of polyester, as nubbly as a bad carpet, with pinstripes, wide lapels, and a flared pair of pants. He imagined that the man had little use for civilian clothes.

They stepped out into the anteroom to greet him. The officer blinked a couple of times, and Santera saw his eyes sweep quickly around the room, taking in the sudden opulence of its furnishings. Then he stepped forward, hand outstretched.

"Grebenshikov, Valentin Nikolayevich," he said, addressing Santera.

Before Santera could shake the hand, Chavchavadze stepped between them and took it first. He introduced himself, making it a point to welcome Grebenshikov to his office. The attempt to reassert some status evidently failed. Grebenshikov shook his hand with all the enthusiasm he would have shown in greeting a leper.

That was the trouble whenever you established a business in a new country, Santera thought. You almost always had to begin dealing with the wrong people, and wait patiently until you figured out who the right ones were. Looking at Grebenshikov's obvious contempt for Chavchavadze, he began to suspect who the right people were in Russia. The army had always been the only institution in the country that worked. At least the old army had.

Chavchavadze, still attempting to pretend he was the host and chairman of this meeting, introduced Grebenshikov to Santera.

"Minister Rogov asked me to convey his regards," Grebenshikov said in Spanish.

"Thank him," Santera said, pleased that they had a common language. "And may I ask your rank and position, please?"

Grebenshikov looked surprised. "Minister Rogov did not tell you?"

"Uh, no, he didn't. He didn't say who would be coming."

Grebenshikov weighed this information for a moment. Santera wondered if he was asking for a breach of security of some kind.

"Colonel General," Grebenshikov replied, presumably having decided that Chavchavadze knew anyway. "And deputy minister of defense."

"Excellent," Santera said, and smiled for the first time in twelve hours. "And where did you learn your excellent Spanish?"

"In Cuba," Grebenshikov replied.

They entered the dining room and sat down around the table. Marina brought more tea.

Grebenshikov took a sip. "Now, how can we help you?" he asked, addressing Santera. "Minister Rogov tells me that you've lost something."

"That's correct," Santera said. "A painting. Stolen. Thanks to these idiots."

Bykov glowered. He had the feeling they were talking about him, and he could sense that what they were saying was not flattering. But he took his cue from Chavchavadze and said nothing.

"And you don't know who has it or where it is?"

"That's correct. But we have an idea."

"An idea?"

Santera turned to Marina. "Tell your uncle to show him the picture," he said in English.

Marina translated. Bykov pulled the picture from his pocket and slid it across the table to Grebenshikov.

It was a black and white photograph showing two women, a mother and daughter probably, smiling in front of a dacha. It was summertime, clearly, and they had on cotton blouses and loose baggy skirts of the type that Soviet women had worn in the seventies. One sat in a wheelchair.

"We don't know where this dacha is," Chavchavadze said to Grebenshikov in Russian. "But the people in the picture were involved in the theft. We searched their apartment. There was no one there, but we found this photo in an album. We think they may be hiding the painting at this dacha."

Grebenshikov shrugged. "But in St. Petersburg oblast there must be thousands of dachas."

"Not many like this one," Chavchavadze said. "See this glassed-in veranda? Pre-Revolutionary construction. And the trees all around in the background? It's set off in the woods by itself somewhere. And it's in use now, unlike most of the dachas. There will be signs of that."

Grebenshikov nodded. "And you think we could find it—"

"With helicopters," Chavchavadze said.

"All right," Grebenshikov said. "My orders are to assist you if we can. But we cannot do the job of the Ministry of the Interior. It would cause too many political problems in Moscow. I can order some helicopters to search for this place. We can patrol the Finnish border and the harbors to make sure no one smuggles it out. But if we find this picture, you'll have to call the *militsia* to make the arrest."

"Or take care of it ourselves," Chavchavadze said.

Grebenshikov looked at him squarely. "Don't tell me what you don't want me to know," he said.

Chapter Thirty-one

IT WAS HARDER TO FIND MCCOY'S GALLERY IN the car than it had been on foot. In the hour before dawn the sky was blackest and the little street address tags on the sides of buildings could barely be seen. It took Burke a couple of passes up and down Nevsky Prospekt to spot the right alley leading to the right courtyard.

At least, he thought, the chore of finding the building distracted him. There was no such succor for the woman who sat in the seat next to him, staring at the windshield but seeing nothing.

Numbly, she helped him unload the copy from the car and waited while he fumbled with the lock that opened the door. Finally, it swung open, and he flipped on the lights. Recessed fixtures illuminated the gallery's wares and left the rest of the room in shadow. It seemed gloomy and foreboding.

He unlocked the office door with the second key on the small ring McCoy had given him. Then he lugged the painting inside and looked for a place to hide it. She had an enormous, sleek desk of polished blond wood, probably birch, that looked like it belonged in a Scandinavian design studio. No doubt, Burke thought, it had been made in Virginia rather than in Sweden. And, no doubt, it had a few secret drawers. In front of the desk there were

Eames chairs, in brown leather and chrome, for clients. Rather than paintings, the walls held tapestries, showing Russian church scenes.

The biggest tapestry covered half the wall on the far side of the room. Behind it he found the door of a sizable vault with a lever handle and a black combination lock. He tried the lever. It did not move.

He could find no place else to hide the painting but a coat closet, so he stashed the copy there, between a couple of old parkas, resting on a pair of black pumps. The figure of Leda looked vaguely obscene in the closet, as if he were hiding her nakedness, or perhaps the way her left hand caressed the neck of the smug swan beside her. He stared vacantly at the picture for a second, marveling at the skill that Andrusha and Nadyezhda Petrovna had put into it.

Having held the real Leonardo in his hands, Burke could see no difference between it and this imitation. He had been in enough museums to know how paint looked as it aged, showing fine lines like an aging face. This one had precisely that kind of web of cracks. It looked about five hundred years older than it actually was.

It was, in fact, distinguishable from the real thing only because of a little mark on the back. That, suddenly, reminded him of what he had yet to do.

Like the vault, the desk drawers were locked. But on the desktop, in a small ceramic pot that McCoy used for pencils and pens, he found a letter opener.

He went back to the closet and turned the picture around. To his surprise, the back of the panel was littered with letters and numbers, seemingly written long ago in pencil or some kind of charcoal. Some he recognized as Russian, and he saw a date—1767. That, presumably, was the date when this panel, whatever it had originally contained, was added to the Hermitage collection. Some were in Latin characters, but he could make out no words.

"Right upper corner," he murmured to himself. The mark would be small, discreet. He scratched it in. The wood gave way grudgingly under the dull point of the letter opener. He rubbed a thumb over the letter, taking a little of the newness off the mark. It would have to do.

He heard Lyubov behind him, and when he turned around, she was standing there, her face still frozen in grief, her shoulders hunched under the burden she was carrying in her mind. Her eyes were a pale, painful red, but she'd stopped crying. Her hair fell in sweaty strands and tendrils around her face, and her hands hung down in front of her waist. She was twisting them together, making the skin over her knuckles turn white, then fiery red, then white again.

"Now it's perfect," she said, and started to cry.

Lyubov sobbed quietly at first, and then loudly, with a keening cry of pain interspersed with gasps for breath. She did not move. She stood with her shoulders caving in, her hands in front of her, and cried until tears were pouring copiously down each cheek.

He felt helpless, as he always did when a woman cried. Finally, he put his arms around her and drew her to his shoulder.

"I'm sorry," he said. "If it's any consolation, I know you've suffered a terrible loss. I know how angry you must be."

She continued to sob, but she raised her face and fixed him in the glare of her raw eyes. "Why? Why my mother? She never hurt anyone."

"I don't know," he said.

Lyubov's face contorted. "Is it us? Is it Russians? Why is it always we who suffer this way?"

"I don't know," he said.

It seemed to him that she was right, that Russia did have a tragic penchant for destroying her best people, that for every Nadyezhda Petrovna, she produced a Bykov, for every Sakharov, a Lenin. But he doubted that this would comfort her.

"All I can tell you," he continued, "is that I think, little by little, the pain subsides. It doesn't go away. Nothing is ever the same. But if you're lucky, I think, you start to remember some good things, and you hang on to them and you realize that for all the pain of the loss, the good things outweigh it and you're glad that you had them."

She stopped crying. "How long does it take to feel that way?"

He gently squeezed her shoulders. "I don't know. When I get there, I'll let you know."

The faint hint of a smile flickered quickly across her face, and she gestured to the new mark on the back of the painting.

"Why did you do that? What does it matter now?"

"Because unless we divert them, I think they're going to find your dacha sooner or later. It may take them a day or two, but there have to be records somewhere that show that you have it. They'll look there. Or they'll find one of us. Before they do, I want to figure out a way to send them here somehow. Let them find this. Maybe they'll fall for it."

Visibly, she pulled herself together. "Wouldn't it be nice if they did," she said. "I think it would make Mama happy."

"She wouldn't be the only one," Burke said.

When he saw that traffic, under the glowering gray sky of dawn, was all but nonexistent, he remembered that it was Saturday. He accelerated to 130 kilometers an hour, and the drive to the dacha took less time than he'd anticipated.

The landscape changed quickly and abruptly. One mile held the stately, pastel buildings of riverside St. Petersburg and a bridge over the Neva. The next was lined with tired *trushchobi* of dun colored brick, the instant slums built in the Khrushchev period. Then there was a mile or so of Brezhnev-era high rises, crumbling at the edges, interspersed by high walls and factory gates. And then the road burst into the countryside, dotted with cottages, covered in a thick layer of white snow, blowing softly into drifts behind the wind off the sea. The road narrowed to a rough blacktop, two lanes wide, but without a stripe down the middle.

Trying to get his bearings, Burke looked for the sun. It was nothing more than a silvery smudge behind some of the low-lying clouds to his right. And as he looked for it, he saw the helicopter.

It was a big, bulbous-nosed attack helicopter with red stars painted on the tail, the kind that had become the favorite prey of the mujahedeen in Afghanistan. He once had known its NATO designation—Mi-20-something. It was flying low and slow, a few hundred feet over tree level, perhaps two hundred meters in from the road. As he watched, it arced to the right, made a tight circle, and kept going. He slowed the car a bit, letting the copter move ahead until it was a small specter toward the horizon.

He looked around. In the distance, to his left, he saw another copter, flying at the same altitude. He looked at Lyubov. If she'd noticed anything, it didn't register on her face. After her brief surge of vitality at the gallery, she had subsided into the same shocked and numb state she'd been in when they left the Hermitage. He pointed to the helicopter until she saw it.

"Military base around here?"

"No," she said. "Unless there's something secret I don't know about."

"Maybe," he replied, "it's just the National Guard, out for weekend maneuvers."

"National Guard?"

"Don't have one here, do you?"

She shook her head.

"Then we've got worse problems than I thought," Burke said.

She seemed uncomprehending.

They sped by a gateway made of some kind of piping, with rust poking through the flaking, pale blue and red paint that once adorned it. He saw the words "Legacy of Ilyich," formed in steel ribbons above the gateway, and beyond it, a long, low white barn. There was no sign that anyone was working.

"The turn is up ahead," she said, "about a kilometer. On the right."

They passed from the farm field into a mixed forest of pine and birch trees that blocked most of the faint light from behind the clouds. He turned on the headlights.

"Slow down," she said.

The road led straight off into the woods, and he could see the tracks McCoy had made in the snow when she arrived.

He checked in the rearview mirror. There was no one behind them. He turned right.

The dry snow presented no traction problems. After he had traversed a hundred yards, the driveway curved and he spotted the dacha through the trees. The early sun was glinting off the windows of the sun porch. It was larger than the modest, rickety little cottages of two or three rooms that were the pride and salvation of some of his friends in Moscow. It must be quite old, he realized. There was even a barn behind the house which, the tire tracks told him, served as a garage.

Before he reached it, he could see McCoy standing warily inside the door, and she stood that way until they had parked the car and emerged from it and she was certain they were alone.

She looked haggard and edgy. "Thank God you made it," she said, simultaneously hugging him and grabbing the computer from his hand as if she were afraid he would drop it. "Did you get into the palace?"

Burke nodded.

"And did you find her?"

She looked at Lyubov then, and understood. Lyubov stood mute.

McCoy reached out and embraced her. The Russian woman leaned softly into McCoy's shoulder for a moment, then straightened up again. Her bearing said she was ready to postpone the rest of her mourning and get on with what had to be done, the task of protecting the painting her mother had died trying to save.

"Where did you put the Leonardo?" Lyubov asked.

"Don't ask."

McCoy's reply struck Burke as abrupt and harsh in the context, even making allowances for the stress she was under.

"Where is Andrusha?" Lyubov asked.

"Asleep," McCoy said.

Lyubov shook her head ruefully. "How typical."

McCoy, to Burke's mild surprise, took up for him. "He deserves a rest," she said. "He worked hard until just a little while ago. All night. And he worked well. He's a very capable man."

"I know, but . . ." Lyubov let the sentence trail away, leaving the impression that there were things about Andrusha that were less than ideal.

McCoy did not pursue the subject. She took the computer from its case, set it down on a table and turned it on. Then she started to type.

Lyubov walked off toward the back of the house. Burke, searching for the kitchen, followed her. When he caught up to her, she was staring, mouth open, at one of the walls.

Burke looked around the room. Like Nadyezhda Petrovna's parlor in St. Petersburg, it had the look of a small museum. But the art on these walls was all modern, abstractions of shapes, patterns, colors, and textures.

He followed her eyes to two particularly large canvases, and he understood.

"New paintings?"

Like a diver breaking the surface of the water, she brought her thoughts back from wherever they had been and focused her attention on him.

"Yes. Er, no. I mean, I did them," she said, hesitating between each phrase.

Burke could not be angry at this weak attempt at a lie. He wanted to say something that would not be unkind but would let her know he hadn't been deceived. But that kind of tact had always been hard for him, and he hesitated.

As he did, they heard two sounds—an anguished curse from McCoy and the beat of helicopter rotors, growing louder overhead.

He hurried back to the front room, to the windows.

McCoy's eyes were jumping from the computer screen in front of her to the view outside.

"What's the matter?" he asked.

"This damn thing won't be usable for another four hours, till a satellite comes overhead. And now . . ."

"Somebody else is overhead," he finished her sentence.

She nodded and joined him at the window.

The rotor noise faded slightly and then grew louder again.

"They're coming back," she said.

They could briefly see the underside of the huge machine, its missile mounts empty. It still looked powerful and dangerous.

"It's flying very low," Burke observed.

"Yeah," McCoy said. "Maybe it's just a training exercise."

They waited for the sound of the rotors to fade, but they did not.

"Either it's a hovering exercise, or we've been spotted," Burke said.

She nodded grimly. The rotor sound was directly overhead now, and they could see the snow blowing furiously in the yard, whipped up by the downdrafts.

"Oh, we're spotted," she said. "It's my own damn fault for lighting the stove. I didn't think they'd have choppers."

He wondered if the helicopter could land in that small clearing. Probably, he thought, if the pilot was skillful.

He had a vision of armed men in boots clambering out of the helicopter and he wondered how much interrogation would be required before he would tell them about the painting on the wall in the studio. Perhaps a minute, he thought. Maybe two if he were feeling especially plucky.

Then, like summer storm clouds that vanish quickly, the rotor noise started to fade again. This time, the helicopter did not circle and return. It moved steadily away until all that was left was the faint sound of the wind blowing through the birches and pines outside, and of their own ragged breathing. He felt a couple of drops of sweat trickle down his forehead and he wiped them away. His skin felt greasy.

"Well, they certainly had time to give us a good look," he said to McCoy. "So you think Chavchavadze has connections with the air force?"

"Of course he does." The speaker was Lyubov, who had returned to the front room while their attention was focused above. "He owns everything."

"We have to assume you're right," McCoy said. "They'll pass on our location, and Chavchavadze will be here in—about fifteen minutes."

"That's how long we took," Burke confirmed.

"All right, then," McCoy said.

Her voice, Burke thought, was remarkably calm and commanding for someone who had been on edge for twenty-four consecutive hours. He would not be so calm in her position.

"Here's what we need to do. Colin, I need you to get to a phone and make a call for me."

"There's no phone out here?"

"No," Lyubov said. "It's almost impossible to get one installed, even in the city, unless you pay bribes."

Burke thought, briefly, about insisting that he stay and help her. Romantic as it sounded, it would also be stupid.

He nodded. "Of course."

"Good. Take down this number: 235-26-12. Find a phone, but don't go to your hotel. They'll probably be looking for you there. Call that number. It's the duty station for the FBI liaison here in St. Petersburg. Tell whomever answers the phone that you're call-ing about a visa for a friend who wants to visit your cousin in North Dakota. North Dakota. Got that?"

Burke pulled out his notebook and wrote down the number. "North Dakota. Got it."

"They may tell you to wait and speak to someone else. When they do, tell them who you are, where I am, and that I need help. Immediately. All right?"

"Okay," he said.

"Take Lyubov and Andrusha with you," McCoy said. "Then all of you go somewhere they're not going to look for you—a friend's place. Not back to your own places or to the hotel. All right? Wait there. I'll call your hotel, Burke, and leave a message when it's safe. You can call in and get it."

"No," Lyubov said. "I'm not leaving."

"Lyuba?"

It was Andrusha's voice, coming from another room, muffled by a wall.

In a second he burst into the room, his clothes rumpled, hair tousled, eyes bleary from sleep.

"I dreamed I heard a helicopter," he said. "Then I heard your voice. How is Nadyezhda Petrovna?"

Lyubov looked away.

Burke walked up to Andrusha. "She's dead, I'm afraid," he said, and put a hand on the man's shoulder.

Andrusha looked too shocked to cry, or to react in any way. "She's dead?"

Burke nodded.

Tears welled in Andrusha's eyes. "She was like my mother," he said to Burke.

Then he stepped across to Lyubov and hugged her. Her arms remained limp at her sides, but she seemed to take comfort from his closeness. Finally, she raised her hands to his shoulders and clung to them, trembling.

"We'll be all right," Andrusha said to her. "We'll be all right."

"Not if you don't get out of here," McCoy said.

"I'm not going," Lyubov said again.

"You have to," McCoy told her firmly.

"No," Lyubov replied, sounding adamant. "My mother died to protect this painting. I won't leave it."

"You won't do any good here," Burke said. "And I might need help in St. Petersburg."

"I won't go, either," Andrusha said.

"You have to come, Andrusha," Burke said. "For one thing, you've got to help me find a place to hide."

Andrusha seemed uncertain.

"Go," Lyubov said. "He needs you."

"And you?"

"I'm staying here."

McCoy shrugged. "There's no time to argue. If you want to stay, you can."

There was one more thing Burke wanted. "What's the combination to the vault in your office?" he asked McCoy.

"Why?"

"Might be useful to me," Burke said. "Don't ask. Trust me."

McCoy smiled through tight lips. "It's empty," she said.

"All the better."

"It's my mother's birthday. Six left, twenty right, thirty-seven left."

"Got it," Burke said.

"Take the Zhiguli," McCoy said. "It's in the barn out back. The helicopter couldn't have seen it."

She handed him the keys and they went outside. The snow felt soft and fluffy against his feet, but the wind sliced through his jacket and stung his cheeks.

Burke and Andrusha slid open the heavy wooden door to the barn. Burke turned around and found McCoy standing two feet away. He stepped toward her, and she put her arms around him and squeezed, for perhaps five seconds. Then she stepped away.

"Take care of yourself," Burke said, wishing he could think of something more eloquent.

"You, too," she replied.

Quickly, Burke got in and started the old blue Zhiguli. Its seats were so cold he thought they were going to bond to his thighs. Andrusha got in.

They backed straight down the drive, past McCoy's gray Volvo, through the snowy, shadowy woods, toward the road. Burke had a last glimpse of McCoy, standing with her hands on her hips in front of the sun porch before the drive curved and trees blocked his view. He did not envy her the chance to remain behind.

"They killed her," Andrusha was muttering. "Killed her."

Burke poked the car out into the road and checked for traffic. There was none. He set out for St. Petersburg, aware of the way the rattling Soviet car strained to do eighty kilometers an hour, where the Volvo had cruised at 130.

He'd covered a mile when he noticed headlights approaching. The lights closed the gap between them with astonishing rapidity.

He hunched down in his seat and pulled his collar up against his cheek. He told Andrusha to do the same.

Then the oncoming traffic blew by them. In the lead was a black ZIL limousine, the one he'd seen in front of the Hermitage, looking like a houseboat on wheels. Then came a Mercedes, only slightly smaller. A black Volvo roared close behind. The caravan must have been doing close to 150 kilometers an hour, he thought. As it roared by, the Zhiguli shuddered and rocked in the turbulent air flow. Burke struggled to keep it on the road.

He looked in the rearview mirror. The cars were not slowing. Presumably, he hadn't been recognized.

"What was that?" Andrusha said.

"Tourists, I guess," Burke said. "Taking a drive in the country."

Chapter Thirty-two

RAFAEL SANTERA STOOD CLOSE TO THE WARM stove in the dacha kitchen and studied the two women sitting a few feet away from him on straight-backed wooden chairs.

They were both attractive. One was dark and the other was fair. They reminded him of vanilla and chocolate ice cream, and of a time when he was eleven and scraped together enough money selling old bottles to buy a cone with a scoop of each kind. That had been a memorable day.

It would be so interesting to interrogate them together that he almost hoped Miguel did not discover the painting.

As if in answer to his unspoken wish, Miguel, Bykov, Chavchavadze, Marina, and three other Colombians converged on the kitchen, hands empty save for the semiautomatic pistols each of the men except Chavchavadze carried.

"If it's here, it's well-hidden," Miguel said to him in Spanish.

"We looked in the barn, all over the dacha, and we did not see it," Chavchavadze added. Marina translated into English. "We may need to tear the house apart."

Santera shook his head. "I don't think that will be necessary."

He took two casual paces to his left and issued another order in Spanish.

Quickly and precisely, Miguel and three Colombians surrounded Bykov, pointing their guns at his head from a range of
about a foot. Miguel had a tight smile on his face. He grabbed the
barrel of Bykov's pistol and tried to take it away from him.

Bykov, his face glazed with a look of surprise and consternation,
clenched the gun tightly.

"Tell him to give it up," Santera told Chavchavadze. "Or we'll
blow his head off. And then yours."

Marina, stuttering and pale, translated. Chavchavadze hesitated.
All of his men had been detailed to the hotels and other points in
the city where Burke or Andrusha might show up. He had only
Bykov to back him.

Santera looked at him and knew exactly what he was thinking
and exactly what he would respond.

"Give it to them, Vanya," Chavchavadze said. "It'll be all
right."

Bykov's gun had been trained, casually, on the dark woman. If
he fired it, he might hit her. But he would be dead before he got
a chance to fire it again. He could struggle. But again, he would
be dead before he could do any damage to the people who had
turned against him.

He was a man capable of calculating the odds quickly and acting on them. The odds were not good if he gave up his gun. They
were worse if he kept it. Slowly, his fingers gave up their grip and
relinquished it.

Miguel, still smiling, slipped the gun into his jacket pocket.

"Good," Santera said. "I'm happy you agree with me."

Chavchavadze, his face pale, nodded at Marina's translation.

"Now," Santera went on, turning his head slightly and raising
his voice to include Lyubov and McCoy. "We have here three people. One is the daughter and assistant of the woman who painted
that brilliant forgery. The second, the black one, says she is an art
dealer. I suspect she may be telling the truth about that. The third,
your friend Bykov, was in charge of security at the Hermitage and
had the woman's studio under video surveillance."

Chavchavadze nodded mutely as he heard the translation.

"I didn't know anything about a forgery," Bykov snapped.

Santera ignored him. "I suggest to you that all three must have been involved in this."

Chavchavadze nodded. When he did, Bykov's flush deepened and the veins stood out on his neck.

"Bastard!" he hissed. He was, Santera noticed, beginning to tremble. It would be best to move quickly.

"Now we could tear this place apart, but that would take a lot of time and it might not be successful. I suggest instead that we get these three to tell us where the painting is."

Chavchavadze nodded again.

Santera nodded at Miguel. This was a scene that, with slight variations, they had played before. As soon as he had seen the birch trees outside the dacha, he quietly told Miguel to prepare for it. Miguel knew exactly what to do. Equally important, he wanted very much to do it, and had since the moment Bykov had humiliated him in Chavchavadze's dining room.

Quickly, Miguel lowered the barrel of his pistol and fired one precise shot. The blast echoed and reverberated in the small room, deafening them all for a moment and filling the air with acrid smoke. Marina screamed.

The bullet tore through Ivan Bykov's left knee, shattering the patella and severing the anterior cruciate ligament. Bellowing in pain, Bykov fell heavily, clumsily, onto his left side. He reminded Santera of a bull in the final stages of a corrida, falling for the first time.

The remaining four Colombians each covered someone with his pistol: Chavchavadze, Marina, and the two women, the daughter and the art dealer. They all remained still, too shocked to do anything and aware that they would probably be shot if they tried.

Bykov writhed on the floor, instinctively reaching down to his knee to staunch the bleeding and hold it together. Blood started to seep through his brown trousers and into his fingers.

"All right," Miguel said in Spanish. "Get him outside."

Two of the Colombians unceremoniously picked up Bykov's shoulders and feet. They did not bother to raise the torso off the ground. They dragged him out the front door. Bykov bellowed, then whimpered. Then he was quiet. He was, Santera realized, going into shock. They deposited him in the snow in front of the house.

The other two Colombians ran to the barn and emerged a minute later carrying half a dozen lengths of rope, a sledgehammer, and a pair of iron stakes.

Miguel, watching them through the kitchen window, grinned when he saw the equipment. He covered Chavchavadze and the two women for another moment, then gestured to them with the barrel of his gun, instructing them to walk outside. They did.

Outside, in the cold air, Miguel hunched his shoulders inside his parka. He looked for the likeliest spot, and selected two young birch trees, each thin, whippy, and about twenty feet high, growing eight feet apart, about ten feet from the south wall of the dacha.

"Those two trees over there," he said to the two men who had dragged Bykov outside. They nodded, picked him up again and dragged him to a point equidistant between the trees.

The pair of Colombians with the ropes began lashing them to Bykov's ankles. He revived enough to groan, raise his head and see what they were doing. But as soon as he began to thrash in the snow as if trying to escape, one of the men twisted his left foot, putting pressure on the shattered knee. Bykov gasped and his head fell back. His skin was pale and sweat was forming on his forehead, despite the freezing temperature.

The three women and Chavchavadze watched, still uncertain as to what was about to happen.

Santera stepped outside only long enough to address Chavchavadze and the two women. "This is something we do in Colombia to extract information, only with slightly different trees. It almost always works."

He nodded to Miguel and then stepped back inside. He did not generally enjoy watching this form of interrogation, and he particularly did not like the cold.

At Miguel's command, the Colombians who had emerged from the barn began to shinny to the top of the two birch trees. They lashed two more lengths of rope to the tops of the trunks, where the bare branches were. Then, hanging onto the trees with one hand, the rope with another, they shifted their weight and dropped, so that the two trees bent under their weight, toward each other. Their body weight alone had relatively little effect; the trunks remained about six feet apart at the top. Then the two men let go of the trunks and leaped the remaining eight feet to the ground, holding onto the ropes. The other two Colombians grasped the ropes, too, and with all four men pulling, they bent the two trees farther, until the tops touched and intersected about eight feet off the snow-covered ground.

Two of the Colombians lashed the ropes around Bykov's ankles to the tree trunks, at nearly the same high point as the ropes held by the climbers.

Slowly, the two climbers relaxed the tension in their ropes, and the trunks began to rise toward their natural position. Bykov's body was pulled upward, until he hung, moaning, upside down between the two trees.

Miguel nodded again at the men holding the restraining ropes, and they released more tension.

Bykov's body rose higher still, and the two trees began to pull his legs farther apart, until they were stretched wide, like the two prongs of a wishbone about to snap.

Bykov screamed in fear and pain, and the sound seemed to hang in the freezing air, contained there by the surrounding curtain of snow-laden fir trees.

McCoy winced. Lyubov trembled. Marina bit her lip. Chavchavadze watched, impassive.

The trees were still bent at a forty-five-degree angle, and it was clear what would happen if the two Colombians released the ropes.

"Now. Ask where painting is," Miguel said to Marina.

Marina swallowed visibly, but said nothing.

"Ask now," Miguel said. He looked around, and his lips curved upward slightly, just enough for Marina to see the pleasure this exercise was affording him. "We have many trees," he said.

Marina blinked, opened her mouth and tried to speak. No sound came out. She coughed and opened her mouth again.

"Uncle, tell them where the painting is," she said.

Bykov's face narrowed slightly. "I don't know," he whispered. He was wavering on the edge between consciousness and unconsciousness, torn between the pain in his knee and his knowledge of what would happen if the trees were released. "Tell him he has the wrong person. The girl knows."

Marina translated.

Miguel listened, nodded again, and then gestured toward the sledgehammer. The two idle Colombians began pounding the stakes into the ground near Bykov's shoulders. It took them a few blows to pierce the frozen surface, but in a minute it was done. They wrapped the ends of the restraining ropes around the stakes and left Bykov there, hanging and groaning.

Miguel turned to Lyubov and McCoy. "Do you want to tell me now?" he asked. "Or do you want to be next to play in the trees?"

Chapter Thirty-three

BURKE PULLED THE ZHIGULI OVER AND parked next to a low mound of crusty black snow on the outbound side of Nevsky Prospekt, two blocks from McCoy's gallery. The street had filled with Saturday shoppers. They clogged the sidewalks, peering into shop windows, trying to spot something affordable through the filigree of frost that had formed on the glass during the night. He kept the engine running. The heater had finally begun to produce a little warmth, accompanied by a faint odor that he hoped was not carbon monoxide.

The crowds would make it impossible, Burke realized, to tell whether someone was watching the gallery.

He turned to look at Andrusha Karpov. The Russian was chewing on the nail of his right index finger. His eyes looked glazed, and he was staring straight out through the windshield, as he had throughout their ride into town from the dacha.

"Andrusha," Burke said. "How're you feeling?"

The words seemed to startle the Russian. He jerked his finger out of his mouth and clasped his hands together atop his belly, grinding them together like meshing gears.

"Fine," Andrusha said. "I feel fine. What do you want me to do?"

The words had come out too quickly and mechanically to be even remotely convincing, but Burke appreciated the effort behind them.

He pulled McCoy's keys from his pocket and dangled them in front of Karpov's face until Karpov mechanically reached up and took them. Then he gave Karpov the scrap of paper on which he had written the combination to the vault.

"Andrusha," he said, enunciating each syllable as if talking to a drunk. "We've got to split up. I've got to find a phone to call for help. You've got to go into the gallery. You see the entrance? It's up there under that old sign that says *Gastronom*. See it?"

Andrusha nodded slowly.

"You go up there, into the courtyard, and look for the McCoy-Fokine Gallery sign on the ground floor. Okay? Then you go inside and into her office. You open the vault, using that combination. Okay?"

Andrusha did not respond.

"Okay?" Burke grabbed his shoulder, and Andrusha let out a heavy sigh.

"Understood," he said.

"Good. Then you go into the closet and find the copy that Nadyezhda Petrovna painted. I've fixed it so it's now exactly like the original."

He paused, wondering if Andrusha would ask how. He did not.

"Take that picture, put it in the vault, and get out of there," Burke said.

"Why?" Andrusha looked as if his brain had engaged for the first time since he'd gotten into the car.

"Packaging. They're not going to believe we'd keep a painting like that in a closet if we have a vault to store it in," Burke explained.

"Okay," Andrusha said. His face had lost its blank look, and his jaw seemed a little tighter.

"Remember. Don't go back to your own apartment," Burke said. "Go someplace they won't look for you. Ride the Metro all day if you have to."

Andrusha smiled tightly at him, reached over and patted

Burke's shoulder. "Don't worry," he said. "And don't shout. I can hear you."

Burke blinked. He hadn't realized he had raised his voice, but in the echoes of his memory he could hear it, and he knew that Andrusha was right; he'd been almost shouting. And he was startled by the sudden gathering of wit and energy that Andrusha had managed. For the first time since leaving the dacha, he began to feel confident that Andrusha would do what he was supposed to do.

He was relieved that Andrusha had not asked why he didn't simply make his phone call from the gallery. The reason, as perhaps Andrusha realized, was that someone might be there waiting for them. They could not take the chance.

Without another word, Andrusha opened the door into the snowbank, squeezed his bulk through the opening like an eel squeezing through a hole, and walked off toward the gallery. Burke watched his large rear end sway for a moment, then he put the car into gear. He wanted to get a few blocks away before he stopped again.

He drove two blocks to Uprising Square and parked the car in front of the Moscow station, figuring that the crowds waiting for trains would provide good cover.

He edged past the array of money changers, cabbage sellers, shell-game players, and bottle buyers at the entrance to the station and went inside, through brown doors with fingerprints worn into them by the pressure of countless hands. The station hall was noisy and chaotic. A family of four fetid Komis, their pink faces grimy, snored on a bench directly in front of him, their belongings wrapped up in bundles and tied by string to the forefinger of the largest of the four, who appeared to be a woman. Behind them, other waiting passengers sat or stretched out, like a drowsy congregation on rows of benches. Beyond them he could see the black and yellow display board with the train schedule. And behind it, a few clusters of boys playing pinball. Travelers crisscrossed the hall, carrying cardboard suitcases.

He looked for the red neon M that marked an entrance to the subway. There were always phones at subway entrances.

He found a row of nearly a dozen phones, gunmetal-gray with round dials and big, clunky black earpieces, and he groped in his pocket. He sighed with relief. He still had half a dozen phone tokens with him.

He pulled out his notebook and dialed the number McCoy had given him. He got a busy signal. He dialed the number again, very carefully. Busy again.

Trying to remain calm, he hung up the phone and looked for another. Maybe this one was defective. He saw an open phone and moved to it. He dialed again. Busy again. He dialed one more time. Still busy.

"Shit," he muttered, and hung up.

He stepped back and watched an old woman walk up to the same phone, dial a number, drop a token into the slot, and begin an animated conversation. A train roared into the station below, and the noise drowned out what she was saying, except for the words "oatmeal prices."

Obviously, the phone worked.

He waited for the old woman to finish, and when she did, he picked up the phone again. He dialed. The same buzz, sounding like a personal taunt, filled his ears. Angry, he smashed the receiver down on its cradle.

"What's the trouble, man?"

It was a kid, the kind who hustled in train stations for a living, wearing bad Polish imitations of Wrangler jeans, genuine Adidas basketball shoes with the laces artfully undone, and a greasy, rabbit-fur *shapka* with the ear flaps pulled halfway down.

"Can't dial a number. Always busy," Burke said.

"Too bad. Where you calling?"

The kid was obviously aware that he was a foreigner, and Burke hoped that he was just interested in helping. "It's a place on Ultisa Petra Lavrova," he said.

The boy nodded. "Does the number begin with 274, 215, or 235?" he asked.

Cautiously, Burke nodded. He hated giving away this much to someone who could be a plant.

"You can't call there from here, man," the boy said. He grinned, showing off a gap where one eyetooth should have been.

"Why not? It's in the city."

The boy shrugged. "Phone system's fucked up, man. Try somewhere around Pushkinskaya. You can get through from there."

"I don't get it," Burke said.

"This is a Third World country now, man," the boy said. "Not much works. Try Pushkinskaya."

He shouldered past Burke and picked up the phone, starting his own call.

Burke watched him for a few seconds. The kid waited for someone to pick up the phone on the other end, inserted his token, and began a conversation that included a persuasive number of grunts and one loud snort. There was no reason to believe he hadn't been telling the truth.

But Burke walked very warily back to the Zhiguli, half expecting to hear footsteps behind him and feel a strong hand clamp down on his shoulder.

Nothing happened. He noticed only the usual passing travelers eyeing his shoes or his overcoat as he walked by and making instant judgments about whether he was a foreigner or a rich Russian.

He knew vaguely where Pushkinskaya Station was. He turned the Zhiguli around and headed back down Nevsky Prospekt, a sense of urgency overtaking him. He pushed the gas pedal to the floor, overtook a clanking tram, and made an illegal left turn onto Liteyny. The tram's brakes squealed and the driver angrily blew a horn at him. He barely heard.

He pulled up to Pushkinskaya and left the car without bothering to check whether he was in a legal parking zone. He hustled down the broad, gray granite steps dusted with muddy snow, taking them two at a time, and found a phone bank nearly identical to the ones in the Moscow station. But this one was more exposed to the outside air. He shivered as a cold gust blew against the back of his neck.

This time the phone on the other end rang, and he exhaled slowly and completely. He had his token ready, but somehow he dropped it.

He didn't bother to pick it up. He jammed his fingers into his pocket and fished out another one, but by the time he inserted it into the slot at the top of the phone, the line was dead.

Cursing, he dialed again.

This time he got through.

"Connors."

"Uh, hi. This is Colin Burke," he said. He felt suddenly foolish. He had never used code words. They reminded him of the old black and white movies about World War II. That was not his generation.

"Yes," Connors prodded.

"I'm calling about a visa for someone to visit North Dakota," Burke said.

"Who are you and where are you calling from?" Connors asked, sounding more interested.

"The name is Burke, and I'm calling from Pushkinskaya Station on behalf of Desdemona McCoy."

"Shit," Connors said. "What is it?"

"She's in major trouble and she needs help," Burke said. He told him about the location of the dacha and the number of cars in Chavchavadze's entourage.

"Shit," Connors said again. "Your timing is impeccable. All hell's broken loose in Moscow, and nearly everything we have is down there."

"All hell?"

"Riots. A crowd occupied part of the Kremlin. The government's trying to find troops willing to root them out of there."

"Spontaneous?"

"Who the hell knows?"

"So can you help McCoy?"

Connors paused, and Burke could hear his exhalation.

"We'll do what we can. I take it she doesn't have a phone out there."

"Right."

"Well, I don't have a Delta Force platoon standing by. I'll round up what we can and get out there."

To Burke, the man sounded like a bureaucrat, and he knew as well that the FBI liked helping the CIA about as much as Hutus liked helping Tutsis. "How long will it take?"

"I don't know," Connors said. "Hopefully half an hour."

"But maybe longer."

"You're in this country. You know how long it takes to organize anything?"

"Can I do anything?"

"No," Connors said. "Go back to your hotel. Stay there. Or better yet, come to the consulate. You'll be safe. Someone will give you lunch."

"Thanks," Burke said, "but I'm not hungry."

Burke looked at his watch. Roughly twenty-five minutes had passed since the trio of black cars had roared by the Zhiguli en route to the dacha. Give them five minutes to arrive and secure the place and perhaps ten more for a search. If they hadn't found the painting, that would mean for the past ten minutes they'd have been interrogating Lyubov and McCoy.

Would it do any good to go out there?

The grainy, black and white image of Bykov torturing Nadyezhda Petrovna, snapping her collarbone between his fingers, rose, unbidden, into Burke's mind. She had let him kill her rather than divulge the information he demanded.

Her daughter, he sensed, would do the same. So would McCoy.

He did not know whether what he had with McCoy amounted to more than one pleasant night, but he knew he couldn't abide the thought of leaving her out there.

And if he could give McCoy and Lyuba fifteen or twenty minutes of grace, the cavalry Connors was hopefully arranging would ride over the horizon and save the day.

Fifteen or twenty minutes. The picture in the vault would give them that.

When he'd insisted on taking the copy from the Hermitage, when he'd carved the C in the back of the panel, he thought there would be another, safer way to divert Chavchavadze's attention to it. But there wasn't.

Burke looked at his watch again. It was nearly midnight in Washington. There was still time to go to another hotel, find an international phone, and dictate a quick story for the final edition.

But as he tried to envision the story he would write, he could not get through the lead paragraph, could not get around the sentence that would have to admit that he didn't know with certainty the identity of the buyer; he'd only assumed that the man he observed in the surveillance camera was Santera. He didn't know the connection between the sale of the painting and the assassination of Marshal Grachenko. He didn't even know for sure that Slema Chavchavadze was involved in that.

Besides, he had promised Nadyezhda Petrovna he wouldn't write about the picture until she told him to go ahead. He could claim, he knew, that her death dissolved his obligation. But in truth it hadn't. He now had to remain faithful to the spirit of his promise. He had to decide when publishing the story would not jeopardize the painting.

Burke knew he had precious little to show in return for devoting his life to journalism—a failed marriage, a son whom he rarely saw, a mortgaged house in a bad neighborhood, a few of the lesser prizes that the profession handed out in lieu of decent wages, and the liver of a much older man. He also had interesting memories and a reputation. It was not a glittering reputation, but it wasn't a bad one. He was a reporter who filed stories without errors, intemperate prejudices, or holes. He kept his bargains with his sources.

That was worth something, too.

He got into the car again and made the tires skid on the slick cobblestones as he took off. He weaved for a minute between the pedestrians lugging their bags and packages into the subway, then broke clear into Liteyny Prospekt. He cut off another tram turning left on Nevsky Prospekt, pushed the speedometer as close to a hundred kilometers an hour as it would get, then jammed on the brakes.

Ahead of him a wall of humanity was slowly marching down the boulevard, red banners waving in the wind from the river. Two *militsia* cars, their blue lights flashing, rode as escorts in front.

Quickly, Burke turned right, off Nevsky Prospekt, and stalled the car, forgetting to put the clutch in as he applied the brakes. He looked at his hands. They were trembling.

The marchers drew closer, and above the wind he could hear them singing a marching tune from the Communist era, "The Working Class Is Coming!"

They carried Soviet flags, the bright red banners set off by the gold hammer and sickle. There were pictures of Lenin and Stalin, rescued from the back of some closet. One handmade sign, held by the marchers in the front rank, read, "All Power Back to the People."

But it was not a big crowd, or an organized one. After the first two rows it consisted of a loose mass of stragglers, men in *shapkas* and parkas, women with their hair tied in scarves. There were no more than a thousand of them.

About the same number, he recalled, as the Bolsheviks had in 1917.

On the sidewalks, people stared. Some were mute. Some shouted encouragement. A couple jumped off the curb and joined the march.

As the front rank reached the side street where Burke was parked, something curious happened. A band of about a dozen men broke off from the crowd and ran up to a closed kiosk set in the shadow of a bread store. He saw a club swing and heard the sound of shattered glass.

In a second the men were reaching through the broken window and passing out bottles to their comrades. Others on the sidewalk seized the unexpected opportunity. An old man, greasy gray curls streaming from underneath his *shapka*, nearly knocked Burke over as he sprinted toward the ruined kiosk. In a few seconds he returned, a bottle clutched in each hand. One, Burke saw, was Polish vodka. The other was a cheap American bourbon. Behind him, Russians swarmed around the kiosk like bees around a hive. It fell over with a loud crash.

Before he could think, before he knew what had happened, Burke had gotten out of the car and walked to the shattered kiosk. He stepped past a couple of men burrowing at the rubble like dogs trying to get under a fence. He looked inside. He saw shattered glass, a profusion of Snickers candy bars, and a couple of untouched bottles of Four Roses.

He picked up one of the Four Roses bottles and broke the seal. Mechanically, he unscrewed the cap and put the neck of the bottle to his lips.

The cheap bourbon burned as it covered his tongue and started down his throat, and he nearly coughed and spit it up. But he suppressed the urge and swallowed until the level of the whiskey had fallen to the point where the neck of the bottle met its body.

He inhaled, sensing the alcohol working its way into his stomach, and soon out to his bloodstream. It gave him a feeling of peace and well-being.

Then he screwed the cap back on the bottle and turned around. He stuffed it, like a quarterback handing off a football, into the hands of a man with a thin, brown beard and a grimy gray parka. The man had detached himself from the marchers and was moving toward the downed kiosk at a trot.

The man stopped and looked back at Burke in utter surprise.

"My donation to the cause, comrade," Burke said.

The man's face registered befuddlement. "But it's yours," he said, not certain whether to hand the bottle back.

"It's okay," Burke said. "I've quit."

Andrusha Karpov stood in Desdemona McCoy's office, trying to figure out what the American journalist had meant when he said the copy had been fixed and was now exactly like the original. He stared at it, then picked it up and moved it directly under the light recessed into the ceiling.

He could see no change.

He knew, or thought he knew, every inch of the painting, almost as if he had painted it himself. In a sense, he thought it was his own work, since a forgery, to be successful, must marry the art of the painter with the technical expertise of the scientist. He ran his fingers lightly over the surface of the painting and felt the faint, rough texture of the *craquelure*. No difference. He stared for a long moment at the eyes of the woman in the picture. That was the most remarkable thing. Nadyezhda Petrovna had captured everything that Leonardo had poured into those eyes. Leda's eyes proved the genius both of Leonardo, who had created them, and of Nadyezhda Petrovna, who re-created them.

He shook his head, perplexed. There was nothing to do but the job he'd been assigned to do.

He turned the picture around to pick it up, and immediately he saw it, the small letter *C* carved into the back of the panel. He did not think he had seen that before.

He tried to call to mind all his memories of the back of the panel. They were fragmented; he hadn't paid it much attention. Like the original, this panel was half covered with old scrawls, in French and in Russian, placed there by royal and imperial curators as they checked the painting into their collections and catalogued it. But he thought the C was new.

He picked at it with a fingernail. The sides of the gouge in the wood seemed not to have taken on the thin layer of grime that covered the rest of the panel. Most likely it had been carved recently.

He thought for a moment, then rummaged around on McCoy's desk for a pencil. Very lightly, verging on making no contact at all, he ran the point of the pencil back and forth in the groove of the C. He worked with the pencil for a minute or two. When he was satisfied, he picked up the picture and carried it into the vault.

Then he closed the heavy vault door and spun the tumblers. He pulled the tapestry down in front of the door again: packaging, as Burke had said.

He looked at his watch. Eighteen hours had passed since he'd last eaten. Nearly ten minutes had gone by since Burke had dropped him off.

Now he was supposed to go somewhere and hide. Spend the day in the subway, Burke had said. They probably thought he would go somewhere to eat.

People always underestimated him; they stereotyped him as the fat boy with the peculiar flair for science. Lyubov certainly did. Nadyezhda Petrovna, almost alone among the people in his life, had recognized his real worth. Now she was dead.

He had to do something. He had not asked Burke about his plan as they rode into town. He had still not entirely emerged from his shock. Now he was ready to take the initiative. He didn't need to ponder much to determine that Burke was going to try again to pass the copy off to Chavchavadze and his buyer. They would come to this room to examine it. They would be coming soon.

But he had a little time. His apartment was only ten minutes away. He could use the basement entrance; no one would be watching it. He could get there and return with a souvenir that he had kept from his miserable stint as a reserve army officer—his pistol.

Andrusha locked the doors behind him and stepped out into the courtyard. A new snow squall was blowing in from the Gulf of Finland, dropping the kind of tiny flakes that threatened an accumulation of half a meter. The sky in the east was still only half covered with clouds, and he could see isolated shafts of sunlight beaming down like spotlights through the haze.

He left the courtyard and hurried off, pushing his way awkwardly through the crowds of people coming in the opposite direction, vaguely aware that they were demonstrators of some kind.

Chapter Thirty-four

Burke was halfway back to the legacy of Ilyich kolkhoz when snowflakes started to hit the Zhiguli's windshield, and he realized that someone had stolen his wiper blades while he was outside the car, scrabbling in the kiosk for a drink. The naked metal wiper arms scraped across the glass like chalk scraping across a blackboard. Involuntarily, he shivered. He wasn't sure if it was from the freezing cold, the fear, or the Four Roses.

He slowed down, unable to see well. The metal arm made a small, clear slit where it scraped the glass, and he hunched down until his eyes were level with it. It was like trying to see through a crack in a wall into a fog.

He rolled down the window on his side and poked his head out. The snowflakes blew into his eyes and stung his cheeks, but he could see slightly better. He pushed ahead.

He should have kept better track of the distance from the city to the kolkhoz, he told himself. That would have enabled him to at least know when to look for the driveway to the Naryshkina dacha.

He wished he'd worn a hat.

The snow was accumulating quickly, and he found it harder to distinguish the side of the road from the shoulder. He slowed down further, until the needle on the speedometer was wiggling around thirty kilometers.

Three minutes down the road he spotted the gray outline of the steel posts of the kolkhoz gate. He rolled the window down on the right side and peered out to be certain. He could just make out the words, "Legacy of Ilyich." Now he was close. He slowed down to a crawl until a gap in the trees told him that the driveway to the dacha was at hand.

Again he stopped. Forlorn, he looked in the rearview mirror, hoping for the unlikely sight of Connors and his men arriving. There was only the snow and the empty road.

He drove slowly down the drive, and when he'd gone twenty meters, he saw the tail of Chavchavadze's caravan, a black Volvo sedan. The ZIL and the Mercedes were parked ahead of it, dusted white except where the falling snow had melted on the hot metal over the engine.

He got no closer before three of the swarthy men he assumed to be Chavchavadze's Ossetians detached themselves from the area of the dacha and sprinted toward him, semiautomatic rifles in their hands, seeking the cover of the trees.

He stopped the car and got out, keeping his hands visible.

The trio of men emerged from the trees and walked down the driveway toward him. Their weapons looked well-oiled and well-used. He could see a little gray around the end of the barrels, as if the paint had faded.

"What's the protocol here?" Burke asked. "Do you want my hands up?"

None of the trio replied. Instead, they walked toward him in a triangular formation, one training his rifle on Burke and the other two peering over Burke's shoulder.

They were not, he could now see, Ossetians. They had broader, flatter noses than people from the Caucasus. When they reached him, the point man in the triangle jabbed a rough hand inside Burke's coat, removed his wallet, and patted him down. Finding nothing, he reached up and grabbed Burke by the collar.

"Vamanos," he said, and Burke understood that his escorts were Hispanic.

They walked past the cars, came within sight of the house, and Burke involuntarily stopped.

In front of him, in the copse of birch trees, Ivan Bykov hung upside down between two trees, legs splayed improbably wide. Bykov was whimpering softly and incessantly, and the left leg of his trousers was stained dark with what Burke assumed was not perspiration. The trees bobbed gently in the wind, bearing Bykov's weight easily. Burke saw the ropes holding the trees down. He could imagine what would happen if those ropes were cut. Involuntarily, he extended a protective hand toward his crotch.

Ten yards to one side, another of the Hispanics had placed Lyubov between a similar pair of young birch trees. One of her ankles was encircled with rope, and another length of rope hung from the man's left hand. The right hand held a pistol, trained on both Lyubov and McCoy. Both of the women were staring at him, consternation on their faces.

"I always suspected that Bykov had some peculiar hang-ups," Burke said to them. "But who knew it was this bad?"

"Oh, Colin," McCoy said, anger and fear vying for dominance in the tone of her voice.

"Sorry," Burke said. "I didn't know you had a problem with puns. Connors didn't mention it when I talked to him."

He looked at his watch. Fifteen minutes had elapsed since his conversation with Connors.

He addressed the man with his hand on his collar, trying to remember the bits of Spanish he had known as a boy.

"Donde esta Chavchavadze, por favor?"

The man gestured with his head toward the house and said something in Spanish that Burke did not understand.

McCoy edged close enough to whisper. "What are you doing? Why'd you come out here?"

"An elaborate mid-life crisis," Burke said. "What about you?"

They pushed him toward the house. He stumbled and a bit of snow kicked up over the boots he was wearing, melted against his leg and began to seep into his shoes.

Chavchavadze, Rafael Santera, and Marina were standing in the glassed-in porch, out of the weather, watching as he came through the door.

The leader among Burke's escorts stepped forward and handed his wallet to Santera, who opened it, flipped through it, and paused over Burke's press card.

"Washington Tribune," he said in his lightly accented English. "What are you doing here?"

"Colin Burke," Burke said, extending his hand. "And whom do I have the pleasure of addressing?"

The man looked at Burke's hand but did not extend his own. "I am Rafael Santera Calderon."

"From Cali?"

Santera smiled thinly. "That's right. And what are you doing here?"

"You mean here at the dacha or here in St. Petersburg?"

Santera nodded slightly to the man holding Burke, who stepped around, wound up his right hand, and delivered a punch three inches below Burke's belt buckle.

Burke fell to the ground, writhing. He felt bile and alcohol rise from his stomach and burn the back of his throat, and a trident of pain shooting down both legs and into his penis and scrotum. Before it subsided, two of the Colombians grabbed him by the shoulders and pulled him to his feet. His head swam and his knees fluttered, and they held him up until his balance returned.

Burke swallowed and took a few tentative breaths until he was certain he had the hang of it again and his knees felt firmer.

"Please spare me the demonstration of your wit," Santera said mildly.

Burke swallowed some bile and nodded. When he started to speak, his words squeaked out of his throat for a moment. "I came out here to offer you a deal. The painting in return for letting us go," he said.

"And how do you know where it is?"

"A reporter I worked with came to St. Petersburg a couple of weeks ago. She interviewed Fyodorov. He showed her the painting. Bykov followed her to Washington and killed her before she could publish the story. But before she died, she told me what she'd learned. I came here to get the story. I found out that those two out there, McCoy and Naryshkina, were planning to fob a fake off

on you and smuggle the real painting out to America, where Mc-
Coy would sell it."

Santera's eyes betrayed no judgment of this story. "And you
threatened to expose them?"

Burke nodded. "Yeah. So we agreed to a deal. I hold the story
until they get to America and sell the painting."

"And the other part of the deal?"

"What other part?" Burke wanted to make Santera pull this de-
tail out of him.

"What was in it for you?"

"I was going to get a cut."

Santera nodded, and Burke could see he was buying the story.

"And why do you suddenly come here and offer this deal?"

"I was here when the helicopter came over," Burke said. "I see
you've got the army in on this. And the government. That means
we're not getting out of this country until you get what you want."

Santera stood impassively.

"This way, I still get my story," Burke said. "Plus, I have a thing
for Lyuba."

Burke watched Santera's face carefully, and he could see a slight
relaxation. Greed and lust, Burke thought, were credible details in
any story.

"All right," Santera said. "Where is the painting?"

"It's in the vault at the McCoy-Fokine Gallery on Nevsky
Prospekt. Number 80. Go in through the courtyard, ground floor,"
Burke said.

"You can go there and call back here. I assume you've got a
phone in your car. Leave it and take one of the others. Once
you're there, call, and I'll give you the vault combination when you
release McCoy and Lyuba. Then, when you've got the painting
and you're satisfied with it, you let me go."

It was a deal with no guarantees for him, Burke thought. But it
was the best he could think of under the circumstances. It should
buy at least twenty minutes.

Chavchavadze tapped Marina on the shoulder, and she translated the gist of what Burke had said into Russian.

"We can blow open any vault," Chavchavadze said. "Three
minutes."

Santera scowled as Marina translated. "And damage the paint-ing," he said, as if addressing a dunce.

"No," Chavchavadze objected. "We have the best people! KGB-trained!"

Santera ignored him. "I'll make you a counteroffer," he said to Burke. He was smiling confidently. "You tell me the combination now and I will refrain from having Miguel remove your testicles."

Burke looked at the balled fist of the man escorting him. "Under the circumstances, I accept," he said.

Santera nodded. "Good. I thought you would."

"The combination is six left, twenty right, thirty-seven left."

"I can send some men if you like," Chavchavadze persisted. "They can get the picture."

Santera brushed him off. "Leave your men where they are," he said. "They've done enough damage. And how would they know a real picture from a photograph?"

He turned to Burke. "You will remain here. When I have the picture, I will call from this gallery."

Burke nodded. His groin area throbbed quietly, beating time for the persistent doubts that popped into his mind and told him this scheme could not work.

Santera turned and said something to a man in the door-way, who had just come silently into the house. He called him Miguel.

Miguel nodded, took a length of rope and bound Burke's hands behind his back. Then he pushed Burke outside.

Burke hesitated at the top of the steps leading from the veranda down to the snow path trod between the dacha and the cars. Miguel pushed him again, and, without his hands to balance him, he tumbled headlong into the snow.

The cushion of the snow prevented him from breaking his face open on the frozen ground below. But the impact stunned him and he lost consciousness.

When he came to, he managed to raise his head out of the snow enough to see that only a few seconds had passed. Santera and three of his men were getting into the ZIL, leaving Miguel and one more Colombian behind.

Chavchavadze and Marina were standing by the limo, apparently arguing about something with Santera. But the argument ended abruptly, before Burke could manage to hear anything. Looking angry and vengeful, Chavchavadze stomped toward the dacha. Marina trailed him. The ZIL's engine rumbled, and the big car backed slowly out toward the road.

Burke managed to roll himself over onto his side. But without the use of his arms, he could not get up. For a minute he floundered in the snow like a fish thrashing about on the deck of a boat. He could hear the laughter of Miguel and the other Colombian. He could see Chavchavadze's face break momentarily into a smile as he walked past him.

He just could not get up.

Panting miserably, he fell back into the snow, feeling the cold moisture seep through his trousers. He started to shiver.

Then he heard one of the Colombians say something in Spanish, which he could not understand. He heard him repeat it, more urgently.

He twisted and craned his neck to see what it was.

McCoy, her own hands bound behind her back, was walking toward him. Lyubov was a few steps behind.

The Colombian was gesturing angrily at them with his rifle, trying to make them return to their places in the copse of birch trees, but he was not shooting

McCoy reached him and squatted in the snow next to him, her back toward him.

Lyubov arrived a second later and took the same position on his other side. Each of them hooked her bound hands under his arm and straightened up.

Burke struggled upward, but as he twisted, he slipped out of McCoy's grasp. He did, however, manage to get a knee underneath himself and to right himself in the genuflection posture.

The Colombian watched angrily, a few paces away, but he did not interfere.

Cautiously, Burke rose the rest of the way, until he was standing in the snow, swaying slightly, trying to suck in enough cold air to make his brain feel normal again. Lyubov and McCoy stayed at his side, steadying him, as they obeyed the Colombian's gestured order and walked slowly toward the birch trees.

McCoy leaned closer to him and whispered in his ear. "They're on the way?"

Burke nodded.

"What's that on your breath?" she asked.

"Breakfast of champions," he muttered.

He had no stomach for telling her of the lack of urgency in Connors's response. It wouldn't get help there any faster.

As they approached the trees where Bykov was suspended, Bykov recognized Burke, and the sight seemed to energize him.

He revived enough to unleash a stream of Russian obscenities, directed at Burke and Chavchavadze. His face was purplish-red, and the dark, sticky stain on his trousers had spread almost to his crotch.

The effort of shouting taxed Bykov, and he subsided into tortured whimpering.

"Well, whatever happens," Burke said to Lyubov as they looked at Bykov, "I'll have this moment to remember."

Chapter Thirty-Five

THE APARTMENT, ANDRUSHA KARPOV SUDdenly realized, had become frightfully chaotic in the year since his mother's death. While she lived, she had maintained a singular kind of order. The apartment had been crammed with the odds and ends of his life and interests—tubes of paint, computer components, bits of ceramics, and the pride of his adolescence, two long shelves containing samples, in carefully labeled jars and beakers, of three fifths of all the elements in the periodic table. Once, before he knew much about radioactivity, he had dreamed he might actually complete the whole set.

While she lived, he had at least known where everything was. Now the clutter was total. Moldy potatoes and rusty magnetos lay in mixed piles by the kitchen sink. Bits of canvas were strewn over clumps of dirty clothes on the floor of the single large room that had once housed all three members of the Karpov family. Computer chips and dumbbells gathered dust in the corners.

Somewhere, he knew, there was a box full of glue chips. He had to find it.

He stood, uncertain, in the center of the apartment's one large room and looked at his watch. He had very little time.

While she was alive, the glue had always been kept in the bottom drawer of the desk he'd inherited from his father. Maybe there still was some.

He opened the drawer and looked. He found some alligator clips, two diodes, a blank videocassette, a bootleg videocassette of the American film *2001*, and a diagram of the wiring for the video security system at the Hermitage.

No glue.

When was the last time he'd used it? He could not remember.

But since the glue required heating before use, he'd probably taken it into the kitchen and heated it on the stove.

He walked into the kitchen and tossed all the dirty pots and pans from the stove into the sink. Nothing.

He pulled open the cabinet under the sink and checked the plastic tray that contained his mother's detergents and cleaning rags.

And there they were, six chips of high-density polypropylene glue, dirty, dark, and yellow, in a small cardboard candy box. He pulled the box out.

The glue was Russian-made and not ideal for the task ahead of him. He would have preferred a cyanoacrylate. But Russia did not manufacture cyanoacrylate, at least not for the general public. He had a small, imported tube of it back in his lab at the Hermitage. But that was too far away and too risky to go after.

And he knew how to make this glue stronger.

He wiped the crusts of old kasha from a saucepan and set it on the stove. He turned on the gas underneath the pan, found a match and lit it, jerking his hand back as the gas caught, then turning the flame up as high as it would go. Then he dropped in three chips of glue.

Moving quickly now, he dashed from the apartment down the stairs to the basement. It was dark, because the lightbulb had long since been pilfered, but he knew the way into the corner where the pipes from the city's central heating system entered the building. He had done this often enough. He found a crate and pulled it into the corner. He stepped up onto the crate.

The insulation wrapped around the pipes was tattered. It dangled in strips that hung in front of his face, visible as dark shadows in the gloom of the basement.

He probed with his fingers into the insulation tatters until he encountered fresh fiberglass. As if pulling meat from the bones of a chicken, he stripped it off. When he had a handful, he stuffed it into his pocket and ran back upstairs.

Panting, he burst into the kitchen. The glue was liquefying. He tore the fiberglass into the smallest shreds his stubby fingers could manage and tossed it into the saucepan with the glue. He grabbed the cleanest spoon he could find and mixed the glue and fiberglass until the mass had the consistency of motor oil. Mixed with fiberglass, the glue would be three times its normal strength.

He felt a bit of peace settle over him, and he thought that this was the sort of thing he should do with his life. He should open a little shop and solve little problems for people, like how to make glue stronger, or how to make a satellite dish that would receive Finnish broadcasts and an adapter that would show them on Russian television. It would be a quiet but productive life, full of small satisfactions.

He opened the cabinet above the sink and rummaged around amid the dishes until he found one of his mother's old preserve jars. Every summer of her life she had put up late summer tomatoes, peppers, and squash so that her family would have vegetables through the winter. It was one of the things he missed most keenly since her death.

He capped the jar and slipped it into his pocket. Then he had a second thought. He grabbed the electric immersion heater he used to boil water for tea when the gas was cut off. If his timing was the least off, he would have to heat the glue again at the gallery. He saw a paintbrush snug against the wall at the edge of the counter and he grabbed that, too.

There was one more thing to get, and he had no doubt about where it was.

The pistol had been stored in a ski sock under his bed ever since his return from his last stint with the army reserves. Now he was glad that once in a while he had oiled it. He checked the clip. Full. He loaded it. He was ready to go.

The Makarov felt very heavy in Andrusha's right pocket, much heavier than the jar of slowly cooling glue in the pocket on the left side of his parka. He thought that its weight must be dragging the right side of the coat below his knees, giving him a slightly oblique look as he shuffled down Ulitsa Shedrinskogo toward Nevsky Prospekt.

It was a narrow, mean, little cobblestone street, probably born as an alley full of servants' quarters in old, imperial St. Petersburg. The five-story buildings seemed to tilt toward one another, closing off any possibility of sunshine in the winter. The snow that was falling settled wearily atop crusty, icy drifts, gone gray and pockmarked with footprints. No one shoveled anything on Ulitsa Shedrinskogo. There were trucks called *kapitalisti*, with conveyor attachments that scraped all the snow from the curbs of the city's boulevards and greedily whisked it all away. But they were too wide for this street. In the spring, when the thaw started, the winter's accumulation turned to grimy slush.

But Andrusha had lived there all his life, and as he reached the end of the block, it struck him that there was at least a chance he would never see it again. He turned and felt a hot tear well in his eye. He removed his hand from his left pocket and wiped it away.

That made him more aware of the drooping right side of his coat. He glanced around. A boy whom he did not know, perhaps nine years old, was dragging an ancient sled over the sidewalk, with a cracked clay pot atop it. He could not guess what was in the pot, if anything, but the boy seemed preoccupied. Andrusha decided that no one would notice his pocket drooping, or care if they did. People carried guns all the time in St. Petersburg now.

He put his head down, studying the patterns of ice and snow, shuffling in search of reliable footing, as Russians do in the winter. His urge to hurry competed with his fear that if he slipped and fell, the gun might go off. He could just imagine shooting himself in his big rear end and the way the nurses would quietly grimace in disgust when they removed his clothes to sew him up.

Shuffling that way, he needed five minutes to traverse the three long blocks between Ulitsa Shedrinskogo and Nevsky Prospekt, and four more, walking on ice and snow trod nearly to the pavement, to make it to the McCoy-Fokine Gallery.

He stopped and carefully inspected the sidewalk and the street outside number 80. They looked just as they had when he left. The tire tracks Burke had made earlier that morning when he drove into the courtyard were nearly covered with new snow. They were just soft ruts. There were no new tracks.

Cautiously, he walked through the alley between numbers 80 and 78 and peered around the corner into the courtyard. He saw nothing except for softened footprints outside the gallery door.

Andrusha took out his key and walked in, locking the door behind him and keeping the "Closed" sign in place. Once again he checked the room.

The McCoy-Fokine Gallery displayed its sculpture and pottery on more than a dozen white pedestals. Some were tall and narrow. Others were cubes the size of small tables.

Andrusha walked up to the largest of the cubes, which stood against the brick wall on the east side of the display room, about five meters from the door. He removed the heavy bronze sculpture of a sleeping woman that lay on it. Beside the sculpture was a sticker with a number on it: 19. No doubt there was a list somewhere that identified each object by number and gave the price. He put the sculpture on the floor. Then he reached down and tried to lift the cube.

As he expected, it was hollow, constructed of particle board overlaid with a gleaming white veneer. It was more than a meter long on each edge. If he sat down and hunched over, he should be able to fit beneath it.

He put the cube down and looked again about the room. His eyes fell on a delicate glass bowl, hand painted with vaguely religious figures. He recognized it as an example of Karelian peasant art. There were a few pieces like it in the Hermitage collection. He hefted it. It was heavier than he had hoped, perhaps two kilos. He looked around again, conscious of the fact that his heart was beating and he was beginning to sweat. There was nothing lighter on display.

Quickly, he set the bronze sculpture on the pedestal that had held the glass bowl. It barely fit.

A drop of sweat trickled from his forehead onto the sculpture as he tried to center it as best he could upon the pedestal. He cursed softly and wiped it off with the sleeve of his coat. Then he went back to the large cube and turned the glass bowl upside down.

He took the paintbrush and the jar of glue from his coat pocket. He tilted the jar, and cursed. The glue had hardened, not to the soaplike hardness it had when stored at room temperature, but close enough to gelatinous to be impossible to spread thin.

He opened the jar and snatched the immersion heater from his pocket. It was, essentially, a single metal rod, bent into a U and attached to an electrical cord. Now he needed an outlet.

He found one in the desk in McCoy's office. He plugged in the heater, stuck it in the jar, and waited for it to warm up.

The pause in his activity disquieted him. Suddenly, he could hear the wind blowing down Nevsky Prospekt and smell the gradually warming glue. He looked at his watch. Time must be short.

Finally, the metal warmed up and started to melt a small fissure in the glue. He waited until there was a small, gooey puddle, perhaps a centimeter across.

Then he pulled the heater from the jar and whisked the glue back into the showroom. Using the paintbrush, he coated the bottom of the bowl with the adhesive, working as quickly as he could. He knew that at this temperature a thin layer of glue would dry very quickly. Timing was critical. He counted to twenty, slowly. Then he turned the bowl up again and laid it on the surface of the cube, as close to the center as he could manage in his haste.

He closed the jar and stuffed it and the rag paintbrush back into his pocket. Then he looked at his watch and counted off thirty seconds.

If the bond had been made, he would know now. Gently, he put his fingers around the rim of the bowl and tugged upward. He half expected, half hoped to see the bowl rise and a gooey mess underneath. But nothing happened. The bond held. Despite his fears, Andrusha smiled.

He turned out the lights and took one more look around the gallery. He could see nothing he'd left behind, except the faint outline of a wet footprint on the floor. That would dry, and even if it didn't, the people he was waiting for would have no reason to be overly suspicious of some wet footprints. They would make their own as they entered.

He heard the sound of a car engine coming from the alley. The sound was low and powerful, so much so that it seemed to make the brick wall vibrate.

Frantically, Andrusha tipped the cube backward. He watched to see that the bowl stayed where he'd placed it. It did. Quickly, he tested the balance. The cube seemed willing to stay tilted while leaving him enough of an opening to get underneath it.

He saw the nose of the limousine enter the courtyard just as he sat on the floor, holding the bottom edge of the tilted cube in both hands, and prepared to wriggle back underneath the cube. Frantically, he squirmed to get his head underneath. It banged against the underside of the cube. His sweating left hand lost his grip and he felt the cube start to topple backward. He clamped down harder with his right hand, feeling the cube teeter. He had an instant, dreadful vision of the cube toppling backward, the glass bowl shattering, and the men in the limousine entering the room, guns drawn, while he looked for another place to hide.

He wiped his left hand on his trouser legs and regained his grip with it just as he felt the cube start to slide from the grip of his right hand. Desperately, he pulled down and hunched over.

The effort of bending his torso squeezed the breath from his lungs like juice squeezed from an overripe melon. He could only hear now, rather than see, his surroundings, and he heard the sound of voices, speaking Spanish, and a key turning in the lock of the gallery's door.

He pulled the cube downward, tipping the balance until it began to move downward of its own weight. He kept a hand under the leading edge as it fell toward the floor, lest it move too fast and make a noise. The band of light under the edge, the dim light shining through the gallery's window from the courtyard, grew slowly narrow—and then froze.

The cube had settled on his shoulders and neck. There was still a band of two centimeters between the bottom edge and the floor. The cube was askew, and anyone looking closely at the room would be certain to notice it.

Trembling, Andrusha tried to drive his shoulders into his knees, bending until pain shot from his lower back and his hamstrings. Slowly, too slowly, the band of light narrowed again, until the bottom edge of the cube hit the floor with an audible thunk.

Then the men were in the room.

The backs of Andrusha's legs were in pain. So was his neck, jammed up against the top of the cube.

He tried to force himself to concentrate. There were at least two men, because he could hear them talking to one another in Spanish, though he could not understand what they were saying. He could hear them walking around the gallery. From the purposeful pace of their strides, and the way the sound receded and rose again, he could sense that they were walking around the gallery and the office, inspecting it.

He pulled the pistol from his pocket and laid it on the floor by his hip.

His plan, insofar as he had one, was to wait until the right moment, throw the cube up over his head, and emerge firing.

But when was the right moment?

Beads of sweat trickled down his nose. They itched. But did he dare raise a hand to his face to wipe them away? Or would doing so raise the cube and attract attention?

He felt a sneeze coming on. He dared.

He wiped the sweat away from his face and used a finger to press on his nose until he was fairly certain the urge to sneeze had passed.

He could hear the footfalls and the two Spanish voices, coming now from the direction of McCoy's office. He remembered the jar of glue and the immersion heater, still on McCoy's desk. He froze.

What if they noticed it? Surely they would. What if they wondered what a warm jar of glue was doing in a closed art gallery?

And what if they found the list of art objects, identifying numbers, and prices, and started comparing them to what was actually on the pedestals? What if they realized that number 19 should be a bronze sculpture instead of a glass bowl?

No, that was crazy. These were criminals, not curators. He was losing touch with reality.

"Calm down," he whispered to himself.

But the words only brought to his mind the memory of the firing range at the army base near Minsk. He had been assigned to a tank division, because of his knack for coaxing the balky engines in the T-54s to start and perform. But the belt buckle and epaulets of a *tankist* had never really fit him. His fellow officers were tough. But he remembered how alien and uncomfortable the pistol had felt in his hand and how rarely he had hit the target. That was what his instructor had told him. Calm down. Loosen up. He'd never been able to do it.

Suddenly, the feet of one of the men in the gallery moved in his direction, passed within a meter of his cube, and moved on toward the door. He heard it open, and then more words in Spanish.

In a moment a third voice entered the room. It spoke in shorter, clipped Spanish sentences consisting only of a word or two.

"*Bueno,*" he heard.

This, he realized, must be the man he had been waiting for. This was the target. The first two men had come into the gallery to check it, to make certain it was safe. Now, the boss had entered.

This was the moment to strike, to avenge the death of Nadyezhda Petrovna.

But there would be three of them.

There was no way he could expect to survive if he jumped out into the face of three armed men and started firing.

The nerves in his neck and shoulders were all but shrieking now, and his legs had begun to tremble. He would be firing blindly, wildly, unsure even whom to fire at.

There was another way, a better way.

His quarry had come here to get the painting. He had two subordinates with him.

Once they got the painting, the two subordinates would be required to carry it. They would put their guns away. Their leader would be easily identifiable. He would be the one not carrying the painting. And as they walked toward the door, their backs would be turned.

That would be the moment.

He waited.

The voices and footfalls moved past him, close enough so that it seemed to him he could smell them. Then the sounds receded somewhat, and he knew they were in the office.

Faintly, he could hear the Spanish words for numerals, and he realized that they were not forcing their way into the vault. They had the combination. They must have gotten it from McCoy, he thought, the dark-skinned woman. That meant they had already been to the dacha. They had Lyuba. He wondered if she was still alive.

Now, he regretted the whole plan. It would never have happened if he hadn't assured Nadyezhda Petrovna that between them they could create a perfect copy. And even though he'd been right, it would have been better to let the foreigners have the painting, let Chavchavadze and Bykov have the money, let the Hermitage go to hell, let the whole country fall apart.

His muscles ached from their enforced position, and he yearned to stretch. If he had to stay in this fetal position another second, he would holler out loud from the pain. Desperately, he permitted himself a slight movement upward.

His cube was pushed up off the floor a couple of centimeters, and again he could hear the voices more clearly. They were still in the next room.

This time there was a low, excited quality to their words, and he could imagine them pulling the copy out of the vault and into the light. It would captivate them as it had captivated him and everyone else in the small circle of people who had seen it. Leda was easily the most beautiful figure he had ever seen on canvas, and he had spent the past fifteen years working with one of the greatest art collections in the world.

He felt, for a moment, a rush of pride. They were both his pictures. The original and the copy. They were both great works of art.

They could have simply made the copy and kept it, he thought. What was the damn difference? They were indistinguishable to anyone who looked at them. They should have made the copy, kept it, and let the buyer take the original for his private collection. That would have been the Russian thing to do. Suffer losses, live with a lie, but survive.

Two of the voices fell silent, and then he heard the leader's voice. He was having a conversation, but Andrusha could not hear the other half of it. A telephone, he thought. He was talking to someone on the telephone. To whom? To someone at the dacha?

The man's voice sounded calm, but Andrusha could hear a note of triumph in it. Now he thought he had what he'd come to Russia for.

Andrusha hunched down lower, letting the gap between the cube and the floor close again. The time was at hand. He picked up the Makarov, curled his fingers around the butt, and pushed the safety catch off.

His right hand was trembling. His legs were trembling. His breath was coming in short, desperate gasps. He could not tell whether it was nerves or simply the effect of waiting in a cramped, unnatural position. He waited for the sound of footfalls again.

And then he heard them, shuffling now, coming past his cube. He imagined that the leader would step ahead of the two subordinates and open the door.

He counted. One. Two. Three. Four. The footstep sounds were receding. Five. Six. He heard the sound of the door being pulled open, a few words in Spanish. Now or two more seconds? Two more seconds. Eight. Nine.

He started to rise. But somehow his backside had gotten wedged into the contours of the cube like a soccer ball mashed into the opening of a sewer grate. When he tried to straighten his legs, the pressure on his rear end increased, and he could not break it. He panted and trembled. He could not push free.

Ten. The door closed.

He squatted lower, until he felt a gap between his back and the wall of the cube. He tried to rise straight up. His head bumped suddenly against the top side and he lost his balance, falling backward until he was lying on his back, wedged between the walls of his cube, hands above himself, floundering for balance.

He heard, out in the courtyard, the faint sound of car doors opening and a trunk door slamming shut.

He turned over and curled, preparatory to rising on his hands and pushing upward.

Then he heard the sound of an engine pulling slowly away.

In the darkness, still in his fetal position, Andrusha wept bitterly.

Chapter Thirty-six

"**W**HAT COULD BE KEEPING THEM?" MCCOY hissed.

Burke shifted his feet, making a faint squeaking sound in the snow. The snow in his shoes had melted. The water had soaked through his socks. He could barely feel his toes.

"I don't know," he said. "The demise of chivalry?"

She looked at him and half a smile formed on her lips. "It's not quite dead," she said. "Thanks for trying to help."

Burke, McCoy, Marina, and Lyubov were standing, hands tied behind their backs, under the guard of a silent Colombian with a black and lethal-looking semiautomatic rifle.

A few yards away, out of earshot, the other Colombian, the one called Miguel, poked in a languid rhythm at one of the taut ropes holding the birch trees down and preventing Bykov from being torn apart.

Each time he did, the trees bowed slightly and then sprang back up, stretching Bykov's legs, causing him to groan and whimper. The wind shifted briefly, and Burke could smell that Bykov had urinated in his bloodied trousers.

"I wish he would stop torturing that man," Lyubov broke in,

shuddering at the sight before them. "Kill him if they must. But not this. Not even Bykov deserves this."

"Oh, yes, he does," Burke said.

Inside the Mercedes, a telephone chirped. The Colombian guarding them heard it and called softly to Miguel.

Miguel turned away from Bykov immediately and trotted through the snow to the Mercedes. They heard half of a brief conversation, which consisted largely of Miguel saying "*Si,*" to the man on the other end of the line.

Miguel hung up the phone and strode toward them, pulling his own pistol from the pocket of his parka. He spoke quickly to the other Colombian.

That man prodded Burke toward the dacha with the barrel of his gun. Burke looked at his watch. It had been at least forty-five minutes, more nearly an hour. Where was Connors?

The Colombian jabbed him again, right over the kidney, and Burke started walking toward the dacha. Miguel prodded Lyubov, and the three women fell into line behind Burke.

Now the thought Burke had been trying to avoid crowded everything else out of his mind. Suppose Connors didn't come?

"Did your boss get the painting?" he called out, hoping Miguel would answer.

There was no answer.

They could scatter and run for the woods, Burke thought. The odds were they would all be shot dead before they got twenty feet away. The odds still favored waiting.

He found that his mind refused to contemplate his own demise, that it focused stubbornly on ways to remain alive. As soon as the thought that he could die here took shape, something banished it from his consciousness, and he seized ever more tenaciously on the hope that Connors would arrive, or that Santera would order Miguel only to detain them until he had the picture out of the country.

This intense desire to remain alive vaguely surprised him. Life had not thrilled him for a long time. Now there was very little he would not offer up in return for another twenty minutes of it.

Slowly, planting both feet on each step, he ascended the stairs to the veranda and entered.

"Stop," Miguel told them when they had all made it inside. Burke savored the warmth.

Miguel said something in Spanish to the other Colombian. In a few seconds the man was trotting out into the snow and scooping up the remaining rope. He trotted back in, squatted on the floor and pulled a long hunting knife from a sheath under his pant leg. He cut the rope into lengths about two feet long.

Then the man went into the dacha, returning with two straight-backed wooden chairs under his arms. They came, Burke recognized, from the kitchen. He left them by Miguel, retreated back toward the kitchen, and returned with one more.

Four captives. Three chairs. Burke wondered which one would not be seated here. He felt a soaring, irresistible hope that he would be spared. He flushed with secret embarrassment.

Miguel prodded him with the gun. "Sit," he commanded.

"You've got the picture," Burke said. "The deal was, you were supposed to let us go."

Miguel snorted briefly, not deigning to reply.

"That's right," McCoy said. "That was the deal. I thought you were men of honor."

Miguel slapped her across the face, and she fell backward against the window, stunned.

Miguel turned to Burke. "Sit or I shoot you," he ordered.

Burke sat.

The other Colombian went to work quickly. He tied Burke's feet to the legs of the chair. The rope bit into his ankles. Burke looked down. The knots looked like the work of a man who knew what he was doing. A former Boy Scout, no doubt.

When Burke was trussed firmly to his chair, Miguel ordered Lyubov to sit. She did, and was bound in the same way. Finally, he gestured at McCoy. She got the same treatment.

It occurred to Burke that Miguel could simply have shot them all. Maybe he would simply tie them up and leave them there. It made no sense, but Burke wanted to believe that he would. He wished he weren't so damn cynical.

He looked at Lyubov and McCoy. Both of their faces were taut with fear, but he sensed they were hanging on to the same hope.

Miguel turned to Marina. She, too, was pale and fearful. She had momentarily stopped crying. She, too, he guessed, was calculating the number of chairs, the number of captive bodies, and hoping she would be spared.

"Outside," Miguel said, and Marina lurched into motion. She walked mechanically down the stairs and out into the snowy yard. The two Colombians followed her, carefully closing the front door behind them.

At a word from Miguel, the second Colombian took his rifle butt and began methodically smashing the windows of the dacha, starting with the windows of the veranda on which Burke, McCoy, and Lyubov sat.

Burke felt the cold wind from the Gulf of Finland rush through the ruined wooden frames and chill him further.

"Why do they do this?" Lyubov asked. She seemed indignant at the vandalism and on the verge of tears, as if she were thinking that tying them up at gunpoint was one thing, but destroying the summer home of her childhood was more than she could bear.

Burke listened for a moment to the sound of breaking glass from the other side of the building.

"They want to make sure we get enough fresh air," Burke said.

"Why?" Lyubov's voice trembled slightly.

"Stop making it worse for her, Burke," McCoy said. "She doesn't deserve wisecracks."

"Cross ventilation," she replied to Lyubov.

"Cross ventilation?"

"I think they mean to burn the place down," McCoy said.

As if in confirmation, the Colombian got into the Mercedes and backed it twenty feet closer to the dacha. Then he got out of the car and walked around toward the back side. When he returned, he had an old brown garden hose in his hand.

They watched as he opened the gas tank of the black car and jammed one end of the hose into it. For a minute he sucked on the other end.

The man jerked backward, spitting and coughing, as the fuel began to flow out of the tank. Then he took the hose and directed the trickle of gasoline to the wall of the dacha. The wind blew the fumes into the veranda, and for a moment the aroma reminded Burke of gas stations he'd stopped at when he was a kid, putting three dollars' worth into an old car at seven o'clock on a summer evening full of promise.

"Why do they want to burn us?" Lyubov's voice quavered.

"Easier to say we died in an accident," McCoy said. "No bullet holes to explain."

The trickle of gasoline stopped, and the second Colombian asked something of Miguel, who shook his head. Evidently, that was enough gas.

Miguel grabbed Marina's arm and dragged her to within a few feet of where her uncle hung, upside down. A gust of wind caught the tops of the birch trees and they swayed. Bykov moaned loudly. Then Burke could hear him alternately cursing and imploring Marina to cut him down.

"Translate," Miguel commanded the girl. "We have the picture."

Marina only sobbed. Miguel slapped her lightly.

"Translate!"

Stuttering, Marina translated the words into Russian.

They seemed to energize Bykov again, and he burst out with a flood of Russian words that not even Burke could understand, so slurred was the pronunciation.

Marina turned to Miguel and, with great economy, translated. "He wants you to cut him down."

Miguel only smiled. "Translate," he commanded again. "First, we are going to set this house on fire."

Burke swallowed. He couldn't see his watch, but imagined that at least five minutes had gone by since Miguel received his phone call.

"Where the hell are your people?" he hissed at McCoy as Marina translated.

McCoy, eyes wide, chin set, only shrugged.

Burke scowled. "Well, under the circumstances," he said, "I wish I'd taken another shot of bourbon."

"I'm sorry," she replied, and it sounded sincere.

Outside, Miguel hunkered down so his face was only a foot or so from Bykov's.

"At first," he said, "you will roast."

He waited for Marina to translate.

Marina did. The veins in Bykov's neck bulged and his complexion turned an uglier shade of purple.

Miguel leaned down and put a hand on one of the iron stakes holding down the ropes, which, in turn, held down the birch trees. He jiggled it a bit.

"Then, the heat from the fire will melt the snow and the ground will get a little slippery." He paused. "Translate!"

Marina translated.

"The stakes will pull loose."

Marina translated again.

Miguel spat on the ground. "I hope you are still conscious enough to feel what happens."

He patted Bykov's cheek.

"Fuck your mother," Bykov said in Russian. His voice was hoarse and weak. He was trying to shout, but the sound came out muffled. Marina translated.

Miguel stood up. He laughed. "No. I'm going to fuck your niece. In the backseat of the car. On the way to the airport."

He reached into the pocket of his trousers and pulled out a few crumpled bills. He stuffed them in her coat pocket.

"There," he told her. "You're already paid for, but that's a tip."

"No," she said, voice unsteady.

He slapped her face, hard, then turned and walked toward the car, pulling her by the arm. Still crying, Marina stumbled, almost fell, then followed him and got in the car.

The second Colombian, meanwhile, was holding a match to an oily rag. It caught fire. He walked tentatively, mincingly, up to the house, holding the burning rag in front of him like a dead animal. From a range of four or five feet, he tossed it at the gasoline-soaked side. Burke could hear the whoosh as the gasoline caught, and see the flames reflected in the man's face as he leapt backward. In another instant he could see the first curling, orange finger of flame, and smell the acrid odor of burning gasoline.

The Colombian stood where he was for a second, making certain that the dacha had caught. Then he sprinted toward the car. In another thirty seconds the car disappeared down the drive, trailing a small plume of snow.

Burke struggled with the ropes that held his hands. They remained tight. Outside, he could hear a guttural howl of feral rage and fright from Bykov, a counterpoint to the churning fear growing inside himself.

He pressed his heels into the floorboards and found that by squirming he could move his chair backward an inch or two at a time.

"See if we can get back-to-back," he told McCoy, who was squirming against her own bonds.

The smell of smoke rose into his nostrils as he began the laborious process of reorienting the chair. The scent, for some reason, turned his fear into visceral, intense panic. He stopped moving and tried again to break free of the ropes by force. He succeeded only in making himself tremble.

Don't panic, he scolded himself. He looked over his shoulder. McCoy had twisted her chair around until her back was to him, and she had started inching toward him. He put his head down and concentrated on the movement of his feet and toes and hips, the movement that turned the chair.

He could see smoke now, rising into the veranda through cracks in the floorboards. And he could hear the crackling sound of wood in flames. The dacha itself was burning, not just the gasoline. Outside the dacha, in the copse of birch trees, Bykov's howling rose in pitch and intensity, until it sounded more like a screech.

Burke felt McCoy's groping fingers and pushed over the last inches separating them.

"Let me work on yours first," she shouted. He complied.

He could feel her fingers clawing at the knots around his wrists. The ropes remained tight.

"Relax your arms!" she yelled.

He tried to relax, but could tell it was a feeble effort. The posture he was tied in meant that his arms were stretched behind his back, tightening his chest and the entire front of his torso. His heart pounded. Sweat poured off his forehead into his eyes. His lungs sucked in great drafts of air. Every muscle in his body cried out for release, in vain. He felt as if the veranda walls were closing in on him.

"Damn," she said, and he could hear the same kind of strain in her voice. "I can't move them! Try mine!"

She let her fingers go limp, and Burke began picking at her bonds. As he started, flame began to curl in over the windowsills. The smoke intensified. He coughed—a great, racking, continuous cough that he could not stop for several seconds.

He willed himself to concentrate on the knots he could feel in his fingertips. He traced the contours of the rope with the forefinger of his right hand. He found a spot where one strand seemed to loop under another, and he started to tug at it.

But he could apply only a thumb and forefinger, and the rope easily resisted his efforts to tug it free. It kept slipping from his grasp.

He wanted to get both hands on it, to push against the knot with one and pull with the other, and he squirmed and twisted to raise his left hand to do that.

He succeeded only in pushing the rope deeper into his wrists. His fingers flailed vainly, trying to come together. Pain rose in his shoulders and lower back, until he dropped his hands for a rest.

"Can't quite do it," he gasped. The smoke was getting thicker, searing his lungs. He coughed again and this time could not stop until he hung his head and forced himself to take short, shallow breaths. His eyes watered and burned.

He took another crack at the knots. His efforts were weaker. His fingers had grown slippery with sweat, and he could barely get a grip on the strand he was trying to loosen.

"Not going to work," he said, more to himself than to her. He let his fingers dangle.

Lyubov's stoicism cracked under a similar barrage of coughs. She started to sob.

"We have to do something!" McCoy yelled.

Heat was rising now, along with the smoke, and the interior of the veranda was suddenly hot. The flames jumped higher on the wall where the gasoline had been spread, until the view through the windows on that side was all orange. The fire turned the corner of the dacha and began to eat at its front side.

"Let's try working on the door," Burke yelled, though McCoy was only a foot away.

"I'll go first. I'm pointed that way," she wheezed.

A probing tongue of flame entered the room on the far side, snaking up from the window and engulfing the ceiling.

Frantically, they inched toward the door, McCoy in the lead. Burke closed his eyes, trying to protect them from the smoke, which gushed from the burning walls in ever thickening waves, seeking the outside air.

He bumped into McCoy.

"Don't push, goddamn it!" she screamed. "You'll knock me over!"

He opened his eyes and looked over his shoulder. The smoke was thicker now, and he could see flames starting to rise from the floorboards at the far side of the veranda, perhaps twenty feet away. The room was getting hotter, like the inside of an oven.

Behind him, he could see McCoy, her eyes shut, smoke clinging to her hair and coat, struggling with grim determination to squirm and push her way to the door.

The door was thick and wooden, and it had a round knob. Quickly and roughly, he gauged the height of the knob. It was at least a foot higher than their hands.

McCoy reached the door and scratched at it, trying to lift her hands high enough to reach the knob. She failed and fell back to her original posture, hunched over, coughing, trying to keep the smoke from her eyes and lungs. She tried to get her feet on the floor and raise herself up, but the rear legs of the chair bumped against the door and she pitched over, face first, managing at the last instant to twist enough that her shoulder hit the floor first. She lay there, stunned and unable to move.

Burke took this sight in and suddenly thought of a nightclub fire he had covered years ago, in Oakland, a fire that killed fourteen people. He had asked the fire chief where the bodies had been found.

"They were all near the door," the chief told him, "piled up on top of each other like a cord of wood."

Now flames were marching toward them in phalanx formation across the floor. Half the distance between the far wall of the veranda and their position was on fire. He could feel his skin start to redden and cook. In a minute more it would be blistering. He could barely breathe now, and it was even becoming hard to hear, so loud was the sound of the flames engulfing the dacha. They rumbled and crackled in the air around him.

Lyubov's chair bumped into his. She was scrabbling desperately toward the door, shrieking something in Russian that he could not make out.

His pants legs, he could see, were beginning to smolder.

He had to reach the door.

He closed his eyes, trying to remember where McCoy lay, and set about inching around her. He tried to breathe through his teeth, hoping they might screen out the smoke and let in some oxygen. There was no oxygen there.

His chair bumped against something, probably McCoy, and he pushed his toes into the hot floor, trying to maneuver around her. The cuff of his right trouser leg began to burn, and he could feel the hair on his leg start to singe.

His chair lost its balance, or he did. He couldn't tell. He was aware of the sensation of falling, clumsily, to his right, falling over McCoy, but slowly, like a leaf floating briefly above a fire before settling slowly down and turning to ash.

Then he felt cold air on his neck and thought that someone had opened the door.

Hands grabbed his shoulders and pulled him down the steps of the dacha, jarring his shins and shoulder, and into the cold, clean snow. He wanted to bathe in it, to get naked and roll in it forever. He opened his mouth and sucked in all the air he could. His body spasmed with coughs, expelling the smoke from his lungs. The cold air tasted like chilled white wine.

Burke opened his eyes. He was lying on his left side, still bound to the chair. In front of him, the right half of the dacha was completely in flames and the left side was smoking.

He saw the wide backside of Andrusha Karpov in the dacha doorway. He was positioned like a dog digging under a fence, his arms working furiously in front of him, getting a grip on McCoy and pulling her from the building. As he had with Burke, Andrusha dragged her and her chair down the steps. McCoy groaned.

"Lyuba!" he called, and went in again. Burke watched helplessly. McCoy, a few feet away, regained consciousness and started screaming.

His right trouser leg, the one high and clear of the snow, was still burning. He squirmed, trying to roll over and kill the flames in the snow. He could not.

Then, from the doorway, Andrusha's backside appeared yet again, this time dragging Lyubov in her chair. For the third time he pulled a body down the steps and into the snow. Lyubov's skirt and parka were both on fire. She looked almost like a torch.

Feverishly, Andrusha pulled out a pocketknife and slashed at the ropes binding Lyubov to the chair. McCoy was still screaming. Burke could not see her, but he assumed she was on fire as well. His own leg was beginning to burn.

Andrusha finally severed Lyubov's bonds and ripped her from the chair. He rolled her limp body in the snow.

Then he cut McCoy's and repeated the process. Finally he came to Burke, slashed quickly at the ropes, parted them, and with a swift jerk helped Burke free himself from the chair. Burke rolled free and flopped like a fish in the snow, feeling the cold and the moisture like a healing balm where his skin had begun to smolder.

Andrusha by this time was hunched over Lyubov, trying to bring her to. Coughing, McCoy rose onto her hands and knees. She crawled through the snow to where Lyubov lay on her back, pushed Andrusha gently aside and lowered her face to Lyubov's. Burke saw her pinch the nostrils shut and begin to blow into the smoke-filled lungs.

For a full minute she worked over her, pausing periodically to inhale and exhale herself. "C'mon," she said each time. "C'mon, girl."

A stunned and frightened man walked stiff-legged over to the two women on the ground, joining Andrusha in mute observation. Burke looked beyond him and saw a taxi, doors open and motor running. He could only imagine how Andrusha had prevailed on the driver to come out here.

And then Lyubov coughed. McCoy waited until the coughing had gone on for a few seconds, then turned the Russian woman over, helping her to spew the remaining soot and smoke from her lungs and mouth.

Andrusha rose to his feet, his eyes on the burning dacha. Three-fourths of the veranda was up in flames, and the main section of the building was also afire.

"The painting! *Leda!*" he shouted. "I can still get it."

McCoy rose, wobbly, to her feet. She planted herself, swaying slightly, between Andrusha and the door. She raised her arms and pressed lightly against his chest.

"No, Andrusha," she said. "You've done enough. It's gone."

"I can save it!" he insisted, and he pushed past her. "Help me!" he yelled at Burke over his shoulder.

Burke staggered after him. His knees felt watery and he almost fell. But the effort to move quickly forced fresh air into his lungs and helped revive him. He stopped coughing.

They stumbled madly through the snow, heading around the dacha to the back side, where the studio was.

Ahead of him, Andrusha slipped and fell, facedown. Burke, following, barely managed to avoid tripping over him. He reached down and pulled Andrusha to his feet.

Andrusha's face was red, his eyes filled with both tears and the fearful reflection of the flame. Burke could sense that he did not want to go back in there again.

"Hurry!" Andrusha said, and started running again.

Turning the corner, the Russian reached the large, south-facing windows that lit the studio. Burke came up behind him and peered inside.

"It's there, on the wall," Andrusha said.

The room was full of smoke, and it was hard to tell whether the paintings on the wall had caught fire yet or not. Burke saw flames, but they appeared to be flickering at the edges of the studio, concentrating for the moment on the immolation of the kitchen and veranda area in front of the house. He stood as tall as he could, his chin over the windowsill, and looked down. The flames were starting to flicker through the chinks between the floorboards.

"We have to hurry," he said. "Is there a back door?"

Andrusha shook his head. Then he turned and pointed toward

a bench under a linden tree in the back garden. "Help me get it," he rasped.

Together, they stumbled through the snow to the bench and picked it up. It was staggeringly heavy, laden with snow. As they moved it, a cubic yard of snow slid off the bench and fell over Burke's head. He felt it trickle down below his collar, cold and wet. He shook his head. His wet hair began to freeze to his forehead.

As Burke and Andrusha moved, carrying the bench back toward the dacha windows like pallbearers at a funeral, McCoy and Lyubov came around the corner.

"Pick it up! Over your head!" Burke shouted. Andrusha's tongue came out of his mouth as he struggled to push the weight over his shoulders. Burke nearly fell in the snow, but managed to get his end up. He could feel his shoulders trembling.

"Into the window! Now!" Burke yelled, and together they thrust the bench forward.

He heard the sound of shattering glass and looked up. The bench had lodged itself halfway into the room.

"Pull it out!" Burke yelled, and they struggled to free it. But the bench's leading leg caught on the sill, and thirty seconds went by before they could get it out. Burke could hear the flames reacting to the new source of oxygen, moving into the studio. When he looked again, the room had turned from gray to orange.

"I'll go in!" Andrusha yelled.

He stepped onto the overturned bench. With the bottom of the window at his chest now, he put his hands on the sill and tried to pull himself up, but he couldn't. Feebly, he swung a chubby leg against the wall and tried to raise it to the height of the sill. It flailed helplessly.

Burke stepped in behind him, grabbed his legs by the ankles and lifted. Slowly, Andrusha's body rose, his head and shoulders disappearing inside the window. Burke could hear the sound of more glass breaking. His arms trembled beneath the load.

With a convulsive shove, Burke thrust his arms high and Andrusha tumbled, head first, through the window. They heard a thud. Then nothing.

"Andrusha!" Lyubov screamed.

Burke stepped up onto the bench and looked down. Flames

were dancing through the floor. The far wall, the one that held the paintings, was beginning to burn. Dimly, through the smoke, he could see Andrusha's body on the floor.

"He's not moving!" Burke yelled to McCoy. He put his hands on the sill. The wood was hot. "Give me a boost!"

He could feel her hands underneath his feet, and he pulled himself up, as best he could, trying not to cut himself on the shards of glass that littered the sill.

His shoulders went through, and then he felt the heat, like a furnace, and heard the roar as the flames began to devour the studio. McCoy pushed again, and he went through, putting his hands out to break his fall, trying to somersault over Andrusha's body.

The floorboards singed his hands, and he jerked them up, but managed to tuck his head and roll over Andrusha's prostrate body.

The smoke filled his lungs as he sprawled atop the Russian, and he started to cough again, in a way he'd wanted three minutes ago never to cough again.

He rolled over. Keeping his head as low as possible, he bent over and got his arms around Andrusha's thick torso. He pulled upward. It was like trying to wrestle a couple of fifty-pound sacks of cement; Andrusha was dead weight. But he got Andrusha's head up to the window, where he saw Lyubov's and McCoy's faces peering in. Hands reached in and grabbed Andrusha's jacket lapels.

A cough racked his body and Burke lost his grip for a second. Andrusha slipped back down, nearly dragging the two women through the window. Burke gasped for some clean air through the window and held his breath. Behind him, he heard the sound of wood collapsing. His eyes, filled with smoke, were burning.

Desperately, he heaved upward, and Andrusha's body slowly scraped over the windowsill and out.

He poked his head out and looked. The three of them were sprawled on the snow below, Andrusha's body atop the two women. McCoy saw him.

"Get out!" she yelled. "Now!"

Then Lyubov stood up, climbed slowly onto the bench and held up her hands.

"Pull me in!" she screeched. "Please!"

Burke turned from the outstretched hands and looked back into the dacha.

The entire perimeter of the wall was burning now, and flames were consuming the floor. Behind the studio he could see daylight where the roof had collapsed over the front part of the house. The roar of the fire overwhelmed his hearing.

He could remember, rather than see, where the two large, new paintings hung, perhaps twelve feet away. He looked down at the floor. His trouser legs were smoldering again.

He turned toward the shattered window, sucked in a deep breath, pivoted and lunged across the floor, head down, eyes closed, hands groping in front of him, feeling the flames start to consume his shoes. He reached the wall and ran a hand across it. His hand struck a picture.

He could not open his eyes to look at it, not that it would have done any good. He jerked it from the wall, feeling the nail tear from the plaster. It was heavy. It felt like the painting he had carried from the Hermitage.

His lungs were close to bursting and he could feel the hair on his head start to singe. The heat was the most intense thing he'd ever felt. He could almost sense the skin on his neck starting to blister. He lunged for the window. One step, two steps, three, and he was there, hurling the picture out the window, grabbing the sill with both hands, sticking his head out into the air like a whale coming to the surface for oxygen, and then he felt hands on his shoulders, hands pulling him through.

———

Burke got his legs underneath him and rose to the crawling position. Slowly, he planted first one foot, then the other, and stood up. He looked down at his right leg. The pants had burned away below the knee, and the skin was red and blistered. Second degree burns, he thought.

He turned and found McCoy a foot from him, sprawled on her back. He must have knocked her over, he thought. Her brown eyes had reddened and her face was blackened from the fire. Limp strands of hair hung down her forehead. He picked her up.

Saying nothing, she opened her arms and fell against him, clutching tightly, trembling, her face resting in the crook between his shoulder and neck.

Gradually, the trembling eased and her grip on him relaxed.

"You know," he said, "that guy on television who says you can walk across fire and not feel it?"

She nodded.

"Well," he said, "what a load of crap that is."

She smiled at him and shook her head.

Behind her, he could see Lyubov ministering to Andrusha, who had a bruise the size of a plum on his temple. His eyes were open, and they were both crying, looking at the picture that lay in the snow beside them, a painting singed brown around the edges, a painting of assorted, brightly colored stripes that looked, to Burke, vaguely clownish.

"That's an ugly picture," he said. His voice sounded like sandpaper scraped against concrete. "Who painted it?"

"I did," McCoy said. "In the manner of Morris Louis. He's becoming my favorite artist."

"It's the right one?" he asked her.

She kissed him. Her lips were sooty and he could smell smoke in her hair. He didn't care.

"It's the right one," she said.

"You know I'm going to write about it, and do my best to make a scandal."

She patted him on the cheek. "You go ahead. And if people don't like it, the hell with them."

Burke stumbled over to where Andrusha was, in Lyubov's arms, dazed. He thanked Andrusha, but he wasn't sure Andrusha even heard him.

Then he walked on stiff and unsteady legs around the side of the dacha to the copse of birch trees.

Bykov hung there. His clothing had not burned, and Burke wondered why he had not gone up like a marshmallow held too close to a campfire. Then he felt a small gust of wind and had his answer. It was blowing from behind Bykov, toward the dacha.

Bykov was still and limp, though his legs were splayed at an angle so wide that Burke winced to look at it. Approaching, Burke thought he was dead.

But he stepped closer, bent down and saw that Bykov's round eyes were open wide with terror and moving against the purple background of his skin. His lips opened.

"Cut me down," he said in a hoarse, weak voice.

Burke followed Bykov's eyes to the stakes holding the birch trees in their bent position. He could see a half-inch band of dark moisture on their gray surface, just above the level of the snow. They had started to come loose as the ground melted, just as Miguel had predicted. He wondered how long it would be before they pulled free and let the trees snap skyward. Maybe a minute. Maybe two.

"Cut me down," Bykov repeated.

"Well, actually, I thought this might be a good time for an interview," Burke said, leaning in closer. "Who got paid off in Moscow on this deal?"

"Krimyagin. Minister of Culture," Bykov breathed. Burke had to lean very close to make out the words. "Others. Chavchavadze knows."

"And how much was the Leonardo sold for?"

"Four hundred million," Bykov rasped.

The figure startled Burke, and he looked for a second at the flames consuming the dacha. It was an expensive fire.

"Dollars?" He had to be sure.

"Dollars," Bykov confirmed.

"Who killed Grachenko?"

Bykov winced at the effort of talking. "A man named Vladimir. Chavchavadze hired him."

"And you set up Jimmy Duxbury?"

"Yes," Bykov mumbled.

"Was Chavchavadze working with Marshal Rogov?"

"Yes."

"How?"

"Rogov sold weapons to Santera. Indirectly. Chavchavadze was the middleman, smuggled them out of Russia to Colombia. Got a cut."

"What?"

Burke was almost talking in his ear as Bykov wavered on the edge of consciousness.

"A cut—fifteen, twenty percent probably," Bykov whispered.

"You have any documentation for that?"

"No," Bykov said, and fell silent.

Burke reached out and touched one of the stakes. "Not hammered in very well, you know?" His tone was conversational. "I'm not sure those guys really like you too much."

Bykov's eyes opened wider when Burke's hand touched the stake. His lips opened and closed spasmodically a couple of times. Then he opened his mouth again. "In director's office safe. Hermitage. Bills of lading."

Burke nodded. "The combination?"

Bykov concentrated for a moment, then slowly enunciated four numbers: eighteen, twenty, forty-five, and ten. Burke repeated them until he'd memorized them. The safe, he was certain, would be no problem for Andrusha.

"One more question," he said. "Did you kill Fyodorov and Jennifer Morelli?"

Bykov hesitated again, but not as long as he had before, when deciding whether to tell Burke about the bills of lading.

"Yes," he said. His voice sounded like sandpaper on steel.

Burke straightened up. "That's all," he said. "No more questions."

"Now cut me down." Bykov's voice rose as loud as he could make it, but barely loud enough to be heard over the rustling of the wind in the birch trees and the crackling sound of the flames finishing off the dacha.

Burke struggled to keep his mind focused on the memory of Jennifer Morelli's apartment on the night he found her body.

"I'm sorry," he said. "But a reporter only observes events. He doesn't participate. They teach you that in Journalism 101."

He walked away.

Chapter Thirty-seven

SHE WAITED UNTIL HE HAD TRANSMITTED THE piece and the scanned photographs and was unplugging the computer before she walked up behind him, put her arms around his neck and kissed the back of his right ear.

"Done?" she asked him.

He nodded, enjoying the smell of her hands and hair.

"Come to bed," McCoy said. "I need you."

Smiling, Burke turned around. She was wearing a white T-shirt, COLUMBIA on the front in blue letters. Underneath the shirt her legs were long and bare.

He kissed her, and she tasted like honeysuckle on a summer night.

They walked into the bedroom, and before he could get his socks off, he fell asleep in her arms.

It was a dreamless sleep.

The sound of the telephone awakened him.

He turned toward the sound, groping, and found McCoy's shoulder with his hand. He opened his eyes. She lay with her hair bunched against the cool blue pillowcase, the phone at her ear.

"Yes, he is," she said. "I'll put him on."

"Your office," she mouthed to him as she handed over the phone.

Burke rubbed his eyes and looked at the window. McCoy's blinds were drawn, and he had no idea what time it was or how long he'd slept.

"Burke," he said.

"Piece's got a hole in it, Colin."

It was Graves.

Burke tried to keep his annoyance out of his voice. He made a practice of always allowing editors to feel that they'd made a contribution. It got his stories better play.

"What's that, Ken?"

"Well, this woman paints an exact copy of the Leonardo. Fools everyone. From your pictures, you can see they're identical. So why is one worth four hundred million and the other a buck ninety-eight? Same aesthetic experience, right?"

"Pictures turned out, huh?"

"Yeah. Nobody's going to confuse you with a photographer, but we can enhance the resolution, and they'll do. So, anyway, what's the answer to my question?"

He was serious, Burke decided. "Damned if I know," he said. "That's just the way it is. I guess I could call some aesthetics expert and get an explanation."

"I was just kidding," Graves said.

Burke found that it was not hard to chuckle. He did. "Okay. What else?"

He could all but hear Graves smirk. "Well, you know, it's a helluva piece. A holy shit piece. Congratulations."

Burke expelled a little air. "Thanks."

"There is one potential problem, though."

"What's that?"

"They're going to have a press conference today to show off the picture, right?"

McCoy, in fact, had insisted that Andrusha and Lyubov hold the press conference immediately, at the Hermitage, before the opening of the business day in Colombia. Santera, she calculated, would see it and refuse to make the money transfers to complete the deal. If no money changed hands, and the Leonardo was safe in Russia, the ensuing scandal could be contained short of the president's office.

Burke looked at his watch. It was six in the morning.

"Yeah," he said. "It's due to start in four hours."

"Well," Graves demanded, "what do we do if this Santera claims he's got the real picture?"

"Well, it's not in the story, because Karpov made me promise not to put it in. But before he stashed it in the vault where Santera got it, he added a few Cyrillic letters on the back—N, P, N, E, K, S. They blended in with the other writing on the back."

"So?"

"So, in Russian, they stand for, *Nadyezhda Petrovna Naryshkina etu kartinu sdyelala*—'Nadyezhda Petrovna Naryshkina made this picture.' "

"Clever," Graves said.

"Yeah. He's a clever guy."

"I wouldn't want to be near this Santera guy when he finds out," Graves said.

"He'll get over it," Burke replied. "I hope."

"I figure it's still going to shake things up in Moscow when the Russians hear about it," Graves went on. "What do you think'll happen?"

"I think," Burke said, "that Rogov will go. Some ministers will go. They'll have to bust Chavchavadze. Nothing will happen to the president. Maybe he'll be reelected. I don't know. But I think that the Russians have a greater capacity for muddling through than we give them credit for. There's not going to be a new Cold War, as much as some people would like one."

He pulled McCoy closer to him and buried his nose in her hair.

"You're probably right," Graves was saying. "And the guy that gave you the bills of lading that link Chavchavadze to Santera and Rogov. Where's he now?"

"To be honest, I don't know," Burke said.

"Probably long gone," Graves said. "If I were in his position, that's what I'd do. I'd split."

"That's probably what happened," Burke replied. He rolled his eyes at McCoy.

"Helluva story," Graves repeated. "I'm going to recommend we strip it across the top of A-one and fill up a couple of inside pages with the jump."

"Thanks," Burke said. "We'll be a day ahead on the story."

"Where's the painting now?"

"I don't know," Burke said. "I'll see it at the press conference. Until then, I didn't want to know."

"Well, here's one thing I know," Graves said. "You were supposed to be back here today. Now I suppose you'll want a few more days off."

"Yeah," Burke said. "I would."

"You can have two," Graves snapped. "I suppose you'll take 'em with that voice that answered the phone."

"I hope," Burke said.

"Well, I guess you deserve it. One more thing," Graves went on. "You sure you want this double byline, 'By Colin Burke and Jennifer Morelli'? Isn't it a bit too, um, maudlin?"

"That's my New Year's Resolution, Ken," Burke said. "To be more maudlin."

"New Year's?" Graves sounded surprised. "Christ, it's halfway through February."

"I know," Burke said. "But I've always been a slow starter."

ABOUT THE AUTHOR

A reporter abroad and in Washington, D.C., for two decades, ROBERT CULLEN won an Overseas Press Club award for foreign reporting during his stint as *Newsweek*'s Moscow correspondent. His novels include *Cover Story* and *Soviet Sources*, a *New York Times* Notable Book of the Year. He is also the author of *The Killer Department*, which was made into an HBO original movie under the title *Citizen X*. Cullen makes his home in Chevy Chase, Maryland.